Praise for C.L. Taylor

'Fans of C.L. Taylor are in for a treat. *The Fear* is her best yet.'
Clare Mackintosh

'Claustrophobic and compelling.'
Karin Slaughter

'...kewering portrait of obsessive love and psychological manip-
...on, this book gets under the skin from the outset and won't
...u go until you've gasped at THAT ending. With characters
...eal you feel you ought to text them and a plot that keeps
you tearing through the pages, this is Taylor's best book yet.'
C.J. Cooke

'A thoroughly enjoyable read, a highly original and timely tale
that kept me utterly enthralled and entertained from beginning
to end.'
Liz Nugent

'...loved *The Fear*! It's my favourite of C.L. Taylor's novels now.
...ouldn't put it down. Tense, twisty, terrifying – with one of the
best premises I've read in ages.'
Julie Cohen

'...any thrillers claim to be compelling: *The Fear* absolutely is.
...eathtakingly bold, shockingly tense, you won't be able to tear
...urself away from this book. It's dark, emotionally-charged and
...led with characters who will make you question everything
you think you know about them. *The Fear* will delight C.L.
Taylor's fans and win her an army of new ones. What a book!'
Miranda Dickinson

'What an absolutely cracking read! Pacy, well-written,
and anxiety inducing.'
Lisa Hall

'*The Fear* is a compulsive read, that forces the reader to consider
just how far they would go to protect themselves and those
...around them. I could not put this book down!'
Emma Kavanagh

'...and disturbing: this is a book I will remember
for a long time.'
R....

'A terrifying glimpse into a dark subject. This brilliant book stayed with me long after I finished the last page.'
Cass Green

'It's a close call as the bar's set so high but this has to be C.L. Taylor's best yet. SO entertaining, high on the shock-factor and yet totally 'real'.'
Caz Frear

'*The Missing* has a delicious sense of foreboding from the first page, luring us into the heart of a family with terrible secrets and making us wait, with pounding hearts for the final, agonizing twist. Loved it.'
Fiona Barton

'*Black Narcissus* for the Facebook generation, a clever exploration of how petty jealousies and misunderstandings can unravel even the tightest of friendships. Claustrophobic, tense and thrilling, a thrill-ride of a novel that keeps you guessing.'
Elizabeth Haynes

'A dark and gripping read that engrossed me from start to finish.'
Mel Sherratt

'Kept me guessing till the end.'
Sun

'Haunting and heart-stoppingly creepy, *The Lie* is a gripping roller coaster of suspense.'
Sunday Express

'5/5 stars – Spine-chilling!'
Woman Magazine

'An excellent psychological thriller.'
Heat Magazine

'Packed with twists and turns, this brilliantly tense thriller will get your blood pumping.'
Fabulous Magazine

'Fast-paced, tense and atmospheric, a guaranteed bestseller.'
Mark Edwards

'A compelling, addictive and wonderfully written tale. Can't recommend it enough.'
Louise Douglas

See what bloggers are saying about C.L. Taylor . . .

'An intriguing and stirring tale, overflowing with family drama.'
Lovereading.co.uk

'Astoundingly written, *The Missing* pulls you in from the very first page and doesn't let you go until the final full stop.'
Bibliophile Book Club

'*The Lie* is an utterly gripping psychological thriller that you won't forget for a long time. Dark, creepy and wonderfully written.'
Alba in Book Land

'Tense and gripping with a dark, ominous feeling that seeps through the very clever writing . . . all praise to C.L. Taylor.'
Anne Cater, Random Things Through My Letterbox

'C.L. Taylor has done it again, with another compelling master-piece.'
Rachel's Random Reads

'In a crowded landscape of so-called domestic noir thrillers, most of which rely on clever twists and big reveals, [*The Missing*] stands out for its subtle and thoughtful analysis of the fallout from a loss in the family.'
Crime Fiction Lover

'When I had finished, I felt like someone had ripped my heart out and wrung it out like a dish cloth.'
By the Letter Book Reviews

'Be prepared to be consumed by *The Escape* – you'll want to read it in one sitting. Just brilliant.'
Bookliterati

'Incredibly thrilling and utterly unpredictable! A must read!'
Aggie's Books

'A gripping story.'
Bibliomaniac

C.L. Taylor is a *Sunday Times* bestselling author. Her psychological thrillers have sold over a million copies in the UK alone, been translated into over twenty languages, and optioned for television. C.L. Taylor lives in Bristol with her partner and son.

By the same author:

The Accident
The Lie
The Missing
The Escape

For Young Adults:
The Treatment

C.L. TAYLOR

The Fear

avon.

AVON

A division of HarperCollins*Publishers*
1 London Bridge Street,
London SE1 9GF

www.harpercollins.co.uk

A Paperback Original 2018

1

A catalogue record for this book is
available from the British Library

ISBN (UK): 978-0-00-811809-9
ISBN (ANZ): 978-0-00-824813-0

Set in Sabon LT Std 12/15 pt by Palimpsest Book Production Limited,
Falkirk, Stirlingshire

Printed and bound in Great Britain by
CPI Group (UK) Ltd, Croydon CR0 4YY

MIX
Paper from
responsible sources
FSC™ C007454

This book is produced from independently certified FSC™ paper
to ensure responsible forest management.

For more information visit: www.harpercollins.co.uk/green

To my friend Scott James
who never backs down from a dare.

Chapter 1

Lou

Saturday 24th March 2007

I hate surprises. So much so that when Ben rang me at work on Monday and told me to keep the weekend free because he was going to surprise me, I almost ended the call. Instead I pretended to be thrilled.

'You okay?' he asks now. 'You don't get travel-sick do you?'

If I look pale it's got nothing to do with the fact that we are rocketing down the A2 in Ben's battered VW Golf.

'I'm fine,' I say. 'But I wish you'd tell me where we're going.'

He taps a finger against the side of his nose and smiles. 'You'll find out soon enough.'

Ben was never meant to be more than a one-night stand. I figured he'd be straight out of my bed, and my life, the moment our sweat-slicked bodies cooled.

1

But he stuck around. He stayed all night and then insisted on taking me out for breakfast the next day. I said yes, partly because it was less awkward than saying no. Mostly because I was hungry and I didn't have any food in the house. We ended up staying in the café for over two hours. I learnt that he was a self-employed graphic artist, he'd never been to a gig, and his dad was a massive hypochondriac. He learnt that I was an only child, a project manager for an eLearning company and that my dad had recently died. Ben immediately reached across the table, squeezed my hand and said how sorry he was. When he asked if we'd been close I changed the subject.

I need to go back there at some point, to my child-hood home in the rolling green Worcestershire countryside, to clear and clean the farmhouse and put it on the market, but there's a good reason why I haven't been back in eighteen years.

'Not long now,' Ben says as a sign to Dover/Channel Tunnel/Canterbury/Chatham flashes past us. 'Any idea where we're going yet?'

My stomach tightens but I keep my tone light. 'Canterbury has a nice cathedral. You're not planning on marrying me, are you? I haven't packed a dress.'

If Ben knew me well, he'd realise that my voice is half an octave too high and my smile is pulled too tightly over my teeth. He'd ask if I was okay instead of laughing and making a quip about Gretna Green. But Ben and I have only been seeing each other for a month. He barely knows me.

I try to quell my anxiety, first by singing along to

Ben's Artic Monkeys CD, then by talking crap. As the miles speed by we discuss the DVD boxed set we've been binge-watching for the last week, the latest celebrity scandal that's been splashed all over the broadsheets and where we watched the lunar eclipse. Logically I know that I have nothing to fear. I'm thirty-two, not fourteen. And Ben didn't ask me to pack my passport. But the knot in my stomach remains.

'Are we nearly there yet?' I ask, as Ben presses a bottle of water to his lips.

He laughs, spraying the steering wheel with a fine mist. 'Are you five?'

'No, just impatient.'

'I knew I should have blindfolded you. No,' he nudges me lightly. 'Gagged you.'

I tense but force a laugh. 'Please tell me you're not into all that S&M shit.'

'Who says it's shit?'

More laughter. We laugh a lot. We have since we met, in a pub in Soho. I was at a work leaving party and I'd just managed to spill the best part of a glass of red wine down my top. Ben came out of the men's toilets as I swerved into the ladies', dropping my purse in my haste. He waited outside so he could give it back to me. He was a nice-looking bloke, friendly and, because I was drunk, I said yes when he asked if he could buy me a drink.

One month since we met. Two months until we split up. If that. Thirty-two years old and I haven't been in a relationship that's lasted longer than three

3

months. Sooner or later I'll fuck things up. I always do.

The sign as we leave the M2 at junction 7 says Canterbury/Dover/Margate/Ramsgate. I can't imagine he's taking me to Margate for the weekend, although it could be fun. Canterbury then. It has to be. Maybe I should have packed a white dress.

'Please tell me where we're going,' I plead.

Ben smiles but says nothing. The grin doesn't leave his face as we exit the roundabout onto the Boughton Bypass and rejoin the A2.

'No peeking,' he says as I reach for my phone. 'If you look on Google Maps you'll spoil the surprise.'

Which was exactly my plan.

My grip on the hand rest tightens as we speed past the junction to Canterbury and I spot a sign saying 'Dover 17 miles'. The only reason we could be going there would be to get a ferry to Calais. But Ben didn't ask me to bring my passport. He must have discovered some kind of idyll nearby, a picturesque fishing village maybe, out of sight of the ferries and the boats.

'Nearly there,' he says as we drive through Dover and a grey stretch of sea appears between the buildings. 'Trust me, you're going to love it.'

Trust me. You need to trust me, Lou. I will keep you safe, I promise. I love you. You know that don't you?

'Ben.'

We're only a couple of hundred metres from the ferry terminal now, a slab of grey, slapped up against

4

the sea. We speed along the seafront then Ben slows the car as we approach the customs gates.

'Ben, I—'

'Don't stress.' He slows the car to a halt as we join the queue. 'I've got your passport. Don't kill me but I swiped it from your desk drawer when you were cooking dinner the other—'

'I can't do this.'

'What?'

I yank on the door pull but the passenger door doesn't open.

'Lou?'

I try again. And again. Pull. Release. Pull. Release. The piece of black plastic flaps back and forth but the door doesn't open. He's locked me in.

It's going to be okay, Lou. It's what we wanted. Just you and me. A new life. A new start in a place where no one will judge us. We can be together, forever.

The window then. If I open it, unclip my seat belt and lean out, I'll be able to open the door from the outside. I'll be able to get out.

'Lou?'

I try and turn the handle on the passenger door but my hand is slick with sweat and it keeps slipping from underneath my fingertips.

'Are you going to be sick or something? I've opened the door. Sorry, it's central locking and—'

A cold gust of air whips my hair around my face as I leap out of the car. In an instant I am fourteen years old again.

Mike is the love of my life and I am his. He's taking me to France for a romantic weekend away. This morning I put on my school uniform as usual but, instead of getting the bus all the way to school, I got off a stop early on the corner of Holy Lane. Mike was waiting with his car. He'd told me to bring toiletries, a change of clothes and my passport in my school bag. He said he'd take care of the rest.

Chapter 2

Wendy

'Monty!' Wendy Harrison lays down her shovel, dusts the soil from her gardening gloves and stands up. 'Monty, I'm going in now!'

At the sound of her voice, her piebald springer spaniel comes bounding out of the bushes and pads across the grass towards her, his pink tongue lolling.

'Hello, Monts.' Wendy rubs a hand over the top of his head. 'I think we both deserve a treat, don't you?'

The dog's ears twitch at the sound of the word treat and he trots obediently beside his mistress, his eyes never leaving her face, as she makes her way inside the small terraced house on the edge of Great Malvern.

Wendy takes a bite of her custard cream, chews, swallows and then pops the other half in her mouth.

7

When that's gone she sips at her tea and picks up another biscuit. She was only going to have one. She'd even entered it into her Slimming World diary – custard cream, 3 syns – but somehow half of the packet has vanished.

Sod it, she thinks as she moves her finger over her laptop's mousepad. *I'll start again tomorrow.*

For the last hour she's been flicking back and forth between the same three websites – Facebook, Twitter and Instagram. It's the fourth time today that she's logged on and it's only 2 p.m. She tries to distract herself – with gardening, her part-time bookkeeping job and walking Monty – but her mind always drifts back to those websites. Has something new been posted? An update, photo or location? The panic builds in her stomach. What if the information is deleted before she reads it? What if she misses something important?

She can't remember what first prompted her to google Lou Wandsworth. It might have been a passing conversation she'd had with her friend Angela about finding an old school friend on Facebook, an article she read in the paper, or maybe she was having one of those days where she woke up feeling as though a dark cloud had settled in her brain and nothing brought her joy, not even when Monty laid his head on her knee and stared up at her with his searching brown eyes.

It didn't take Wendy long to track Lou down. She was the only Louise Wandsworth on Facebook. The trouble was, she could only see her name, an image

8

of a cartoon character as her profile picture and a list of her friends. Nothing else. Angela had shown her how to set up her own Facebook page but she couldn't use that to try and connect with Lou. She made a new page instead, called herself Saskia Kennedy, and added a few photos of a woman that she'd found online who was about the same age as Lou.

Wendy's heart trembled in her chest when she pressed the 'add friend' button. But nothing happened. Her request was ignored. Days went by, then weeks. Wendy did some more googling: *How do you get someone to accept a Facebook friend request?*

She discovered that it looked suspicious if you didn't have many friends, or any in common, so she set about adding random people who lived in London and looked about the same age as Louise. Men were easy – the woman in her fake profile picture was attractive – but it took a little longer for women to start accepting her requests. Once she had fifty friends and had filled her wall with memes, silly photos and the same sort of updates as her 'contemporaries' she tried adding a few of Lou's friends. To her surprise they accepted her, at least half a dozen of them. When she tried adding Lou for a second time her friend request was accepted.

She was in.

She felt jubilant as she clicked on Lou's photo albums. All those months of detective work and she'd finally found what she had been looking for. Not just one photo of her but dozens and dozens. Lou had long brown hair pulled back into a ponytail. A hint of make-up around the eyes but no lipstick. Skinny. But not in an attractive way. Her jacket sloped away from her shoulders and her skirt bagged below her knees. There was a pinched, haggard look to her cheeks, despite her youth – the hollowed face of a long-distance runner or one of the dieters in *Slimming World* magazine who've lost four or five stone in a matter of months.

As Wendy clicked through the photos, a weight settled in her stomach. Lou might not be conventionally attractive but she was surrounded by people in every shot. There were photos of her in dim bars, chinking cocktail glasses with dewy-skinned friends. Shots of her running through the waves on a tropical holiday, not an ounce of fat protruding from beneath her string bikini. Lou on top of a mountain with a cagoule hood pulled tightly around her head with a look of triumph on her face. Lou in fancy dress, one foot cocked behind her like a fifties starlet, kissing a dark-haired man dressed like Clark Gable. She was vivacious, well-liked, well-travelled and content. Everything that Wendy was not.

Wendy didn't go back on Facebook for a week after that first discovery. She didn't even open her laptop. Just walking past it made her feel sick.

But then curiosity got the better of her.

'I'll just have a quick look,' she told Monty as she settled down at her dining room table and opened the laptop lid. 'Then I'll stop.'

That was seven months ago.

'Give me a second, Monty,' Wendy says now as her dog nudges at her knee. 'We'll go for a walk in a minute.'

She reaches for a custard cream and pops it into her mouth. Outside, storm clouds are gathering in the sky. If they don't go out now they'll be in for one soggy walk. *One last refresh of the screen*, Wendy tells herself as she clicks the trackpad button, *and then I'll get my coat on.*

What she sees on the screen makes her inhale so sharply a tiny bit of biscuit whizzes down her windpipe, making her cough. Lou has just updated her Facebook page.

I got the job in Malvern and I'm moving in a month's time. London, I'm going to miss you.

Chapter 3

Lou

Saturday 21st April 2007

I've spent the last month trying to ready myself for this moment but nothing could have prepared me for the cloud of memories that descend as I catch sight of the Malvern Hills, curving like a dragon's back, as I head down the A4440: buying penny sweets in white paper bags from Morley's, laughing at the girls from the local boarding school in their brown 'Batman' cloaks, walking up to St Anne's Well with Mum and Dad feeling like I was climbing a mountain, and stepping into The Martial Arts Club for the first time, feeling sick with nerves. An image of Mike, smiling and holding out a hand in welcome, flashes into my brain. I try to blot it out by focussing on the road as I speed past Malvern and along the A4103 towards Acton Green. It's not a journey I've ever driven before – I passed my test in London –

12

but the road is imprinted in my memory from all the times Dad ferried me to and from karate lessons. My phone bleeps on the passenger seat as I pass Dad's favourite drinking haunt, The Dog and Duck. I snatch it up, hoping it's a text from Ben, knowing it won't be.

I haven't seen or heard from him since that awful afternoon in Dover four weeks ago. He caught up with me after I fled, half a mile or so along the seafront.

'Louise?' He abandoned his car on a double yellow line and ran after me, grabbing my hand, forcing me to stop. 'What's wrong? What's the matter?'

I shook my head, hating myself for what I was about to do.

'What is it?' he asked. 'What just happened?'

When I told him that I didn't think we should see each other again, the concerned expression on his face morphed into confusion. Why, he wanted to know. What had he done wrong?

'Nothing,' I said. 'Nothing at all.'

He searched my face for an answer. 'Then why?'

I couldn't tell him. Not when I've spent the last eighteen years pretending that Mike Hughes doesn't exist. Instead I mumbled something about things moving too quickly. I wasn't ready for a relationship. We wanted different things.

I cried on the train back to London, turning my face to the window so the man sitting next to me couldn't see my tears. Ben didn't deserve what just happened. Neither did any of the men I'd dumped, run away from and lied to. If I didn't face up to what happened to me when I was fourteen I was going to spend the rest of my life alone.

I glance at my phone. The text is from my best friend Alice, asking if I've got to Dad's house safely. I drop the phone back on the seat and indicate left, taking the road towards Ledbury – and Mike's house – instead of continuing on to Acton Green. I've never been to his house before. Why would I? He was a respectable member of the community, a karate teacher who raised money for charity through fun runs and tournaments. And besides, he lived with his wife Dee. Mike was very good at keeping our 'affair' secret. Our first kiss was in the changing rooms behind the dojo. I was fourteen and it was almost one year to the day after I first started karate, but we first fucked in—

Don't use that word again.

Mike's voice cuts through the memory.

Fucking is sex without emotion, Louise. That's not something I do and it's certainly not something we're going to do. When we spend the night together for the first time it's going to be because we love each other and we'll express that by—

I turn the radio on and twist the knob round to the right. The sound explodes out of the speakers in a fury, making my eardrums pulse, but I don't turn it back down. It's a song I barely know but I sing along anyway, shouting nonsensical words as Mike's voice creeps through the space between notes, demanding to be heard.

Mike might not have taken me to his house but I

14

knew where he lived. I knew everything about him, or as much as a fourteen-year-old girl could without access to the internet, and I wrote it all down in my diary. I listened in to conversations between the parents and the other senseis. I casually quizzed the older students about him and, during the rare moments I was alone with Mike, I'd listen, enrapt, to anything he told me. This was way before we kissed for the first time. A long time before that.

As I turn right off New Mills Way – one street away from Mike's house – my resolve vanishes and empty terror replaces it. What am I doing? My plan was to give myself a couple of weeks to sort out Dad's house and start work before I tracked Mike down. I googled before I left, to check he hadn't changed his name or gone underground. But no, he lives in the same house he lived in eighteen years ago and he's got his own business – Hughes Removals and Deliveries – on the outskirts of Malvern. No karate club though, thank God.

I park up, then slump over the steering wheel as all the air leaves my body in one raggedy breath. I've got no idea what I'll walk into when I knock on his door. Mike's wife could answer. One of his children – if he has any. What do I say if that happens? Hello, I'm Louise, the girl your dad groomed. Is he in?

I don't know why you're blaming me for everything. You knew what you were getting yourself into.

Shut up, I tell the voice. I was fourteen. I had no idea.

15

If I did such a terrible thing why didn't you testify at my trial?

Because I was terrified of what you might do if you weren't convicted.

That's a lie, isn't it? You didn't testify because you loved me.

No, that's not true.

You were the one who said 'I love you' first. You said you wanted to marry me and have my children. Do you know why you can't make a relationship work? Why you had to send Ben packing? Because you still love me.

'No.' I slam my fists against the steering wheel, pounding the horn to block out the soft murmur of Mike's voice in the back of my skull. 'I don't. I don't.'

Sweat prickles at my armpits as I push open the gate to Mike's house and walk up the path. If his wife answers, I won't recognise her. There are no photos of her on the internet and Mum made sure I didn't get so much as a peek at the news or the front page of a newspaper after the trial. I didn't have a mobile phone or home computer back in 1989 either.

But what if Dee Hughes recognises me? She never went to the dojo or to any of the matches but she must have tried to find out who I am. What if she screams in my face and tells me that I ruined her life? When I look at photos of fourteen-year-old me, I barely recognise myself. My face was soft and round, my hair dark and cut into a jaw-length bob with a thick heavy fringe. These days it's lighter and longer, with pale tendrils that hang over sharp cheekbones and a tight jaw that I didn't have eighteen years ago. But it's not just my face that has changed. The softly curved body I despised so much as a teenager has gone. On a good day, I can look in the mirror and tell myself that I'm slender. On a bad day, my body looks wizened and androgynous, as though the years have eaten away at my femininity.

I knock three times on the front door. I've imagined this moment a thousand times. Sometimes Mike looks shocked to see me. Occasionally he starts to cry. Once I stabbed him before he could speak. I concentrate on the thick, glossy red paint and take a deep breath. If Mike peeks from behind a curtain, I want him to see me standing here confidently, not twitching and shifting. I want to get this over and done with now, before any more memories overwhelm me. I have to do it while I'm still feeling brave. We can talk on the doorstep or in the pub down the road. If he invites me in, I'll say no. Even if he's home alone. *Particularly* if he's home alone.

That's her, someone shouts as I step out of the French police station. Flashbulbs light up the dark sky as I'm sandwiched between four police officers and shepherded into a black car. That's the girl who ran away with her karate teacher.

'Hello?'

I am vaguely aware of a voice, a male baritone, shouting hello, but it doesn't register. Nothing does.

I need to find out where Mike is. Did they bring him here too? Is he being interrogated behind one of these flat, beige doors?

'Hello! You at the door of number fifty-nine!'

I turn slowly. There's a man in his mid to late fifties, hanging out of the first-floor window of the house next to Mike's. The upper half of his body is naked and his hair is slicked back, like he just stepped out of the shower. I try to erase the image of Mike's face from my mind, to mentally shake myself forward in time, but the memory's still holding me tightly, like the last vestiges of a dream. Or a nightmare.

'Were you after Mike?' the man asks.

Do I say yes or no? I have no idea who this person is.

'I was, yes.'

'Friend are you?'

I smile tightly. 'Old friend.'

His eyes flick the length of my body and he smiles lasciviously. 'Lucky Mike.'

I ignore him and head back down the path to my car.

'He's at work,' the man shouts, making me pause as I touch a hand to the driver side door. 'Greensleeves, the garden centre. He does their pick-ups on a Saturday.' No mention of Mike's wife, but I'm not about to ask.

'Fancy going for a drink sometime?' he adds as I get into my car. 'Thank me properly?'

I consider shouting something abusive but I haven't

got time to explain why no sane woman would date a prick who slathers at women out of a window. It's half past five. I need to find out where the garden centre is and get there before it closes. I need to find Mike. Now. Before the fear sets in again.

Chapter 4

Lou

I change out of my uniform in the car, wriggling out of my school skirt and pulling on my jeans. When I undo my seat belt so I can take off my shirt, Mike snaps at me.

'What the fuck are you doing? We're on the motorway for God's sake.'

I quickly plug my seat belt back in but tears prick at my eyes as I struggle to pull on my jumper. It was supposed to be a romantic weekend away and he's just snapped at me like I'm misbehaving in class.

'I'm sorry.' Mike rests a hand on my knee. 'I didn't mean to make you cry. I just don't want anything to happen to you, Lou. You mean the world to me. You know that, don't you?'

I nod, but I don't squeeze his hand. It remains on my knee like a dead weight until he has to lift it up again to tap the indicator and change lanes.

* * *

I push open the doors to Greensleeves Garden Centre. As I step inside the woman behind the counter, dressed in a red polo shirt, shouts that they'll be closing soon. I ignore her and speed through the shop, barely registering the shelves of bird food and ornaments and the displays of garden furniture and houseplants. The only other customer is a heavily pregnant woman pushing a trolley full of fertiliser and decorative fencing with bedding plants piled on the top.

I glance at my watch as I step through the large double doors next to the restaurant. 17.53. Seven minutes until they close. If Mike's not out here, in the yard amongst the plants, shrubs and timber, I'll head round the back, see if there's some kind of loading bay. I don't want to have to come here again or go back to his house. I want to get this over and done with now.

I walk along the length of the aisles, pausing to peer down each one as I pass. The place is deserted. I'll just do one last loop of the yard and then head round the—

It's the flash of blue amongst all the brown and green that makes me pause. I'm at the far end of the yard, standing beside a raised pallet full of shaped bushes and willow-like trees in decorative pots. There are six sheds and summer houses, standing in a row like sentries, directly to my left – no more than a couple of metres away. A grey-haired man wearing a blue T-shirt just ducked inside the summer house.

A sharp pain cuts across my chest, like cheese wire

being pulled tight around my ribcage. It's him. It's Mike. I only caught a glimpse before the door closed behind him, but it was enough for me to take in the thick grey hair, the deep lines either side of his mouth and the pronounced limp as he walked. He must be forty-nine years old but he looks older. So much older than I remember, but I know it's him. I'd stake my life on it.

I crouch down and peer from between two bushes. Unlike the two wooden sheds on either side of it, the summer house has white PVC double doors and two long windows. As Mike appears in one of the windows, someone else steps out of the shadows. As she reaches a hand to touch Mike's face, he glances over his shoulder, back towards the yard. For one terrible second I think that he's seen me, but he turns back to face the woman. He sweeps the hair from the side of her face, then, cradling the back of her head, leans in for a kiss.

They kiss for several seconds, then the woman pulls away and I catch a glimpse of her face. Bobbed brown hair with a thick fringe. A soft jawline. Full, plump cheeks. Jeans that cling to thick thighs. A red polo shirt pulled tight over large, weighty breasts. She's not a woman at all. She's a child, no more than thirteen or fourteen years old.

I don't burst into the summer house and scream at Mike to get his hands off her. Nor do I run off in search of a staff member. Instead I turn and flee, flying through the aisles of trees and bushes, brushing past plants and dodging statues. I don't stop running until I'm back in the safety of my car, then I smash my fists against the steering wheel until my skin is red and throbbing.

I have never hated myself more than I do right now.

I should have felt anger when I saw Mike kiss that girl. Or disgust. Instead I felt betrayed. He was kissing her the same way he kissed me: the smoothing away of the hair, the cradling of the back of the head, the teasing lip brush followed by a deeper, harder kiss as he pulled her into him.

I had to wait so very, very long for our first kiss. He pulled away so many times before our lips finally met, denying me, telling me that I was too young and it wouldn't be right. His reticence only made me want him more. I'd lie in bed and relive every touch, every lingering look and every soft word. I'd run a finger over my mouth, then push two fingers against my lips, imagining the weight of his mouth on mine. Fourteen years old and I'd never been kissed. I never admitted it to anyone at school but teenagers can sniff out weakness and fear the same way pigs can sniff out truffles and, somehow, everyone knew. The bullying began when I was thirteen, just before Mum and Dad split up. I've got no idea why. One moment I was invisible, the next I was on the bullies' radar. It was Dad that suggested the karate lessons. They'd give me an air of confidence, he said, even if I never used the moves. An air of confidence? That's a joke.

23

I start as a dark green estate car pulls into the car park. It does a U-turn, then parks near the exit. The driver doesn't get out but he does open a window and flick cigarette ash on the floor. As he does, the door to the garden centre bursts open and the girl I saw in the summer house runs down the path.

'Chloe!' the man in the green estate bellows, leaning out of the window.

The girl sprints across the car park. 'Sorry, Dad, sorry,' she calls as she rounds the car.

'I've been waiting bloody ages. Get in.'

That's a lie.

'They needed me to work late,' the girl says as she pulls at the car door. 'I couldn't just . . .' The rest of her sentence is lost as she slides into the car and slams the door shut.

As the car inches forward, its right indicator blinking, I look back at the door to the garden centre. Do I wait for Mike to come out or go after the girl?

The green estate pulls out into the road and I start my engine.

Chapter 5

Chloe

Chloe endures her dad's rant all the way home. She's a stupid girl. She's got no sense of responsibility. She's selfish. She's fat. Most thirteen-year-olds would be grateful to have an after-school job. He hopes she's more punctual when her boss asks her to do something. Mike's his friend but he didn't have to help him find his stupid daughter an after-school job. If she gets the sack, it will reflect badly on both of them.

She tries to block him out by glancing out of the window and losing herself in the green blur of the hedgerow, but each time she turns her head her dad snaps at her to look at him when he's talking to her.

I hate you, she thinks as she looks into his eyes. *You're a bully. You bully Mum and you bully me. The only person you don't bully is your precious little mini-me Jamie.* At seven years old he's too young to realise that his dad's an arsehole. He thinks his dad

25

can do no wrong, not while he's still impressed by tickets to see Wolves play, packs of football cards and father–son trips to McDonald's. She'd like to think that when Jamie hits his teens, the scales will fall away from his eyes and he'll understand that it's not okay to talk to women like they're shit. Then again, just yesterday, when she asked him to put his plate in the dishwasher after dinner, he said, 'Why should I? Dad doesn't.'

Chloe's spent a lot of time trying to work out why her dad and Mike are friends. They couldn't be more different. Her dad, Alan, is harsh and abrasive. Mike is gentle and kind. Her dad criticises her and makes her feel like shit. Mike tells her she's beautiful and makes her feel like she could do anything she wanted to in life. She didn't always feel so warmly towards Mike. She used to ignore him if he came round to their house for a BBQ or to have a few beers with her dad in the garden. Putting up with her dad was bad enough, why would she want to chat to one of his arsehole mates? And when her dad suggested she get a weekend and after-school job at the garden centre she was horrified. A garden centre? How boring was that. And anyway, she had homework to do after school. 'It's not like you'll ever be an A-grade student,' her dad had snapped, 'even if you did homework for the rest of your life. Get retail experience now, while you can.' It was her mum who finally talked her into taking the job. 'It'll get you out of the house,' she said softly, 'and you might make some new friends.' Chloe wasn't sure she wanted to be friends with people who worked in a garden centre, but the idea of avoiding her dad for sixteen hours a week did appeal. And earning some money of her own so she didn't have to ask him.

When the car finally pulls up on their street, Chloe sits tight, waiting for her dad to tell her that she can get out, then she runs up the path and into the house.

'Mum!' she calls. 'I'm back!'

She pops her head into the living room to find Jamie sitting on the rug in front of the TV, the PS4 remote welded to his hands.

'Jamie, where's Mum?'

'Having a lie-down. She's got a migraine. Again.'

She takes the stairs two at a time, then gently pushes at her parents' bedroom door. The curtains are drawn and the room is dark but she can make out the shape of her mother lying curled up on her side on the bed. She's fast asleep. Chloe reaches into her back pocket for her phone and checks the time. 6.17 p.m. She wonders if Mike will be home yet. Not that she knows where that is. When she asked him where he lived and if he had a family, he shook his head and said, 'All you need to know is that my life is a lonely one. Tell me if I'm wrong, but I've got a feeling you can relate?' She'd looked away then, unable to cope with the intensity of his gaze.

'Chloe!' her dad yells from downstairs. 'If your mum's not able to make the dinner you'll have to do it.'

Chloe glances at her mum, her face slack, her shoulders relaxed and her breathing heavy and slow, then she makes her way back down the stairs.

Chapter 6

Lou

Any tension between me and Mike lifts the moment the ferry pulls away from the terminal and we're free to get out of the car. He grabs my hand and half-leads, half-pulls me up the stairs to the deck.

'Let's find the arcade.' He beams, dimples puncturing his stubbly cheeks. 'If they've got those grabby games, I'll try and win you a toy.'

We move from game to game – shooting, driving and dancing. Mike wins the shooting. I win the dancing. I win the driving too when I cheat and yank on his steering wheel, making him do a U-turn. He doesn't care. He pulls me onto his lap, then without bothering to check if anyone is looking, he covers my face in kisses. When we've exhausted all the games, we drop shiny ten-pence pieces into the penny shove. We work as a team first, then race each other to see who can get the most coins in. As our winnings tumble over the edge, Mike wraps

28

an arm around my waist and lifts me clean off my feet.

'Let's celebrate in style!' he laughs. 'The burgers are on me!'

He leads me to the restaurant and orders burgers, fries and milkshakes. I get Mike to dip his fries in his milkshake ('disgusting') and he challenges me to see who can take the biggest bite out of our buns. I've seen lots of different sides to Mike's personality in the eighteen months since I've known him. I've seen him thoughtful, sensitive, kind and strict (but only at the club). But I've never seen him like this before. The playful side of him is amazing. It's like we're the same age.

It doesn't last forever. The closer the ferry gets to Calais, the quieter Mike becomes and as the car pulls off the rank he snaps at me to 'wait' when I ask where we're going. When the customs officers check our passports, his whole body tenses and he holds himself very still. He's worried, but he shouldn't be. As far as Mum and Dad are concerned, I've gone on a karate camping trip. As long as I'm back by Sunday night they'll be fine.

'My niece,' Mike says as the uniformed man looks from him to me.

'Oui,' I say and flash him a smile. Mike twitches, ever so slightly, like he's annoyed with me, but he keeps his eyes fixed on the man's face.

'Merci.' He gives the passports back and waves his hand for us to move on.

*   *   *

29

I almost threw up when I pulled into the parking lot of Malvern Police Station but anger propelled me out of the car and into the building. God knows what the duty sergeant made of me as I flew up to the desk and demanded to speak to someone urgently. My heart's still pounding and I babble rather than speak, my voice filling the small, beige room. DS Hope doesn't say a word. Instead she listens intently, her eyes on me, her pen poised over the notepad on her lap.

'It happened at Greensleeves Garden Centre near Powick,' I say. 'Just before closing. The man's name is Michael Hughes. I don't know the girl's surname but her first name is Chloe. I heard her dad shout to her when he picked her up. I followed them home in my car. Her address is 29, Missingham Road. It's just off the—'

DS Hope raises an eyebrow. 'You followed the girl home?'

'Of course. I was worried about her. I thought if I found out where she lived, then I could pass the information on to you.'

'Why not ask another employee? You just told me you thought she worked there. That she was wearing the same red polo top as the woman on the tills.'

'The woman on the tills wasn't there when I left.' My chest tightens as the lie leaves my mouth, but what else can I say?

DS Hope is looking at me like I'm unhinged. Did I do something weird? Would a normal person not have followed Chloe home?

30

'What did you do after you followed her?'

'I drove straight here.'

'Right, okay. So, let's go back to the start.' DS Hope lays her pen down on her notepad. 'You were walking around the garden centre and you saw an adult man kissing a teenage girl?'

I try to swallow but my mouth is too dry. Being in this windowless beige room is bringing back memories I'd rather forget and it's taking all my willpower not to run from the room.

'Yes, as I said. He went into a summer house. She was already in there, like she was waiting for him. He looked around to see if anyone was watching and then he kissed her.'

'And what time was this?'

'Nearly six o'clock.'

'And this . . .' she glances down, 'Michael Hughes. Does he work at Greensleeves Garden Centre too?'

'No. He's got a delivery company. But I think he does some of their deliveries.'

'You know him then?'

'I . . .'

I can't tell her the truth. I told the duty sergeant that my name was Lou Smith, not Lou Wandsworth. I don't want to talk about what happened between me and Mike. I just want the police to stop it from happening again.

'Lou? Are you okay?' DS Hope sits forward in her seat, her eyes scanning my face.

'I'm just a bit hot.' I grab a tissue from the box on the table and wipe it over my forehead. Mike kissing that girl is all my fault. If I'd testified against him, he might have been given a longer sentence. He might still be in jail. I've spent the last eighteen years telling myself that what happened was a one-off, that it was because of me. I wouldn't – couldn't – let myself believe he'd do that to anyone else.

'What is it you're not telling me, Lou?' DS Hope asks. 'What's your relationship with this man?'

'I haven't got a relationship with him. I came here to report what looked like grooming. That's all. I thought it was the right thing to do.'

'How do you know his name then, and what he does for a living?'

'Because I've used his company for removals before.' The lies are coming thick and fast now. Why did I think this was a good idea? I didn't think it through properly. I never should have stepped foot in here.

'And you recognised him, when you saw him in the summer house?'

'Yes. Why are you asking me all these questions?'

'I'm just trying to establish what happened.' Her gaze doesn't waver. She doesn't say anything for several seconds. She's trying to get me to talk but I've said too much already. 'The thing is, Lou, we need evidence to arrest someone and if there's something you're not telling me you're going to make my job more difficult.'

'He's a paedophile. He's served time for abducting . . .' I pause. My heart's beating so quickly I feel like I'm on the verge of a panic attack, ' . . . another girl.'

DS Hope raises her eyebrows as she scribbles in her notepad. 'When was this? Do you know?'

'A long time ago. Look, I've told you everything I know. I was just trying to do the right thing, coming here and telling you what I saw.'

She gives me a lingering look then stands up.

'All right, Lou. I've got enough to go on for now. I'll be in touch.'

Chapter 7

Wendy

Tuesday 24th April 2007

Wendy stiffens as two young men glance her way as they walk into the café. Her preferred table, a single-seater in the window, was occupied when she came in and she had no choice but to take a four-seater in the corner. It's a quarter past one and the café is filling up. Sooner or later someone's going to ask if they can share her table. What if Louise Wandsworth herself took one of the seats opposite her? Wendy's stomach clenches with a mixture of fear and excitement.

But there's no sign of her. When Lou came into the café yesterday just after one, she went straight up to the counter and ordered a black coffee, a chicken roll and a tub of fruit salad. Wendy watched discreetly from behind her paperwork as Lou frowned over her mobile phone and picked at her food.

It was the first time she'd seen Lou up close and she was dumbstruck. It reminded her of the evening she'd been having drinks in the Royal Malvern hotel with Angela when Michael Ball had walked in. Wendy had raised a hand, waved and flashed him a smile. Michael Ball didn't even acknowledge her. Instead his gaze swivelled across the room, to a large, raucous group of lovies by the bar. Wendy was mortified. Angela told her that she wasn't the first person to mistake a celebrity for a friend but Wendy insisted they leave immediately. It had been the same when she'd first seen Lou – the surprise and the hollowing in her stomach – only that time she'd managed to grip the table rather than thrusting her arm into the air.

When she'd read on Facebook that Lou was going to start a new job at Consol eLearning, she'd imme-diately checked out the company online. According to the website, they developed eLearning solutions for the public and private sector, whatever that meant. Lou's friends seemed to be as surprised as Wendy by her proposed move from London to Malvern. There were lots of ridiculously effusive comments begging her not to go and several 'we'll miss you soooooo much.' When asked by one friend why she was making the move, Lou had replied, 'I'll DM you.' That had frustrated Wendy almost as much as her initial attempt to add Lou as a friend. Wendy didn't comment. She never did. Instead she lurked, reading and analysing everything she found.

She hadn't planned to sit in the café directly oppo-site Consol eLearning on Lou's first day but she'd woken up at 5.30 a.m. and hadn't been able to get back to sleep. With her car in the garage, Monty walked, and no meetings until that afternoon, she had found herself at a bit of a loose end.

I probably won't see her, she told herself as she settled herself into the single window seat at 8.15 a.m. with a pot of tea. *And if I don't, that's fine. I have work I can catch up on before I meet up with Judith.*

But Wendy's briefcase of paperwork sat untouched by her feet for an hour. She couldn't tear her gaze away from the window and the people walking past. And then she saw her, Lou, walking down the street. She'd watched, her heart pounding in her chest as Lou had pulled at the door to Consol eLearning, then slumped back in her seat, exhausted and spent, as the door closed behind her and she disappeared from view.

Wendy made a snap decision. She would stay in the café until lunchtime to see where Lou went. No one could have been more surprised than her when she actually came in.

Now, she looks at her watch – 1.32 p.m. Lou's late. Yesterday she came in at 1.05 p.m. But there's no way Wendy can hold on for another second. She really must use the toilet. She grabs her handbag, snatches up her coat and speeds across the café.

When she walks back out again, Lou Wandsworth is standing less than five metres away from her. Shock almost propels Wendy straight back into the ladies'. Across the room, her table has already been snapped up by a family of three and there are no free seats available. She has two choices – leave without paying the bill or join the queue behind Lou?

She moves closer. She has never run off without paying a bill in her life and she's not about to do so now.

Lou doesn't so much as glance round as Wendy silently slips behind her and rests a quivering hand on the top of the glass cake display. Up close, Wendy is able to measure herself against the other woman. Louise Wandsworth is tall, at least five inches taller than her, and her hips – swimming in a too large skirt – are narrower than Wendy's waist. There is mud on the heels of Lou's shoes and the ends of her hair are split and tangled. The compulsion to reach into her bag and pull out a comb is almost more than Wendy can bear. She never leaves the house without checking that her shoes are clean and her hair is neat.

'Order to go, please,' Lou says as the café owner, a smiley woman about Wendy's age in a blue and white striped apron, gives her a nod. 'Black coffee, chicken roll and a fruit salad pot.'

'Not stopping today?'

'No, I need to prepare for a client meeting at three. Well, it's more of a pitch for new business.'

'Sounds important.'

'It is. The boss wants me to bring in more money.'

'Well, fingers crossed it goes well.'

Wendy stands very still, her eyes fixed to the floor as the café owner bustles about, putting the order together, and Lou stands silently beside her, waiting. After an interminable five or six minutes, she hears the clink of money changing hands, the dry rustle of a paper bag being handed over and a soft, breathy 'thank you'.

'Yes?' the café owner says. 'Hello, yes. How can I help you?'

Wendy tears her eyes away from the thin figure sprinting across the road and fixes the other woman with a big smile. She's just had the most wonderful idea.

Chapter 8

Lou

I can't believe I get to spend a whole weekend with Mike in France. First stop, a hotel room just outside Calais. I've been in hotel rooms before, mostly on holiday with Mum and Dad, but this is only the second time I've been to one with Mike. The first time was to a Travelodge in Birmingham. The carpet was blue and there were stripy curtains but they weren't what caught my attention – it was the double bed in the middle of the room. It was finally going to happen. Mike and I were going to have sex for the first time and I was utterly terrified, despite him reassuring me that we'd take our time and he'd be ever so gentle.

We've had sex loads of times since then, sometimes in the dojo changing rooms but mostly in his car after class. When Mike offered to start dropping me home, Dad couldn't say yes fast enough. He said it would give him more time to get some work done but we both knew he meant more time at the pub.

When we reach our hotel room, Mike opens the door, chucks the bags in, then holds up a hand when I try to enter.

'No, no. I need to carry you in!'

I laugh. 'We're not married!'

'We will be one day!'

I try to wriggle away as he reaches for me. I'm far too heavy and I'd die of embarrassment if he drops me. But Mike scoops me up and into his arms as though I'm as light as a feather. He kicks the door closed behind me and half-drops, half-throws me onto the bed. I land on my side and twist round to pull him close for a kiss. He pecks me on the lips, then flips me onto my stomach and pulls me towards him so I'm bent over the bed.

'Mike!' I laugh, as he starts unbuttoning my jeans. 'Let's at least go out for dinner first. I thought this weekend was supposed to be romantic.'

He looks at me but it's as though he doesn't really see me. His cheeks are flushed and his eyes have this weird glassy sheen to them. He's got this jubilant expression on his face, like he's climbed a mountain or won a race.

'It will be,' he says as he yanks my jeans and knickers down to my ankles.

A couple of minutes later he slumps on top of me, roaring as he comes. It's the first time we've had sex and haven't looked each other in the eye.

* * *

40

Three days ago I caved and texted Ben. Mostly because I still feel so awful about what happened and partly because my friend Alice encouraged me to. She rang me on my mobile as I was walking to my car after work. Just for a chat, she said, but we both knew she was fishing for gossip. First she chastised me for not updating Facebook since I left London, then she told me she'd bumped into Ben in the pub. Apparently he was frosty when she asked how he was.

'He said, *I've been better.* Those were his exact words. I think he still likes you, Lou. Are you sure you can't sort things out with him?'

I haven't told Alice the truth about what happened in Dover. I said we'd had an argument and decided to end things. She doesn't know about Mike. None of my friends do.

'I've told you, I'm a screw-up when it comes to men. I can't even become a mad old cat lady because I'm allergic to them. Cats, not old ladies, although I've never had one rub themselves up and down my leg.'

Alice laughed. 'Okay, well, first off, we're all screwed up. Some people are just better at hiding it than others. Secondly, what you and Ben had was pretty intense. I barely saw you when you were with him. Maybe you both just need a bit of a breather. Has he texted you since you split up? Have you texted him?'

41

No, I told her. I haven't heard from him. And I haven't texted him either. But I still feel really bad about what happened.

'Text him then. Say sorry. You obviously like him. If you didn't we wouldn't be having this conversation. Anyway, what's it like being back? How's the farmhouse?'

She listened as I told her how I'd almost driven straight past my old family home, it had changed so much. That the neatly clipped hedges, gnarly apple trees and bright daffodils that lined the lane up to our house had been replaced by a tangle of green foliage and weeds. The trees dipped so low, their branches so tightly tangled, it was like driving through a dark tunnel. I told her how my heart had caught in my throat as I'd pulled into the driveway and spotted Dad's parked Volvo.

'For a second, I thought he was still alive,' I said. I didn't tell her how freaked out I was when I walked into the living room and saw his old chair.

'Bloody hell, Lou,' she said when I finally stopped talking. 'Sounds traumatic. Oh mate, I knew I should have come with you, at least for your first weekend.'

By the end of the phone call I felt calmer than I had done in days. I hadn't realised how much I was bottling up my emotions or how isolated I was. Alice was the first person I'd spoken to in a week. Properly spoken to, I mean. Superficial conversations with my new colleagues at work didn't count.

I took Alice's advice and texted Ben before I got into my car.

I'm sorry for what happened in Dover. There are reasons why I reacted the way I did that I can't explain right now. You didn't deserve the way I spoke to you afterwards. I hope you're okay. X

I read the message again, deleted the kiss at the end and then sent it. Ben had twenty minutes to reply before I reached the countryside and the technology dead zone that is Dad's house. There's no reception, no Wi-Fi and no neighbours for at least a quarter of a mile. If someone bludgeoned me in my bed, no one would hear me scream. There's a landline phone downstairs that works, but that's it.

It's Saturday now and I still haven't heard back from Ben. I haven't heard anything from DS Hope either. When I rang for an update, she told me to ring back this afternoon. The wait has been torturous. I can't stop thinking about Chloe, and the look on her face as she ran out of the garden centre. Her cheeks were flushed and she was smiling. I remember how that felt – the adrenaline rush of an illicit meeting, the warmth of the kiss, the wretchedness of saying goodbye. I thought I was so grown up. That my life was a romantic movie. That I was in control. I couldn't have been more wrong.

Chloe looked so damned joyful that it makes me feel sick. Sick with guilt. She should have been smiling because she'd just been kissed by a boy her own age, not a man old enough to be her father. I just pray things haven't progressed any further. If he's put her through what he put me through I'll never forgive myself.

43

This morning I decided to try and distract myself by getting on with some of the jobs I've been putting off. I've scrubbed the bathroom from top to bottom and sorted through Dad's wardrobe and chest of drawers, bundling jumpers, jeans and suits into black plastic bags for the charity shop. I had a bit of a cry when I found a framed photo of me face down in the bottom of a drawer. There was nothing else that shed any light on who he was or the life he'd lived. Just a few piles of change, some painkillers, half a tube of Deep Heat, betting slips, newspapers, an alarm clock, a radio.

I was fourteen the last time I saw him. It was the weekend before Mike's court case. Mum waited in the car at the bottom of the track while I walked up to the house that I hadn't called home for nearly a year. I dumped the cardboard box I was carrying outside the garage, then knocked on the side door. When no one answered, I turned the handle and let myself in. I found Dad slumped in a chair in front of the television, horse racing blaring and an empty bottle of whisky on the table beside him. He didn't open his eyes when I said his name and he didn't stir as I shook his shoulder. Only when I turned off the TV and slapped him, hard, on the back of his hand did he open his eyes.

'I'm going, Dad,' I said. 'To London, with Mum. We're not coming back. I've left a box of my things by the garage. Can you keep it here? Mum says there won't be enough space in our flat in London.'

His eyes swivelled towards me. They were red-rimmed and puffy, dark pinpricks in a rough, doughy face. He was only forty-seven but he looked twenty years older. 'Have fun,' he murmured, then he closed his eyes again.

Now, I push open the door to my old room and throw the bin bags on the growing pile on the floor. Other than the piles of Dad's crap, it's exactly as I left it eighteen years ago. I hate this room. Mike never came to the house but he's in here. He's ingrained in the fabric of the faded yellow curtains, the peeling wallpaper and the bleached faces of the popstars I pinned to the wall. The number of nights I'd lie in bed, staring into the darkness, losing myself in my imagination. A smile during a kata, trouble finding my things as I got changed, coming out of the changing rooms to discover that I was the only one left in the dojo. Mike appearing behind me and lifting my hair from my neck and—

I back sharply out of the room and slam the door shut. I need to make the call. I can't wait anymore.

My hand shakes as I pick up the landline and dial the station. If Mike's been arrested and charged I'll need to tell the truth about who I really am. And if he hasn't . . . No, I'm not even going to go there.

'Hello,' says a male voice I don't recognise. 'This is DS Walters.'

'Oh, I was expecting to speak to DS Hope.'

'DS Hope's not in until later. I'm her colleague. How can I help?'

He listens as I tell him my fake name and summarise what I told DS Hope, then asks me to hold the line. I can barely breathe as I wait.

45

'Right, well,' he says. 'It looks like the CPS haven't authorised the charges.'

'What?'

'We carried out a thorough investigation and referred it to the CPS, but I'm afraid there won't be a prosecution.'

'But he's a paedophile! He's abusing a young girl. I saw him!'

DS Walters sighs heavily. 'I don't know what to tell you. Well, I can't actually tell you anything because of data protection rules, but let's just say that the CPS can be a strange beast sometimes.'

'Can I speak to them? Tell them what I saw?'

He laughs dryly. 'I'm afraid not.'

'So that's it? He just carries on doing what he's doing?'

There's a pause then, 'Our hands are tied, I'm afraid. Is there anything else I can help you with?'

'No, there's nothing else.'

I end the call and stare at the phone in my hand. How can this have happened? Mike was sent to jail for five years for what he did to me. Why haven't they locked him up again? It's my fault. I screwed up again when I didn't tell the police who I really am. But it's not too late to put things right.

A tall man with hollow cheeks, thinning hair and an angular face opens the blue door at 29 Missingham Road. He looks me up and down, sighs and rests against the door frame.

'Yes?' He doesn't say 'what do you want?' but it's written all over his face.

'I was wondering if I could have a word with you and your wife. It's about Chloe.'

His expression darkens. 'What's this about?'

'If I could just come in I'll tell you. It's . . . quite sensitive.'

'We've already spoken to the police and if you're a journalist you can fuck right off.'

'Alan!' a woman calls from the back of the house. 'Who is it?'

'No one!'

'Please, I'm not a journalist or police. Maybe I could talk to your wife?'

'She's ill.'

A curtain twitches at an upstairs window.

'Please,' I say as Alan moves to shut the door. 'A man called Mike Hughes is having an inappropriate relationship with your daughter and I'm worried about her.'

'Who the fuck are you? If you're not police or journalist . . .' His eyes narrow as he looks me up and down. 'Are you the one that reported him?'

'I . . . I . . . yes, I am.'

'Are you now?' He shakes his head slowly, his lips pressed into a tight, thin line. 'Got a soft spot for him have you, love? You wouldn't be the first bored housewife to try it on. Turn you down, did he? Is that why you thought you'd get your revenge by spinning a little story?'

'It's not a story. I saw Mike and Chloe—'

'You disgust me!' He lurches towards me, forcing me to step back. 'That man's like a dad to my girl.

I'd trust him with my life. And hers. And I've had it up to here,' he jabs at his throat with a flat hand, 'with gossips, do-gooders and shit-spreaders.'

'I'm not—'

'Mike Hughes is a good man. He spent five years in jail because he tried to keep one of the kids at his club safe when she ran away to France. The stupid bitch was so scared of her alky dad that she lied to the police about what had happened and I won't let you,' he jabs a finger at me, 'or anyone else put him through that kind of hell again. If you ever come back here again I won't be responsible for my actions. Do you hear me? Now piss off.'

The door slams in my face. As the heavy stomp, stomp, stomp of feet on stairs rattles the house, the curtain at the upstairs window twitches again. This time I catch a glimpse of a face. It's Chloe and she looks scared.

48

Chapter 9

Chloe

Monday 30th April 2007

Chloe walks with her head down and her book bag gripped to her chest. Normally she'd drag her feet as she walked from the bus stop to school, but today she can't get there quickly enough. Anything is better than being at home with her arsehole of a dad, *anything*. He went spare after that stupid woman turned up at the door. She tried to listen to their conversation but all she could hear was the woman pleading to come in. The second the front door slammed shut, her dad stormed up to her room. She threw herself onto her bed just as he flung open the door.

'Is this down to you? Have you been talking shit about Mike at school?'

'No.' She grabbed her pillow and hugged it close. 'I wouldn't.'

'Because she looked like a teacher. Sounded like one too.' He crossed the room in four strides and yanked open the curtains. 'She's gone.' He turned back to look at Chloe. 'Who was she? I know you were eavesdropping.'

'I don't know. I've never seen her before.'

Chloe hugged her pillow tighter. Could it be the police again? Her dad hadn't met the woman who'd knocked on the door the other day. She was wearing normal clothes but she said her name was DS Anna Hope, from West Mercia police. Chloe felt sick with fear when DS Hope asked if her parents were in. She hadn't taken anything big from the garden centre – just a few small ornaments she thought were cute and a packet of fairy lights. They were hidden in the bottom of her wardrobe, wrapped in an old dressing gown. But that wasn't what DS Hope wanted to talk to her about, she wanted to talk about Mike. Was there somewhere they could have a little chat? Just a few questions. It wasn't a formal interview. She said that Mum was welcome to join them if that was something Chloe wanted. It wasn't, but her mum insisted she sit in on the conversation before she could say a word.

The next few minutes were the most excruciating of Chloe's life. DS Hope started by asking her which her favourite bands were and which member she fancied the most, but she could feel her mum's worried eyes boring into the side of her head as the police officer switched to using phrases like, 'unwanted attention', 'inappropriate comments' and – worst of all – 'touching that made you feel uncomfortable or scared'. Had Mike ever asked her to do anything that made her feel bad? Had they spent time alone together? Had he bought her gifts? Had he asked her to keep something secret? Had he threatened her or her family? Chloe did her best to meet the police officer's eyes but she could feel her cheeks burning as she answered the questions. Mike was her dad's friend, she told the police officer. They'd chatted but only ever in front of another adult. He hadn't touched her or done anything inappropriate. He was a nice man who said hello to her if her saw her at work and that was all. DS Hope wrote everything she said down in a little notebook, then made Chloe and her mum sign it. After that she asked to speak to her mum in the kitchen.

When they came back into the living room, her mum had a weird, vacant expression on her face. She didn't say anything to her though, not even when DS Hope asked if she could have a look through Chloe's room and made them sign her notebook again to say that they'd agreed. Chloe stood next to her mum at the door to her bedroom, hands clenched into tight fists, as the detective searched her jewellery box, homework books, bed and chest of drawers. Panic rose in her chest as DS Hope lifted up her dressing gown in the bottom of the wardrobe but she didn't unfold it and her stolen stash remained hidden. When she asked if she could take a look at her mobile, Chloe handed it over. She deleted all the texts Mike sent her as soon as she'd read them (as well as the ones she sent him) and he'd warned her not to keep a diary or any mementoes of the time they spent together. But she couldn't stop herself from reaching up behind her hairline to touch the necklace around her neck. Mike hadn't bought her many gifts – a couple of CDs, a book, plus he'd given her forty pounds after he found her crying in one of the sheds at work. She'd accidentally run up a huge bill on her mobile by buying game add-ons and she was too scared to tell her dad. After listening to her sob, Mike reached into his wallet and handed her the money to cover it. 'Now you don't need to tell him,' he said. 'And you don't need to cry anymore.'

Her gave her the necklace after Chloe got upset about a list the boys at school had made. It ranked the girls in her year in order of the fittest. One of her friends had managed to sneak a look at the piece of paper and Chloe's name was last. Mike had hugged her close while she cried, then reached into his pocket and pressed something into her hand.

'It's beautiful.' She ran a finger over the delicate edges of the silver daisy pendant. It was the loveliest present anyone had ever given her.

'It is. And so are you. Those boys are idiots. When they grow up, they'll kick themselves for not realising how stunning you are.'

She'd shivered as he fastened the necklace around her neck, his fingers brushing her skin. Then, embarrassed by her reaction, she'd pulled away. If Mike noticed her reaction he didn't mention it. Instead he looked from her face to the pendant, nestling above the top button of her work polo shirt and smiled.

'It suits you.'

Chloe presses a hand against the cold chain at her neck as she spots a small group of boys hanging around the school gates. They're the ones who started the stupid list. Five weeks she's had the necklace and her parents haven't said a word. There was a time when her mum would notice every little thing about her – a scrape on her knee after a fall at primary school, a new hairstyle after they took turns to braid each other's hair at break, a spot on her chin, a rash on her chest – but it's been a long time since her mum did more than give her a passing glance. Sometimes, when it's just her, Mum and Jamie at home, she feels like a ghost.

'Chloe?'

She turns sharply as someone says her name. A tall, thin woman with her hair pulled back into a tight ponytail is hurrying along the pavement towards her. It's the woman who knocked on her front door the night before.

'Chloe, have you got a second?'

'No.' She continues to walk. Two girls she doesn't recognise laugh as they overtake her and her stomach clenches with anxiety. Great, another reason for people to laugh at her.

'Please, Chloe, just five minutes. It's important.'

The hand on her arm makes her stop just long enough to shake it off. 'I've got to get to school.'

'I know. I won't take up much of your time. Please, just hear me out.'

It's the woman's suit that makes her pause. She looks smart, like a lawyer or something.

'What do you want?'

'I need to talk to you about Mike Hughes.'

'Oh god.' She sighs dramatically. 'Not that again. I already talked to the police.' She lowers her voice as a boy from her year swerves around them. 'He hasn't done anything wrong.'

'He has,' the woman says. 'I saw him kiss you.'

Chloe stares at her, her throat dry, her mind empty. 'You're lying.'

'I'm not. I was in the garden centre. I saw him kiss you in the summer house.'

'No you didn't.'

'Chloe,' the woman touches her on the shoulder again. 'I know what you're going through. I know what he's like. He makes you feel special, doesn't he? Beautiful? You feel understood and cared for, like he's the only person in the world who really gets you.' The woman is speaking softly and quickly, like she's running out of breath, and she's leaning in far closer than Chloe is comfortable with. 'Has he told you that he loves you yet?'

She shakes her head. 'I don't know what you're talking about.'

'Yes you do. I can see it in your eyes. You need to tell the police what's going on. He's a dangerous man. You think he's kind and generous and caring but he's manipulating you. He's a paedophile, Chloe. This is all about control and nothing to do with love. Have you slept with him yet?'

'What? No!' The horror in Chloe's voice is real

54

and the other woman seems to sense it because she raises her eyebrows.

'Good. Don't. Whatever's going on between you and Mike Hughes, you need to end it now. No good can come of it. You need to trust me on this.'

'Trust you? I don't even know who you are.'

'I'm—'

'Chloeeee!' A red-haired girl with thick black eyebrows barges between them. 'Sorry, Miss, I need to talk to Chloe. Chlo, did you do last night's biology homework because I, like, well, didn't. I need to borrow yours. Is this it?' She yanks at one of the books Chloe is clutching to her chest. Normally there's no way in hell she'd let Misty Engles anywhere near her but right now she'd take an atomic bomb over spending one more minute talking about Mike Hughes with this weirdo.

'Course you can borrow it,' she says, then she threads her arm through Misty's and heads for the gates.

'Chloe,' the woman calls from behind her. 'Let me give you my phone number. You can call me if—'

'Fuck off!' Chloe shouts without looking back. 'Just fuck off.'

Misty Engles giggles. 'Who was that?'

'Just some freak. I think she fancies me.'

Chloe's laughter lasts all of thirty seconds, then her phone bleeps with a text from her dad. She's been sacked from the garden centre. They know about the thefts. And so does he.

Chapter 10

Wendy

It's six minutes past nine. Wendy's irritation at being late is reflected back at her in the bathroom mirror, along with a face of carefully, if heavily, applied make-up.

'Warpaint,' Wendy says to her reflection, then sighs heavily. Monty, the springer spaniel at her feet, nudges her leg with his nose and she reaches down to rub him behind the ears.

She's being ridiculous, she knows she is. Wearing a faceful of make-up isn't going to impress Lou Wandsworth. Nor will it give her the upper hand. In fact the only message it'll give Lou is that Wendy needs to get down to Boots for a new mascara because the clumpy eyelash look isn't fetching on catwalk models, never mind on fifty-nine-year-old women. She reaches for a make-up wipe and roughly scrubs at her cheeks, lips and eyes. She doesn't need make-up for what she's about to do.

She walks into the office with her shoulders back, her chin tipped up and an uncomfortable prickling sensation under her arms. After she dropped Monty off at her sister's house she had to put her foot down to compensate for the ridiculous amount of time she'd spent applying, and then removing, her make-up, but she parked up outside Consol eLearning right on time. And with a minute to spare too.

'Good morning,' she says merrily to the matronly-looking receptionist. 'My name is Wendy Harrison. I'm here to see Louise Wandsworth.'

'She's expecting you. I'll just ring through. Would you like a coffee or tea?'

'A cup of tea would be lovely. Milk no sugar.'

There's something very pleasing about people making a fuss of you, Wendy thinks as she sits back in her chair and sips at her tea. Ever since she arrived at Consol eLearning ten minutes ago, she's been greeted with warm smiles and firm handshakes. She was even given a plate of nice Marks and Spencer biscuits as she was shown into the meeting room by Lou and a rather balding man who introduced himself as Gary Lambley, head of sales. Wendy felt a wave of disappointment as he thrust a sweaty hand at her. She'd assumed her meeting would be with Lou and Lou alone, but actually the presence of someone else in the room has meant that she can study the other woman without being too obvious.

'Well, that's pretty much everything about us and

what we do,' Gary says as his presentation finally draws to a close. 'Do you have any questions?'

'No, I think you've covered pretty much everything.' Most of the presentation went over Wendy's head but she's not about to admit that.

Lou gets up from her seat and switches on the lights. She smiles warmly at Wendy as she sits back down. 'As I mentioned on the phone, I am quite new here, but I've got over seven years' experience in managing eLearning projects and I'd be your first port of call.'

'It sounds as though I'll be in very safe hands.'

'You would. Absolutely. So, now we've told you all about us perhaps you'd like to share a bit more about the training you'd like us to develop. You said on the phone that . . .' her hair falls over her face as she glances down at her notebook '. . . the nursing faculty at the University of Worcester are considering adding some eLearning to the bachelor's degree?'

'That's right yes.' Words tumble out of Wendy's mouth like stones from a bucket. Her nursing degree is over thirty years old but she can still recall the fundamentals of her training. And besides, she practised for this question when she was out walking Monty yesterday. When she'd come up with the idea of finding out a little bit more about Lou Wandsworth by masquerading as a new customer, she'd worried that there was a flaw in her plan – that Lou might ask for a landline contact number in addition to the mobile number she'd provided, or the details of someone more senior at the university. She hadn't. She'd taken Wendy completely at her word.

It's astonishing how gullible and naïve some people are, Wendy thinks as Lou nods and smiles at everything she says. They're traits you'd associate with the weak and vulnerable – children and the elderly – and yet here is a woman that's neither of those things. Is she really that gullible? Or – Wendy sits up a little higher in her chair and looks towards the door – it could be a trap. She'd assumed that Lou wouldn't know who she was when she walked into the office. Why would she? They'd never met before; Lou hadn't even glanced at her when she was behind her in the queue at the café. They'd never spoken other than Wendy's initial enquiry about a meeting and there are no photos of her on the internet for Lou to google but there's still a small chance she might know who she is.

'That all sounds great, Dr Harrison,' Lou says and Wendy suppresses a smile. It was a bit of silliness, deciding to award herself a doctorate seconds before she picked up the phone to ring Consol eLearning, but she has to admit that she quite likes the sound of it.

'Wendy, please.'

'Do you have any questions for us?'

The male voice makes Wendy twitch. She'd been so focussed on Lou – on the muddy green hue of her irises, the enlarged pores on either side of her nose, the visible tendons in her neck and the sharp collar-bones beneath them – that she'd quite forgotten they weren't alone in the room.

'I'd love another cup of tea please.' She smiles tightly as she pushes her saucer in his direction.

Lou moves to get up from her seat. 'I'll get one for you.'

'No, no.' Wendy flashes her eyebrows at Gary. 'I'm sure he wouldn't mind, would you Gary? I've got a few questions for Lou. If that's okay?'

'That's fine. No problem at all.'

Wendy registers a fleeting glance between Lou and her colleague as he leaves the room, but the second the door closes behind him, Lou is all smiles again. Wendy reaches down beside her and pulls her handbag onto her lap. *I could have a knife in here*, she thinks as she unclips the fastener and reaches in for her Laura Ashley glasses case, *and no one would ever know. I could plunge it into her chest and make it back out onto the street, before anyone realised anything was wrong.*

Gosh, she thinks as the case opens with a satisfying pop and she takes out her glasses. *That was a bit of a dark thought. I don't know where that came from. I'm just here to find out a little bit more about Lou Wandsworth. That's not a crime, is it? I could have introduced myself to her in the café instead but social situations are so awkward. She could have excused herself and walked away. Office protocol means she's got no choice but to sit here and talk to me. Whether she likes it or not.*

'So,' she says as she hooks her glasses over her ears and pushes them up the bridge of her nose. 'Tell me a bit about you, Lou.'

The other woman shuffles awkwardly in her chair. 'Well, um, as I said, I've got seven years' experience—'

'No, no. Not all that corporate stuff. You as a person. If we're going to be working together for a while it makes sense to get to know each other a little better. Doesn't it?'

'Oh, um. Sure. What . . . er . . . what sort of thing do you want to know?'

'Anything you want to tell me!'

Wendy's chest tightens as the younger woman glances towards the door. She's overdoing it. Her convivial tone sounds forced and she's making Lou feel ill at ease.

'Me for example,' she says quickly as she picks up her pen, 'I'm fifty-nine, no children, live alone with my little dog Monty. I'm a big fan of gardening, crosswords and crime dramas.' She laughs lightly but the pen in her hands is strained to breaking point. If the other woman notices, she doesn't let on. 'How about you?'

Lou shrugs. 'There's not much to tell you really. I'm thirty-two and er . . . I live just outside Malvern.'

'Oh yes. Whereabouts?'

'Near Bromyard.'

'Oh, out in the sticks.'

'Yes. It is a bit.'

'And do you live there with your husband?' Wendy's gaze flicks towards the naked ring finger of Lou's left hand.

'I live alone.'

'That's something we have in common then.'

And it's not the only thing.

'Woah!' Lou jerks back in her seat and raises her hands to her face as something flies across the desk towards her. 'Your . . . your pen.'

'My what?' Wendy is genuinely surprised to look down and see two halves of a biro in her hands. She's snapped it clean in two.

'Tea!' Gary walks backwards into the room, carrying a tea tray in his hands. 'What did I miss?' He looks at Lou as she stands up. 'Bloody hell. What happened to you?'

'It's ink.' She pulls the white shirt away from her body, but the sticky red ink isn't only on the crisp white cotton. Her cheeks, her forehead and her throat are splattered too. 'Wendy's pen broke. I'd better go and clean myself up.'

'I really am very sorry,' Wendy says as Lou slips from the room. 'I don't know what happened.'

'It's fine,' Gary says as he places a fresh cup of tea in front of her. 'Accidents happen.'

Wendy picks up her tea cup and raises it to her mouth.

'They do, don't they?' she says, then she takes a small sip.

62

Chapter 11

Lou

When we woke up this morning we had breakfast, but not in the restaurant. We ate sandwiches in bed – Tesco sandwiches that Mike bought before he picked me up yesterday – and washed them down with warm Fanta. Afterwards, Mike told me to shower and pack up my things because we were off to Rouen. I was a bit disappointed that we weren't going to Paris (if you have to go to France you should at least see the Eiffel Tower), but I tried not to let it show on my face. I don't care where we go, as long as I'm with Mike.

Not that I've seen much of Rouen, just a few old buildings and a glimpse of the river on the way to the hotel. We had sex again, pretty much as soon as we walked into our door. This time we did it face to face and Mike didn't roar when he came. He did cry though, after he rolled off me, which I thought was a bit weird. When I asked him what was wrong he said that he'd never loved anyone as much as he loved me and that it would break him if I ever left him. I wiped the tears from his cheeks, covered his face with kisses and told him that would never happen. He was the love of my life and we were going to spend the rest of our lives together. He looked at me then for a really long time without saying anything, then he rolled away from me and got out of bed. When he started pulling on his clothes, I moved to get out of bed too but he told me to stay where I was. He had a surprise planned and he'd be back soon. I begged him to tell me what it was but he refused, laughing and saying it wouldn't be a surprise if he told me. When he left the room, I heard the key turn in the lock.

That was six hours ago. The sun is going down, it's seven o'clock and I'm really pissed off. I thought we'd go sightseeing together or something, walk hand in hand along the river, visit a few shops and see the ruined buildings Mike was talking about on the way here. Some romantic break this has been. It's Saturday and we're due to go back to the UK tomorrow and all we've done is have sex twice and eat sandwiches. And I've been stuck here alone all day. There isn't even a TV and I didn't bother bringing a book. All I've done is nap, throw balled-up socks into the bin, write my diary in the back of an exercise book and stare at the stupid painting on the wall opposite the bed. I could probably draw it with my eyes shut now. I can't ever remember being so bored in my life.

I sit up sharply, pulling my knees into my chest as

the locked bedroom door rattles and Mike steps into the room. He looks exhausted, and a tiny bit pissed, but he smiles as our eyes meet. 'Hey, hey. How's the love of my life then?'

I don't return his smile. 'Where've you been?'

He takes a step back, as though I've just landed a punch in his belly. 'What?'

'Where the fuck have you been?'

'Woah.' His smile vanishes. 'You don't get to speak to me like that.'

'I do if you leave me locked in here so you can go and get pissed.'

'Who said I'm—'

'You are! I can smell it. You smell like my dad. You're a—'

'Don't you dare compare me to him. Don't you dare!'

'Get out!' I reach for the pillow and launch it across the room. It hits him weakly on the hand and drops to the floor. 'Get out and leave me alone. I want to go home.'

Mike crosses the room, his hands clenched into fists, jaw tight, nostrils flaring. I scoot as far back on the bed as I can and wrap my arms around my body. But he doesn't touch me and he doesn't say a word. Instead he stops at the end of the bed and glowers at me until I break eye contact, then he marches straight back out of the room and turns the lock.

I stare at the door, too shocked to react, but the numbness doesn't last long and I howl with frustration and despair, then burst into tears. I cry, curled up on the bed, until the world beyond the window turns black and I pass out with exhaustion. It's still dark when I wake but the radio alarm clock on the bedside table glows red with the time. 1.13 a.m. I pull the thin duvet up to my chin and roll over. As I do, I catch sight of a figure sitting in the armchair on the other side of the room. It's Mike. And he's watching me.

I've been living in Dad's house for over a week now but, despite hours spent hoovering, cleaning and scrubbing, the smell still hits me the second I open the front door and step into the porch. Dampness, mustiness and cold. It's the scent of neglect.

I glance at my watch as I step into the kitchen. Twenty to six. Mike said he would be here a little after six thirty.

I trail from the kitchen to the living room and sit down on the sofa. Dad's chair, in all its horrible tweedy green worn glory, is closer to the TV, but I haven't sat in it once since I got here. I'm trying to work up the nerve to throw it away.

Dad's friend Bill was the one who found him. He realised something was wrong, he told me on the phone, when the local pub landlord told him that Dad hadn't been in in over a week. He went to check on him after closing time. The curtains weren't drawn, the lights were on and the TV was blaring away in the corner of the room. Bill said he could tell by the way Dad was slumped in his chair that he was dead. A heart attack, the coroner said.

It wasn't hard to pick Bill out from the mourners at Dad's cremation. Other than me, the only other people in the room were the celebrant, the funeral director and three elderly men. Unsure what to do after the ceremony ended, I stood by the door and shook hands with the scant group of mourners as they left. Bill gripped my hand in both of his.

'I know your dad was a grumpy old bugger,' he said, his voice rough and rasping, 'but he was proud of you. He told me a few times that he had a daughter living the high life and earning herself a small fortune in London.'

I smiled and thanked Bill for his good wishes. I didn't mention that Dad and I hadn't spoken in over ten years – other than a brief and awkward phone call when I rang him five years ago to tell him that Mum had died of cancer – and that he had no idea what I was doing or how much I was earning in London (certainly not a small fortune). I did cry though, when I got back to my car. *Proud* was not a word in Dad's vocabulary when it came to me. Disgrace – yes. Embarrassment – that too. While Mum rushed up to me and wrapped me in her arms after I was brought back from France, Dad could barely look at me. When he did it was to ask whether I had been harmed. Harmed. He meant, had I had sex with Mike? I could tell by the way his eyes swept the length of my body then focussed on a spot on the floor near my feet. Afterwards, Mum and I went back to our flat. We stayed there, locked together on the sofa with the TV on loud while the phone rang off the hook and journalists tapped at the kitchen window and thumped on the front door. One night I heard an argument between Mum and Dad on the phone. She was trying to keep her voice down but I heard her snap, 'I can't believe you'd suggest that, Steve. This is your daughter we're talking about and she's fourteen years old.' Dad thought I'd brought it all on myself. He wasn't the only one who thought that. I did too.

Mum tried to convince me to testify against Mike. She said she knew that I loved him but what he had done was wrong and he had to be stopped from doing it to anyone else. I started to cry then, not because of what she'd said but because she'd got me so wrong. What I felt towards Mike wasn't love. It was a strange limbo emotion – a longing for the love I thought we'd had, wrapped up in guilt, regret and fear. When Mum, and the police, finally accepted that I wouldn't testify against Mike, she decided that we should move to London before the trial started. Mum said it was for the best.

I turn on the TV, watch a couple of seconds of a game show, then change the channel. I watch a couple of seconds of a period drama, then press a button on the remote. I change the channel once more, then turn it off. I look at my watch again.

6.08 p.m.

Not enough time to go for a run.

Mike will be here in less than forty-five minutes.

After Chloe told me to fuck off this morning, I was so frustrated I drove to the nearest phone box, rang

Mike's work and asked to speak to him. If the police weren't going to prosecute, and Chloe and her family refused to listen to me, the only option I had left was to confront him directly. Ringing from the phone box was a deliberate decision. It meant Mike wouldn't have my number or any way of contacting me. He'd be shocked to hear from me, wrong-footed, and I'd be the one in control. I'd call, tell him who I was and say that I needed to speak to him in a public place (a park maybe or St Anne's Well on the Malvern Hills). I'd tell him how he'd ruined my life. How I'd end a relationship as soon as a boyfriend told me they loved me because I associated love with control. How I'd freak out if anyone so much as brushed my neck with their fingers. How promiscuous I'd been because my self-worth was in the toilet. How I'd only have sex if I was the one who initiated it and it took place in my home. I'd tell him all of these things, and more, and then I'd scream in his face that it was his fault. That he'd made me like this. That I'd spent eighteen years denying how much of a fuck-up I was, but I wasn't going to do it anymore. And especially not when he was about to screw up another innocent girl's life as much as he'd screwed up mine.

I was shaking – with anger and fear – as I tapped the number out on the buttons and waited for the call to connect. My voice wavered as I asked to speak to Mike Hughes. The receptionist had to ask me to repeat myself. When she said he wasn't in – he was already on the delivery run – I slumped against the glass side of the phone booth.

'You could try his mobile,' she said.

It took me three attempts to call his number. Twice I slammed the phone down before the call connected.

'Mike Hughes speaking.'

I pressed myself up against the glass as though pinned by his voice.

'Hello?'

Tears burned beneath my closed eyelids.

'Hello, is there anyone there?'

My courage had vanished. I could barely breathe.

'Are you after a delivery or a collection? Hello? I'm going to put the phone down now.'

'Do you know who this is?' Panic forced the words out of my mouth.

'No? Should I?'

A pause. A silence that stretched eighteen years. I didn't have any control. The moment I told Mike who I was he'd have a choice. He could tell me to fuck off. He could refuse to meet me and put the phone down. The only way to help myself, and save Chloe, was to take away that choice and put him in a situation where he had to listen.

'My name is Milly Dawson. I'd like to arrange a collection please.'

'What is it and where are you?'

'An armchair. It needs to go to the dump. I live in Acton Green.'

'That's a way out so it'll be pricey. Forty quid.'

'That's fine. When can you get here?'

'Six thirty all right?'

I told him it was fine and gave him my address. I

held my breath, waiting for that spark of recognition, for him to comment that he'd been to the farm before. Instead he said,

'All right then Milly, I'll see you later.'

Then the call ended, just like that.

By the time I got to work I didn't have more than five minutes to run a comb through my hair and print out my emails before Alison buzzed me to tell me that Dr Wendy Harrison was waiting in reception for me. That was a strange meeting. I've met some interesting clients in my time – including the man who talked to my chin rather than looking me in the eye, a woman who continuously tapped a pen against her teeth and the man who addressed all of his questions to my male colleagues rather than me – but I've never met anyone like Dr Harrison before. She had a very odd manner for someone with a background in nursing – clinical, rather than caring. I could feel her watching me while Gary gave his presentation and then, after she'd ordered him from the room to make more tea, she stared at me like a specimen under a microscope. Then she started asking me personal questions, her strange, fixed smile not faltering once. As I wondered if she might be on the autistic spectrum, she sprayed me with ink.

Let's just say I won't be gutted if we don't win the bid.

6.12 p.m.

After a week's worth of tidying, the house finally looks as I remember it, but it doesn't *feel* like the

71

house where I grew up. I always used to feel safe here – until the arguments started between Mum and Dad anyway. It was always draughty and the ancient cracked tiles in the kitchen were so cold I'd hop from foot to foot as I poured out my cereal, but the sounds were reassuring. It was always so noisy – the radio babbling away in the kitchen, the television blaring in the living room and Dad chopping logs in the garden while the dog barked at birds. All those noises have gone now and it's eerily quiet. It's true what they say, about people making a house a home. I never really understood that until now.

'Right.' I grab the arm of Dad's old green armchair and pull. 'I'm not letting Mike in this house, which means you're going in the barn.'

I am dripping with sweat by the time I reach the back garden. The lawn is more weeds than grass and the bright pots of flowers that Mum spent hours planting and tending are long gone. The only decorative touch Dad added is a pile of abandoned car tyres and a collapsed pile of logs. The gate at the back of the garden is almost rusted shut. I have to give it a good shove before it swings open, then I drag the armchair into the yard. When this was a working farm, there would have been tractors, trailers and farm machinery filling the space, but all that's left is a huge dilapidated barn and the three fields that wrap around the house. Dad was an architect but he had designs about becoming a farmer when he bought this place. He swiftly changed his mind after the chickens he kept in the back garden were wiped out by foxes. His next bright idea was to try and convert the barn. It's accessible by a track that runs down the side of the house as well as through the garden, but the council rejected his planning application. He pretty much gave up on the place then, and himself.

The chair's wheeled feet creak and groan as I drag it over the concreted yard and pull at the barn door. It's the first time I've been inside since I came back. Mum hated this building. I did too.

I brace myself as the barn door swings open, but the row of steel cages still makes me catch my breath. Dad's decision to allow the local hunt to house some of their dogs here caused the biggest argument I can ever remember my parents having. Mum, an out-and-out city girl who'd met Dad at a wedding, was horrified at the idea.

'Fox hunting!' she screamed as I perched at the top of the stairs in my pyjamas. 'I'm not supporting fox hunting.'

'No one's saying you have to support it. You're not going to be shoved onto a horse and made to blow a bloody horn. We'll just be looking after the dogs. Geoffrey needs somewhere to keep them for a little—'

'I don't want animal rights protesters throwing paint at our car and shouting and blowing whistles outside our house. We've got a thirteen-year-old daughter, Steve. What if they set fire to our house like they did to Geoff's barn?'

'That's not going to happen, and anyway, there's no proof that they burned—'

'Of course it was them. It was the same people who threw red paint all over William's haulage trucks last year. If it was some random arsonist, why wait until the dogs were on a hunt?'

'Oh, for god's sake. No one's going to burn the barn down or hurt Louise. Anyway, it's just for a few months, until Geoff's barn is rebuilt. You were the one who said we need to make more of an effort to be part of the community and it's not like we're doing anything with it.'

'It's our barn. We don't have to—'

'*Whose* barn is it?'

The cold silence that followed made me shiver.

'I knew you'd do this,' my mother said tightly. 'Lay down the law when it suits you.'

'I did buy the house, Maggie.'

'You think I don't know that?'

I'd long stopped asking my parents why they weren't married. They both claimed that they didn't need a piece of paper and an expensive wedding to prove how much they loved each other, but I'd once heard my mum confess to a friend that she was sad she'd never got to have her big day.

When Mum and Dad split up, she told him that he should sell the house so she could buy somewhere for me and her to live. Dad said he wasn't going anywhere and if she was that worried about me living somewhere nice she should leave me behind. Mum said she'd rather bring me up in a hovel.

The sound of their argument was still ringing in my ears as I trudged down the stone steps that led to the dojo and opened the door. Mike was sorting the pads and gloves in the corner of the room. He took one look at me and asked what was wrong. The concern in his voice made me burst into tears. My parents were splitting up. It was the end of my world.

He put an arm around my shoulders and squeezed the top of my arm. His palm wasn't touching the soft material of my gi for more than a couple of seconds but the warmth of his touch remained—

A violent shiver courses through me. The sun has disappeared and the sky is thick with heavy, black rain clouds so, mustering all the energy I have left, I drag the armchair into the barn. The cages are even bigger and more imposing than I remember. They're tall enough for a man to stand up in and almost as wide, with huge great padlocks hanging from the doors. They look like somewhere to house prisoners of war, not animals. The musky, yeasty smell of dogs is long gone but the air is rich with the sour, musty scent of sawdust, hay and ammonia.

When I reach the other side of the barn, I abandon the armchair, push open the door and peer outside. Rain is bouncing off the tarmac and puddling in the cracks. The field at the end of the yard is already flooded where it dips down into the lake. Much more of this rain and the roads will flood too. I'd be cut off from the world and no one other than my solicitor and a handful of friends in London know that I'm here.

A loud, angry, insistent sound cuts through the soft pattering of the rain.

It's a car horn.

Mike is here.

Chapter 12

Lou

I spot the white transit van through the gap between the house and the garage as I run across the lawn. The van windows are misty with condensation and the windscreen wipers are sweeping back and forth. My hair is stuck to my cheeks, my hoody is clinging to my back and my trainers are caked in mud. I slow my pace as I reach the house and duck under the eaves, out of sight of the van. My chest is tight and I've got pins and needles in both of my arms. I have never, ever felt more scared in my life. Why did I think this was a good idea? I've got no mobile signal, no neighbours and no way of calling for help. Mike never threatened me, but I know how dangerous he can be. If anything happened to me, it would be days before anyone sounded the alarm. But why would he turn on me? When the police arrested him, he was still in love with me. I didn't testify against him. And he has no idea that I'm the one who reported him to the police for kissing Chloe.

The horn sounds again, making me jump. There's no way Mike could have seen me. I could just stay here, out of sight, until he gives up and drives away. I don't have to do this.

But what about Chloe? a small voice whispers at the back of my brain. *Mike will continue to abuse her. If she's not already broken, she soon will be. Could you live with that, knowing you could have stopped it?*

I tried. I rang the police. I visited her parents. I spoke to her. Even if I do talk to Mike there's no guarantee anything I say will make a difference.

You wanted to do this. You wanted to confront him, to make him face up to what he did to you. You wanted him to know how much his 'love' fucked up your life. That's why you moved up here, Lou. To exorcise your demons. If you don't, you'll spend the rest of your life screwing up relationships with decent men like Ben. Just get it over and done with.

I step back into the rain, through the gap between the house and garage, and walk up to the van. The driver side window opens slowly. An elbow appears, swiftly followed by a face.

'Milly Dawson?'

'Mike.'

I brace myself, waiting for his eyebrows to raise and his jaw to drop. He didn't react on the phone when I gave him my address but he had to recognise the house as he drove up the track. And he has to know who I am.

But there's no spark of recognition in his eyes as they flit over my face.

It's the strangest sensation, staring into the eyes of the man I once loved and feared in equal measure. It's him and yet it's not him. His face, once so familiar, has been stolen by a much older man. There's a sagginess to his jawline that wasn't there before and a hollowing beneath his cheekbones. His eyebrows are thicker and wirier, the hoods of his eyes are heavier, almost obscuring the bright blue of his irises. There's no passion or love behind his gaze. As I continue to stare, the edges of his lips curl up into a smile and he gives me a little nod. He doesn't recognise me at all.

'You might want to get a coat on,' he says. 'Although I'm not sure you could get much wetter.'

He laughs then and the sound catches me by surprise. His face may have changed and his voice may have become a little raspier but his laugh is the same.

'I'm . . .' I pull my hood over my head and plunge my hands into the pockets of my hoody. 'I'm okay.'

'Well, if you're sure.' He gestures at the house with his thumb. 'In there, is it?'

For a moment I have no idea what he's talking about but then I remember – I asked him to take the armchair to the tip.

'It's in the barn.'

'Interesting place to keep a chair.' He raises an eyebrow. 'Where's the barn?'

'In the yard, past the garden.'

He moves to look out of the window even though there's no way he can see into the garden from the angle of the van.

'Or you could take the track round the house and I could open the gate to the yard.'

He looks back towards the garden, as though considering his options. A dimple appears in his chin as he presses his lips together. I used to push my little finger into that indentation to try and make it disappear.

'My left leg's a bit fucked. I'll drive. Get in.'

The command makes my blood run cold but, after a moment's hesitation, I do as he says.

We are sitting so close that, when he just changed gear, I had to lean to my left to avoid his forearm brushing mine. A wave of panic courses through me. The last time I was in a car with this man we were driving through France. But Mike doesn't recognise me. He did a quick sweep of my body as I rounded the van, a casual appraisal any man might do to a woman he's never met before, but there was no spark of interest when I opened the passenger door and got in. Why would there be? I'm a grown woman, not a child.

As he navigates his way back down to the road and up the muddy track to the barn he chatters away about nothing in particular – the weather, the flooding, the news. I nod and shrug but I'm not really listening. I can't stop staring at his face. He's forty-nine now and his hair is more grey than black, but it's still thick and wavy, cut short above the ears and at the nape of his neck. Deep lines stripe across his brow and fan out at the corner of his eyes. He looks old and tired.

I was afraid that all the feelings I'd had as a teen-ager would come flooding back and overwhelm me, but I don't feel love or desire. Not even hate or fear. What I feel, as I look at his long, thick fingers curved over the steering wheel, is revulsion.

'Here we are then.' He pulls on the handbrake and turns off the engine. We're in the yard. Parked up outside the barn.

'In here is it?' Mike says, gesturing at the barn, as he gets out of the van. It's raining heavily now and there's an air of impatience in his voice. Am I keeping him from something? An illicit meeting with Chloe perhaps?

'That's right.'

He doesn't say anything as he lollops past me – there's definitely something wrong with his left leg – but his head turns sharply as he opens the barn door. He's spotted the cages.

'Got dogs, have you?'

'No,' I say. 'They were—'

But he's not interested. He's already halfway across the barn. He grunts as he squats to pick up Dad's green armchair. He was the strongest, fittest man I knew eighteen years ago. Now he's unfit and wheezy, with a stomach that hangs over the belt of his jeans.

'Mike, before you put the chair in the van you need to—'

He grunts again as he lifts the chair up. 'I'm a bit pushed for time at the moment, but if you need to

81

book in another job give Joy a call and she'll sort something out.'

'It's not about a job.'

The expression on his face switches from friendly to irritated as he takes a step towards me. 'I'm sorry, love, but I haven't got time for a chat.' He pauses to take a breath. 'I have to be somewhere after this.'

'I'd rather you stayed, Mike. And it would be in your best interests to listen.'

I'm not going to let him walk away without hearing me out.

'Look,' he sighs heavily, 'I don't know what this is about but this is heavy and—'

He's interrupted by the tinny sound of a mobile phone ringtone. He lowers the chair to the ground, reaches into his pocket and presses his phone against his ear.

'Hello Chlo, are you okay?'

I stiffen at the sound of her name. I was right. He was trying to get away so he could meet up with her. The sick bastard.

'It's okay, it's okay,' Mike says. He's lowered his voice but I can still hear every word. 'Take a deep breath. All right . . . now tell me what's going on.' He pauses. 'What? Oh no. Oh, Chlo, there's got to be a mistake. There's no way you would . . .' He pauses again. 'What woman? What did she say?' He turns, almost in slow motion, and his eyes meet mine. He scans my face, his eyes clouded with confusion, as the tinny voice in his ear rattles on. The confidence I felt

82

less than a minute ago vanishes. Why is he looking at me like that?

'Mike,' I say as the confusion on his face is replaced by shock. 'Mike you need to—'

He holds out a hand, silencing me.

I don't breathe a word. Instead I take a step backwards, towards the door. I shouldn't have done this.

'I'll give you a ring back in a bit, Chloe. Okay? Stay where you are and I'll come and get you. It's going to be okay. I promise.'

I take another step back. My heel catches on something and I have to steady myself on the wall.

'It's you, isn't it?' Mike says, looking straight at me as he hangs up. 'You fucking bitch.'

Chapter 13

Lou

It all happens so quickly. One second Mike is on the other side of the barn, the next he's speeding towards me, a look of absolute fury on his face. With no time to run, all I can do is raise my hands in self-defence and brace myself. In a heartbeat he's right next to me but he's unsteady on his feet and I'm quicker and fitter than he is and, as his fingers grasp at my hair, I swerve out of reach. Before he can regain his balance, I shift my weight to the left and kick out with my right leg. The sole of my trainer smashes into Mike's bad leg. It's like felling a tree with a single axe blow, the way he lurches to one side, his left leg crumpling beneath him. I kick out at him again, this time landing my foot square in his chest. The force of the blow sends him reeling backwards and through the open door of one of the cages. His arms flail at his sides as he tries and fails to weave his fingers through the metal bars, then SMACK, the back of his head makes contact with a pile of bricks stacked up next to a bucket.

He's not moving. His eyes are closed, his neck tilted to the left, his head propped up on a brick, his fingers unfurled and slack at his sides. Across the barn the armchair lies on its side; Mike's mobile phone is half-buried in the straw beside it. I reach into my back pocket for my mobile. No reception.

'Mike?' I take a step towards the cage. My heart is beating so hard I feel sick. When his head hit the brick it sounded like a watermelon being hurled at the floor. If he's not dead he's badly injured. I need to call an ambulance.

I move towards the entrance to the barn, hesitate, then walk back to the cage. I should lock it. Just in case he comes round and tries to find me. Mike's eyes are still closed and he hasn't changed position.

'Mike!' I shout his name. 'Mike, wake up!'

When he doesn't stir, I cross the barn and pull a bamboo stick from a pile propped up in the corner. I push it into Mike's leg. He doesn't so much as twitch. I prod him harder. Nothing.

I step into the cage, not taking my eyes off his face as I crouch down and reach for his wrist. His eyes remain closed, his lips slightly parted as I extend the first two fingers of my left hand and feel for his pulse. If he's got one, I'll lock him in and ring an ambulance. If he's dead, I'll ring the police.

My hand is shaking so much I can't hold my fingers still against the thin skin of his wrist. I try again, wrapping my thumb around to anchor them in place, but I can't feel anything. I've only ever taken my own pulse before. Rain is battering against the roof of the shed and the wind is whistling through the open door. Was that a dull throb I just felt beneath my fingertips? I close my eyes to concentrate. Yes, there's a pulse. It's strong and deep and—

A scream catches in my throat as Mike's arm twists beneath my hand, his fingers close around my wrist and he looks straight at me.

'It's you.'

It's not the tone of his voice that makes me scrabble to my feet, run out of the cage and slam the door shut. It's the hate in his eyes.

I grab at the padlock, dangling from the catch, but I'm shaking so much I drop it. As I crouch down to pick it up, Mike presses his hand to the back of his head and rolls onto his side. He groans as he gets to his knees.

'Lou! What the fuck are you doing, you stupid—'

He slams up against the door and tries to grab my hand through the bars but he's too slow.

Click.

I squeeze the lock shut and jump away from the cage.

Mike grabs hold of the bars and shakes the door. All six cages rattle and shake and, for one horrible moment, I think the whole thing is going to tip over and pin me to the ground, but it holds firm. It must be bolted to the floor.

'Open the fucking door!' Mike shouts. He reaches a hand behind his head, then looks at his fingers.

They're slick with blood. There's blood on one of the bricks in the pile in the corner too. He sees me looking and picks one up.

'The police are going to have a field day with you,' he says as he walks back to the door. 'Assault and imprisonment. Five years is nothing compared to what you're going to get.' I inch to my left, preparing to run. He's going to push the brick through the bars and try and smash the lock off.

But the brick won't fit between the bars, no matter which way he turns it. The gap is too small.

'Fuck's sake!' He takes two steps back, then hurls the brick at the door. It bounces straight off, narrowly missing his foot as it lands.

Mike launches himself at the door. SMASH! He drives his shoulder into the bars. The padlock swings back and forth, but it doesn't open.

'Open the fucking door!' He grips the bars and shakes the cage. 'Lou . . . Louise . . . what are you fucking doing? Just open the fucking door.'

I'm as far away from him as I can get, backed up against the barn wall, my hands pressed against the wood. Rough, spiky splinters scratch at my fingertips.

'Lou, please.' He softens his tone. 'Just open the door. I know you didn't mean for this to happen. I promise,' he holds up his hands, palms out, 'I won't lay a finger on you. I'll just get back in my van and go home. Neither of us need ever mention this again.'

'You'll go to the police.'

'I won't. I swear. I know what it's like inside. I wouldn't put you through that.'

'Yes you would.' I'm surprised to hear myself laugh.

'I really wouldn't . . .' he tails off as he looks me up and down. His eyes linger on my small breasts, then drift southwards. 'You've changed.'

'So have you.'

He raises an eyebrow. 'Haven't forgotten your karate though, have you?'

'There are some things you never forget.'

Mike falls silent, but his eyes continue to search my face. I can't bear it, the creeping sensation on my skin as though he's physically touching me.

'That's my phone,' Mike says as I pick up his mobile, nestled in the hay. He reaches a hand between the bars. 'Give it to me.'

'No.'

'Come on, Lou. I told you I wasn't going to call the police. I just want to go home and forget this ever happened.'

'Liar. You want to see Chloe.'

'What?' He starts at the mention of her name.

'Chloe. Your girlfriend. That's what you call her, isn't it? The child you're grooming.'

'I'm . . . I'm not . . . Lou, I don't know who's told you that, but I'm absolutely not—'

'You kissed her. I saw you, Mike. In the garden centre.'

'That was you? That sent the police round my house?' A tendon pulses in the side of his neck. 'Chloe was upset. She's had a crush on me for a while and she tried to kiss me. It didn't last more than a couple of seconds. I pushed her away. If you saw the kiss you will have seen that too.'

'Funny how that keeps happening, isn't it, Mike? Teenagers throwing themselves at you. What was it Chloe's dad told me? You only went to France with me because I was running away from my alky dad and you wanted to keep me safe.'

'Alan said that?' He raises his eyebrows, pretending to be shocked. It's like an acting masterclass with Ralph Fiennes. If Ralph Fiennes was a really, really shit actor. 'Then he's a liar. I never said that. We were in love, Lou. I never denied that. I loved you.'

'Stop.' I shove his phone into my back pocket then press my hands over my ears. His voice, his tone, his words, they're so insipid, so insidious, so carefully crafted, I feel as though tiny insects are crawling up and down my spine each time he pauses for breath. 'Just stop.'

'But—'

'Just stop I said.'

'Where are you going?' Mike shouts as I turn and walk out of the barn. 'Lou!' he tries as I shut the door behind me. 'Lou, where are you going? Let me out! Lou, let me out!'

A clanging sound follows me across the yard and into the garden. He's throwing himself at the door again.

Chapter 14

Chloe

Chloe looks at her phone. 7.45 p.m. and she's only got 17% battery life left. Where is Mike? It's been over an hour since she called him to pick her up. He said he'd be straight there. So where is he? He knows she's too scared to go home and face her dad. Maybe she shouldn't have told him about the weird woman who stopped her on her way to school and called him a paedophile. He'd sounded angry then. Was that a mistake? Mike always told her that they shouldn't have secrets from each other.

She shivers, despite her blazer, and runs her hands up and down her arms. The sun is still in the sky, hovering above the houses on the other side of the park, but the light and heat are fading. Other than Chloe, there's just one lone dog walker doing loops with his terrier. If Mike turns up now he'll have to park down the street because the gate to the car park has been lowered. Maybe there's been an emergency.

Or a delivery he forgot about. Or maybe he doesn't care. Doubt gnaws at Chloe's heart. She wants to believe that he loves her, but there are some days, like today, when she struggles. She's thirteen years old. She's not good-looking and she'd rather die than wear a swimming costume in public. None of the boys at school fancy her. She's not clever. She's not funny and she can't do banter. Mike told her it was her 'sweetness of spirit' that made him fall in love with her, whatever that means. He's said a lot of nice things to her over the last couple of months. She's had more compliments than she's had her entire life. 13%.

The battery icon on her phone has turned red now. If she's not going home tonight she needs to ring someone. She tries her best friend Eva first. Eva doesn't know about Mike, none of her friends do (he's forty-nine, they'd just laugh at her), but Eva knows about the garden centre job and the fact that Chloe helped herself to a few things. But Eva doesn't answer her phone, or the Snapchat messages Chloe sends her. She tries Freya next. Freya answers but says that Chloe can't stay over. Her brother's got a sleepover with his annoying mate Tyler which means Freya can't have anyone to stay. Panic rises in Chloe's chest as she calls Kirsteen. If Kirsteen says she can't stay over, she'll either have to sleep rough or go back and face her dad. Tears prick at her eyes when Kirsteen gets back from speaking to her mum and says that yeah, she can stay over.

'I had to lie though,' Kirsteen says, 'and tell her

that your parents had to take your little brother to the hospital. She would have been suspicious otherwise.'

Chloe thanks her friend over and over until her phone runs out of battery. Then she shoves it into her bag, slings it over her shoulder, takes one last look round to check that Mike hasn't appeared, and starts to run.

Chloe scoots up next to Kirsteen on the bed, dips her hand into the bag her friend is holding and shoves a handful of crisps into her mouth. At the far end of the tastefully decorated black and white bedroom is a huge 40" TV showing a romantic comedy Chloe has never seen before.

'I heard your mum on the phone,' Chloe says. 'As I was coming out of the loo. You don't think she was ringing my dad, do you?'

'Why would she? She believes me.'

'But she seemed a bit suspicious when I turned up at the door on my own.'

'No she didn't.' Kirsteen gives her a dismissive look then shoves her hand into the crisp packet. 'You're just being paranoid.'

'I dunno. She definitely gave me a funny look.'

Kirsteen laughs. 'Para . . . para . . . paranoid,' she sings the words in time with the chorus of Coldplay's 'Paradise' as she whirls her forefinger in circles near her temple.

'Para . . . para . . . paranoid.' Chloe joins in, initially because she doesn't want her friend to think she's a headcase, but then the rhythm of the song seeps into her bones and she bounces up and down on the bed as she shouts the words. It's great being at Kirsteen's house. Her mum's really cool and laid-back. Her dad too. She's never heard Kirsteen complain about her parents, other than when they wouldn't let her stay at a party until midnight. She even gets on well with her little sister Sophie. But it's more than that, there's a nice atmosphere at Kirsteen's house. It feels relaxed, just like the people in it. An idea pricks at the edge of Chloe's brain as she reaches for her can of Diet Coke on the bedside table and takes a sip. Maybe she could ask Kirsteen's mum if she could live with them? Kirsteen's room is big enough to fit a second bed in. She'd sleep on a blow-up mattress on the floor if she had to. They could do their homework together and hang out watching films and stuff at the weekend. She can't imagine her own family objecting to the idea. They'd probably be glad to see the back of her.

'Kirst,' she says, but her friend is engrossed in the film and doesn't acknowledge her. 'Kirsteen,' she says again. 'I had an idea. What do you reckon to me—'

'Girls, I'd like a word please.'

Chloe and Kirsteen both start as Rebecca Crowley appears at the bedroom door. Her hands are on her hips and her eyebrows are raised.

'Turn that off please.' She tilts her head towards the TV. The two lead characters freeze mid-kiss as Kirsteen presses a button on the remote. 'Right.' She looks from her daughter to Chloe and back again. 'I just had Chloe's dad on the phone, frantic with worry because his daughter didn't come home after school. Would one of you like to tell me what's going on?'

Chloe and Kirsteen share a terrified look and, in an instant, the comfortable bubble Chloe's been living in for the last two hours pops. Fear grips at her chest. She's going to be in even more trouble now.

'No?' Rebecca says. 'No one got anything to say for themselves? You're lucky it's me talking to you about this and not the police. Alan was on the verge of calling them.'

'Mum, I'm sorry, I—' Kirsteen starts, but her mum interrupts her.

'I don't want to hear it. I'm too angry. Consider yourself grounded. And no Wi-Fi for a fortnight.'

'But I need Wi-Fi to do my schoolwork and—'

'Three weeks. Anything else you want to say?'

Kirsteen shakes her head, then turns to look at Chloe.

She hates me, Chloe thinks. *And I don't blame her. If I hadn't called her, none of this would have happened.*

'Please, Mrs Crowley, don't blame Kirst. She hasn't done anything wrong. I lied to her on the phone and—'

Rebecca Crowley holds up a hand. 'Save it for when your dad gets here. Now, downstairs please. Kirsteen, turn off the TV and go to bed. You've got school in the morning.'

* * *

For ten agonising minutes Chloe sits in an armchair in the Crowleys' front room and picks at her cuticles as Kirsteen's mum drinks tea and watches some kind of cop show on Netflix. She told her her dad would be round to pick her up in twenty minutes and ever since she sat down she's been staring at the clock above the fireplace willing the hands to move slower or stop. The clock paid her no attention and now her cuticles are ragged and bleeding. If her mum was on her way to pick her up it would be okay. She could bear the disappointment in her mum's eyes and her soft sighs of frustration all the way home. But her dad . . . he'd probably lay into her before she even left the house. He'd embarrass her in front of Mrs Crowley and Kirsteen would hear every word from upstairs. It's bad enough knowing that Kirsteen will tell Eva and Freya everything that happened at school the next day without her repeating all the horrible names her dad will invariably call her.

No, she can't take it. And she won't.

She reaches into her school bag and pulls out her phone. She presses the button on the side and holds her breath as the phone flashes to life. A second later the screen goes black again. Shit. Even if Mike has replied to her text messages she can't read them.

'Mrs Crowley,' she says softly. 'Can I go to the toilet please?'

Kirsteen's mum nods her head, her eyes not leaving the screen. Chloe stands up and hooks her bag over her shoulder. *If she asks why I'm taking my bag to the loo*, she thinks as she crosses the living room, *I'll tell her I'm on my period.*

But Rebecca Crowley doesn't say a word as Chloe walks out of the living room, turns left in the hall and lets herself out of the front door.

Chapter 15

Lou

I barely slept last night. After I caught Mike staring at me from across the room I kept my eyes tightly closed. Then I started to cry silently, the tears rolling down my cheeks and wetting the pillow. Our first argument and I'd never felt more alone. All I wanted was for Mike to crawl into bed with me, put his arms around me, pull me close and tell me everything was going to be okay. But he wouldn't. I'd seen how stubborn and ruthless he could be in the dojo – sending kids out of class for failing to bow when they came back from the toilet and not backing down when their parents complained. I knew he was waiting for me to apologise, but why should I? He was the one who'd left me alone all day so he could go out drinking.

When I woke up just now Mike was still in the chair on the other side of the room, watching me. I don't know what to say to him, so I say nothing. Instead I sit up and rub my hands over my face, stalling for time to allow him to speak. He doesn't. Instead he gets up and disappears into the bathroom. So that's how it's going to be then – we're going to ignore each other all the way back to England? Are we over? Have I lost him because of one stupid argument?

My throat tightens with tears again. As a tear rolls down my cheek, Mike walks out of the bathroom carrying a tray. I tense as he approaches the bed and lays it down on my lap. On it is a single red rose, three croissants arranged on a split paper bag, a glass of orange juice and a small black box.

'What's this for?'

'For you.' He perches on the end of the bed. There are dark circles under his eyes.

'Why?'

'Because I love you. And I'm sorry.'

'What for?'

'Losing my temper last night. You had every right to be pissed off with me.'

I should say that it's fine. This is what I wanted after all, for him to apologise to me. But it doesn't change the fact that we're going back to England today and this has been the shittest romantic weekend in the world.

'Are we going anywhere today?' I say. 'Before we go back to England?'

'We're not going back to England.'

'What?'

'That's why I was gone so long yesterday. I was trying to find us an apartment to rent. That was the surprise.'

An apartment? Why would we need an apartment when we've got a hotel room? I don't know what he's on about. Can you even rent an apartment for one night? Mum is expecting me back this evening. And I've got school tomorrow. She'll be really pissed off with Mike if he doesn't take me home when he said he would, even if he does come up with a good excuse. 'When are we going back?'

Mike shuffles closer and takes my hand. 'We're not.'

I snatch my hand away. 'Ever?'

'Aren't you pleased? Isn't this what you said you wanted? To spend the rest of your life with me? We can't do that in England – there are too many complications – but we can do that here. No one knows who we are and no one cares.' Before I can reply, he swipes the black box from the tray, slips off the bed and gets down on one knee. 'Louise Wandsworth,' he says as he opens the box to reveal a silver ring with a tiny silver diamond in the centre. 'Will you marry me?'

I didn't intend to lock Mike in the barn but I'm not going to let him out until I come up with a way to stop him from grooming Chloe. My phone might not have any reception out here but Mike's does. Between 6.52 and 7.45 p.m. six messages flashed up on his mobile, each one more frantic than the last. The phone was locked so I wasn't able to read them all but I could see snippets.

How long do u think ull be?

Is everything ok, u sounded a bit stressed when

Sorry if I said anything to upset u but I needed to

R u still comin?

Am waiting where I said. U comin?

Pls msg me asap.

The messages stopped after that. They were flagged as belonging to 'Jim' but it was obvious that they were from Chloe – from the way they were spelled and the fact she'd rung him in the barn. With any luck, she got fed up of waiting for Mike and went home. Good. Maybe a text would arrive later, after she'd stewed for a while, telling him she didn't want to see him anymore. That was wishful thinking. Of course she wouldn't end things with him. He'd stood me up and let me down dozens of times when we were together and each time I forgave him. I fell for his lies, his apologies and his tears.

I could never hurt you, Lou. Not intentionally. I want to spend the rest of my life making you happy.

I shudder and tuck Mike's phone back into my pocket. Chloe might not want to end things with Mike but she'll have to if I can gather enough evidence to give to the police. All I need is the code to get into his phone. And a torch.

It's after 10 p.m. and the only light outside is from the half-moon in the sky, a scattering of stars and the dull glow of the light from the kitchen. If I thought the house was cluttered, the garage is a hoarder's delight. There's a wheel-less car in the centre, propped up on bricks and surrounded with boxes, bin bags and clutter.

I feel my way around the shelves that line the walls, but there's no torch amongst the drills, trowels, tools and plastic plant pots. I find two toolboxes and carry them outside and into the pool of light cast by the kitchen window. There's no torch in the first box but I find one in the second. I press the button and . . . nothing. The batteries are dead. As I bend over to put it back in the box there's a clattering sound as the phones – mine and Mike's – slip out of my back pocket and drop to the floor. What am I looking for a torch for? I could use one of the phones to light the way through the garden to the yard. Or I could drive up the track. Even with the headlights on full beam, no one will see them. I don't have any neighbours for miles. And I'll be able to see into the barn.

As I turn to go, I spot a cardboard box with my handwriting on the side and feel a sharp pang of regret.

Louise's stuff.

Dad kept it after I moved to London with Mum. Was he hoping I'd come back and collect it? He didn't bother getting in touch with me, but maybe he was waiting for me to make the first move?

I turn on the torch app on my phone and peel back the lid. There are clothes on the top – jumpers, jeans, T-shirts. My skin crawls as I pull out a black and white polka dot halter-neck dress. Once, after karate, Mike said how much he'd like to see me in a dress – I was always in my gi or tracksuit bottoms and trainers – so I bought it to wear the first time we stayed in a hotel. I hurl it away, then look back at the box. What else did I keep?

I put my phone in my mouth, grab the edges of the box and tip it to one side, then upend it completely. Clothes, books, jewellery and ornaments slide out and then I see it, the small wooden box I kept my diary in. I tuck it under my arm and leave the garage. Opening it can wait, I need to get back to the barn.

With my headlights on full beam, I can see straight into Mike's van. There has to be evidence in here that he's been grooming Chloe. The keys are still in the ignition, there's a coat on the passenger seat and a bag in the footwell. I pull them out of the van and drop them onto the ground, then dig around in the glove compartment and the pockets in the doors. It's mostly crap: sausage roll wrappers, flattened sandwich boxes and empty cans of drink. There's not much more in the glove compartment: a couple of CDs, more cans, some documentation relating to the van, a list of addresses, some business cards and a bunch of keys. I look under both seats next, then behind the sun visors, but there's nothing. If any evidence exists that Mike's been grooming young girls it's probably in his bag or coat but I check the back of the van anyway. Nothing there apart from a couple of dirty rugs and some of those elasticated ropes you use to secure furniture to stop it rolling around.

I return to the coat and the bag. Nothing in the pockets of the coat and nothing incriminating in the bag either.

'Help!' Mike's shout rings out from the barn. 'Police! Help!'

I drop the bag as his voice echoes around the yard. I might not have any neighbours for miles but dog walkers and cyclists use the main road. I can't risk anyone hearing him.

I've just run down the track to the main road and you can't hear a peep. Mike's cries for help faded away by the time I drew level with the house. I turn and run back up the track to the yard. He can shout all he wants. No one's going to hear him.

'Thank god,' he breathes, shielding his eyes against the full beam of the car's headlights as I open the barn door. 'Thank god.'

The hopeful expression on his face vanishes as I step closer and he lets out a low groan.

'C'mon, Lou.' He rests his forearms on the bars, his eyes weary. 'Enough's enough. Whatever point you were trying to prove by locking me in here, you've done it. Okay? I'm sorry if I scared you. I didn't mean to. Just . . . please . . . open the door.'

'I could do that,' I begin and Mike looks up hopefully. 'But you need to do something for me in return.'

'Anything.'

I reach into my back pocket. 'Give me the code to unlock your phone.'

Mike doesn't move a muscle. He doesn't even look as though he's breathing, he's staring so intently at the mobile in my hand.

'Why?' he says.

'Because I want to send Chloe a message.'

'Saying what?'

'That you don't want to see her again. That it's over.'

'I told you, I'm not . . .' he tails off. He knows as well as I do that if I look at the texts on his phone they'll prove his guilt. And that's what I need to give to the police, hard evidence. The CPS would *have* to prosecute him then. But I can't give the phone to the police with Mike still locked in my barn. I could end up on a kidnapping charge. If I unlock the padlock how do I get from the barn to my car without Mike catching up with me? He might be seventeen years older than me and lame in one leg, but he flew at me like a man thirty years younger. I could throw the key into the cage and leave it to him to undo the lock. That might buy me enough of a head start.

'How do I know you'll let me out if I give you my code?' Mike asks.

'You don't.'

He stares at me, indecision and frustration written all over his face, then he sinks down to his knees and rests his forehead against his clenched hands.

'Could I have some water please?'

'No. Give me the code.'

'Please. I'm thirsty. And a blanket or something. It's fucking freezing.'

I ignore him and start sorting through all the crap piled up next to the armchair. I examine the paint pots first, prising off the rusty lids with my car key. There's nothing inside. I feel around the lawnmower, then shift the bales to one side. But what I'm looking for isn't here. There's no key to the lock on Mike's cage. I could turn Dad's house and garden upside down looking for it, but the chances of finding it are slim. No one's used these cages for years.

I unhook one of the open locks from an empty cage and turn it over in my hands. Do all these locks have the same key? Even if they do, I doubt B&Q still stock them. The only way to let Mike out would be to give him some kind of saw or some bolt cutters. Either way, I'm not letting him out tonight. He needs to sweat it out a bit longer. Let's see how he enjoys being a prisoner.

I put the lock in my pocket and approach Mike's cage, making sure I stay far enough back that he can't grab me through the bars. 'Are you going to give me the code to your phone or not?'

He shakes his head. 'Not. I've told you, Lou. I haven't done anything wrong. You can't keep me locked up forever. Sooner or later someone's going to realise I'm missing and the police will come straight here.'

'Why's that?'

'Because you tried to fit me up. They'll put two and two together.'

105

'They might, if I hadn't given them a false surname and address.'

Mike seems to shrink before my eyes.

'I'll go and get you that water. And a blanket,' I say. 'You might want to reconsider giving me the code while I'm gone.'

Chapter 16

Wendy

Tuesday 1st May 2007

'Oh for goodness sake!' Wendy Harrison throws the duvet away from her and sits up in bed. She twists onto her knees and pounds her fists against the wall she shares with her neighbour. 'Will . . . you . . . please . . . be . . . QUIET!'

It's 2.34 a.m. and she has only had an hour's sleep. When she turned off her bedside lamp, a little after eleven, she heard someone shouting and laughing outside. It was her neighbour, Jason Marsons, with a cackling blonde on his arm. They were returning, Wendy assumed from the way they swayed down the street, from the pub. Ten minutes later the music started up. A thumping electronic beat that shook her house. She went round immediately, with Monty in tow, and knocked on the flaking red door of number 31. Her neighbour, a young man in his mid to late twenties, opened the door with a gleeful look on his face. He took one look at Wendy, then his expression changed.

'You again, seriously?'

'It's nearly twelve o'clock.' Wendy glanced at her watch to prove her point. 'And this isn't the first time you've kept me awake with your noise.'

The man shrugged. 'It doesn't seem to bother the neighbour on the other side.'

'That's because he's deaf,' Wendy snapped. 'And I, certainly, am not.'

'Jay, where are you?' a blonde woman called from behind him. A second later she hurtled down the hallway, knocking into the walls like a bowling ball thrown by a pre-schooler. 'Oh, there you are.' She looped her arm around his neck and peered out at Wendy through red-rimmed eyes. 'Who are you?'

Wendy tried very hard not to sigh. The woman was obviously drunk and, from the look of her grubby feet, she'd walked barefoot back from the pub. 'I'm Jason's next-door neighbour. I'd like you to turn the noise down please. I can't sleep.'

'But it's his birthday,' the woman wailed before she pressed her smudged lips against the side of his neck. 'Don't be an old killjoy.'

'I'm not an old anything,' Wendy said tightly. 'But I've got work in the morning and I suggest you save your partying for the weekend.'

Jay sighed. 'We'll turn it down.'

'And spoil your birthday? No chance!' The blonde waggled a hand in Wendy's face. 'You need to go

108

home and have sex with your husband. It might loosen you up a bit.'

'Lisa!' Jay tried to extricate himself from her octopus-like grip. 'You can't talk to her like that. Sorry,' he said over his shoulder to Wendy as he attempted to wrangle Lisa back down the hallway. 'She's a bit of a livewire.'

'I'd rather be a livewire than a dried-up prune,' Lisa shouted up at him. 'I don't want to get old. Not if I end up like her. Will you shoot me if I do, please?'

'You'll never be like her.'

Wendy reached forward and tugged on the door handle of the open front door. The glass in the top panel shook as she slammed it shut.

I want to smash something, Wendy thought as she stepped into her kitchen. *I want to whirl round like a dervish, knocking cups and plates to the floor, throwing plant pots against the walls and smashing everything I can lay my hands on.*

She eyed the potted orchid on the windowsill. She'd rescued it, half dead and sorry-looking, from her sister's conservatory. To send it tumbling to the floor would be a travesty. And very unfair on the plant that had finally flourished under her care. The mug then, on the washing-up rack. If Jay and the stupid blonde woman heard that smashing against their shared wall they might think twice about messing with her again. But the mug was part of a set of six she'd bought at a car-boot sale. They were vintage Laura Ashley.

She stared around her small kitchen, desperate to find something – anything – she could destroy, but everything she saw held sentimental value. She'd been living on a budget for years and she'd saved hard for all the beautiful things in her home, or spent hours sifting through tat in charity shops or car-boot sales.

Jam. Her eyes fell on a on a small glass jar on the kitchen counter. It had been a gift from a client but it was the most revolting home-made jam she'd ever tasted – too runny and with a horrible bitter aftertaste. She lifted the jar to head height. Monty, at her feet, looked up expectantly and Wendy paused. If she threw the jar at the floor there was a very real risk that Monty would end up with tiny shards of glass in his paws, even if she did send him out into the garden first and then cleaned up diligently. Then there would be the mess she'd have to sort out. Not to mention the potential damage to her kitchen tiles.

'Damn it!' she shouted as she slammed the jar against the kitchen surface. 'Damn it! Damn it! Damn it!'

As her neighbour's music continues to pound the wall behind her bedhead, Wendy reaches for her laptop, on the bedside table, pulls her headphones over her ears and selects a playlist of eighties hits from iTunes. She tries to sing along as Madonna warbles about keeping her baby, but she can't block out the memory of her neighbour's friend calling her a dried-up prune.

I've had sex, Wendy wants to scream at the shaking wall behind her. *You didn't invent it you know. And I'm only fifty-nine. How dare you call me old, how dare you, you drunken little slut!*

But she doesn't. Instead she grits her teeth and logs onto Lou Wandsworth's Facebook page. Yesterday she'd visited that little madam in her cushy job on Church Street. Other than the small amount of satisfaction she'd gained from the other woman sucking up to her in a professional capacity and her evident discomfort when faced with questions about her personal life, she'd left the office none the wiser about who Lou Wandsworth actually was. And to think she'd been so excited at the prospect of infiltrating her life. It had come to nothing really. After the meeting she'd received an email from Lou saying how nice it had been to meet her and that she was attaching a breakdown of their fees and a pro forma invoice for payment if they were successful in winning the bid. And that was it.

There was no way of taking the matter forward. The pro forma alone was for several thousand pounds and, even if Wendy could afford to pay it, it would look very strange to pay it from her personal account rather than from the University of Worcester. So what next? She's put it off long enough. She needs to confront Louise Wandsworth and tell her some home truths. It might not change Wendy's situation. She won't be magically whisked out of her damp two-up, two-down and into a lovely warm home. She won't wake up each morning in the arms of a loving

111

husband. She won't have a clutch of children running around her feet or, at her age, calling her from university. She won't have any of those things. But she might find peace. Or, at the very least, the opportunity to get a few things off her chest.

There is nothing exciting on Lou's Facebook page. She hasn't updated since she lived in London and, although there are a couple of 'how are you doing?' 'long time stranger!' type posts from friends and acquaintances, the only one that catches Wendy's eye is from someone called Alice.

I hope you took my advice. It's better to regret the things you do than the things you don't (if you know what I mean). Love you xx

Advice? Wendy raises an eyebrow. That suggests Lou has some kind of problem. But what? She has no way of knowing. A number of people have liked the comment and someone has written *Hello, Vague Book! Spill or don't post.* To which someone else has replied *Hey, it's not your conversation. Keep your nose out.* It then degenerates into an argument about the correct Facebook etiquette. Wendy isn't interested in the argument but is curious about Ben Feltham, the only man to like Alice's original post.

When she clicks on his name she isn't surprised to see that they are already friends. Over the last couple of months she's gradually friend requested each and every one of Lou's friends in an effort to get to know more about her. She vaguely remembers Ben's page but, as he hadn't posted any photos of Lou or any posts to her page, she'd dismissed him as an acquaintance rather than someone who meant something to her. But what's this? Eight weeks ago he posted a photo of himself lying under a red Mini, seemingly changing a wheel. Underneath he's written: *The things you do for some people*.

The red car looks familiar. She's definitely seen it before.

Wendy clicks back to Lou's page. Yes, there it is. A photo of the same Mini about a year earlier with Lou sprawled on the bonnet, giving it a kiss.

My new car, Lou has written beneath it.

Her heart beating faster Wendy clicks back to Ben's page. Before the photo of the Mini he's written *Anyone recommend a good musical in the West End? (Don't laugh!)* :D

Musicals? She clicks back to Lou's page. Three days after Ben's request, Lou posted a photo of them both standing outside *Wicked* in the West End. Ben Feltham is Lou Wandsworth's boyfriend. But she'd told Wendy that she lived alone.

Ben's most recent Facebook post is a meme. She'd scrolled past it originally (believing that memes are for people who are too stupid or lazy to express themselves with their own words) but it's a lot more interesting now she's worked out the connection between Lou and Ben. The background image is of a man sitting alone in an American-style diner. Overlaid are the words *If you are not scared then you're not taking a chance. If you are not taking a chance then what the hell are you doing?* Wendy snorts softly. How very fey. Obviously Ben's friends thought the same as several of the comments beneath the meme seem to be taking the mickey.

U ok, hon? says one.

Stop being such a maudlin bastard and go for a beer says another.

You are so GAY says another (that comment started an argument about homophobia).

Did Ben post the meme because he was planning on moving to Malvern to be with Lou? Wendy's stomach tightens as she clicks back to Lou's photo albums. The Clark Gable alike that she's kissing in the fancy dress photo is obviously Ben. How lovely for them both, moving back to Lou's home town to make a new life for themselves. As a child Wendy was taught that good people are rewarded in life, whilst bad people get their due. It's total bullshit of course. Murderers live out long lives in prison, whilst innocent souls die in childhood. Horrible, abusive women get to have children, whilst kind, loving women don't. There's no such thing as karma and no higher power meting out reward and punishment. The world is a very unfair place. You just have to turn on the TV to see the extent of the devastation wrought on people who don't deserve it. And Wendy hasn't watched the news in years.

She moves her cursor away from Lou's photo and clicks instead on Ben's profile picture. He's a nice-looking man, late twenties possibly with a thick head of dark hair, warm, brown eyes and nice teeth. He looks approachable and friendly, like the type of man who wouldn't allow anyone to sit on their own at a party.

If she messages him what's the worst that could happen? He could tell her to sod off or he could ignore her completely. She has a feeling he won't do either – not when she's pretending to be an attractive blonde with a very enticing smile.

Chapter 17

Lou

I thought Mike was joking yesterday when he said we weren't going back to England, but he was deadly serious. He was serious about marrying me too. I was shocked when he opened the ring box and proposed. I know we've talked about spending the rest of our lives together, but I'm fourteen. And Mike's already married – legally anyway (he's told me he doesn't love her and they never have sex). I mean, obviously I was pleased and when I said yes he pulled me into his arms and kissed me, then he looked into my eyes and stroked my face, and said I'd made him the happiest man alive. It was amazing, seeing him so happy, and I love him and everything but he makes me nervous too. He's changed since we got to France. I don't know if he's going to kiss me, shout at me, ignore me or have sex with me.

From the way Mike kept kissing me after we got

engaged, I thought he'd want to have sex again but he didn't. Instead he shooed me towards the shower and told me that we were going to spend the whole day celebrating.

And we did. We walked along the river hand in hand, we dared each other to try the stinkiest cheese at the market and we had lunch in a posh bistro with haughty waiters. I even tried snails (gross) and champagne (amazing!) for the first time. After that we went shopping and Mike bought me a new dress (I didn't really like it – it was really tight with horrible glittery stuff on the front – but I didn't tell him that). Everything was brilliant until I asked if we could find a phone box.

'What do you want a phone box for?'

'To ring Mum. We were supposed to go back today and she'll be worried.'

He shrugged and tugged me up the steps of an old cathedral. 'She'll be fine.'

'She won't, Mike. She'll call the police.'

'Let her. We're together. That's all that matters.'

He pulled me close and wrapped his arm round my shoulders. His fingers dug into the top of my arm.

I wake with a start and reach for my mobile phone. 4.55 a.m., Tuesday morning. There's no light creeping from between the closed curtains and the living room is still wrapped in shadows. I sit up and rub my left shoulder. I've spent every night on the sofa since I got here – there are too many memories in my old room and I'd feel weird sleeping in Dad's bed – and my body feels old, tired and cramped. I reach for the glass on the table beside me and take a swig. Urgh. It's gin, not water. I must have drunk half a bottle before I finally passed out.

I went back to the barn at around 10.45 p.m. to see if Mike had changed his mind about giving me the code. He screamed abuse at me as I opened the door, replied 'fuck off, fuck off, fuck off,' to every question I asked him, then hurled himself at the bars as I threw a bottle of water, a packet of biscuits and a blanket at the cage. I sprinted all the way back to the house and burst into tears the second I set foot in the kitchen. When I finally stopped crying I opened the gin. My teenaged memory box was on the counter where I'd left it earlier. I tried to ignore it. I even went into the living room and turned on the TV but, after my third gin, I admitted defeat. I had to open it.

It took me a while to get the lock off. The hacksaw blade kept slipping and I couldn't get the teeth to bite into the metal. I tried unscrewing the hinges instead. They were rusty and I sweated, swore and broke two screwdrivers, but two screws in each hinge came free, then I jemmied the others off.

The contents of the box spilled onto the table as I tipped it to one side. My diary, once a rainbow of pink, blue, yellow and orange butterflies, was faded with age. There was a blackened silver bracelet in there too – a gift from Mike – a couple of cinema tickets, my karate licence, and a tiny teddy bear holding a heart (also from Mike). The police seized the box, and pretty much everything else in my room, when Mike and I disappeared. That's why they knew to look for us in France. I'd diarised all of it, even down to the time and place that Mike would be picking me up. After it was returned to me I screamed at the police that they'd invaded my privacy. It wasn't Mike who'd violated me, it was them.

I examined everything but I couldn't bring myself to open the diary. Just holding it in my hands made me feel sordid, so I dropped everything back into the box and closed the lid. It's still there now, on the kitchen table, a terrifying portal to the past.

I put the glass of gin back on the side table and stand up. I need water.

A loud creaking noise makes me turn sharply as I step into the hallway. It's coming from the kitchen.

'Hello?' I stand very still.

I hold my breath as I listen. Is it Mike? Has he managed to get out of the barn?

'Mike?' His name is a soft squeak at the back of my throat.

The house has never been burgled as far as I know, but thieves broke into the garage when I was a child. They stole Dad's ride-on mower and some power tools.

I reach for the landline and rest my thumb on the number nine button. 'I know you're in here. Leave now or I'll call the police.'

Nothing.

If there is someone else in the house they're standing very, very still. Unless it wasn't a person. Old houses creak and moan all the time.

'I'm coming into the kitchen now.'

I step towards the dining room that connects the hallway with the kitchen. The floorboards creak beneath my weight and the grandfather clock, its face pale and spectral in the half light, watches me from across the room. The floor-length velvet curtains that hang at the window look more bulbous than normal. As a child they were my favourite hiding place.

'Hello?' I clutch the phone tighter. I could turn around and run out of the front door. But then what? Jump in my car and wait? Run to the barn and see if Mike is still there? Ring the police and hide? Since that first creak I haven't heard a thing. And if it's not Mike, if he's still shivering beneath his rough blanket, the last thing I need is the police turning up on my doorstep.

It was nothing, I tell myself as I walk through the dining room and touch a hand to the kitchen door. My imagination's gone into overdrive. I'm bound to be jumpy, given what I've done.

Then there it is, as I open the kitchen door, another noise. A high scraping sound like something being dragged across the floor.

'Get out!' I shout. 'The police are on their way.'

But the scraping sound continues.

I don't know if it's idiocy or bravery that propels me across the kitchen, but one second I'm standing at the kitchen door and the next I'm pulling at the handle to the porch. And there he is . . . staring up at me with amber eyes, top lip rolled back and teeth bared – a fox with its front paws on one of my recycling bins. Behind him the side door is wide open.

'Out!' I shout, kicking at the recycling bin, my foot only inches from the fox's open mouth. 'Out! Out! Get out!'

For one terrifying second I think it's going to launch itself at me. The next it's turned tail and is sprinting across the driveway. As it continues to run, I step around the recycling bin, slam the side door closed and turn the key in the lock.

I keep an eye out for the fox as I traipse through the garden a little after six o'clock, but there's no sign of it. I can't believe I left the side door open. I must have forgotten to shut it last night, with all the toing and froing to the garage to get tools.

'Idiot,' I say under my breath as I open the garden gate and step into the yard.

It rained heavily while I was asleep last night. The soles of my wellies are caked in mud and, beyond the barn, the lake has risen part way up the field. It's drizzling and my jacket is misted with rain. I've got Mike's mobile in my pocket. When I looked at it earlier there was a missed call from a Malvern number on the locked screen. But no more texts from Chloe. I was surprised. Most teenaged girls would have reacted badly to hours of silence, I know I would, but maybe Chloe's made of sterner stuff. Still feels odd though.

Mike is already awake and standing in the centre of the cage. The lid of the cage only clears the top of his head by an inch or so and he looks huge in such a small space. He regards me silently as I approach him.

'I brought you this,' I reach into my pocket and pull out a bacon sandwich wrapped in silver foil.

Mike looks at it.

'Don't worry,' I say. 'I didn't poison it.'

Still Mike doesn't speak. He doesn't move an inch. But his eyes flick from the foil-wrapped parcel to my face. They're so blank and expressionless, I look away.

'It's there if you want it.' I crouch down and slide the sandwich through the bars then snatch my hand back quickly. 'And two more bottles of water.'

I push those through too, then retreat to the wall opposite the cage and sit down, resting my back against the rough wood.

'Silent treatment is it today?'

Mike continues to stare at me.

'You're not doing yourself any favours, Mike.'

I sound more confident than I feel. There are moments where I feel like I'm caught up in a dream and none of this is real. Several times last night I woke up drenched in sweat with my heart pounding. What if Mike continues to refuse to give me the code to his phone? I can't keep him locked up forever. He was given a five-year sentence for battery, abduction and unlawful sexual intercourse with a child under sixteen. How much would I get for kidnapping? The same? More? If I let him out now – assuming I can buy a bolt cutter somewhere and run to safety before he gets out – he'll go straight to the police. He'll say I have a grudge against him (a grudge the police might possibly understand, but then again, who knows) and I fabricated reports about him grooming a child, then lured him to my house so I could imprison him. If I'm arrested, he's free to keep grooming Chloe. She says she hasn't slept with him yet. But she will if I don't keep them apart and, if that happens, she really will be in danger.

'Mike, give me the code to your phone and I'll let you go. I promise.'

He continues to stare at me but his blue eyes are no longer expressionless, there's an unnerving coldness behind his fixed gaze.

'Mike.' I get to my feet. 'Staying silent isn't going to make me magically open the door.'

As I speak a memory flashes up in my mind – of Mike, ignoring me after an argument. It was the first time he mentioned us running off to France. I wasn't keen on the idea, despite being good at

French (my teacher told me that I could easily get an A* in my GCSEs if I kept working hard). I told Mike that going to France would feel too much like homework and I'd rather spend our romantic weekend away in the UK or Ireland. He told me I was being ridiculous. That I'd enjoy practising my French. I bit back, saying he sounded like my dad. He went quiet then. We were at the cinema in Kidderminster, on the pretext that I was taking part in a karate tournament, and Mike ignored me throughout the film. When I placed a hand on his knee, he moved it off. When I told him to talk to me, he shook his head and folded his arms. Only when I burst into desperate tears did he turn to look at me.

'Is it worth it?' he said. 'Insulting me when all I'm trying to do is make you happy?'

I shook my head dumbly.

'I only want what's best for you, Lou. I'm the only person who does. You need to trust me to make the right decisions. You trust me, don't you?'

'Of course I do,' I said between sobs.

I cried some more when he put an arm around me and pulled me into his chest. His silence was the worst possible punishment. Although he was sitting right next to me, I'd felt utterly alone and abandoned.

'It's not going to work,' I say now. 'Giving me the silent treatment. I'm not fourteen.'

Mike continues to stare, but I can see by the rise and fall of his chest that he's breathing deeply. Is he trying to keep his temper? I need to keep doing what I'm doing. Eventually he'll snap.

'You know Chloe sent you some texts last night?'

His lips part. Of course he didn't. He hides his interest quickly but I saw it. It was there.

'Yeah,' I say. 'You've got her in your phone as Jim, but it was obviously her. She sounded worried. She was waiting for you to pick her up. I hope you didn't arrange to meet her somewhere public. She might have gone off with some other pervert.'

'Give me that!' Mike throws himself against the bars, but I'm too far away for him to grab the phone.

'Oh,' I feign surprise, 'are you worried about her? Give me the number and I'll call her to check she's okay.'

'Jesus Christ.' He sinks to his knees and rests his head against the bars. 'Why are you doing this?'

'Because I don't want you to hurt Chloe like you hurt me.'

'I loved you.'

'You groomed me.'

'No.' He shakes his head but he doesn't look at me. His jawline and top lip are dark with stubble and, despite his tanned arms and neck, his face looks wan in the early morning light. 'No, I didn't. I fell in love with you. The same way you fell in love with me. I didn't leer over you like some dirty old man. I didn't put my hand up your top and make you cry. I didn't force you to do anything. I never would have let myself love you if I thought you didn't love me back.'

'I was vulnerable and you took advantage of me.'

'I tried to help you!' He raises his head and looks straight at me. 'Your dad was the worst kind of bastard. When you came to me for karate lessons your confidence was destroyed. You couldn't look me in the eye for the first six months. I thought you were shy. A lot of the kids were, particularly the girls, but I saw the startled look in your eyes when he came to pick you up.'

'Stop justifying—'

'The first time I spoke to him, I could smell the booze on his breath. I tried to make light of it, said that if he'd had a couple in the pub maybe he should leave the car behind and get a lift back with me. He laughed in my face, then told you to hurry up and get your shoes on. I barely slept that night for worrying about you.'

'That's not true.'

'Of course it's bloody true! He smelt like a brewery. He could have killed you both.'

Now it's my turn to fall silent. He's right, about Dad drink-driving. When Mum would pull him up on it, he'd say, 'Everyone does it in the countryside. We know the roads, it's fine.' That didn't stop me being utterly terrified each time I got into the car with him.

I look back at Mike. 'You can't use my dad as an excuse for what you did to me.'

He holds his hands out, palm up. 'Lou, what happened between us would have been perfectly legal eighteen months later. Yeah, so there would still have been a seventeen-year age gap, but who cares. No one bats an eyelid if a thirty-year-old goes out with a forty-seven-year-old.'

'But I wasn't thirty. Or sixteen. I was fourteen and what you did—'

I break off and look towards the door. There's a strange noise outside. A dull chopping sound. Mike hears it too and a slow smile spreads across his face.

'Helicopter,' he says. 'A police helicopter,' he adds as I move towards the door.

It's definitely a helicopter, speeding over the trees near the back field, but it's so far away I can't tell if it's a police helicopter. Not that I know what one looks like. Do they say Police on the side like the cars?

I press a hand to my chest and try and calm my breathing. It can't have been a police helicopter. It's only been twelve hours, thirteen tops, since Mike got here and I'm pretty certain that the police don't launch a missing persons enquiry unless someone's been missing for at least twenty-four hours or they're vulnerable or a child. And they certainly wouldn't send a helicopter out to look for a forty-nine-year-old man in a white van. They'd start by triangulating the location of his phone and—

I stare at the mobile in my hand. It's Mike's.

Shit.

Shit.

Shit.

I open the back and slide out the battery and SIM card but it's too late. The last call Mike received was

127

in the barn. As soon as the police start looking for him they'll trace him here. I need him to give me the code to the phone. I don't have much time.

Chapter 18

Chloe

Chloe's lungs are burning and her legs are so weak she stumbles every dozen or so steps, but she forces herself to keep running.

When she left Kirsteen's house she headed for the centre of Malvern. She felt conspicuous in her school blazer and knee-length skirt as cars zoomed past so took off her blazer and tie. The wind bit at her skin through her thin cotton shirt as she continued to walk, her head down, her hair whipping around her face. Town was quiet but there were still a few people around, standing outside pubs and restaurants puffing on cigarettes and vapes and, although she received a few concerned glances – mostly from older women – she was largely ignored. That changed when the pubs kicked out. Suddenly groups of men roamed the streets, laughing, shouting and weaving back and forth on the pavement. 'Lost your boyfriend have you love?' shouted one man. When she'd turned to look at him, hopeful that he'd help her find Mike, he said, 'I'll be your new boyfriend if you want!' and nudged his friend. She'd quickened her pace, tears pricking at her eyes, as their laughter followed her.

If the high street was scary then the park was worse. Tucked away from the road, the only light was the dull glow of the theatre but, as Chloe ventured further in, darkness wrapped her like a shroud. She gripped her dead phone to her chest as she passed the abandoned swings and slides and then sprinted across a stretch of lawn. As she reached a dark clump of trees and bushes she dropped to her knees and began to crawl, brushing sharp branches, nettles and brambles away from her face. For a worrying couple of seconds she feared she was in the wrong place, it wasn't the secret hideout she'd shared with her best friend Martha when they were eight, but the foliage gradually parted to reveal a small hollow, four foot high by four foot wide with a tree trunk in the centre. Finally hidden from the world, she started to cry.

It was all her fault. Everything that had happened was down to her. Mike had been on at her for a while, asking her to come back to his after work or one afternoon after school. He said he wanted them to have some alone time, away from the prying eyes of the world, but she knew what he really wanted. He wanted to sleep with her. She might be stupid but she wasn't that stupid. She'd told him that she wasn't ready, when the truth was she was worried that he'd lose interest in her after they'd had sex. She'd seen it happen to a few girls at school. Their boyfriends told them they loved them and made out like they were really into them and then dumped them after a couple of shags. Sometimes they made out it was because the girl got really clingy afterwards. The really cruel ones spread rumours that the girl was shit at blow jobs or they didn't want to go out with her because she was a slut. Chloe was pretty certain Mike wouldn't call her a slut but she might be shit in bed. She'd watched videos on her phone, to learn how to do stuff, but he was forty-nine years old. How could she possibly compare to the other women he'd been with? He told her he'd only slept with seven people. Six girlfriends and his wife. He said he hadn't loved any of them the way he loved her. They had so much baggage. They were bitter and twisted from the other relationships they'd been in and they'd taken it out on him. They weren't like her – so optimistic and hopeful, so kind and so loving. He kept telling her he wished he could rewind time or be born again so he could be thirteen too and they could lose their virginity to each other. He said he wished she could have met him when he was thirteen. He was really good-looking back then, with a flat stomach and jet-black hair. Secretly she'd wished that too, even though she told him that he was still good-looking for his age. It was weird, the first time, kissing a man who was older than her dad, but he was so kind to her. So gentle and so understanding. And he made her feel safe. She couldn't remember the last time she'd felt like that.

But he hadn't turned up to meet her. He'd told her

over and over again not to ring or text his work phone unless it was an emergency and she'd promised him that she wouldn't. But he'd ignored his other phone and it *had* been urgent. She'd done everything else he'd asked. She'd listed his secret phone as Liam in her mobile and made sure she deleted his messages the second she read them. Maybe he was ignoring her because she wouldn't sleep with him yet. Maybe she'd pushed his patience too far and he'd lost interest in her. The thought made her cry harder.

'I'll sleep with you,' she whispered as she laid her head down on her school bag and pulled her jacket over her shaking shoulders, 'just please, please come and find me.'

But Mike wasn't there when she woke up. She was still alone: cold, stiff and soaking wet, buried in the heart of a bush. Rain wasn't the only thing that had seeped through her clothes as she slept. Despair had too. Mike wouldn't save her. He wouldn't stand between her and her dad and stop him from screaming at her. He wouldn't drag her mum out of bed or heal her never-ending migraines. He wouldn't jump to her defence when she was called a loser or a freak at school. Life was shit and it was going to continue getting shitter. And now she had to deal with it alone, just like she had to deal with everything. Or not deal with it at all.

I don't care, she thought as she scrabbled back out of the bushes and started to run. *I don't care anymore. I just don't care.*

* * *

132

There is a light on in the front room as Chloe walks down the garden path but she doesn't falter or slow her pace. Instead she turns the front door handle and walks into the living room. She doesn't react as her mum leaps off the sofa, screams, 'Oh thank god!' and throws her arms around her. She doesn't blink as her Auntie Meg, who is standing by the window, snatches up her phone and shouts down it, 'Mum, she's here. She's back. She's just this second walked in.' And when her dad bursts in, fifteen minutes later, and hugs her, then shakes her and screams in her face that she's a bloody stupid girl and does she even know how worried they all were, she looks him in the eye and doesn't cry.

'Why?' he shouts at her. 'Why did you do this to us? First stealing, then running away. I give up. I absolutely give up. Give me your phone.' He holds out a hand.

Chloe reaches into her pocket, pulls out her mobile and gives it to him. She waits for a twang of pain or regret to pull at her heart. But there's nothing.

'I'm cancelling your contract. And you're grounded,' her dad says. 'You're not going out for a month and I'm going to pick you up from school every day. You're lucky Greensleeves decided not to press charges or you'd have a criminal record to your name. At *thirteen*! How fucking stupid are you?'

Chloe doesn't reply. She knows exactly how stupid her dad thinks she is.

'And I'm cancelling the holiday to Majorca,' he adds.

'No!' her mum whines from the sofa. 'Oh Alan, that's not fair. Jamie's been so looking forward to it. I have too.'

'Well . . .' he pauses. 'We'll see about the holiday. But you're not going anywhere.' He prods Chloe on the cold, clammy skin of her chest, just below her collarbone.

Chloe doesn't react. She feels as though a transparent film has formed around her, separating her from the rest of the world. Nothing can touch her anymore and nobody can hurt her. For thirteen years she's lived for 'if only'. If only I had a nice boyfriend I'd be happy. If only my dad stopped being an arsehole I'd be happy. If only I was clever/beautiful/thin I'd be happy. All along the solution to her misery was right there in front of her but she'd never seen it. The only cure for unhappiness is to stop caring.

She looks from her dad to her mum to her aunt. *They think they're still in control. They think I'm upset. They think I give a shit. But none of them know that on the inside I'm dead.*

Chapter 19

Lou

Last night Mike really scared me. He'd been out all day, looking for somewhere for us to stay. He locked me in the hotel room again, saying I'd get bored, traipsing around looking at apartments. When I told him I'd be bored staying behind on my own, he kissed me on the nose and told me be patient. We had the rest of our lives to spend together.

I knew it hadn't gone well, the second he walked back into the room. He was all sweaty round his temples and his blue eyes looked dark. I didn't ask him how it went. Instead I patted the space beside me on the bed and give him a sympathetic smile. He slumped beside me, crossed his hands under his head and stared up at the ceiling. His bad mood was like a black cloud that covered both of us.

'I fucking hate French people.'

'So why did we come here?' The words were out

of my mouth before I could take them back and I tensed, waiting for him to snap.

'Because I love France. But I hate the people.'

'Why?'

'Because they're up their own arses. Arrogant pricks. Everyone I tried to talk to in French acted like they couldn't understand me and the only person I could find who spoke English laughed when I told him what our budget was.'

'Maybe he—'

'He fucking laughed at me. I should have taken his head off. Fuck it. Maybe we should leave Rouen and go somewhere else.'

I didn't know what to say. I didn't want him to snap at me if I said the wrong thing and if I said nothing he'd think I didn't care.

'Why don't we . . .' I slid my hand over his stomach and wriggled it under the waistband of his jeans.

'Don't.' He grabbed my wrist and threw it away from him. 'I'm not in the mood.'

Neither of us said anything for the longest time. Mike continued to stare at the ceiling while I lay curled up on my side, watching his face. It was horrible and awkward and I wished I could magic myself out of that cold, boxy little room and back into my bedroom with my warm duvet, my TV and all my stuff. I even missed Mum shouting at me to stop messing about and do my homework.

'Maybe . . .' my voice sounded small and weak. 'Maybe we should go back to England?'

'What?' Mike turned his head to look at me, lightning fast. I'd said the wrong thing.

'You . . . you don't . . . you don't seem very happy.'

'And why's that then, do you think?'

'I don't know . . . the French . . . the Frenchman. You didn't—'

'Has it ever occurred to you, Louise . . .' Mike propped himself up on one elbow and looked down at me. 'That perhaps you're part of the reason why I'm not happy?'

'Me?'

'Ever since we've got here you've done nothing but bitch and moan about how bored you are, how there's no TV, how you want to ring your mum. You've thrown things at me, you've shouted at me and you've insulted me. I did this for YOU, Louise. I did it because you told me that I was all you ever wanted. That you loved me. That you wanted to spend the rest of your life with me. I have given up everything for you. EVERYTHING. My home, my marriage, my club. And how do you repay me? You ask if we can go back to England?'

'Mike I'm sorry.' I burst into tears and threw myself at him, burying my face in his chest, wrapping him with my arms and legs. 'I didn't mean . . . I'm sorry . . . I just, I just . . . I just want to make you happy.'

He flipped me onto my back and sat astride me, pinning my arms either side of my head. He was red in the face, eyes gleaming.

'You are everything to me, everything. Don't you get it?'

I nodded dumbly.

'You need to trust me, Louise. I keep telling you. You need to start trusting me.'

'I do. Mike I really do.'

He shifted off me, pulled at his belt buckle and took off his jeans and boxers. He flipped up my dress – the one he bought me on Monday – and pulled down my knickers.

'Prove it,' he said as he sat astride me. 'Prove how much you trust me.'

'How?' Tears rolled down my cheeks as I reached up and touched his face.

He gently moved my hand from his face and laid it on the pillow by my head, then he wrapped his hand round my throat. I instinctively tried to pull his hand away but he shook his head.

'You need to trust me, Louise. Remember? I'm not going to hurt you. I'm going to do something to you that's going to feel amazing. You'll feel giddy, light-headed and more pleasure than you've ever felt in your life. It might scare you but I will . . . not . . . hurt . . . you. I promise. This is your opportunity to prove how much you trust me. Do you?'

As I nodded my head he shoved himself inside me and tightened his grip on my neck.

Wednesday 2nd May 2007

I speed round the supermarket, chucking bread, milk, ham and cheese into my basket. It's Wednesday

138

morning and the second time I've phoned in sick at work. Mike has been in the barn since Monday early evening. He's still refusing to give me the code to his phone. Yesterday, after my freak-out about the helicopter, I drove around until my phone picked up 4G, then I googled how to unlock a phone. I spent hours following different YouTube videos, and read through pages and pages of forums, but none of the suggested hacks worked. There's only one more thing I can try – one of those phone stalls that unlock phones and replace screens. There aren't any in Bromyard but I'm pretty sure I'll find one in Worcester.

With my basket half full I hurry to the tills. It's a small shop and there's only one cashier working so I'm forced to queue. There are two older women in front of me, dressed in near identical puffy anoraks, and they're deep in conversation.

'Do you go there, do you, Mavis?' says the taller of the two.

'I used to, but they put their prices up so I go to Crossman's now.'

'Do you? I like the staff in Greensleeves, they know their stuff.'

My ears prick up at the mention of the garden centre. That's where Chloe and Mike work.

'Did he work there then, did he?'

'I think so.' Mavis, the shorter woman, starts unloading her basket onto the conveyor belt. 'Delivery driver apparently.'

'How long's he been missing?'

'Since Monday night. He was supposed to check

139

his van back in at work but he didn't show and he didn't answer his phone. Sandra was telling me all about it yesterday. Her neighbour's niece works there. Apparently he rang his receptionist to say that he had one last delivery to do, then he disappeared off the face of the planet. He didn't turn up to do any of his Tuesday deliveries. Sandra said they're really worried about him. He had some heart problems last year and they're worried he might have had an attack and ended up in a ditch.'

'Oh gosh. Poor man. I do hope they've gone to the police.'

'Oh yes. They reported him missing yesterday.'

I keep my gaze fixed to the conveyor belt as a pint of milk, tin of baked beans and a packet of bacon travel towards the cashier but my heart feels like it's about to beat out of my chest. Mike can't have told his receptionist where he was going or my door would have been the first one the police knocked on. But it's only a matter of time until they do. And Mike's van is parked up in my yard.

'Sorry,' I drop my basket full of food into the metal holder beneath the conveyor belt and shoot an apologetic look at the cashier. 'I've got to go.'

'Someone's in a hurry,' one of the chatty women comments as I head for the door.

There's no way I can hide Mike's van in the garage, not with a wheel-less car and all the junk filling it. That gives me two options – drive it as far away as I can and dump it or hide it in plain sight. Dumping it's too much of a risk. Too close to the farm and it'll look dodgy, particularly as the last call Mike took on his phone was in my barn. Too far away and someone might spot me hitchhiking back. I'll have to hide it, and there's only one place where I can do that.

Compared to my Mini, driving Mike's van is like manoeuvring a tank. I can't see anything in the rearview mirror and the wing mirrors make everything behind the van seem miles away. Still, there's not much I can reverse into out here, other than a few fences.

Mike starts shouting as I start the engine. 'Lou! Lou, what are you doing? That sounds like my van. Lou! Lou!'

I touch my foot to the accelerator and drive towards the rear field. The van easily fits through the open gate and rolls and bumps down the steep incline. The field, like all the others surrounding the house, is unkempt and unloved with grass that's at least waist height. It's raining heavily but I don't bother turning on the windscreen wipers. I'm not going to be in here for long.

I stop the van halfway down the field, pull on the handbrake, pull up my hood and get out. It should look miserable, the murky lake at the edge of the field, reflecting the black sky but there is something almost beautiful about the way the rain lands on the water, painting concentric circles that appear and then vanish in less than a heartbeat. It's deep. Mum was terrified I'd drown in it as a kid and insisted Dad put a fence around it. He did a half-hearted job and it's all but rotted to nothing now.

I half expect a helicopter to drop down through the clouds but there isn't so much as a bird in the sky. For now. I reach into the van, release the handbrake and jump back out, scared I'll be swept down the field with it. But the van doesn't speed anywhere. It lurches forward and then stops. I'm going to have to give it some help.

'Please,' I raise my eyes heavenward. My hood has slipped down, my hair is plastered to my head and my waterproof is clinging to every part of my body. 'Please work.'

I trudge back up the hill, turn, and ready myself.

'One . . . two . . . three . . . go!' I run towards the van, hands outstretched and launch myself at the closed back door.

The wheels groan against the wet grass and, for one terrible moment, I think the van isn't going to move, but it lurches forward. I ready myself to give it another shove but it gathers pace and suddenly it's off, hurtling down the field towards the lake. Please, I pray, please don't stall partway into the water. I won't be able to get it out again.

My prayer is answered. The white van speeds towards the lake and then SPLASH, the front end goes in and a huge brown wave of water leaps into the air. The van travels halfway across the lake and then slowly begins to sink. The lake ripples as it swallows it whole then it's still again. Still, apart from the gentle dimpling of the rain.

I don't know whether to punch the air or sink to my knees. The whole thing was so surreal I can't believe it just happened. How can I have gone from living in a nice flat in London, dating a decent guy and doing a good job to locking a man in a cage and sinking his van? It's like one of those dreams where you kill someone and wake up desperately hoping it didn't happen.

But Chloe is real. What Mike did to me was real. And there's no waking up from that.

Chapter 20

Lou

'Did you enjoy it?' Mike asked this morning as I opened my eyes to find him staring at me from the other pillow. 'What we tried yesterday?'

I forced a smile.

He stroked my hair away from my cheeks. 'The look on your face as you passed out was mesmerising. You looked almost . . . blissful. Do you want to do it again?'

I kept the smile fixed to my face. 'Maybe later.'

That thing he did, squeezing my throat while we had sex, was the most terrifying thing that's ever happened to me. First I felt light-headed and dizzy then, as he increased the pressure, it was as though a grey veil was separating us. As it got darker I pulled at his fingers. I was dying. He was strangling me to death. And then I woke up, still lying on my back on the bed with my skirt up round my waist. Mike was lying on his side, staring at me with this weird fascinated look on his face. I tried to twist away, so I wouldn't have to look at him but he said, 'No,' and reached for my hand. 'I want to fall asleep looking at you. Don't ever turn your back on me, Lou. It's not fair.'

I closed my eyes and kept them tightly shut until Mike started to snore softly. When we checked in on Saturday, the woman at reception told us in French that the night porter would be there overnight if we needed anything. I had to find him. There was no way Mike was ever going to let me go home and the porter was the only person who could help me.

Mike stirred in his sleep as I inched away from him towards the edge of the bed. I froze and waited for his breathing to slow again, then I gently tried to slip my fingers from his but his knuckles were large and vice-like, and I had to yank my hand free.

'Where are you going?' He caught me by the wrist and opened his eyes.

'Toilet.'

'Be quick. You woke me up.'

I shuffled across the bedroom, my heart pounding in my chest. The door to the bathroom was right next to the door to the hallway. I could run for it. I could scream that I'd been abducted and hope someone came out of one of the other rooms. Or Mike could spring out of bed and bundle me back into the room before the scream had even left my mouth.

'Good girl,' he said as I came out of the bathroom.

He tapped the empty space I'd left in the bed. 'Now let's go back to sleep.'

'Would you like anything else, love?' the waitress asks as she puts a cup of coffee on the table in front of me.

I shake my head. 'I'm fine thank you.'

I'm in a small café in the Shambles, Worcester. Fifteen minutes ago I walked out of a grotty-looking electrical and mobile phone shop with Mike's unlocked phone in my hand. The shop owner didn't give me a second look when I told him that it belonged to my mother and she'd forgotten her security code. Instead he told me it would cost twenty quid, then he disappeared into the back of the shop. Five minutes later he returned and slid the phone across the counter towards me.

I practically ran into the nearest café and pressed the home button continually as I placed my coffee order, terrified the phone would lock again before I could check the messages. I've seen them all now. There were the six I caught glimpses of on the screen and one that must have arrived just before Chloe rang Mike. It's the most interesting.

I no I shdnt use this number but its an emergency and ur not replyin to ur other phone. I need to talk to you. ASAP.

I went through all Mike's contacts, his photos, downloads and emails. There wasn't a single piece of incriminating evidence anywhere. No photos of Chloe, no emails and no text messages other than

146

the flurry she sent on Monday. All of the texts were either work related – what time would he be arriving, how much for a delivery, change of address etc – or they were from friends asking if he fancied a pint or a night at the races. I considered whether George, Bill and Nick could be more pseudonyms for Chloe but those messages were written in a completely different style, using full English and some of the messages stretched back years.

After I'd been through the phone, I rang 'Jim', the number that definitely belonged to Chloe. It went straight to voicemail. I tried again. Voicemail again. Damn it. She was probably at school with the phone in her locker.

But what if she wasn't? What if she was in danger when she asked Mike to call her ASAP? I stopped Mike going to her aid.

I re-read her first message.

I no I shdnt use this number but its an emergency and ur not replyin to ur other phone. I need to talk to you. ASAP.

How long was there between that message and her phone call? Sixteen minutes according to the phone. What could have happened that was so urgent?

Mike's got another phone. One he uses for personal calls. She obviously rang it first, but I didn't hear another phone ring when Mike was getting out of the van and he can't have it on him or he would have rung for help by now. It wasn't in his van or his stuff so it has to be hidden somewhere. And hidden well, or the police would have found it when they questioned him about Chloe a few days ago. It could be anywhere.

I push my chair away from the table and stand up. What do I do? Go back home or check Chloe's okay?

Alan!

A name flashes up in my mind.

Alan is Chloe's dad's name. His wife shouted it when I went to their house. If he and Mike are friends his landline number might be in the phone.

And there it is. Alan Meadows. A mobile number *and* a landline. That has to be him. I tap on the latter and hold the phone to my ear. It rings several times and then, 'Yes,' says a tired-sounding female voice.

I lower my voice. 'Is Chloe there please?'

'She's at school.'

'Oh, okay.'

'Can I ask who's calling please?'

I end the call before she can ask me again, then I turn the phone over and take out the battery and SIM again. If the police do track Mike's calls they'll think he's been in Worcester.

The stench of shit hits me the second I open the barn door. Mike is sitting in one corner of his cell with the blanket pressed over his nose. In the opposite corner of the cell he's piled bricks around and over the bucket.

I can feel him following me with his eyes as I cross the barn and scoop up a big armful of hay.

'Here.' I drop it next to the cage. He only needs

to reach out an arm to grab it. 'Use it to smother the smell.'

He shakes his head. He looks dead behind his eyes, like all the fight's gone out of him.

'You can lie on it too.' I pick up a handful and shove it through the bars. 'It'll make it more comfortable for—'

Mike is lightning fast. One moment he's curled up in a blanket in the corner of the cell. The next he's on his feet with his fingers wrapped around my wrist. He yanks on my arm, slamming me up against the bars of the cage.

'Open the cage!'

I struggle to twist free but he's holding me too tightly. 'I can't.'

'Open the cage or I'll break your wrist.' He pushes my hand back against my arm, making me cry out in pain.

'I can't!' I scream. 'I haven't got the key.'

'Liar!' He pushes harder on my hand. The pain is unbearable. The muscles in my elbow and shoulder feel as though they're being ripped from my joints.

'There's no key. I swear! Not here anyway. It might be in Dad's garage but it's full of stuff. I'd need to—'

Mike's other hand grips my throat. As he squeezes, I pull at his fingers with my free hand.

'Stay still!' he shouts, yanking on my trapped hand, making me yelp in pain.

Somewhere at the back of my brain I know he can't kill me. If he does he'll never get out. But I'm in too much pain to think clearly. I don't know how either of us are going to get out of this situation. I just want it to stop.

'Stop fighting or I'll snap your fucking neck!' Mike shouts.

I don't know if it's fear, the tone of his voice or the pressure of his fingers on my windpipe but I stop squirming and twisting and my hand drops away from my throat. As I go limp, the angry buzzing in my mind quiets and then stops.

'Where's the fucking key?' Mike screams in my ear. There's desperation in his voice now. Fear too. He knows as well as I do that he's either going to have to let me go or kill me. Either way he stays in the cage.

After what feels like forever he lets go of my throat but he keeps hold of my hand. He reaches through the bars and plucks at the pocket of my hoody. I plunge my hand in first. My thumb pricks against the sharp edge of a metal keyring. It's an owl in flight, a present from Alice when I left London. The tips of its wings are as barbed as a knife edge. I gather it into my fist, then twist sharply and plunge it into Mike's cheek.

He roars in pain and shoves me away from him, sending me sprawling to the ground. I lie still, panting and sweating, my whole right side throbbing, then I scrabble to my feet.

'Tell me where the other phone is!' I scream. 'Tell me where it is! Tell me!'

Mike grips the bars of the cage, one hand pressed

to the side of the face, blood trickling through his fingers. His lips curl into a smile.

His laughter follows me out of the barn and into the garden.

Mike's eyes flick from my face to the coil of green garden hose in my hands. There's dried blood on the side of his face but the keyring didn't cause more than a scratch.

'Lou,' he retreats to the back of the cage, 'don't do this.'

'I won't, if you tell me where the other phone is.'

He holds his hands out, palms up. 'I've got no idea what you're talking about.'

There's that laugh again.

I uncurl the hose and squeeze the trigger.

Mike strips off his wet sweatshirt and throws it to the floor. 'You've lost the plot. You know that don't you?'

He didn't say a word as I soaked him. He turned his back and took it, gallons and gallons of freezing cold water. He undoes his trousers and slips them off too. His legs are hairy and the skin is mottled. His quads used to be so strong they looked carved into his skin but he's lost all his muscle tone.

'When the police find me,' he says, 'which they will, they'll do you for torture as well as kidnapping.'

'Not if you're convicted of paedophilia. I'll probably get a medal.'

There's a hollow ring to my words. I'm no closer

to finding the second phone than I was this morning and if the police turn up before I find evidence that he's been abusing Chloe, then he's right – I will be the one that ends up in jail, not him.

I throw a towel at the cage – there's no way I'm getting within grabbing distance again – then sit with my back against the barn wall. There's something I need to ask him, something that's been bothering me for a while. 'How did you get your probation officer to agree to let you work at the garden centre? I thought sex offenders weren't allowed to work anywhere near children.'

'I haven't got a probation officer and I'm not a sex offender.' Mike crouches to grab the towel.

'Don't be ridiculous.'

He stands up. 'I'm not. I got out of prison in 1994. The register wasn't set up until 1997.'

He's not on the sex offenders list.

That can't be right.

Or is it? I was fourteen in 1989 when Mike was sent to prison. Even serving the full five-year sentence he would have got out before 1997. Which means . . . he's right. He's slipped through the paedophile net.

He meets my gaze. 'I served my time, Lou. Most people have let me move on with my life.'

'I'm not most people.'

I hurl some of Dad's clothes – items I can't remember him ever wearing – at the cage. Much as I'd love Mike to suffer, I need to keep him alive. He runs a hand through his wet hair, then crouches down and drags them through the bars. As he pulls them towards him I notice the ugly scar on his right thigh, thick and ribbed, like a pirate's scar, and at least three inches long.

'What happened?' I ask as he pulls on his trousers.

He touches his scar. 'This? Car crash. Well, articulated lorry. My first job after I got out. I fell asleep at the wheel and careered off the motorway.'

'You could have killed someone.'

'Yeah, me. When the doctors said they didn't think I'd walk again I wished I had died.' He does up the trousers. They're too big and drop to his hip bones. He looks across at me as he reaches for Dad's T-shirt and jumper. 'You know I was beaten up in prison?'

'And?'

He crouches down in the cage and rubs his hands over his face. He looks pitiful, draped in the folds of my father's oversized clothes.

'I'm sorry,' he rubs his hands back and forth over his face, 'if I hurt you earlier. I can't live like this, shitting in a bucket and eating scraps of food.'

'Well—'

He holds up a hand. 'Just hear me out. Please. I've done a lot of thinking, trying to work out why you'd do this to me. It's revenge, isn't it? You think I ruined your life. Am I right? Do you hate me, Lou?'

I meet his gaze, but only for a second. Hate is such a powerful, all-consuming word. What was that quote I read? Hate is like a poison you make for your enemy that you end up swallowing yourself. Hating him gives him too much power, too much control

153

over the way I live my life. And I've spent far too many years doing that.

'Was it so awful?' he says softly. 'What we had? It must have been for you to hate me this much. I was rough with you when I shouldn't have been. I was hot-headed and angry, frustrated that you couldn't – or wouldn't – understand all the wonderful things I had planned for us. I never meant to hurt you, Lou.'

'You revolt me.'

To my horror he starts to cry. I turn away as fat, dirty tears spill down his cheek. I can't watch this.

'Look at me,' he begs. 'I loved you. I really did. You were my whole world, my greatest love. I wanted to spend the rest of my life with you.'

'Mike, don't—'

'Being with you was the happiest I've ever been in my life. You made the world a better place. You made me feel optimistic and hopeful, like anything could happen. Since I lost you I've stumbled through life lurching from one disaster to another. I've lost jobs, homes and relationships. Some women ran as soon as they found out who I was, they wouldn't have anything to do with me. And the women who stayed . . . they either saw me as some kind of lost cause they wanted to fix or they wanted to dress up as schoolgirls and shit.'

'I don't want to hear—'

'I'm sorry. That's all I'm trying to say. I'm sorry, Lou. What I did was wrong. I see that now. I was the adult. I never should have let it happen.'

'No, you shouldn't.'

154

'I just . . .' He stands up and grips hold of the bars, his eyes damp with regret and self-pity. At least, that's what I think he's feeling. I've got no idea anymore. He's such a manipulative bastard. 'I just hope that you're happy, Lou. I only ever wanted the best for you. I wanted you to feel safe and looked after. Is someone doing that for you now? Do you have someone who loves you? Someone to take care of you?'

This is where I tell him how screwed up my life is. How many failed relationships I've left in my wake. How I feel like permanently broken. But I can't. I can't let him know how much damage he's done. I can't give him that much power. Instead I turn my back on him and walk towards the door. He's never going to change. He's never going to take responsibility for what he did. His apology, his attempt at remorse, it's all lies. I might not be able to make Mike see what a monster he is but I haven't given up on Chloe. Not yet.

'Lou, wait!' Mike shouts. 'I . . . I've probably got no right to ask you this but . . .'

I don't stop walking.

'Did you love me? At all? Or did you say that because it was something you thought I wanted to hear?'

I turn to look at him, the first man I ever loved. 'This isn't about me anymore.'

Chapter 21

Chloe

Chloe stands on the pavement outside school with her head down and her arms crossed over her chest as the other kids mill around her, laughing, chatting and nudging each other. When her he dad dropped her off before school he told her wouldn't be able to pick her up until after four but she was to stand outside the gates and *not move a muscle* until he turned up. She didn't reply, she just nodded, then swiftly said, 'Yes, Dad. I promise I won't go anywhere,' when she saw the look on his face.

Tomorrow she has to skip school so she can go on holiday to Majorca for a long weekend to celebrate her dad's birthday. When her dad first mentioned it she'd tried to get out of going. She was thirteen, she'd insisted, and she didn't want to miss any school. She was sure Granny and Grandad wouldn't mind if she stayed with them. She was hoping her parents would jump at the opportunity to get rid of her for a couple of days – days she could spend with Mike – but her dad insisted she come. If it was bad before, it would be hell on earth now. She'll have to share a room with her brat of a brother and her dad wouldn't let her out of his sight. She'll be forced to wear a swimsuit and play with Jamie in the pool before being dragged along to hideous evening entertainment events.

The numb, dead feeling inside hasn't abated since she returned home. If anything it's got worse. Yesterday hope flickered inside her when she heard a car pull up outside her house. It was Mike. He'd turned up under the pretence of seeing her dad but secretly he wanted to check that she was okay. But it wasn't Mike's black 4x4 parked up beneath her bedroom window. It was an Amazon delivery driver in a white van. It was ages since she'd last spoken to Mike, even longer since she'd seen him. At first she'd made excuses for his silence – he'd lost his phone, or his voice, he'd got caught up at work – but the longer the silence stretched, the more she feared the worst. He'd dumped her without even bothering to tell her. He'd met someone else. He was involved in a terrible accident and couldn't get a message to her. He was dead. Out of those options only the accident was acceptable but death was preferable to the idea that Mike had gone off with someone else. He'd told her so many times how special she was, how he'd never met anyone like her and how he'd never felt so much love for another person. And she'd believed him. She'd tucked his precious words away in her heart and cherished them.

He was the only person in the world who loved her completely.

Now she turns at the sound of her name, fully expecting it to be Misty Engles, asking if she can copy her homework again. But it's not Misty that runs down the street towards her, her cheeks flushed, arms pumping at her sides, her long fair hair streaming behind her. It's the weird woman again. The one who stopped her on the way to school the other day. The one she rang Mike about.

Chloe's hands twitch at her sides. She wants to run but if her dad turns up and she's not outside the school he'll kill her.

'Leave me alone.' She holds out a hand towards the woman and turns away. 'I'm not interested in anything you have to say.'

'I know. And I totally understand.' The woman has a soft, calm voice. It reminds Chloe of the police-woman who asked her about Mike. 'I just want to give you something, that's all.'

Curious, Chloe turns to look at her.

'Here,' the woman holds out a white plastic bag.

'What's in it?'

'Something you need to read.'

'I don't read books.'

'It's not a book. It's a diary.'

A diary? Chloe's gaze flicks towards the pink shape in the bottom of the bag. 'Whose is it?'

'It belonged . . .' The woman suddenly seems lost for words. 'It belonged to a girl who was in exactly the same situation as you.'

'What, stalked by some random woman?'

The woman laughs. 'No, someone who fell in love with an older man. I think you should read it, Chloe. I think it might help you.'

'I don't need your help.' Chloe turns away again and crosses her arms over her chest.

'I think you do. And if you ever need to talk I'm here for you. I've written my number in the front of the book. Give me a call.'

Chloe's heart quickens as a green estate car turns into the road. Her dad is behind the wheel.

'Whose diary is it?' She turns to look at the older woman but she's already halfway down the street, getting into a red Mini, and doesn't look around. At Chloe's feet is the white plastic bag. 'Freak,' Chloe says under her breath as she picks up the bag and shoves it into her school bag.

'Who's a freak?' her dad says from behind her.

'No one,' Chloe breathes. 'Just me.'

Chapter 22

Wendy

Wendy can feel Ted standing at her shoulder, breathing heavily. She can smell him too, the obnoxious scent of aftershave layered over cigarette smoke and sweat. Every single one of his white shirts is yellowed under the armpits. She's never asked about his marital situation but she's pretty certain there's never been a Mrs Ted Barton.

'Everything okay?' she asks.

Ted leans over her and prods a stubby finger at the screen. 'I think you've made a mistake there.'

She leans away from his armpit. 'What mistake?'

'You've got the VAT incomings and outgoings in the wrong columns. Are you sure you know what you're doing?'

He laughs, the low, chesty gurgle of a smoker. The sound makes Wendy want to clear her throat.

'What?' She bends closer to the screen. He's being ridiculous. Of course she hasn't—

Her heart sinks as she looks from the screen to the ledger on the desk and back again. 'Oh.'

'Aha!' Ted looks victorious. 'I'm right aren't I? I did my own returns for twenty-five years you know. Not much gets past me.'

But you employed me to start doing them for you, Wendy thinks, *how about you just let me get on with them? Or better still, let me take the ledgers home so I can do this in peace and quiet.* She doesn't say that though. Instead she says, 'Sorry Ted. You're right. It's my mistake. I won't charge you for the time to correct it.'

'I'd hope not.' He crosses his arms over his thick chest. 'Anyway, I'll let you get back to it. I need to go into the factory.'

Wendy keeps the smile fixed to her face until the door closes and Ted's rotund profile passes the window. It vanishes the second he disappears.

'Patronising arsehole.'

She reaches down for her handbag, lifts it onto her lap, and pulls out her phone. It's been an hour and a half since she last checked Facebook and her concentration level has been shot for at least forty minutes.

This is getting ridiculous, she thinks as she taps on the app icon. *The amount of times I log onto Facebook each day. I can't even walk Monty without checking it.* She clicks on the Facebook message icon. She sent a message to Ben yesterday and she can tell that he's read it but he still hasn't replied. He hasn't updated his page either. Neither has Lou.

I'm going to delete this stupid app, Wendy decides

as she drops her phone back into her bag. *Just as soon as I'm done with all this*. Only she isn't entirely sure what 'done with all this' means. She still wakes up each morning with a strange gnawing sensation beneath her ribs and she gets the most terrible indigestion whenever she so much as pictures Lou Wandsworth's face. Dr Google says it's anxiety, but she's not so sure. It's acid, the ache she feels inside. It's been gnawing away at her for years. For a couple of days after she visited Lou at work the pain dissipated – probably because she felt in control for the first time in her life – but now it's back, and it's worse than ever.

She gets up from her desk, glances down the corridor to check that Ted isn't on his way back, then snatches up her phone again. She waited in the café until well after 10 a.m. this morning. She'd run through what would happen dozens of times. She'd spot Lou from the window of the café, hurry to the door and shout her name. Lou would stop, turn around, smile – maybe in surprise – then raise a hand in greeting. Wendy would run across the road and tell her that she really needed to talk to her. She'd suggest a chat – perhaps as they walked around Priory Park (it was important they weren't overheard). Only Lou hadn't shown up today, had she? Or yesterday. Last night Wendy hadn't been able to sleep for worrying. What if Lou had jacked in the job and started somewhere else? Even worse, what if she'd moved back to London? The woman had literally been within Wendy's grasp and she'd let her slip away like a thief in the night. She should have acted while she had the chance instead of skipping around like an awkward teenager. She'd cursed herself for her cowardice over and over again before finally, she fell into a broken sleep.

'Hello, yes,' Wendy says now. 'I'd like to talk to Lou Wandsworth please. It's Dr Wendy Harrison from the University of Worcester.'

The receptionist makes a sad little sighing sound. 'I'm afraid Lou's off sick.'

'Off sick?' She feigns surprise. 'I do hope there's nothing seriously wrong.'

'No, no,' the receptionist says quickly. 'I think it's just a tummy bug. Although she has been off for a couple of days now so maybe it's a little more serious than she originally thought.'

You are the *soul* of discretion, Wendy thinks as she pretends to sigh sympathetically. At the same time the knot in her stomach untwists. So Lou hasn't left. That's excellent news.

'Could I have her address, do you think?' she asks. 'So I could send her some get well flowers.'

The receptionist pauses. 'I'm . . . I'm not sure I can . . .'

'If you're not sure what you can and can't do, I suggest you need a little more training,' Wendy snaps. 'Could you put me through to Gary Lambley please?'

'Yes, madam. Straight away.'

Madam. Wendy smiles to herself. Bet she said that between gritted teeth.

'Hello, hello,' a bombastic voice says a couple of

seconds later. 'Wendy Harrison! Great to hear from you.'

'Hello, Gary,' Wendy attempts to put what she hopes is a seductive purr into her voice. 'Are you well?'

'I'm great. What can I do you for, Wend?'

She tenses at the shortening of her name but forces a smile. 'Actually I'm after Lou's home address. I hear she's ill and I'd like to send her some flowers.'

'Flowers?' There's a question mark in Gary's voice. Why would a prospective client want to send flowers to her potential account manager? Surely it would be the other way round. Wendy holds her breath. It's a long shot but worth a try. Gary makes a clicking sound with his tongue as though he's made up his mind. 'That's very kind of you. Just give me a sec, Wend.'

She hears the clunk of a phone being placed on a desk, a couple of seconds of background chatter then, 'I've got it. It's . . .'

Her forced smile melts into a real one as she scribbles down Lou's address on the back of a notepad.

'Thank you so much, Gary. You've been incredibly helpful.'

'No problem. I don't suppose you've had a chance to fill out a pro forma yet have—'

Wendy puts the phone down before he can finish his sentence.

The house is much, *much* bigger than Wendy was expecting. From the address she'd imagined a little cottage crammed in the centre of a terrace with a mess of roses growing up the outside and a roof in need of attention. She didn't imagine an enormous detached house with a sprawling driveway and its own private lane. The house is so isolated she drove past it several times before she finally spotted the track, almost hidden between overgrown apple trees and bramble bushes.

It's late afternoon and, with the sun still high in the sky, Wendy tucks the car well into the trees to avoid being seen. Not that it would matter if Lou *does* see her. She's carrying an armful of flowers and wearing an expression of concern. If Lou asks why she's there she'll say she was in the area and thought she'd drop a small gift by to cheer up the ailing patient. It's a little unusual, admittedly – a home visit from a new work acquaintance – and Lou might raise an eyebrow, but it's certainly nothing Wendy could be locked up for.

That house though. Wendy sighs deeply. It's enormous. It must have at least five bedrooms and four receptions. If not more. So much space – inside and out – and no other houses for miles. Unlike her and her hideous excuse for a neighbour. She caught him throwing snails over the fence into her back garden the day before and stood on a bucket and shouted at him to stop. And what was his excuse? 'Sorry, I didn't think you were in.' Absolute imbecile! Lou doesn't have to deal with obnoxious neighbours inflicting their music and throes of passion on her. Oh no, she's landed on her feet nicely: a huge house, a handsome boyfriend, friends who adore her and a good job. And what's Wendy got? A tiny two-up two-down with thin walls, a couple of friends who routinely moan about their husbands/children/ ailments, a job that barely makes ends meet and a permanent cold patch on the right side of the bed. It's so unfair. All her life Wendy prided herself on being warm, loyal and fair and where had it got her? At the bottom of society's heap, that's where. At least Lou hasn't got children. If she'd waltzed back to Malvern with small brood or a swollen stomach . . .

Wendy briskly wipes away the tear that's appeared in the corner of her right eye. Now is not the time for self-pity and regret. Now is the time for confronting Lou Wandsworth and telling her exactly what she thinks of her. There's a tired-looking Volvo parked up outside the house. Wendy takes a steadying breath, steps back out onto the path and heads for the door.

There's no one in. Wendy knocked, hard, several times on the front door and then the side door. When there was no answer, she peered in at the windows. All the lights were off and the inner doors were closed. She tried shouting out Lou's name but none of the curtains in the upstairs windows so much as flickered. Even an ill person wouldn't be able to sleep through the racket she's made. Despite the car, Lou is definitely not at home.

Wendy has completed a lap of the house and is now standing in the garden. It could be a beautiful space. There's a weeping willow on the right and several apple trees on the left, but that's all that's attractive. The beds and borders are overgrown and riddled with weeds and there are piles of rubbish everywhere. Anger burns in Wendy's stomach as she surveys the huge space. If this were her garden she'd turn it into a magical, restful place. She'd order chairs and tables from John Lewis, maybe install a water feature or a pond and plant rose bushes. She'd sit outside with a nice G & T and read the papers at the weekend. Monty would love it too.

She wanders to the far end of the garden and peers over the gate. There's a bloody enormous yard beyond it, with a barn ripe for conversion. She glances back towards the house. It wouldn't hurt to take a peek inside, would it? If Lou discovered her creeping about she'd say she'd been looking for her. She does still have the flowers in her hands after all. She reaches for the latch, then freezes as the sound of car tyres on gravel travels up the garden towards her.

It has to be Lou.

Wendy's heart double beats in her chest as she touches a hand to her hair, smoothing it down. The barn will have to wait.

'Wendy Harrison,' she tells herself as she turns and marches back towards the house, 'you can do this. You've waited long enough.' But as she gets closer to the gap it's not Lou she sees walking up to the side door. It's the bloody postman with a clutch of letters in his hand and a parcel under his arm. Wendy waits, out of sight, until the letter box clatters, the van's engine starts up and she can no longer hear the sound of wheels on gravel, then she steps through the gap between the house and the garage. She looks from the house to the track and sighs. She could sit in her car and wait, but Lou might not be back for hours. And there's always the possibility she might bring someone back with her. If Lou had been in, then Wendy would have been the one in control, with the element of surprise on her side. Waiting around will strip her of control and she can't deal with that. Not again. Maybe she'll come back again tomorrow, after checking she is home. Gary was quick enough to give her Lou's address, he's bound to give her her phone number if she asks for it.

Wendy lays the flowers down on the doorstep and reaches into her bag for a pen and the blank card the florist gave her. She puts the pen in her mouth and pulls off the cap. What should she write? Should she let Lou know she'd popped round? No. It would look odd when she returns for a second time. What then?

She smiles as she plucks the pen from her mouth and scribbles on the card, then she carefully places it between the cellophane wrapper and the flowers and walks away.

Chapter 23

Lou

Mike wanted to pack up our stuff this morning and drive to another city but I convinced him to stay.

'You'll have the same problem communicating wherever we go,' I said. 'And my French is quite good. I've been predicted an A star.'

'I don't know, Lou.'

I could tell he was wrestling with himself. He was nervous about leaving me alone in the hotel room again, but he couldn't find an apartment without my help. He knew I was trying to escape last night. I could hear it in his voice when I came out of the bathroom and he called me a good girl. He meant, 'good girl, you didn't try and leave'.

Finally, after a lot of pacing and several visits to the window to look outside, Mike relented. We would stay in Rouen and try to find an apartment together.

'Voilà! Le chambre,' the letting agent says now, casting an arm wide as we walk into the tiny room.

'This is the bedroom,' I say, glancing at Mike.

'Yes,' he hisses from between his teeth. 'I worked that out when I saw the bed. You should have a GCSE in stating the fucking obvious.'

His mood has been darkening since we left the letting office. He held my hand very tightly as we sat across the desk from Jean-Pierre and I explained, in faltering French, that we were looking for somewhere to live. Out of the corner of my eye, I could see Mike squinting in concentration, his gaze flicking from the older man to me as he read our expressions. For someone who goes on so much about trust he doesn't trust me at all.

'C'est très jolie,' I say to Jean-Pierre, who raises his eyebrows.

'What did you say?' Mike hisses, tightening his grip on my shoulder.

'That it's a pretty bedroom.'

'Don't lie, it's a dump.'

Jean-Pierre responds but he speaks so quickly I have to ask him to repeat himself. I don't understand everything he says but I catch the gist of it. He's asking if we want to see the next place. Maybe his English isn't quite as non-existent as he made out. Or he can read the unimpressed look on Mike's face.

'He wants to know if we want to go on to the next place,' I tell Mike.

He sighs and clicks his neck to the left, then the right. 'I need a piss first.'

I point my finger. 'The bathroom's over—'

'There are four fucking rooms. I don't think I'll get lost.'

I wait for the bathroom door to click shut, then hurry across the room to Jean-Pierre who's standing by the window.

'Aidez-moi,' I say desperately. 'Je suis . . . Je m'appelle Louise Wandsworth. J'habite en Malvern, Angleterre. Je dois returner. Mike Hughes,' I point towards the bathroom. 'Ca . . . cette homme. Il me . . .' I pause. I don't know the word for kidnapped. 'Je suis prisoner. Je dois . . . escape.' I make a pumping motion with my arms. What's the word for run? 'Courir! Je dois courir. Je dois appeller ma maman. Aidez-moi! S'il vous plaît!'

I can't tell from the way the letting agent is staring at me whether he's confused or horrified. I pull on his arm. 'Aidez-moi.' Help me, I say again. 'J'ai peur.' I'm afraid.

Jean-Pierre touches my shoulder and speaks rapidly. I don't catch much but I do hear him say the word 'police' and rapidly nod my head. Yes, take me to the police. Ring the police. But please, please help—

'Who's ringing the police?'

Mike's at the door, his thick arms crossed over his chest. His eyes swivel towards Jean-Pierre's hand, resting on my shoulder.

'Get your fucking hands off my girlfriend.'

'Monsieur.' The letting agent holds up both hands as Mike steps towards us. 'Nous ne discutons que—'

Mike swings at him before he can finish his sentence, smashing his fist against his jaw. Jean-Pierre

171

stumbles backwards but, before he can recover, Mike hits him again.

'No!' I grab Mike's arm but he swats me away with a backhander that knocks me off my feet and onto the bed.

I scream as Mike grabs Jean-Pierre by the hair and smashes his knee into his face, then lifts him up and slams the back of his head into the windowsill. The attack seems to last forever and there is blood everywhere – on the walls, the carpet, the bed. When it finally ends, with a kick to the stomach, Jean-Pierre is unrecognisable. His face is a bloody mess: his nose shattered, his lip cut and his eyes – two swollen red eggs – blackened and shut. Mike shoves him away from him and he falls to the floor, unconscious. Mike looks at me, curled in terror on the bed.

'We're going.'

Thursday 3rd May 2007

It's risky, driving past Mike's house. He's officially a missing person now. I heard the news report on the radio this morning, after I'd visited the barn to check he hadn't escaped and to throw a bottle of water and a couple of ham sandwiches into the cage. The reporter said he was vulnerable as a result of several different health conditions. Vulnerable? I almost laughed as I filled a vase with water and cut the ends off my flowers. My heart leapt when I got back from seeing Chloe yesterday afternoon and saw a bouquet of germini, gypsophila and white roses on the doorstep. I had no idea who they were from. I hadn't been off sick long enough for my boss to send them. And they definitely weren't from Ben, much as I hoped they might be. He still hadn't replied to my text. Alice then? It was just the kind of thoughtful thing she'd do. I plucked out the card.

In Deepest Sympathy.

In Deepest Sympathy? Dad died nearly three months ago and none of his friends had called at the house since I'd moved in. I wasn't even sure if they knew I'd moved in. Dad's solicitor then? But there was no name on the handwritten card. Maybe they'd been delivered by mistake? I took them inside anyway; they'd cheer the house up a bit.

I slow the car as I turn onto Mike's road. Not so much that I look suspicious but enough that I can get a good look at his house. I'm not sure what I expected – a police car outside perhaps and people streaming in and out the front door – but everything looks normal. All the doors and windows are closed and the curtains are pulled back. Somewhere, beyond that front door, is evidence that Mike's been grooming Chloe. Yesterday, before I gave her my diary, I finally worked up the courage to read it. Most of the entries were so raw and painful I couldn't do more than flick through them, but there was one that stood out. It was a conversation I'd had with Mike about secrets. Mum had come close to discovering my diary when she'd cleaned my room. I knew Mike would be angry with me if I

173

admitted to keeping a diary about our relationship so I told him a white lie. I said I had some precious possessions that I didn't want anyone else to find. Where would you hide them, I asked. If you were me? He'd laughed and said, in a shoebox under a pile of clothes in the wardrobe. That's where he kept everything he didn't want his wife to find. Or I could just buy myself a box with a lock on it.

Mike's second phone is hidden in his house. I'm sure of it. Getting in is going to be difficult, but not as difficult as getting the key.

Before I drive back to the farmhouse I pull into a parking space in Ledbury town centre and check my phone. There's an email from Ian at work saying he hopes I feel better soon and a couple of messages on Facebook asking how I've settled in and whether I fancy meeting up the next time I'm in London. I tap out replies – I'm fine, busy with work, cleaning the house is hard work, I'm definitely up for a night out in London once life has calmed down a bit. There are no messages from Ben. For days I've been trying to push him out of my mind but, after what Mike said yesterday about hoping I was happy and being cared for, I couldn't sleep last night for thinking about him. I'm pretty certain Ben had nothing to do with the flowers but it gives me a good excuse to contact him again.

I tap out a message quickly.

Hello! I don't suppose you sent me a bouquet of flowers yesterday? The florist included a 'In Deepest

Sympathy' card which was unsettling. Anyway, I hope you're ok. Take care. X

I press send before I can change my mind, drop the phone back onto the passenger seat then start the engine.

The lake has crept further up the field over the last couple of days, thanks to all the rain, and leaves, twigs and insects are floating on the surface. The van. That's where Mike's house keys are. I remember seeing keys dangling from the ignition and in the glove compartment. I'd be able to grab them in a flash if it weren't for the fact that the van is two feet below water. I could kick myself for not taking everything out before I pushed it in the lake. Especially now, when water is spilling over the top of my wellies and soaking my jeans.

I slip several times, wheeling backwards into the water, then scramble up again, painted with thin brown mud. It's everywhere – on my arms, my chest, my face. I can taste soil in the back of my throat: dark, bitter and gritty. I want to give up, to go back to the house, strip off my clothes and step into the shower, but I continue onwards, arms outstretched, moving gingerly. The water is deeper now and each step sucks at my boots, anchoring them to the muddy field. I bend at the waist and grab each boot top to stop them from being pulled clear off my feet, but it doesn't take more than a couple of steps before the water level is too high and the suction is too strong. I'm going to have to leave the boots behind. I pull my feet out, then launch myself, chest first, into the water. The cold makes me gasp and my hoody billows out around me like a life jacket, rising up under my chin, forcing me to tip my head back and stare up at the cloudy, grey sky. I kick out with my legs and curve my hands through the water. Swimming fully clothed through a muddy lake is exhausting and I tip to the side several times but, somehow, I move through the water.

I feel like I've been swimming for hours when, finally, my right hand connects with something solid. The top of the van. I grip the trim with one hand and reach down with the other. Slowly, slowly I inch my way forward, feeling for the ridge of the driver side door. When I touch it, I stop, then slide my hand down. The solid surface of the van disappears and my fingers curl through the water. It's the open window. I could try swimming through it but if I got stuck in the cab I might never find my way out. I need to open the door. I stretch my hand further down the side of the van, pressing my right ear into the water to extend my reach, but I can't find the handle. I'm going to have to go under the water to open the door.

My first attempt ends in failure. I panic the second my head is under the water and break through the surface, coughing and retching. On my second attempt I get lower. I keep my eyes screwed shut as I feel along the side of the van. My fingers graze the handle but my lungs are burning, so I kick for the surface. On my third attempt, I grab the handle and brace my feet against the side of the van to give me leverage but I've got too much air in my lungs and I keep bobbing upwards.

'Come on.' I slap at the water as I surface. 'Come on!'

I breathe out, emptying my lungs, then push myself back down into the water. My fingers latch onto the handle, my socked feet press against the side of the van and I pull. The door opens and I reel to one side. A second later my head breaks through the surface and I suck in a lungful of air. I reach for the rim of the van but my fingers are so cold I can't extend them. My teeth are chattering, my chest is tight and every breath hurts. If I stay here much longer I'll get hypothermia and I still need to swim back. But I have to get those keys.

I kick out with my legs, pushing myself away from the van, then I dip my head into the water and pull with my arms. I open my eyes, to check I'm heading for the open doorway but all I can see is a brown swirling mist. Then the pain starts, a stinging sensation around my eyeballs that makes me want to claw them out of my face. Closing them makes no difference and I grit my teeth against the pain as I drag myself forwards, into the cab.

My lungs ache as I wave my hands through the water. I can't feel anything. Not the passenger seat, not the seating and definitely not the glovebox. Where is it? I open my eyes again and regret it immediately. It stings so much I lash out with my left hand, then quickly snatch it back as it scrapes against something sharp. The speed of the movement makes me whirl in the water and I reach for the doorway to steady myself. But the doorway's not there. How can I have lost all sense of direction in a matter of seconds? Fear floods through me. I'm not going to get out. I'm going to run out of air.

No. I have to get out. I have to.

I reach one arm above my head and the other to my side. Both of my hands make contact with something solid but my right hand touches something softer than the left. A seat back? I reach my left hand in front of me. Nothing. I move the hand up and down. First the back of my hand, then the palm, hits something hard and smooth. It's the closed passenger side window. In my panic I've moved across the cab. Keeping my chin tucked low I twist round and push myself back across the cab. I grit my teeth, bracing myself for impact but none comes. I slip through the open driver side window back out into the lake. As I pull myself up through the water my lungs start to burn. I'm not sure how much longer I can hold my breath. The urge to inhale is unbearable.

Just when I think I can't stand it a second longer, I break through the water.

And breathe.

Three hours have passed since I dragged myself out of the lake, gasping, shivering and crying. I didn't so much as glance at the barn as I passed it. Instead I headed straight for the house. I peeled off my clothes in the kitchen, wrapped myself in a dusty blanket

178

from the back of the sofa and walked up the stairs to the bathroom on heavy legs. I stayed in the bath for what felt like hours, then crawled into bed in the spare room and shivered beneath a single duvet that smelled of damp and mildew. I started to cry then, not the tears of relief I'd shed as I'd crossed the field, but tears of rage and frustration. It was over. Without the keys and the phone I had no way of proving that Mike had groomed Chloe. For a brief moment, when I locked him in the cage, I felt like I finally had control over my life, but it was all an illusion. I'd have to let him out and pray that the courts would give me a lenient sentence or . . .

I could kill him.

I dismissed the thought almost as soon as it crossed my mind. I might have taken him prisoner but that was accidental. And hosing him down with cold water wasn't torture, no matter what he might think. Murder was something else though. That would be premeditated. I'd spend years in prison. When . . . *if* . . . I got out, I'd be in my late fifties. I wouldn't have children or a family. I'd be completely alone.

And I couldn't do it. I couldn't take someone else's life and live with myself afterwards. I wasn't that sort of person.

But I never thought I'd be the sort of person to imprison someone either. If Mike died I wouldn't have to worry about him grooming Chloe – or anyone else – ever again. But what about his van? Even if I could get rid of Mike's body, how the hell would I get a huge water-logged transit out of the lake? If the police got a warrant to search the farm it wouldn't take them long to find it.

No, it was a ridiculous thought. Even if I could do it and live with myself afterwards it was too risky. Mike didn't deserve to die for what he'd done. Return to jail? Yes. With any luck he'd get a stricter sentence second time around and this time he *would* end up on the sex offenders list.

I push the duvet away from me and swing my legs out of bed. There's one thing left to try.

Mike doesn't look at my face as I walk into the barn. He looks at my empty hands.

'I'm thirsty,' he says as I settle into my normal spot against the barn wall, directly opposite the cage. 'I finished the other bottle last night and I haven't had a drink all day.'

'Good.'

'Lou.' He wipes a hand over his lips. They look pale and dry, even from this distance. 'Come on. I said I was sorry.'

I shrug.

'Come on, Lou.' He forces a smile. 'At least get the hose out again. I'll catch some of it in my mouth.'

'You're not getting any water.'

His smile slips. 'What?'

'I'm not here to give you water. I'm here to tell you that I'm going to break into your house.'

His eyes widen. 'What the fuck?'

'I need that other phone. You may as well tell me where it is or I'll trash your house looking for it.'

He laughs, gripping his stomach as he throws back his head. 'You're fucking kidding me! You're going to break into my house? And then trash it? Seriously! You're fucking unhinged, Louise. Have you heard yourself? And to think I thought my ex was a psycho.'

'Don't laugh at me, Mike.'

'Why? What are you gonna do? Stab me? Sorry, Lou. Been there and got the scar to prove it, thanks to Dee. She said wanted to talk to me about the terms of the divorce and put a steak knife through my leg instead.'

He rubs his hand up and down his left thigh.

'You told me you got that scar from a lorry accident.'

He smirks. 'So I told a fib. I thought it might make you feel sorry for me.'

'You're scum.'

'Whatever. Doesn't change the fact that you're both psychos. I had to take a restraining order out on Dee. She got Community bloody Service for what she did, and I got a permanent limp. Where's the justice in that?'

I don't believe him. He never made out that his wife was violent. Boring, yes. He told me she was more interested in her garden than him and at bedtime she'd rather do a crossword puzzle than have sex. Their marriage had been over for years, he said.

'I wasted ten years of my life on that woman. I should have listened to my mates when they said she was a bunny-boiler. Jesus. Wendy Harrison, what a bloody mistake.'

'Say that again.'

'Say what again?'

'The name of your ex-wife.'

'Wendy Harrison. Hughes after she married me.'

'But you told me she was called . . .'

All the hairs on my arms go up as all the pieces of the jigsaw fit together.

Dee. Wendy. Wen-Dee.

Chapter 24

Chloe

Thursday 3rd May 2007

Jamie's laughter carries across the pool, over a frantic father–son table tennis match and across to the sun loungers. Chloe plucks at her dress. It's too tight across the bust and sweat is pooling between her breasts. Still, at least Jamie's firing his water pistol at their dad now, rather than her. She glances at her mum, lying on the sun lounger beside her. She's wearing oversized sunglasses and a black swimsuit with a sarong swathed around her hips. She hasn't looked up from her book once in the last hour.

Chloe has never really understood her mother – with her constant migraines, lack of interest in Chloe's life and her permanently exhausted expression – but she does now. She's dead inside too. There's no point talking to her about what's been going on in her life. Even if she could find the words, what could her mum do? At best she'd tell Chloe that everyone has crushes and she should find a nice boy her own age to go out with. At worst she'd tell her dad and the police about Mike. What does her mum know about love anyway? She might have loved her dad once but there isn't any evidence of that now. They never kiss or touch each other. They barely speak other than about the kids. Chloe can't even remember the last time they smiled at each other. Their relationship couldn't be more different to her relationship with Mike. Correction. The relationship she *used* to have with Mike. Even her dad had commented on the fact he hadn't dropped round the house for a while.

Chloe shifts on her sun lounger and sits up. She plucks at the thin material of her dress, clinging to her thighs. The second she lets go, it sticks to her skin again. She's so hot and uncomfortable she feels sick. In another world she'd rip off her dress and jump in the pool with her knees tucked up to her chin and feel the sweet relief of the water washing over her. But it's not another world. It's this world, where she's fat and lumpy and she'd rather die than let anyone see her in a swimsuit.

'I'm going to get a Coke,' she says. 'Do you want anything?'

Her mum shakes her head.

'All right. I'll be back in a bit.'

Chloe hangs back when she reaches the poolside bar. Three teenaged girls are propping it up, sipping cold drinks through straws and gazing around the complex.

They look so confident and relaxed, even the short girl with the thick thighs. They're the sort of girls she'd like to be in another life. And the type of girls who'd whisper about her in this one.

She turns to go.

'Hey, you.'

She keeps walking.

'Girl in the blue dress with the bob!'

Chloe stops walking. If she ignores them they'll only say something the next time she runs into them. Better to get it over and done with now.

She turns slowly and points at her chest. 'Me?'

'Yeah, you,' says the short girl with the thick thighs. 'Come over here.'

She sighs. What does it even matter? There's nothing they can say about her that she hasn't thought herself. They won't beat her up, not with so many other people close by. They'll probably just tell her what a fat bitch she is.

'Hi.' She surveys them through dead eyes as she draws closer. The short one in the middle is definitely the ring leader. The girl on the left has thick black hair, eyebrows that look as though they've been drawn on with marker pen and a sickly pink gloss lipstick. The girl on the right is as skinny as they come but with massive boobs.

'I'm Katie,' says the short one. She gestures to her right. 'This is Leticia. And that's Charlie. Are you on holiday here too?'

No, Chloe thinks. *I'm a Spanish waitress. Of course I'm on holiday here.*

'Yeah, with my family,' she says.

'You don't have an older brother, do you? Like, well tall, totally fit. Brown hair, good abs?'

She shakes her head. 'No, my brother's seven.'

Katie bursts out laughing. 'That's a bit young, even for me.'

'How old are you?' Chloe asks.

'Sixteen. So's Charlie. Leticia's fifteen. How old are you?'

'Thirteen.' To her surprise Chloe finds herself warming to the small girl with the big smile and the chunky thighs. There's a light in her eyes and a warmth to her laugh that makes Chloe feel slightly less dead inside. 'Are you all on holiday together?'

'I wish,' says Leticia, flicking her dark hair behind her shoulders. 'Nah, we got talking what . . .' she looks at the others ' . . . a couple of days ago? Now we're besties.'

They all laugh, even Chloe.

'Do you wanna come to karaoke later?' Katie asks. 'Charlie does a mean Beyoncé.'

The blonde nudges her. 'Shut up!'

'Seriously, it'll be fun. And you can help us stalk the worldy I saw yesterday.'

Chloe shrugs. 'I can't sing.'

'Neither can I, but I can drink. See you there then, yeah? We'll grab a table and save you a seat, 'bout eight o'clock?'

'Okay.' A shy half-smile appears on Chloe's face. 'That would be cool.'

She orders a Coke, says goodbye to the girls and

186

walks back to her sun lounger feeling half a stone lighter.

'Have some.' Katie nudges Chloe's arm and gestures at the vodka bottle she's holding under the table.

'Can't. My dad's over there.'

'What is he – Superman?'

'What?'

'Unless he can see through Leticia how's he going to see what you're doing?'

Chloe shrugs. If her dad catches her drinking he'll kill her. He only agreed to let her sit with the girls when her mum made a rare intervention.

'She's thirteen,' she said. 'She doesn't want to sit with us. And she's made some new friends, Alan.'

Her dad had eyed Chloe suspiciously. 'Just because we're on holiday doesn't mean you're not still grounded. You can sit with those girls, but you're not to leave my sight.'

And she hasn't. For the last half an hour she's been sitting in a booth around a table with Katie, Leticia and Charlie in the large characterless room the reps call 'the theatre'. Charlie is already pissed. She's fallen off her seat twice and she squeezes her boobs and honks with laughter every time Leticia says *patatas bravas*.

'Here,' Katie snatches her glass of Coke from her hands and empties at least three or four shots of vodka into it. She gives it back to her. 'Drink it. You're on holiday.'

Chloe raises the glass to her lips. The vodka is rank

– cheap and strong. Just the smell makes her gag, but she parts her lips and swallows a large mouthful. It hits her throat first, then her stomach. A couple of seconds later it hits her brain and she sits back in her chair and smiles.

'Good, isn't it?' Katie says. 'So what are you going to sing? I'm going to do "Chandelier". Best song ever. Are you into Sia?'

For the next fifteen minutes as the four girls laugh and joke and tease each other, Chloe forgets all about school, getting fired from the garden centre and the weird woman who gave her a diary – which she left at home, wrapped in its bag in the bottom of her wardrobe. She even forgets about Mike. Then four boys approach their table.

'You all right, girls?' says the one with brown hair and an England top.

His eyes scan all four of them and rest on Leticia. She flicks her hair back and stares up at him from under two pairs of false eyelashes.

'We'd be better if you bought us a drink.'

The boy laughs. 'And there was me thinking you'd already brought your own.'

He looks pointedly at Katie who smirks.

'Get your own drinks.'

'We have!' He gestures at the pint in his hand. 'Budge up then, girls. Make room for a big one!'

Out of the corner of her eye Chloe sees her dad stand up. He stares straight at her and cricks his index finger. Her heart sinks. She's having one of the best nights of her life and her dad's going to ruin it.

He's going to humiliate her in front of her new friends. She moves to stand up but, as she does, her mum does something out of character. She reaches out a hand and yanks at her husband's wrist. She says something, looks across at Chloe and then pulls on his wrist again. To Chloe's surprise and delight he sits back down.

'He's gone to the loo with Ed,' Katie hisses. 'Go after him.'

'No way!' Chloe's lost track of the number of vodkas Katie has tipped into her glass, but she doesn't care. She's having the best time. The three girls are the loveliest friends she's ever had and, though she can hardly bring herself to believe it, Sam, who's been sitting next to her for most of the night, was chatting to her non-stop until he left to go for a fag.

'I am *not* going in the men's loos,' she says.

Katie rolls her eyes. 'I didn't say you should go in there. Just, you know, hang around outside. Look casual. Then when he comes out you can snog him without your dad seeing.'

'But . . .' doubt gnaws at Chloe's drunken confidence. 'I don't even know if he fancies me.'

'Of course he fancies you! He wouldn't talk to you if he didn't fancy you, would he?'

Chloe glances across the table. Leticia is sitting on Callum – England top's – knee. There's a lot of tongue and slurping going on. Beside her, Charlie is also getting her face sucked off by Ashley.

'Anyway,' Katie says. 'Ed told me that Sam fancies

you. So there.' She inches her way across the bench, her skirt riding further and further up her thighs as she moves. When she reaches the end, she grabs Chloe's hand. 'Go get him!'

It takes all Chloe's concentration to walk across the room without bumping into someone, falling over, or throwing up. Now she's upright she feels three times drunker than she did sitting down but at least her parents have gone. At some point in the evening her mum came over to the table and asked to talk to her. Chloe shuffled off the bench, cheeks burning, certain her mum was going to bollock her for drinking. But that wasn't why she'd come over. It was to tell her that they were going back to the apartment to put Jamie to bed.

'Your dad wanted you to come back too,' her mum said, 'but I told him to give you a break. I,' she jabbed herself in the chest with a stubby fingernail, 'told him that. So don't let me down, Chlo.' She put her hands on Chloe's shoulders and peered down into her face through bloodshot eyes. Chloe wasn't the only one who'd been drinking. '*I* told him to let you have a night out. You won't let me down. Will you? We both know what your dad can be like.'

Chloe hadn't just agreed to behave herself, she'd sworn on Jamie's life that she'd be back by midnight and she wouldn't do anything to upset her dad. But her dad isn't in her thoughts now as she leaves 'the theatre' and sways down the corridor that leads to the toilets. She's made friends. She's drunk. And a boy her own age fancies her. She's normal. For the first time in her life she feels normal and if she weren't so pissed she'd jump up in the air and click the heels of her shoes together like some kind of twat in a romantic comedy movie.

It's the cigarette smoke that makes her pause as she passes an open fire exit, then the low rumble of voices. One of them sounds like Sam. She grins to herself and prepares to throw herself through the door and shout boo! She can be as funny as Leticia and as spontaneous as Katie. She's good fun too. She's—

'Man, you really lucked out tonight.'

She takes a half step back and presses a steadying palm to the wall. That's Ed's voice.

'I know, man. Four birds and I get the fat one.'

Chloe widens her eyes, but her eyelids feel impossibly heavy and her vision is starting to swim. Sam's met a fat girl? What fat girl? He's been sitting next to her all night.

'Sorry, mate. We owe you. You got the short straw this time.'

Sam sighs. 'I wouldn't mind if she wasn't so fucking boring. She has literally no personality. I'd get more banter talking to a lilo.'

'You could still poke your dick in a lilo.'

Ed cackles with laughter. The sound goes right through Chloe, making her shiver, but she's still in denial. She's convinced she's mishearing things. She has to be. Katie told her that Sam fancied her.

'Mate,' Sam says. 'I wouldn't touch Chloe with

191

yours. She's rank. She's like a fucking blancmange. Have you seen the size of her? She looks like she ate the fucking lilo!'

It takes all the energy Chloe has to push herself off the wall but rage drives her forward, through the open fire exit on wobbly legs and into the courtyard. The cool night air hits her full in the face and she sucks it deep into her lungs.

'You,' she says, pointing at Sam, leaning against the wall with a cigarette between his fingers. 'You are a fucking arsehole.'

Then she pukes all over her shoes.

Chapter 25

Wendy

Wendy Harrison can't remember the last time she felt so full of adrenaline. Her wedding day possibly, maybe the time she was arrested for stabbing Mike, but certainly not for a while. But she can feel it now, the buzz of excitement that's making her skin tingle and her heart beat faster.

Ben Feltham has replied to her message and he's online now!

She pulls her chair a little closer to the kitchen table and takes a sip of her gin and tonic. She's not normally a big drinker but the reply from Ben – which made her phone ping five minutes ago – is cause for celebration. Not that his reply – *Why?* – gave much away, but it's enough. He's curious and now she can reel him in.

She looks at the screen:

Saskia Kennedy: *How much do you know about Lou Wandsworth?*

Ben Feltham: *Why?*

Wendy taps the glass against her teeth. The plan was to tell Ben everything she knows – she's fairly certain Lou won't have told him all about her past – and then watch the online fallout. Only, Ben and Lou have been very quiet on social media recently and she's got a sneaking suspicion that the whole thing would be a huge anticlimax. Ben and Lou could have had the most terrible break-up and she'd never know. Leaving the flowers on Lou's doorstep had given her the most wonderful thrill, but she wasn't there to see her reaction. She needs to get closer. But how? She could try and befriend Lou. Maybe take her out to lunch or accidentally bump into her at the weekend. She could play on the other woman's sympathy. Maybe pretend to be desperately ill. You'd have to be a hard-hearted bitch to turn down a dying woman's requests.

That wouldn't work. Lou Wandsworth *is* a hard-hearted bitch. She had to be to steal Wendy's husband away from her when she needed him most. It had made Wendy's blood boil, seeing how the press had painted Lou as an innocent victim. She wasn't 'just a child', she was a fourteen-year-old seductress who knew exactly what she was doing. She'd used her smooth skin and her soft body to lure Mike away. Then, on the day Wendy turned up at the IVF clinic, supposedly to support Mike as he produced a sample, Lou Wandsworth stole him away to France instead. She didn't just steal Wendy's husband that day. She took her hopes and dreams too.

Wendy takes another sip of her gin, then slams it back down on the coaster. For years it was the girl she hated most. The girl who would appear in her dreams laughing and pointing and humiliating her. Later, Mike appeared in the dreams too. Sometimes with the girl, sometimes alone, but always mocking her.

He protested his innocence of course, in person at first, then in letters and prison visits. Wendy needed to believe in that innocence. Anger and bitterness had burrowed into her heart like termites and, whilst Mike's desperate protestations couldn't dig them back out again, they did ice the pain, ever so slightly. The thought that her kind-hearted (if stupid) husband had been deceived by a manipulative teenager who wanted to escape from her parents was much easier to live with than the idea that he'd been actively enjoying an illicit affair with the girl.

Her friends told her she was a fool for refusing to divorce Mike. Several of them stopped speaking to her when she insisted on attending the trial. Those that did abandoned her after his conviction. They'd flinch if she spoke to their children in the street, almost as though she was the one who'd committed the offence. Guilty by association. Only a dark-hearted woman would stand by a man who did something so terrible to a child, they said. They didn't understand. How could they? Wendy was forty-one years old, with a husband ten years her junior, when Louise Wandsworth had robbed her of her only chance of a child after four terrible, heart-breaking years of infertility. She'd stolen her friends, happiness and her peace of mind. If Wendy left Mike, she'd have nothing. She'd have to sell their beautiful house in Ledbury and that was her sanctuary from the world.

For five long years whilst Mike was in jail, she endured sideways looks, barbed comments and cold shoulders. She gave up her job at an accountants and registered as a self-employed bookkeeper because she couldn't stand the raised eyebrows when she was introduced to a new client. She spent all the free time she had either caring for her elderly mother or working in the garden. She avoided driving past the local primary school at drop-off and pick-up time because her heart tore whenever she saw a small child reach for its mother's hand. And spotting a pregnant woman in the supermarket could make her cry for days.

Mike was released from jail three weeks after her mother died. Wendy drove to the jail to collect him. For the next two months, they shared the house in Ledbury, barely speaking, never touching, orbiting each other, then one day Mike came back from the pub and told her he wanted a divorce. He'd keep the house, he said. And buy her out by selling the flat he'd bought before they were married and rented out. He knew full well that she had no savings of her own to buy him out, and that wound her up so much—

The screen flashes. Ben's written the same thing again.

Why?

Wendy stares at the word. Why indeed? It's a question she's been asking herself for a very long time. She's pretty sure the only reason Mike didn't divorce her sooner was because he needed her to pay in his commissary money. During one of her first prison visits he'd told her he loved her and wanted to rebuild their life together when he got out. His eyes shone with tears and his hands shook as they reached for hers. He repeated the same mantra over and over again for years. He even mentioned donor eggs and adoption, feeding her fantasy of becoming a mother. It wasn't too late.

But it was. And for the second time all her dreams were dashed.

In that moment she hated him more than she'd ever hated anyone in her life.

Why?

She needs to ask Louise Wandsworth that question. Why did you do it? Why him? Why didn't you think about me? How can you sleep at night knowing the damage you wreaked? How can you go on with your life when mine was put on pause? How can you be such a callous, conniving bitch?

Because there's something about her that you don't know, Wendy types to Ben.

Nothing happens for a couple of seconds then an ellipsis appears on the screen. Ben is replying.

Like what?

What do you know about her teenage years?

Just that she moved from Malvern to London with her mum. Why?

Wendy smiles. Lou hasn't told him. This is even better than she hoped.

When did you last see her?

A while ago. What's going on? This is all a bit weird and mysterious. Are you a friend of Lou's?

Yeah, I've known her for years, since we worked together at Knowledge Pool. Hasn't she ever mentioned me?

No

Really? I'm going to have words with her about that! Me and Alice are her best friends. Anyway, when did you last speak to her?

Why do you need to know that? What's all this about?

Strange, Wendy thinks. If she was in a long-distance relationship with a man as attractive as Ben she'd be on the phone to him all the time. To check up on him, if nothing else.

Have you noticed that she hasn't been on Facebook much recently?

There's a pause. The ellipsis remains on the screen for a long time then disappears. Wendy takes a sip of her gin. Has she gone too far? Has he logged off because she hasn't got to the point yet? Her heart skips a beat as the ellipsis appears again and Ben replies.

Not really.

Wendy runs her thumb back and forth across her lower lip. The only thing better than telling Lou a few home truths would be doing it in front of an audience, especially if that audience was the man she loved. It would almost make Wendy's years of suffering worthwhile. Ben's presence might also stop Wendy from doing something stupid. Emotions are strange things, the way they can make a logical woman completely lose her cool. And Wendy's not a violent woman. Well, she was thirteen years ago, but her actions were justified. Any sane woman would have done the same thing.

But how can she orchestrate it so that all three of them are in the same place at the same time? Could she convince Ben to come to a meeting at Consol eLearning? It would be even better if the whole office witnessed Lou's demise. But what reason could she give him for such a meeting? She shakes her head. Too complicated. At Lou's home then? She's been ill. Wendy could pretend to be a concerned friend and . . .

Her stomach twists with excitement. She's had an idea. It's risky. Hugely risky. But it might just work.

If I tell you, she types, *you have to promise not to discuss it with anyone. Lou has only shared this news with her very closest friends.*

Ben responds immediately: *Tell me what?*

She's dying. She's only got a few weeks to live.

You're shitting me.

Wendy takes another sip of gin. She's playing a very dangerous game here. One phone call or message from Ben to Lou and the game is up.

I'm sorry to break it to you like this. It must be a terrible shock. It was for me when I found out.

What's wrong with her? She seemed okay the last

time I saw her. Shit, I can't believe this. I need to speak to her.

Wendy's heart quickens and her fingers dance over the keyboard.

No, you mustn't. Lou doesn't want anyone to know how ill she is and she'd kill me if she knew I've told you but, whether she'll admit it to herself or not, she needs to see you. She'll forgive me eventually (I hope).

I can't believe this.

Can you come up this weekend? I could pick you up from the train station?

Oh god. You're serious about this aren't you? I was hoping it was a wind-up.

Wendy pulls a sad face. She's enjoying playing the part of Saskia the concerned friend almost too much.

I wish it was, Ben. I really do.

Her smile fades as Ben takes his time replying. Even if she's managed to convince him not to ask Lou about her 'illness', what's to stop him from driving up to see her?

You mustn't spring a surprise visit on her without me, she types. *The shock would be too great. Meet me at the station and I'll take you to her.*

You'll have to, Ben replies, *I don't know where she lives.*

Wendy raises her eyebrows. It's almost too easy.

So, she types. *This weekend then? Let me know what time your train gets in. Again, I'm so sorry I had to break the news like this. If I had your number I would have called.*

For several seconds Ben doesn't say anything but then, *I need to think about this. I'll get back to you.*

Wendy grimaces. This isn't a good sign. He's seen through her story and he's going to ring Lou to check on her. Any concerned boyfriend would do so immediately. Ah well. She reaches for her gin and drains the glass. It was worth a go. She'll just have to go back to plan A and confront Lou alone.

She jumps as she sets her glass back down on its coaster. Someone is repeatedly banging on her front door. Her annoying next-door neighbour no doubt. She sighs as she gets up from her chair and heads for the door.

'Yes,' she says wearily as she opens it. Her expression changes the second she sees the two uniformed police officers outside her house.

'Mrs Harrison?' says the one on the left.

'Ms, but yes,' Wendy says. She tries to swallow but her throat's so dry nothing happens.

'PC Bray from West Mercia police. This is PC Broome. Could we come in?'

Wendy stares at him wide eyed. 'What's this about?'

'Your ex-husband Michael Hughes,' PC Bray says. 'He's gone missing. Do you have a minute?'

Chapter 26

Ben

Ben Feltham stares at his phone in disbelief. If it weren't for the string of messages on the screen in front of him he'd swear he was dreaming. When Saskia Kennedy's message had appeared in his Facebook messages folder on Wednesday morning he'd ignored it. It wasn't the first time he'd been contacted by an ex's friend after the relationship had ended and he was pretty certain it wouldn't be the last.

How much did he know about Lou Wandsworth? Sod all apparently. She'd seemed so cool when they'd got talking in the pub – properly laid-back and up for a laugh. It was almost inevitable that they'd end up in bed together, the chemistry between them was so strong, but he'd been surprised by the way he felt the next morning. He wasn't a love 'em and leave 'em type of guy but he disliked the weird vibe after a night of frantic shagging and, if the woman

202

seemed to feel it too, he'd make the move home as soon as he could. It hadn't been like that with Lou. He'd woken up feeling as comfortable with Lou as he had the night before. She'd seemed pretty chilled too.

Lou was great, he really liked her but, more than that, she intrigued him. Despite initially seeming like an open person she was actually quite guarded, especially about her childhood There was something she was repressing, that was for sure. He often woke in the night to find Lou's side of the bed empty. Sometimes he'd find her sitting in a chair in another room, staring out of the window. Once he heard her crying in the bathroom. Nightmares, she said, but she wouldn't go into any detail. Then there was the freak-out in Dover. He had no fucking idea what that was about. She'd seemed so agitated when she'd ended things and he had no clue why. He does now though.

He reads through the message exchange again and shakes his head. It wouldn't be out of character for Lou to keep something so serious to herself, but dying? How long had she known? After she'd met him? Before? It might explain the move back to Malvern.

As a child he'd had a cat called Murphy who'd disappeared after he got ill and was found, dead, in a neighbour's shed. Ben was distraught. He felt as though he'd let Murphy down by not being there when he took his final breath. His mother comforted him, telling him that sometimes animals just want to be alone when they die. Not that Lou could be compared to a cat, but it wasn't beyond the realms of possibility that she'd want to get away from the noise and bustle of London and return to her childhood home.

He clicks onto Lou's page and scans it for updates and messages. After what happened in Dover he'd combed it for clues to explain her strange behaviour. Was there someone else? Had she lost interest? He couldn't find anything to explain her odd change of heart. He checked her page the next day too. And the day after that. Nothing. A few weeks later there was an update saying she was moving to Malvern. After that he stopped checking.

There's nothing on her page now – other than a few messages from friends asking how she's doing. Oh no, wait, there's an interesting message from her friend Alice. Lou talked about her a lot but he'd never met her. He hadn't met any of her friends. She'd laughed when he'd joked that she was ashamed of him, but she didn't explain why she kept the two parts of her life so separate. Maybe she just wanted to take things slowly. He was okay with that. He frowns as he reads Alice's message.

I hope you took my advice. It's better to regret the things you do than things you don't (if you know what I mean). Love you xx

If Saskia hadn't contacted him he wouldn't have given Alice's message a second thought, but there's a weight behind the words, knowing what he does about Lou's health. Does a dying person think about regrets? Of course they do. He clicks away from the page and looks at his messages. The most recent one is from Lou:

Hello! I don't suppose you sent me a bouquet of flowers yesterday? The florist included a 'In Deepest Sympathy' card which was unsettling. Anyway, I hope you're ok. Take care. X

Ben runs his hands over his bare forearms. That's seriously creepy. What kind of idiot would send a deepest sympathy to someone who wasn't dead yet? Poor Lou, how horrible. And to think he'd actually laughed when he first read the message. It sounded like she was playing games with him, hinting that some other bloke was interested in her. God, what a dick. If he misinterpreted that message what else has passed him by? He clicks out of Facebook and opens his text messages. He has to scroll down a couple of pages to find the last one Lou sent him. Thank god he didn't delete it.

I'm sorry for what happened in Dover. There are reasons why I reacted the way I did that I can't explain right now. You didn't deserve the way I spoke to you afterwards. I hope you're okay.

Fuck! He slaps a hand against his forehead. It's all there in black and white – Lou hinting that something was wrong – and he'd completely ignored it, too pissed off to reply.

He slumps forward over his desk and presses his hands over his ears. All around him his colleagues are tapping away at their computers and drawing on tablets with styluses. They're focussed in on their work, probably thinking about what they'll have for

205

dinner or how many hours there are until they can escape to the pub. But his world is crashing around him. The girl he was falling in love with is dying and he's been ignoring her, too wrapped up in his own misery to reach out to her. Too proud to try and put things right.

He sits back up and reaches for his phone. He should send a Facebook message to Alice to ask her what she knows. But what if she's one of the friends that Lou hasn't told? Saskia said Lou had only shared her news with a select handful of people. If he contacts the wrong person he could be opening a whole can of horrible worms.

He could contact Lou though? Saskia said not to but an innocuous text wouldn't hurt. Yeah, that's what he'll do. He'll try and get a dialogue going. She might open up about what's going on with her. That's if she's well enough to even use her phone. Jesus. He runs his hands through his hair. For the first time in his life he has no idea what to do.

Chapter 27

Lou

'*I never meant to hurt you. You know that, don't you?*'

I jump as Mike appears at the bathroom door. The pink stripe that bloomed on my cheekbone last night after he shoved me away to get at Jean-Pierre is now a vivid bruise and my eyes are red and puffy from crying. I sobbed all the way from Rouen to Bordeaux last night. Noisily at first, then silently after Mike shouted at me to be quiet. I couldn't stop thinking about that poor man, Jean-Pierre. All he'd done was try and help me and Mike had beaten the shit out of him. I just hope the woman who peered out from behind her apartment door as Mike dragged me down the stairs called an ambulance.

After we left the apartment Mike drove like a maniac to our hotel, hauled me up the stairs to our room, threw all our stuff in a bag and then ordered me out again. The receptionist gawped at us as we barrelled out the door but she didn't shout for us to come back and I was too scared to cry for help.

'Lou,' Mike says. 'You should answer me when I talk to you.'

'Sorry.' I lower my eyes. 'I didn't mean to—'

'Hey . . .' I flinch as he puts an arm around my shoulders. If he notices he doesn't comment. Instead he puts a finger under my chin and lifts it so I've got no choice but to look at him. 'I love you.'

He waits, expectantly for a reply.

I force the words out of my mouth. 'I love you too.'

'Do you?' He searches my eyes. 'Do you really?'

I nod, dumbly. I just want him to stop looking at me, stop touching me, to just . . . stop.

'I'm sorry that you had to see that yesterday. I thought he was going to hurt you and I'd never let anyone harm you, Lou, never.'

'He wasn't trying to hurt me, Mike. We were just talking about—'

'Ssh, ssh, ssh.' He presses a finger to my mouth. 'I don't want to talk about him anymore. I want to talk about how I'm going to go out and buy you some treats. It's been a while since I've seen you happy and I want to put a smile on that beautiful face.'

My heart leaps. He's going out. I've been praying that he would. When we got in last night the first thing I noticed was the window next to the bed. It doesn't open all the way but I think I could get through it. There's a flat roof about six or seven feet

208

below. I could make it. I could drop down and run away.

'You won't get bored this time,' Mike says as he leads me by the hand to the bed. 'You can watch TV.'

He gestures for me to sit down, then turns on the TV on the other side of the room. I fake a smile. Go, I say in my head. Just go.

'Now, the thing is,' Mike says as he crouches down and rummages through his rucksack, 'we're staying in quite a built-up area and it's really important that we're quiet. We wouldn't want anyone to stop us from finding a lovely place together, would we, Lou?'

'I can be quiet,' I say as he pulls a pair of socks and a roll of thick black tape out of his bag.

He smiles tightly. 'Sadly, not as quiet as I'd like.'

'Mike,' I say as he tears a strip of tape off with his teeth. 'Please, please don't do this. Mike, please, if you loved me you wouldn't do this. Please, Mike.'

'I'm doing it because I love you,' he says as he shoves a sock into my mouth, presses the tape over the top and ties my wrists to the bedposts. 'Sometimes I think I love you too much.'

Friday 4th May 2007

I couldn't sleep last night for thinking about what Mike said. Could the Wendy who came to my office actually be Dee? Wendy Harrison isn't an unusual name. There have to be a ton of them in the UK, maybe even in Worcestershire. Just because Mike's

209

ex-wife is called Wendy Harrison that doesn't mean she's the same woman who sat in a meeting with me.

And yet . . .

There was something about her that made me feel uncomfortable. As soon as Gary left the room to make tea she started asking personal questions. Nothing too weird about that per se, no one likes to talk about business all the time, but she leaned a little too far forward in her seat as I spoke, peering at me over the top of her reading glasses. While I ummed and ahhed she splurged her life history at me, telling me how old she was, what her hobbies were and how she lived alone with her little dog. And all the while she was fiddling with the biro in her hands.

Could it be a coincidence, Mike's ex-wife ringing the eLearning company where I work? We're the only one in Malvern, but the University of Worcester would have its pick of the bunch with a project that size. It wouldn't be unusual for them to use a company in London or Brighton. Maybe she found out I was working at Consol and wanted to check me out? But how would she find out? I'm not even listed on their website. If that was *the* Wendy Harrison, then she had to be as clueless about my identity as I was about hers. Otherwise she would have reacted more strongly. She can't be Mike's ex-wife. But I need to make sure.

I flip open my laptop, log onto the café's Wi-Fi and start up the browser, then type into the Google search box.

Wendy Harrison University of Worcester.

A Janet Harrison is listed. And a Dr Wendy

Messenger. Beneath their names is a link to the University of Worcester.

I click on the link and enter *Wendy Harrison* into the search box.

Zero results.

I didn't think it was strange when Wendy contacted me via her personal email address. University VPN networks can be unstable and she wouldn't be the first academic to get in touch via a Hotmail or yahoo account whilst working from home, but this is worrying.

I navigate to the contact page and tap on the number for the main switchboard. A couple of seconds later a recorded voice tells me to tap 1 for the Humanities and Creative Arts department, 2 for Science and Environment, 3 for Health and Society – I press 3.

'Hello,' says a female voice. 'Institute of Heath and Society, Mary speaking.'

'Hello, I'd like to speak to Wendy Harrison please. She works in the nursing department.'

'Please hold.'

Tinkling music plays in my right ear then, 'Hello, can I just check. Was it Wendy Harrison you said?'

'That's right, yes. She's responsible for organising distance and blended learning. I forget her job title.'

'Okay, please hold.'

This time several seconds pass before the music stops abruptly.

'Hello, sorry to keep you but Wendy Harrison doesn't work in the nursing department. There's a

Diana Harrison who works in midwifery if that's who you're after.'

'No, it's definitely Wendy. I don't suppose you could put me through to someone in charge of learning could you?'

'That would be Fiona Hillier. One moment please.'

I reach for my coffee and take a sip. This isn't looking go—

'Fiona Hillier speaking. How can I help you?'

'My name's Lou. I work for Consol eLearning in Malvern. A lady called Wendy Harrison visited us recently to request a quote for a blended learning solution for the nursing department, but I'm having trouble getting in touch with her.'

There's a pause then, 'I'm . . . I'm not sure who it was that you spoke to, but there's no Wendy Harrison on my team. As for blended learning, well, our students are taught via a combination of in-house training and clinical practice. We use the web to deliver some of our assignments, but we don't use eLearning for teaching purposes and have no plans to do so.' She laughs lightly. 'Nursing is very much a hands-on degree, as I'm sure you can imagine.'

'Yes,' I say. 'Yes of course.'

'Maybe you're thinking of a different department? Is there someone I can put you through to?'

'No, you've been very helpful. Thank you.'

I don't know how long I've been sitting here staring into space but my coffee is cold and I've got pins and needles in my thighs. My laptop is still on the table in front of me but the lid is shut. I didn't find anything when I searched for Wendy Harrison, Malvern or Wendy Harrison, Worcester. Nothing when I entered her email address WHarrison5353@hotmail.com either. Or Wendy Hughes. Or Mike and Wendy Hughes. I've searched for Mike a lot over the years but I've only ever found one article, about famous child abduction cases in the UK, and it didn't include any photos. The internet was still in its infancy when we ran away together. Google didn't even exist.

There aren't any photos of any of us online. Not me, not Mike and not Wendy. But I know it's her, the overly friendly, nervy woman who sat at a table with me. It has to be; the University of Worcester has never heard of her. Her phone number is in the initial enquiry email she sent. I could call her and ask her all the questions that have been going round and round my head since I found out her lie. Why come to my office and pretend to be someone you're not? Why didn't you confront me when you had the chance? Why didn't you tell me who you are?

But I'm too scared to make the call. For so many years she wasn't a real person to me. She was the caricature Mike painted – a dour-faced woman who existed rather than lived. Now I've shaken her hand, inhaled her sickly-sweet perfume and looked her in the eye. I can't pretend she doesn't exist anymore. Any conversation we have is going to be painful and I'm not sure I can deal with that right now.

I sit back in my chair and rub my hands over my face. She must hate me. I'm the reason her husband was sent to jail. I feel guilty, but I shouldn't. I'm as much of a victim as she is. Mike groomed me. He made me fall in love with him, he orchestrated those feelings. Wendy must realise that. Mike said she was his ex-wife, which means she divorced him at some point. Maybe it was curiosity that drove her to my office? Maybe she wanted to say something, to find closure, and then bottled it at the last minute? God knows I can relate to that feeling.

Scared or not, I have to ring her. She's the only one who can help me put Mike away. They were married for a long time. Even if she doesn't have a spare set of keys to his house she might know where he keeps them, or how best to break in.

My phone bleeps as I get up to go. It's a text from Ben.

Sorry I haven't been in touch. Life has been a bit hectic since I got back to London. Are you okay?

I text him back.

I've been better. Can't talk right now. X

I delete the kiss at the end and press send.

Chapter 28

Chloe

Footsteps outside the apartment force Chloe up from the sofa and out to the balcony. For the last three hours she's had the place to herself and now her family is back from their trip to the beach. Her dad's booming voice and Jamie's high-pitched whine explode into the apartment as her mum opens the door. Chloe presses a hand to the side of her head. She's had two paracetamol and countless glasses of water and she still feels as though a small creature is sharpening its claws on her brain. She'd fully expected to see her dad pacing the room when she crept in just after midnight but everyone was asleep. After puking all over her shoes in front of Sam and Ed she'd run off, tripping and weaving her way through the theatre as the sound of the boys' laughter followed her. She puked again when she got outside and then again, into a bush, as she stumbled towards her apartment block. Once inside she'd thrown herself onto the small uncomfortable sofa in the living area and burst into tears. She pressed a musty-smelling cushion to her mouth to stifle the sound but the tears continued to fall for a long time. How could she have been so stupid, believing she stood a chance with Sam? It was the vodka. It had stripped away her inhibitions and self-doubt and made her believe that maybe she wasn't a fat loser after all, that she was as desirable as Katie, Charlie and Leticia. What a stupid bitch. Of course Sam wouldn't want her. Even a forty-nine-year-old man with deep crow's feet and a bit of a gut had lost interest. Everything her dad said about her was true. She was useless, worthless and a waste of space. And that was never going to change.

'Chloe?' her mum says now, making her jump. 'How are you feeling?'

Chloe, holding on to the balcony railing to steady herself, looks over her shoulder. 'Horrible.'

'Oh dear.' Her mum's sunburned forehead creases with concern above her big, black shades. 'Do you think a bit of lunch would help? We thought we'd try that burger place further down the strip.'

'No thanks, Mum. I'd rather just stay here.' She turns away and stares down into the pool below. The girls she met last night are screeching and squawking as the boys dive-bomb and splash them. *They haven't even noticed that I'm missing*, she thinks. *None of them care.*

'If you're sure?' There's a pause, then, 'Chloe, is everything okay?'

She doesn't turn round. She doesn't want her mum to see the tears welling in her eyes. 'I'm fine, Mum.'

'Okay then. Well, if you're sure.' The doubt in her mother's voice tears at her heart.

Just go, she thinks. *Just leave me alone.*

'Jamie, no. Don't take your shoes off. We're going out again.' Her mother's voice fades as she chases her brother into the bedroom.

'Julie!' Her dad shouts from another room. 'Did you pack my Police sunglasses? I can't find them anywhere. These ones from the airport are shit.'

Chloe glances behind her. The living area is empty. Down by the pool Sam strides along the side, chest out and shoulders back. Katie's in the water, sitting on Ed's shoulders. Her hands are interlinked with Charlie's who's on Callum's shoulders. They're trying to wrestle each other into the pool. Several feet away from them a mum is chasing her toddler son round a sun lounger, waving a bottle of suntan lotion at him. Next to them an older woman is trying to read a book as her husband leans over and waves a hand in her face, trying to get her attention. The pain in Chloe's chest eases as she continues to watch the holiday scene below her balcony play out. She feels as though she's watching a documentary on the TV. Life doesn't feel real anymore. *She* doesn't feel real anymore. It's as though a pane of glass has descended, separating her from the world.

She feels dead inside again. She'd been hoping the feeling would come back. But it won't last for long. Sooner or later she'll start to feel again.

She steps closer to the balcony, pressing her thighs against the metal bars. She spreads her hands wide and bends at the waist. Directly beneath her, seven floors down, is a wide patch of concrete. Normally the steep drop would make her feel dizzy, overwhelmed and scared but today she feels . . . nothing.

She moves almost in slow motion, tightening her grip on the balcony and raising her right knee. A mobile phone rings in her parents' bedroom but Chloe ignores it. She can't get her knee over the railings. She's too short, even if she stands on tiptoes. But there's a small table beside her. She drags it closer to the railings and jumps her bottom onto it. It wobbles, but doesn't fall over, as she shifts her weight into the centre. She grips the sides of the table with both hands and twists over onto her knees then shuffles up to the railings. Now she's on the table there's only six inches of metal separating her from a vertiginous drop. All she has to do is tip forwards.

She takes a deep breath, fixes her eyes on the stripe of blue sea on the horizon and loosens her grip on the balcony. As she does, the table wobbles violently beneath her and she snatches at the railings, her heart beating wildly in her chest. She pauses for a moment; her forehead, slick with sweat, resting against the hot metal then she pushes herself back onto her knees. She just has to be brave. In a couple of seconds it will all be over. She has to be—

'Jesus Christ! Julie! Julie!' her father's booming voice – almost directly behind her – makes her jump so violently the table tips to one side and she lands with a thump on the cold concrete floor of the balcony, the table clattering on top of her.

'Julie!' her dad shouts again. 'That was the police. Mike Hughes has gone missing! He hasn't been to work since Monday and no one knows where he is.'

'He's always disappearing off without telling anyone where he is,' her mum shouts back.

'This is different! They've put out an appeal on the radio and everything. He's properly vanished.'

Chloe raises her head from the ground. Her lips part and her eyes grow wide and round. She pushes the table away and sits up. Mike's missing? That changes everything.

Chapter 29

Wendy

Wendy parks up her car, gets out and strides across the business park to Unit 9. Normally her energy levels would be flagging after such a short and broken night's sleep, but she's been fizzing with intrigue and excitement ever since she woke up. Monty must have thought it was his lucky day, leaving the house a little after 6.30 a.m. and taking *three* turns around Priory Park rather than his normal one, but Wendy couldn't keep still. Sitting would make time drag. She had to keep moving. With every step she was another second closer to finding out what had happened to Mike.

Her initial reaction, when PC Bray turned up on her doorstep the night before and told her that her ex-husband had disappeared, was to go on the defensive.

'Well it's nothing to do with me.'

The police officer had smiled tightly and asked to come in. Wendy's wariness of the police had been superseded by her curiosity, so she'd opened the door wider and invited the pair into her living room. They hadn't stayed long, maybe half an hour tops. They didn't give her much information; just that Mike hadn't been to work since Monday, he wasn't at home and he wasn't answering his phone. They asked her a lot of questions. When had she last seen him or spoken to him? Did she know the names of any friends or acquaintances he might have gone to visit? Where were his favourite places? Did she know of any routines he had? Did she know how he was feeling? Had he ever suffered from depression?

Wendy answered 'no' or 'don't know' to most of the questions. She'd actually laughed after the first question – the one asking her when she'd last seen him.

'Approximately thirteen years ago.'

PC Bray raised an eyebrow. 'Are you *quite* sure about that?'

'Perfectly. PC Bray, you know as well as I do that there's a restraining order in place that prohibits me from going anywhere near my ex-husband or his property. I haven't breached that order, not once.'

'And phone contact?'

'About thirteen years ago.'

'So you've had no contact with your ex-husband recently – not in any form, email, social media etc?'

'Not for thirteen years, no.'

'And if we checked your phone and computer . . .'

'You'd discover that I am telling the truth. Look, I have no idea where Michael is or why he's disappeared. My ex-husband and I had an acrimonious

221

split – I'm sure you know that – but we've both moved on.'

She said the last part of the sentence through gritted teeth. Physically she'd moved on – to a smaller house several miles away – and she didn't spend as much time thinking about him and obsessing over the details of their marriage as she used to, but emotionally a kernel of anger was still buried deep within her heart.

When the officers left they told her they'd be in touch. She'd nodded and said, 'please do.' She wasn't Mike's next of kin anymore. The only reason they'd be in touch was if they suspected she was behind his disappearance. Which she wasn't, obviously, but it wouldn't be the first time she'd been treated unfairly by the police.

She stayed up for hours after they left, re-running the conversation in her head. It was all so fascinating. Why would Mike disappear, now of all times? She would have understood if he'd done a runner straight after he was released from jail, or even after their divorce. But now?

She hadn't actually been completely honest with the police. Whilst she hadn't spoken to Mike in the last thirteen years, she had instructed her solicitor to contact Mike's when he defaulted on his maintenance payment eleven years earlier. Her solicitor had informed her that Mike was in the process of setting up his own company and he'd had a temporary cash flow issue which had caused the delay. The next month Wendy received twice the normal payment in her bank account and didn't bring it up again. She did turn detective however, which is how she discovered that Mike owned a removal company.

Now, she pushes open the door to Unit 9 and walks up to the counter.

'Morning,' says a woman of a similar age, her dark hair, streaked with grey, pulled up into a scraggy bun. There's a name badge – Joy – attached to her navy polo shirt. 'How can I help?'

Wendy touches her own hair even though not a strand is out of place. 'I'm concerned about Michael Hughes.'

Joy blanches. 'The police said I wasn't to talk to journalists.'

'I'm not a journalist. My name is Wendy Harrison. I'm Mike's ex-wife.'

'Oooh.' The other woman's eyes widen and she takes a step back from the counter.

Inside Wendy rolls her eyes. Outwardly she forces a smile. 'I see you've heard of me.'

'You can't . . . you shouldn't be here,' Joy stutters, her gaze fixed on Wendy's hands.

Oh get over yourself, Wendy thinks. *If I was going to stab you I'd hide in the car park until dark and wait for you to turn your back, not turn up in the office in broad daylight. Anyway, one little puncture wound does not an axe-wielding maniac make. And besides, Mike provoked me.* She considers telling the wide-eyed woman all this but settles for asking, 'Is Mike here?'

'No.'

'Well then.' She shrugs. 'I'm not doing anything illegal. I just wanted to talk to you about him. See if maybe, between the two of us, we can work out where he might be.'

Joy's hunched shoulders relax, just the tiniest bit, but she remains tucked up against the wall. 'None of us know. I've talked to the other drivers and I've rung Greensleeves and everyone's clueless. Last thing I heard from him was a phone call saying he was doing an extra job. For someone called Milly, he said. He didn't give me the address.'

Milly? Wendy runs the name through her mind but comes up blank.

'Did you tell the police that?'

'Of course I did. They said I'd been very helpful.'

'What else did you tell them?'

'I don't know what you mean.'

'Well, they asked me if he'd been depressed and if he . . .' she raises an eyebrow at the other woman, 'was in a relationship.'

Joy shakes her head. 'I don't know anything about Mike's private life. And I wouldn't ask.'

Of course you wouldn't, Wendy thinks. You don't have a nosy bone in your body, do you? You do your job, keep your head down and go home at the end of the day like a good little girl. She sighs. Honestly, the number of people who go through life wearing blinkers so they don't have to see or experience anything unpleasant. Pathetic, utterly pathetic.

Still, talking to the lifeless 'Joy' hasn't been a complete waste of time. She's got the name 'Milly' out of her. A potential suspect perhaps? Maybe a love interest. Interesting that the police didn't tell Wendy anything about her, unless they think it's her pseudonym. Inwardly she laughs. If she were going to knock Mike off, she'd wouldn't leave a clue like that behind. She'd be much cleverer.

'Okay then,' she flashes her teeth at Joy. 'Thanks for your help. If Mike does reappear, which I'm sure he will, could you ask him to let me know he's okay? Thank you.'

She doesn't wait for the other woman to respond. Instead she turns on her heel and strides out of the unit. As she does, her handbag starts to ring. Wendy sighs, unzips it and pulls out her mobile phone. If it's Ted, having a go at her for getting something wrong again she swears she'll—

She stands stock-still and stares at her phone. An unknown number is flashing on the screen. Could it be Lou? A jolt of fear passes through her. Has Ben figured out that she's Saskia and told Lou all about her elaborate ruse to meet up with him? With all the excitement about Mike's disappearance, she's barely given Ben a second thought. No. Lou can't be ringing? There's no way Ben can know who she is, even if he has contacted Lou to ask how she is. It has to be a work call.

She taps at the green button and presses the phone to her ear. 'Wendy Harrison speaking.'

'Hello Wendy, this is Lou, from Consol eLearning. Are you free to speak?'

Wendy jolts then glances back at the glass door of

Unit 9. Joy has disappeared from behind the desk. 'I am yes.'

'Great. The thing is, Wendy . . . um . . . I was wondering if we could meet? Are you free today at all?'

Wendy sighs. The last thing she wants is to be dragged back into Lou's office for another hard sell from Gary. Tempting though it might be to get another look at Lou, she'd much rather go home and have a nap for a couple of hours. And besides, there's still a chance Ben will take her up on her offer to go and visit Lou together.

'I'm not sure,' Wendy says. 'What is it you want to discuss?'

'It's um . . . it's a personal matter. I thought perhaps we could meet in Priory Park if it's not raining. We could talk as we walk. Or . . . or maybe get a coffee if you prefer.'

Wendy's eyes widen. Lou wants to talk to her about a personal matter? Now this is a *fascinating* development.

'Yes,' she says quickly. 'I'd love to meet, although I'm not sure about a walk. How would you like to come to my house? I cooked the most delicious carrot cake yesterday and it needs eating.'

'Um . . .' She can hear the indecision in the other woman's voice. 'I'd um . . . I'd rather we met in a café if that's okay with you.'

Wendy raises her eyebrows. Lou doesn't want to come to her house. That's interesting. Very interesting indeed.

'I'm afraid I can't,' she says. 'I twisted my ankle yesterday and I'm pretty much housebound for the next couple of days. You'll have to come to me. Or we could arrange to meet another time, when I'm better . . .'

She holds her breath as she waits for Lou to respond.

'Okay,' Lou says. 'I'll come to you. What's your address?'

Chapter 30

Lou

I cry out when Mum and Dad appear on the TV, but my muffled scream doesn't leave my lips. I'm still tied to the bedposts, my mouth stuffed with a sock and sealed with tape. The second Mike left the room, I tried to get free. I wriggled my wrists and twisted and squirmed on the bed, but the tape held firm. I tried to shout, but the sock shifted in my mouth and slipped back towards my windpipe making me jolt forward, terrified I'd suffocate.

'This is a message for Michael Hughes,' my dad says, as my last school photo appears in the top right corner of the screen and French subtitles run along the bottom. Dad is stony-faced and his voice is unusually clear and strong, but his clasped hands bounce lightly on the table as he speaks. He's probably desperate for a drink. 'Mike, I don't know why you took her, but please, please, bring Louise back unharmed. She is our only child and we love and miss her dearly.'

A sob catches in my throat, then I burst into tears. I'm not the only one crying. Mum has tears running down her cheeks. She nods at everything Dad says, then when he says the words 'only child', she gasps and presses her hands to her face. Mum! *I shout her name in my head.* Mum, I'm here. I'm here, Mum. I'm here.

A policeman appears next. He says that they know Mike took me to France and they have reason to believe that he may have attacked a man in Rouen.

'If you see Michael Hughes or Louise Wandsworth, please contact a member of your local police force. Under no circumstances should you approach them. Alternatively, please ring . . .'

By the time the appeal is over I can't see the TV for tears. They know. Everyone knows that he's got me and they're trying to find us. I'm relieved and scared in equal measure. If Mike sees the news, or spots a paper with our faces on, he'll move us on again. He'll take me somewhere where there aren't many people. He'll keep me locked up and he'll—

I try to take a breath but I've been crying so much my nose is bunged up with tears and snot and when I inhale only the tiniest amount of air makes it into my lungs. I exhale forcefully but no air comes out.

I breathe in.

Nothing. Not even the tiniest stream of air.

Panic rises in my chest as I thrash from side to side, dragging my face along the pillow. I've got to get the tape off my mouth. If I don't I'll die. My lungs are already starting to burn. Oh god, please, please. I don't want to die. Please god don't let me—

'Lou! What the fuck?' Mike appears standing in the doorway, weighed down with bags, flowers and a teddy the size of a two-year-old. He drops them, speeds across the room and jumps onto the bed. He rips the tape from my mouth, then forces his fingers between my teeth. As he pulls out the sock, I gasp, sucking air deep into my lungs.

'Lou,' he cradles my head in his arms. 'Oh my god, Lou.'

He hurries back across the room and slams the door shut, then ducks back down and starts rummaging through his backpack. When he pulls out a Stanley knife I scream.

'Stop it, stop it.' He presses a hand over my mouth. 'I'm going to set you free. Don't scream. I'm sorry. I'm so sorry.'

He continues to apologise as he cuts through the thick tape on my wrists, then he holds my hands in his and presses his lips to my red, chapped skin.

'Can I go?' I say. 'Can I go home now?'

Mike gives me a puzzled look. 'Whatever gave you that idea?'

The air is cold and crisp as I cross the yard and head towards the barn. I need to check on Mike before I go and meet Wendy. The terror I felt in the first couple of days – that he'd managed to escape or was waiting to jump out at me from beyond the barn door – has faded but I still feel jittery as my wellies splash through the puddles and drizzle mists my face.

The barn door creaks as I open it. Mike is lying

on his back on the floor of his cage with one blanket over him and another balled up beneath his head. He opens his eyes as I walk in.

'I need water.' His voice is dry and rasping, his hair is lank and there are dark circles under his eyes.

'Here!' I throw him a small bottle of water, only a quarter full.

He groans as he rolls onto his side and slowly sits up. 'Why are you doing this to me?'

I cover my nose and mouth with my sleeve. Even with the straw soaking up the fluids in the bucket, the smell in the barn is unbearably fetid.

'Has Chloe told you that I hurt her? Because I haven't. I swear.'

He's never going to understand. Everything he's said since I locked him in the cage has been an attempt to convince me to let him out. Yesterday he even admitted he'd invented the near-death lorry story so I'd feel sorry for him. Should I tell him that I've arranged to meet Wendy? It might elicit a reaction. No, best to keep it to myself for now.

'The bucket's full,' Mike says, hanging on to a bar and pulling himself up to his feet. 'Could you empty it?'

He retreats to the back of the cage and unstacks the bricks surrounding and covering the bucket. He nestles his face in the crook of his elbow as he reaches down and picks it up. He turns and walks towards me, the bucket swinging from his right hand.

'Mike, how do you expect me to—'

I break off as he drops his arm from his face and

his lips curl into a smile. I turn to run but I'm too slow. Before I can reach the safety of the yard, warm piss, shit and straw rain down on me, soaking my hair, my shirt and my jeans.

'I hope you die alone and in pain,' Mike screams as I slam the barn door shut. 'And if I ever get out, you will.'

Despite washing my hair twice, scrubbing my body with the scratchiest loofah I could find in Dad's bathroom cabinet and covering myself in perfume, the faint odour of urine still clings to me as I get into the car and start the engine. I can't tell if I'm imagining it or it's somehow made its way up my nostrils, but I open the window anyway. Any nerves I may have had about going to Wendy's house – along with any guilt about keeping Mike locked up – vanished the minute he threw his shit bucket at me. Nothing is more important than making him pay for what he's done to me and Chloe. Nothing.

As the car winds its way through the narrow country roads, I replay the conversation I had with Wendy earlier. There was something odd about her reaction when I asked if she'd like to go for a coffee. She sounded breathy and enthusiastic, as though it was the most exciting thing to happen to her all year. If there was any doubt in my mind about who she was, it's gone now. She has to know who I am. But why so excited? I'd be nervous if it was the other way round.

I turn off the A4103 onto the B4219 and glance

at the map on the passenger seat beside me. Wendy lives on Clarence Road which is only five or ten minutes away. I didn't want to meet her at her house but she gave me little choice with her sore ankle story.

My phone bleeps as I pull onto Worcester Road. Please don't let it be Wendy cancelling. I snatch up my phone and glance at the screen. It's a text from Ben.

Where are you? I'm at your house.

What?! I yank the steering wheel to the left to avoid clipping the kerb. The driver behind me sounds his horn.

Thirty seconds later and I'm parked up on the side of the road with the phone's screen inches from my face. I didn't misread Ben's text. It definitely says *Where are you? I'm at your house*. He can't mean the farm. I didn't give him my address. I haven't given it to anyone.

'Hello!' he answers the call a split second after the dialling tone sounds in my ear.

'Where are you?'

'Outside your house. At least I hope it's your house. I got pretty lost trying to find it. Big old farmhouse up a track?'

'Yes, how . . .' I can barely speak I'm so shocked.

'I looked your dad up on the electoral roll. He was the only Steve Wandsworth in Hereford and Worcester. Anyway, how are you? And where are you? You sound a bit breathless.'

'I'm coming back,' I say. 'Stay in your car. Don't move. I'll be there in fifteen minutes.'

* * *

233

I drive like a maniac to Acton Green, my stomach in knots. I shouldn't have told Ben to wait for me in his car. If he gets out and wanders round he'll find Mike in the barn. I should have suggested we meet at The Dog and Duck instead but I panicked. Oh, fuck. Fuck. Fuck. What the hell's he doing at my house? It would have to be something serious to look up my dad to find my address. But what? We're not together anymore. What would he possibly need to say to me that's so urgent? Fuck. Fuck. Fuck.

'Ben!' I jump out of my car and hurry across the gravel to where he's standing beside his open car door. He's not wearing a coat and he's got his arms crossed over his chest. His trainers look too clean for him to have traipsed through the garden but there's a weird look on his face that I can't read.

Please, I silently pray as I stop still about a foot away from him. *Please don't ask me why I've got a man locked in the barn.*

'Ben,' I say. 'What are you doing here? Shouldn't you be working?'

'I took the day off.' He smiles nervously. 'You look well. Really well!'

Why's he being so weird and awkward? I feel sick with nerves. I haven't got the faintest clue what's going on.

'Seriously Ben, what are you doing here?'

His eyes flick from the top of my head to my muddy boots. 'I was . . .' he tails off and shakes his head.

'You were what?'

'Worried about you.'

'Why? I'm fine.'

He runs a hand through his hair. 'In the last text you sent you said you'd been better.'

'And?' I glance towards the garden. The trees and plants are bent towards the house. If Mike shouts for someone to help him, his voice could carry on the wind. I need to get Ben out of here. Or at least into the house. 'Life's been a bit hectic.'

'Hectic?' Ben frowns. 'I know that I'm not supposed to talk to you about this but I just . . . I can't believe how well you look . . . considering.'

What the hell is he on about? And where's all this stuttering and twitching come from? What is it he's not telling me?

I reach into my pocket for my keys. I need to get him into the house. 'Considering what?'

'How ill you are.'

'What?'

'Oh god, Lou. I'm sorry. I'm a bit lost for words if I'm honest. I've never had to deal with this type of situation before. I mean, I lost my gran and grandad in my late teens, but they died quite suddenly. I didn't get the chance to say goodbye.'

I stare at him in disbelief. 'Someone told you I was ill?'

'Yeah.' He glances away, then back at me. 'She made me swear not to tell you.'

'Who said I was ill?'

'Saskia.'

'Who?'

'Your friend, Saskia.' He shifts his weight from one leg to the other, then sighs, bends at the waist and groans loudly. 'Oh fuck. This is a wind-up, isn't it? Jesus, I can't believe I fell for it. Of all the fucking psycho—' He straightens up. 'You told your friend to tell me that you were dying, didn't you? To get me to come up here because I didn't reply to your messages. Jesus, I've met some manipulative women in my time but this takes the absolute biscuit. I genuinely can't believe—'

'Ben!' I snap. 'I have no idea what you're talking about. Number one, I'm not dying. Number two, I didn't ask anyone to try and convince you to come up here. If you remember rightly I was the one who ended things. And who the hell is Saskia?'

Ben stares at me as though he can't quite make up his mind whether to laugh, scream or hit something, then he sighs and says, 'Have you got any beer?'

'Here you go.' I plonk a glass of cheap red wine on the side table next to Ben and take a seat beside him on the sofa. He reaches for the wine, takes a big swig, grimaces and then sets it back down. I do the same.

'Here, look at these.' He hands me his phone. 'I wasn't sure what the 3G was like out in the sticks so I took some screenshots of Saskia's messages before I left London.'

'Why?'

'I thought . . .' he shrugs ' . . . that you might have

nurses or carers and I'd have to convince them to let me in.'

'Jesus Christ.' I stare at him in disbelief. What kind of sicko would convince another person that someone they knew was dying?

'Just read the messages. They'll explain everything.'

We sit in silence for a couple of minutes as I read the message thread. I don't recognise Saskia, or her name, but according to Ben she's a mutual friend. 'She wanted to come here with you. Why didn't you agree?' I ask.

'I don't know her, do I? And anyway, I wanted to drive. When I got your text last night and you said you'd been better and you couldn't talk I freaked out a bit. I thought . . .'

That I was on the verge of death.

'This is nothing to do with me,' I say. 'You believe that, don't you?'

'Yeah.' He reaches for his wine and takes another sip. 'As soon as you threw that line in my face about you ending things.'

'I'm sorry.'

He gives me a sideways look. 'For what you said or what you did?'

'Both.'

A wave of sadness crashes over me. In another lifetime, one where I wasn't such a big fuck-up and I hadn't dumped the nicest man I'd ever met, we'd be curled up under a blanket right now, watching a film and laughing and teasing each other.

'Lou,' Ben says, 'do you think—'

He's interrupted by several sharp knocks on the front door.

I stand up. 'It's probably the postman.'

I hurry out of the room, my mind whirring with everything Ben has just said – and everything he hasn't – and yank on the front door handle.

'Hello—'

'Good afternoon,' says a police officer with closely cropped hair. 'My name is PC Bray from West Mercia police and this is PC Broome. Could we have a quick word?'

Chapter 31

Lou

'A word?' I repeat. My heart is beating so quickly I feel sick.

'Lou!' Ben calls from the living room. 'Can I help myself to some more wine?'

I ignore him. I can't stop staring at the two policemen standing in front of me.

'We're sorry to disturb you,' PC Bray says, 'we were just wondering if you'd seen this man recently?'

He opens the clipboard in his hands and flashes a photo of Mike at me. It looks like it was taken in a pub, with Mike propping up the bar, drink in hand.

'You know him,' PC Bray says. It's a statement rather than a question.

Do they know? Did they send out a helicopter when I was in Worcester yesterday? Did the heat sensor pick up that Mike was in the barn? Or did they trace the last phone call he received? Are all these pleasantries just preamble before they arrest me? There's a police car in the driveway, parked up next to my red Mini, dad's Volvo and Ben's grey Audi. Shit.

Shit. Shit. Shit.

'Yes,' I say. 'I do.'

'How well?' PC Broome asks.

'I . . . we . . .' There's no point lying. They know who I am and what my connection is to Mike. 'He groomed me when I was fourteen. He convinced me to run away to France with him. He was arrested and sent to jail.'

PC Bray's eyebrows flash upwards. Shit. He didn't know. They're just doing house-to-house enquiries and they had no idea who lived here. 'And your name is?'

'Louise Wandsworth.'

'When was the last time you saw Mike Hughes?'

'I haven't seen him for years. Not since we were in France.'

'I couldn't find the wine.' Ben appears behind me and puts a hand on my shoulder. 'Oh.'

PC Bray smiles tightly. 'And your name is . . .'

'Ben Feltham. Why? What's this about?'

'We're looking for this man.' He flashes Mike's image at him. 'Have you seen him?'

'Nope. Why, what's he done?'

'He's missing.' The police officer flips Mike's photo over and shows us another image. 'Have either of you seen this van? We have reports that it was seen in the area on Monday, 30th of April.'

'I just got here today,' Ben says. 'I drove up from London.'

'And you and Miss Wandsworth are . . .' PC Bray tails off.

'Friends,' I say at the same time Ben says, 'It's complicated.'

PC Broome laughs, then turns it into a cough as he continues to scrawl in his notebook.

'Have you seen the van?' PC Bray asks me. He has an unremarkable face: small, green, slightly too close together eyes framed by thick, bushy eyebrows, doughy cheeks, pitted with acne scars, and rubbery lips. I can't shake the feeling that he knows what I'm thinking. He's picturing the van, submerged in the lake. He's imagining how it feels to have your eyes, ears and nostrils flooded with dirty, murky water.

'No,' I say. 'Not that I remember. I've probably seen dozens of white vans over the last couple of weeks but none that stick in my mind.'

'Where do you work, Miss Wandsworth?' PC Broome asks, looking up from his notepad.

'In Malvern. Consol eLearning.'

'I'm a graphic designer,' Ben says.

PC Broome nods but he's still looking at me. 'So you've had no contact with Michael Hughes recently? No phone calls, texts, internet contact. Nothing of that sort?'

'You know that man?' Ben asks, gesturing at PC Bray's clipboard.

'No,' I say, ignoring Ben. 'I haven't had any contact with Mike whatsoever.'

'Right. And how long have you lived here, Miss Wandsworth?'

Just when I think they've finished asking me questions they fire another one at me. My legs feel weak but I'm determined not to rest a hand on the door frame to steady myself.

'A couple of weeks. My dad died and left me the house. I came back to sort it out and sell it. But I'm skint so I took a job in town.'

'Right, right.' He nods then takes a step back and looks over the house, then the driveway. 'No . . . um . . . no estate agent's sign yet though?'

'My dad was an alcoholic and a hoarder. I haven't finished tidying.'

'Anyone else live here?' PC Broome asks.

'No, just me. Ben's visiting,' I add as both police officers glance in his direction.

'Right, well,' PC Bray nods at PC Broome who shuts his notepad. 'I think we're done for now.' He digs into the inside pocket of his jacket and hands me a small, white card. 'If Michael Hughes does get in touch or if you think of anything, anything at all that might be useful, give me a call. Okay?'

He smiles for the first time since I opened the door and gestures at his colleague to return to the car. A couple of minutes later it pulls out of the driveway and disappears.

'Wow,' Ben breathes. 'That was intense. I felt like I was under arrest!'

'Yes,' I say. 'So did I.'

Ben and I are sitting on opposite sides of the sofa. I've got a rug pulled over my legs and a cushion clutched to my chest. He's topping up our wine glasses.

He glances across at me, 'You okay?'

I almost laugh. Okay? I don't know whether to run, hide or cry. I made a huge mistake telling the police my real name and how I know Mike. I should have lied; pretended to be one of my cousins, or a cleaner. They're bound to start digging now, especially as Mike disappeared nine days after I came back. As soon as DS Hope sees a photo of me it'll be over. She'll tell the missing persons team that I made an allegation about Mike and Chloe and that I gave her a false name. They'll put two and two together and turn up on my doorstep with a search warrant. But . . .

I take the glass of wine Ben hands me and force a smile.

. . . That's assuming the police think Mike has been abducted or murdered. They might just be worried about him. Often when men go missing it's because of a mental health issue.

I press my wine glass against my lips and take a sip.

I've still got Mike's work phone. It's hidden at the back of the medicine cabinet upstairs, along with the detached SIM. I could drive out to Gloucester or Birmingham and send a text to Joy from his phone. *Life's not worth living anymore.* Or *I can't live with what I've done.* It might not be enough to throw the police completely off but it could buy me a bit more time. Time to do what though?

A new thought hits me. I didn't meet Wendy. I'll

have to ring her and see if I can go round tomorrow and—

I put down my wine glass, slump back against the sofa and press my hands to my face. I can't do this anymore. Anything I do now will just dig me in deeper. The police just knocked on my door for god's sake. It's only a matter of time until they triangulate his phone then put two and two together and come back. I can't let Mike out because he's too dangerous. I either run or I confess. They're the only options I've got left.

Or I could tell Ben. He might know what to do. But I've screwed up his life enough already without adding accessory to kidnapping to his rap sheet. No. I need to deal with this myself. I'll go to the police station tomorrow and tell them what happened. I've tried my best to help Chloe but there's nothing more I can do.

'Lou?' Ben touches my arm. 'What's the matter? Why are you crying?'

I shake my head.

'Lou?' He gently peels one of my hands away from my face. 'What is it? Talk to me. Please.'

For well over an hour Ben listens as I tell him about Mike. I tell him everything apart from the fact that, as we speak, Mike is lying in a shit-stained cage in my barn.

Ben doesn't comment and he doesn't judge me as the words pour out of me. It's the first time I've told anyone about what happened. When I reach the bit about going to France, Ben smiles ruefully.

'That's why you freaked out in Dover.'

'I'm sorry,' I say. 'I wanted to tell you but . . .'

He reaches for my hand and squeezes it. 'It's okay, we've all got secrets.'

'Have you?'

'Not really.'

I laugh softly.

'Is there anything I can do?' He glances around the room as though he's expecting a solution to magically appear in the patterned wallpaper.

'You could drop me at the police station tomorrow. But I'll totally understand if you want to get back to London.'

'Of course I'll come to the police station with you.' He squeezes my hand again. 'I'll stay for as long as you want. Okay? I want to make sure you're all right. God knows who's been spreading shit about you dying but that sounds like stalker territory to me. You're right to tell the police.'

For a second I've got no idea what he's talking about but then I realise – he thinks I want to go to the police about the weird Facebook messages he received. I don't set him right.

'Lou.' He searches my eyes. 'You can tell me anything. You know that, don't you?'

Nearly anything, I think but don't say.

Chapter 32

Lou

It's late evening. We've been in the hotel room ever since Mike got back from his shopping trip and the only food we've eaten is the small box of chocolates he dropped on the floor when he realised I was suffocating to death.

He's never going to let me go. My only hope is to play along and wait for an opportunity to escape. So far today we've played cards, read to each other (from Mike's really boring book about the Second World War) and played memory games and charades. My stomach rumbles as I pick up the remote and change channel.

'Mike? I'm hungry . . . can we get something to eat?'

'Sure, I'll go out and . . .' He pauses. He's worried that if he ties me up and gags me again I might not be alive when he gets back. But going out is dangerous too. I'm not the only one who's seen the

news, Mike turned it off as soon as Dad started to speak.

'They don't know where we are,' I say. 'No one knows where we went when we left Rouen.

'Look,' I slip off the bed and pick up his baseball hat. 'I could wear this. It would hide my fringe. And you . . . you already look different. You've practically got a beard now.'

Mike drums his fingers against his lips. He's considering jumping in the car and driving somewhere remote. The fewer people there are, the less likely I am to be found. I need to talk him round. Going out now might be my only chance of escaping.

'Mike.' I perch beside him on the bed and rest my head on his shoulder. 'It would be lovely to go to a restaurant. It's dark, no one's going to see us and when we get inside I could face the wall and you . . . you could be on lookout.'

He stares at our reflections in the window opposite the bed. 'I don't know, Lou. It feels risky.'

'Please.' I weave my fingers through his. 'We had such a lovely day the other day when we went out to celebrate our engagement. Being in hotel rooms all the time isn't good for us. And anyway, I might fancy doing that thing again afterwards . . . where you squeeze my neck.'

He twists sharply towards me. 'We could do that now, if you like.'

'No, no. Not now. I'd . . . I'd like some wine first. It would help me relax. Please, Mike, let's go out.' Almost on cue my stomach rumbles again.

Mike turns away and rests his elbows on his knees. He drops his face into his hands and sighs heavily.

'Okay,' he says. 'But you're to hold my hand all the way there, keep your eyes lowered and do as you're told.'

Saturday 5th May 2007

I slip out of bed just after seven, leaving Ben curled around the duvet, snoring softly, and pad into the bathroom. I open the medicine cabinet, snake my hand through the out-of-date medicine bottles, plasters and ointments and reach for Mike's phone and SIM card. I tuck them into the pocket of my dressing gown, then quietly make my way down the stairs. Before Ben drives me to the police station I need to get them back into Mike's bag, in the corner of the barn. I also need to take him a bottle of water and some food. My self-defence plea won't hold if it looks like I tried to starve him to death. I feel calmer now I've made the decision to confess. Whatever the police throw at me, however long my prison sentence is, it can't be worse than waking up each morning feeling sick about what I've done.

I bundle two bottles of water, a couple of apples, some crisps and a few cereal bars into a plastic bag and head towards the side door. I don't open it. Instead I drop the bag onto the kitchen table and walk into the living room. I need to write Ben a note.

I'll give it to him before I say goodbye to him at the police station. I owe him that much.

We didn't sleep together last night – it was a decision I made more for him than myself – but we did share the same bed. He curled himself up around me as we whispered into the darkness. It was mundane, drunken stuff mostly and I cried silent tears as he nuzzled his face into the nape of my neck and planted a kiss on the top of my spine. I hated myself for my selfishness in letting him stay. I'd only told him half my story. He didn't know who I was or what I'd done. But I couldn't spend another night alone in the house, not knowing what was to come. I wanted to pretend my life was normal, just for a few hours.

I lean over a bookshelf and press a biro to an unfilled betting slip I found between the pages of a book. The note won't explain everything, but at least he won't feel hurt when he doesn't hear from me again.

Dear Ben.

I lift the pen from the paper. What do I write? How can I possibly explain what's happened?

Please don't hate me. I wanted to tell you everything but . . .

A creaking floorboard makes me look up. Is Ben awake? I hold my breath as I listen but there are no new noises. The house has fallen silent again.

I couldn't find the words. You'll probably hear about what I did on the news and I want you to know that I never planned on keeping Mike prisoner. I was scared and . . .

Another creak. Ben's walking down the stairs. I snatch up the piece of paper and crumple it into my dressing gown pocket. As I do, Ben walks into the living room.

'There you are!' He runs a hand through his crumpled hair and glances at the carriage clock on the fireplace. 'God, it's early. Are you coming back to bed?'

I shake my head. 'No, I'm wide awake.'

'Oh well.' He reaches his arms above his head and stretches. 'I suppose I'd better get up too. Have you got any eggs and bacon? I'll do a fry-up if you fancy it?'

'I haven't got any but there's some cereal if you're hungry.'

'Are you okay?' He steps towards me. 'You look really pale.'

I force a smile. 'I didn't sleep very well last night.'

He pulls me into a hug and runs a hand across my shoulder blades. 'I'm not surprised. I've been thinking about her too.'

'Her?'

'That Saskia woman. Can you think of anyone who's holding a grudge?'

'Not really.' I shake my head. I haven't given the Facebook messages a single thought since I woke up.

'Ah well.' He kisses me on the top of the head. 'Don't worry about it. The police will sort it out.'

I smile tightly. Yeah, right after they arrest me for kidnapping.

* * *

250

Ben hasn't let me out of his sight for the last two hours. The bag of food and water for Mike is still on the kitchen table, taunting me each time I walk past it. I tried to get rid of Ben for a while by asking him if he wanted to pop to Bromyard to get eggs and bacon but that backfired when he said we should go together. I thought about telling him to watch TV while I did a bit of work in the garden but I can't risk it. If I'm gone too long and he comes after me he might discover the barn. Mike hasn't had any food for a while but I gave him a quarter of a bottle of water yesterday. He'll survive until the police get here.

'Ready?' Ben wraps an arm around my shoulders and pulls me into his side. 'I know you're nervous but the police will be able to put your mind at ease.'

'Yeah,' I say as I open the side door. 'I'm sure you're right.'

The police station car park is full so Ben has to park several streets away, on a busy road. He didn't put up an argument when I suggested we come in his car. In fact he said, 'Of course. I'm more than happy to drive.' At least this way he won't be stranded when I don't come back out.

He unclips his seat belt and puts a hand to the door handle. 'You ready?'

'Actually, Ben, I'm going to go in alone if that's okay.'

'What?' His face falls.

'Please,' I beg. 'I really need you to stay here.'

'But I've got the photos on my phone. I was the one she contacted. They'll need to speak to us both.'

He looks so confused, it's killing me. All I've done since we met is put him through shit and now I'm doing it again. I should have started an argument with him last night and sent him away but I wanted to spend one last night with him. I wanted to feel cared for. I wanted to feel normal.

'Ben, I'm not going to talk to them about the Facebook messages.'

'What?'

'It's something else. Something I need to confess to.'

'I don't understand.'

'I know.' I reach out a hand to touch his arm but it falls away before I make contact. 'And I'm sorry. I made a mistake and I did something terrible. I can't explain it now but I will, one day. I promise.'

I move to open the passenger door. My eyes are swimming with tears and my throat is so tight I can hardly breathe.

'No, Lou. Don't—' Ben's hand brushes the thin material of my coat as I push at the passenger door. I just want to get away from him and get this over and done with.

He shouts my name again as I swing my legs out of the car and stand up. There's terror in his voice, not desperation, as I slam the door shut and step into the road.

I don't see the car – a flash of red in my peripheral vision – until it's too late. Brakes squeal, there's a loud thud and then my legs are whipped away from me and I'm launched into the air.

Chapter 33

Chloe

Saturday 5th May 2007

Chloe stands at her bedroom door and listens. The door is open a fraction of an inch and her parents' voices carry up the stairs from the living room. They're arguing. She's not sure what about but she can hear her dad calling her mum a useless pile of shit and her mum's crying and telling him to go away and leave her alone. They talked about Mike for ages on the flight home. Chloe had her earphones on but the sound was turned down on her iPod so she could eavesdrop. Mike had gone missing. Joy, his receptionist, tried to ring him when he didn't turn up for work and there was no reply. By the second day, when he still hadn't shown, she rang round asking if anyone had seen him. By the third day she was worried enough to call the police. Her dad and mum speculated about what might have happened. Her mum thought Mike had met someone and gone on an impromptu dirty weekend (whatever that was). Her dad said there was no way Mike would have left Joy in the lurch without telling her where he was going. He thought maybe he'd had a heart attack at the wheel and was lying in a ditch somewhere. Chloe gasped so loudly both of her parents peered across the aisle to see what was wrong with her.

'Audiobook,' she said, touching her headphones. 'Something scary happened.'

The moment they looked away again she got up and headed for the toilets. The door had barely closed behind her before she burst into tears. Mike hadn't abandoned her. He still loved her. She hadn't done anything wrong. But with the relief came fear. What if her dad was right? What if Mike *was* lying in a ditch somewhere, unconscious or badly injured? Or worse, dead? Her heart ached at the thought of a life without him. What had happened with Sam had taught her how precious her relationship was with Mike. Their love was unique. He was unique. How could she ever have doubted him when he said he'd never loved anyone the way he loved her?

'Please,' she said, staring out of the small round window at the clouds outside the airplane. 'Please let him be alive.'

'I'm going out!' her dad shouts now. 'You can rot in hell.'

Startled, Chloe pulls her bedroom door closed but not before she hears the front door slam. She presses her face against the cold gloss paint and closes her eyes. Mike has to be alive. Otherwise she may as well open her bedroom window and jump straight out.

She opens her door, steps out onto the landing and listens. She can hear the bleep-bleep-bleep of a computer game from Jamie's room and the soft sound of her mother crying downstairs. She glances at the front door. If her dad doesn't storm back in in thirty seconds, then she's safe. She starts counting . . .

It doesn't take Chloe long to find her confiscated phone. It's shoved in her dad's sock drawer – the same place he hides everything he takes away from his kids. Jamie's Nintendo 3DS is in there too (swiped on the plane journey when he refused to turn it off for take-off). She snatches her phone up, creeps back out onto the landing and darts into her room. Her heart thuds in her chest as she stands at her bedroom door, listening out in case her dad comes back, then plugs her phone into her charger and turns it on. The Samsung logo swirls on the screen. A second later her apps appear. She holds her breath as she stares at the top left-hand corner of the screen, waiting for the phone to connect to the network and the notifications to appear.

Nothing happens.

She clicks on the text messages app. The last message from Mike was over a week ago. Her sent messages folder reveals the texts she sent him when she was desperately waiting for him to join her in the park but, if he ever received them, he didn't reply. There are no missed calls either, just the one he answered when, in desperation, she rang his work phone. She checks the time. That was at 6.36 p.m. The first text she sent him was at 6.52 p.m. How could he go missing in sixteen minutes? Oh god. Was he in the van when he took her call? Her dad had joked about him ending up in a ditch but she's seen the terrifying video of a woman who crashed her car when she was texting instead of keeping her eyes on the road. If her phone call resulted in Mike's death, she'd never forgive herself. Never.

Chloe opens her bedroom door and peers down the stairs. She needs to tell her mum what she's discovered. It might be a vital clue. But . . . she steps back into her room again . . . how would she explain what has happened? What possible reason could she give her mum to explain why she was arranging to meet Mike or why she had his number in the first place? Even if she could come up with a plausible explanation – something to do with the garden centre maybe – her mum would tell her they needed to contact the police and there was no way *they* would buy her story. She can still remember the way DS Hope's eyes bored into her when she'd asked about 'inappropriate touching'.

No, she can't go to the police yet. For one thing Mike might not actually be in a ditch. And two, there's no way he'd forgive her if she accidentally exposed their relationship. She needs to find him. If she sends him a text, he might tell her where he is. Even if he is injured he might still be able to use his phone. Her thumbs fly over the screen as she taps out two messages – one to Mike's private phone and another to his work phone. She waits with bated breath, her heart thudding in her chest, but nothing happens.

'Chlo!' Her mum shouts from downstairs, making her jump. 'I'm going out for a bit. Look after Jamie.'

Her mum never goes out, not without her dad.

'Where are you going?' she shouts as she yanks the phone from the charger, springs back across the landing and hastily shoves the phone back into her dad's sock drawer.

'Out. Look after your brother,' her mum shouts back.

A couple of seconds later she hears the front door slam.

'Chlo?' Jamie pokes his head round his bedroom door, clutching a Minecraft manual. 'What are you doing in Mum and Dad's room? Has Mum gone out?'

'Yeah. Dad too, which means I'm in charge.' She glances at the book in her little brother's hands as she steps back onto the landing. With everything that's been going on she'd completely forgotten about the one thing she does have that might hold a clue to Mike's disappearance.

'I'm hungry,' Jamie whines. 'I want a sandwich.'

'Get it yourself, I'm busy.'

'But—'

'I'm busy,' she repeats, then steps into her bedroom and shuts the door.

Chloe sits cross-legged on her bed with her duvet wrapped around her shoulders. Resting in the hollow of her legs is the white plastic bag the weird skinny woman shoved at her when she was waiting outside school. Chloe plunges a hand into the bag and pulls out the book inside. It's pale pink and decorated with multicoloured butterflies. The corners are grubby, the pages are rippled with damp and it smells musty, but she opens the cover. Someone's written on the unlined inner page

This book is STRICTLY PRIVATE. And it belongs to . . . actually I'm not telling you who it belongs to, but if you're reading it I WILL KNOW. SO DON'T.

Chloe smirks and turns the page. The first entry is dated 2 January 1989.

Dear Diary, it begins, *today I saw M again. I tried to act cool when he smiled at me as I walked into the dojo but my heart was beating so fast I felt sick. I've never felt like this about anyone before. I thought I was in love with X but that was just kids' stuff. Infatuation. This is the real deal. M isn't like the boys in my class, he's different. He's an adult. And he treats me like I'm one. He listens. He understands me. And I understand him. There's a connection between us, even when we're not speaking. I know what you're thinking, Diary, that this is a stupid crush but it's not. IT'S REALLY NOT. I have never been so serious about anyone in my life. Anyway, like I said, I tried to act cool when M smiled, and I didn't smile back. Instead I did a few stretching exercises. But I could feel him watching me. We didn't speak the whole hour, other than him shouting commands at us, but when he touched my leg and corrected my stance I felt like my whole body was on fire. I couldn't even look at him. I was so pissed off when Dad turned up on time to pick me up. I really wanted to talk to M. I probably wouldn't have though. I'd have ignored him. Because that's the kind of dickhead I am. Ha, ha. God, it's a WHOLE WEEK until I see him again. How am I going to cope?*

Chloe fingers the corner of the page. There's a part of her that wants to stop reading, that senses that she should, but her curiosity is stronger than her self-preservation and she turns the page.

Chapter 34

Lou

Other than ordering some food and beer Mike hasn't said a word since we sat down. He's barely made eye contact either. It's like he's some kind of policeman doing a surveillance job, the way he's scanning the room. A couple of minutes ago he almost jumped out of his seat when a waiter dropped some cutlery. Not that I saw anything. We're sitting at a table in the darkest corner of the restaurant and, as I promised, I'm facing the wall. The good thing about Mike not talking is that I've heard everything: the bell tinkling above the door as someone comes in, low voices chatting in French, the shouts and clashes from the kitchen and an Englishwoman – two tables away – bitching loudly to her husband about how rare her steak is. I only caught the quickest glimpse of them as Mike ushered me to our table but what I saw made my heart leap. The man was wearing long shorts with socks and sandals and the woman was wearing a sequinned top and jeans tucked into really ugly high-heeled boots. As soon as I saw what they were wearing, I knew they had to be British. Too scared to scream, I flashed a desperate look at the woman as we passed them, but she was too busy buttering her roll to even glance my way. She might if she hears us talking though. If our disappearance is on the French news it's got to be all over the newspapers back home.

'Mike!' I say in a deliberately loud, cheery voice. 'Could I have another Diet Coke please?'

'Sssh,' he hisses at me from between clenched teeth.

I lower my voice. 'What?'

'Coming here was a bad idea.' He pushes his chair back from the table. 'We need to go.'

'But . . . but . . . we've just ordered, and I'm hungry.'

'We'll find a supermarket.'

'They'll be shut.'

Mike reaches across the table and grabs me by the wrist. 'Then we'll go to bed hungry. We're going.'

'Okay, okay.' I twist my hand out of his. 'But I need the loo first.'

'Wait until we get back to the hotel.'

'I can't. I'm desperate.'

'Fine.' Mike stands up and reaches for my hand. 'I'll come with you.'

My heart sinks as we weave our way through the tables and take the stairs down to the toilets. He's not going to let me out of his sight. Not even to take a wee.

'Here,' he pushes at the door with a silhouette of

261

a woman. As he does, an elderly, but very chic, Frenchwoman comes up.

'Les Femmes,' she says, tapping the silhouette and looking pointedly at Mike. 'Les toilettes des hommes sont là-bas.'

When he tries to object, she shoos him away, speaking quick-fire French that neither of us understand and he's got no choice but to let me enter alone. Once inside I search desperately for some kind of escape route, but I'm in the basement, there are no windows. There are two sinks, a hand dryer and a bin and two cubicles, and that's it. I go into one of the cubicles, lock the door behind me and rummage around in my pockets. I haven't got a pen but I've got a lipstick. As I uncap the lid, I hear the main door creak open and freeze.

'Lou?' Mike says. 'Are you in there?'

'I won't be long.'

I scrawl desperately on the wall:

My name is Louise Wandsworth. I have been abducted. We are staying at La Madeleine. Please get help.

'Lou?' Mike says again. 'What are you doing?'

'Just pulling up my pants. One second.'

I shove the lipstick back in my pocket, then flush the toilet. Mike stands by the open door as I wash and dry my hands. But he's not watching me. He's looking at the cubicle I just stepped out of. Shit. Shit.

'Mike,' I say as he steps into the ladies' toilets. 'You can't come in—'

'Excusez-moi monsieur!' the Englishwoman says, raising her eyebrows as she appears behind him.

Mike turns to the side to allow her in and gestures at me to leave, NOW.

I try to twist back, to see which cubicle the woman's going into, but Mike grabs my hand and yanks me out of the toilet before I can see.

Our waiter stops us as we weave our way through the restaurant. Our food is on the table, he says in English. Are we leaving? Mike remonstrates with him in a low voice, saying the service was too slow and he's not going to pay for something we didn't eat. As the waiter calls for the maître d', I spot the Englishwoman coming back up the stairs. Mike sees me looking, wraps an arm around my shoulders and pulls me into his body, blocking my view. As he reaches into his back pocket for his wallet I hear the click-clack of the woman's heels on the tiled floor. She's getting closer. She must have gone into the same cubicle as me and seen my message. She's going to—

'Did they bring my steak back yet?'

Her husband mutters something I don't catch, a chair scrapes on the tiles and Mike thrusts a handful of euros at the waiter.

'We're getting out of here,' he hisses in my ear.

'Please,' I beg Ben. 'Find the doctor and tell her I want to go home.'

He shakes his head. 'Absolutely no way. You're staying overnight. You heard what the doctor said about your blood pressure.'

263

'There's nothing wrong with my blood pressure.'

'Really? So why did the machine start bleeping like a metal detector? And . . . er . . .' he gestures at the drip in my arm and the saline bag on a metal stand beside the bed, 'why's this here?'

'I'm fine now. I just felt a bit dizzy. I'm sure if they check it again it'll be back to normal.'

'Lou,' he covers my fingers with his, 'just rest. You were run over less than nine hours ago for God's sake.'

Apparently I was out cold for over ten minutes. Ben said the old man who clipped me with his car was distraught, wringing his hands and mumbling that he'd killed me as I lay in the road with my eyes closed and my left arm twisted away from my body at an unnatural angle. I came round before the ambulance arrived and screamed in pain. My whole left arm felt icy cold and like it was burning, all at the same time. I was sick, several times, as Ben gently stroked my hair and told me I was going to be okay. I begged for pain relief as the paramedics shifted me onto a stretcher and lifted me into the ambulance and only stopped when they injected me with something. Once in the hospital I was examined, X-rayed and ferried to the fracture unit. Once my arm was set in plaster I assumed they'd let me go, but no, they were worried about concussion because I was unconscious for so long and insisted I stay the night. Now I'm on a ward along with several snoring old ladies, a woman who talks FAR TOO LOUDLY, a teenager who's watching YouTube videos on her phone without headphones, and a woman who groans intermittently.

'I need to get out.' I try to sit up but black spots appear before my eyes as I raise my head and I slump back against the pillow. It's nearly seven o'clock at night and Mike hasn't had any water except a few mouthfuls on Friday morning. If the doctors aren't going to let me out until tomorrow he'll have gone forty-eight hours without anything to drink. I'm going to have to tell Ben. Someone has to go back to the barn.

'Ben,' I twist my fingers in his so I'm holding his hands. 'Ben, I need to—'

I'm interrupted by the sound of a mobile phone ringing.

'Shit.' He blanches and reaches into his back pocket. 'That's me. Sorry.' He takes one look at the screen and says, 'I'm going to have to take this. Mum?' he says as he hurries out of the ward. 'Mum, what's happened?'

When Ben walks back in fifteen minutes later he's a different man. The light has gone out of his eyes and his skin looks tight and drawn. I touch the chair beside the bed, urging him to sit down but he shakes his head.

'I can't . . . I can't stay. I'm sorry.'

'What's happened?' I've never seen him look this serious before.

He swallows and looks at a spot on the wall just above my head. He looks like he's barely holding it together.

265

'Ben, what is it?'

'You know . . .' his gaze drifts down to meet mine. 'You know I'm always joking that my dad's a hypochondriac? How he'll become convinced a mosquito bite is skin cancer and a cold is bubonic plague?'

I smile nervously. 'Yeah.'

'Well, last week he texted me to say that he'd been having a bit of chest pain. I thought he was just being Dad and texted back that he should take an antacid. That it was probably indigestion or something.'

I tense. I know what's coming next.

'Well, about an hour ago he had a heart attack. He's in intensive care. Mum doesn't know if he's going to pull through.'

'Oh Ben.' I reach for his hand but he's too far away for me to touch him and he doesn't move to close the gap between us. 'I'm so sorry. That's really scary. Are you going to go and see him?'

'Yeah. He's in the Royal Infirmary in Manchester. If I leave now I can get there in about three and a half hours.'

'Go. He needs you. Your mum needs you.'

'But . . .' He rubs his hands over his anguished face. 'But we didn't . . . we haven't been to the police station yet and I'm worried that . . .'

'I'll be fine. Honestly. Whoever it was that sent those messages they didn't threaten me, did they? It was someone having a sick joke. Honestly, Ben. I'll be fine. Please, don't worry about me. You need to go.'

He perches on the edge of my bed and pulls my

hand onto his lap as his eyes search mine. 'Are you sure? How will you get back? We brought my car.'

'I've got friends. I'll ask one of them to give me a lift.' I pause. Unless I ask Alice to drive all the way up from London I'm going to have to get a taxi to get back to Dad's. 'Honestly, Ben,' I add. 'It's not me you should be worrying about. My arm will heal, that drip will sort out my blood pressure and I'll be out of here before I know it.'

'If you're sure?' He's so desperate for me to reassure him it hurts. There's absolutely *no way* I can ask him to check on Mike now and I wouldn't anyway. For all Ben's jokes about his dad's hypochondria I can tell that he means the world to him, to their whole family, and they'd be broken if they lost him. This is my fuck-up and I need to sort it out alone.

'I'm absolutely sure,' I say. 'Now, stop wasting time with me and get going. But drive carefully. One of us needs to stay fit and well.'

Some of the tightness and strain in Ben's face eases and his lips curl into the smallest of smiles. 'I knew there was a reason I came up to see you.'

There is a softness in his eyes that wasn't there before; an intensity to his gaze that makes my stomach clench and my chest tighten. He looks like a man who's falling in love. At any other time, in any other situation, I'd reach up and kiss him, but not now.

'You only came up to see me,' I say, 'because you thought I was half dead.'

The effect of my words is immediate. Ben laughs and the intimacy of the last couple of seconds vanishes.

'Totally not true. Although I was kind of hoping you'd left me your Mini Cooper in your will.'

'It's being buried with me.'

He laughs softly, leans towards me and kisses me softly on the lips. 'I'm going to go. With any luck I'll be back tomorrow. Maybe the day after.'

I shake my head. 'No. Stay with your family. We can text.'

'Not if you're back in the arse end of nowhere we can't.'

'Call then. I'll text you my landline number. Seriously, Ben, no more surprise visits.'

He recoils, as though physically stung by my words and there it is again, the hurt and confusion in his eyes. But what else can I say? I won't be at Dad's tomorrow. I'll be in a police cell. If Mike's still alive when I get back to the barn, I'll be on a kidnap charge. And if he's dead . . . No, I can't think about that.

'Please give my love to your family,' I say. 'And look after yourself.'

'Yeah.' He nods curtly and stands up. 'Look after yourself too.'

I watch him go, his body stooped forward as though he's carrying the weight of the world on his shoulders, as he crosses the ward and disappears into the corridor. Only when I'm sure he's gone do I let myself cry.

Chapter 35

Wendy

If there's one thing Wendy hates more than husband-stealing bitches it's husband-stealing bitches who don't turn up when they say they will. It's Saturday evening and she still hasn't heard from Lou. She waited in for hours on Friday, even denying Monty his afternoon walk because Louise bloody Wandsworth didn't deign to visit her house. When Lou was ten minutes late, Wendy had to steal herself not to ring her because she didn't want to appear too desperate. When she was thirty minutes late, Wendy pressed one of her favourite Laura Ashley sofa cushions to her mouth and screamed as loudly as she could. She snapped and rang when Lou was a whole hour late. That wasn't desperate. That was the behaviour of a sane, rational person whose time was being wasted. Only Lou didn't reply, did she? By eight o'clock Wendy had had enough. She stormed into the kitchen, flung open her crockery cupboard and threw her least favourite mug at the floor. Poor Monty was *terrified*. He hightailed it out of the kitchen, exiting the dog flap at a speed Wendy had never witnessed before, and he wouldn't come back in until she'd swept up all the broken shards of porcelain *and* produced a whole handful of his favourite treats.

Wendy stares at her phone and sighs. It's 5.35 p.m. and she has already checked Facebook five times. On Friday evening she was this close to going round to Lou's house before she realised Lou hadn't actually ever given her her address and it would look unhinged. But why ignore her after Lou was the one who requested a chat? It's as though she's disappeared off the face of the earth. Wendy reaches down and rubs Monty behind his ears. Now that's an interesting thought. Lou and Mike, both pulling missing persons acts within days of each other. It's like history repeating itself. It's a ridiculous thought, that the two of them would reconnect almost eighteen years to the day after their little sojourn to France. Lou has Ben for one. Although Ben still hasn't replied to Wendy's invitation to visit Lou with her. He'd seemed so shocked and concerned when she'd broken the news about his girlfriend's prognosis but maybe she'd read that wrong.

She taps on the Facebook app and re-reads their conversation. Yes, there it is, the bit where he wrote *I was hoping it was a wind-up*. He'd ended the conversation saying *I need to think about this. I'll get back to you*. Maybe he was convinced it was a wind-up. Or maybe he and Lou weren't as close as she'd assumed. It would explain why their statuses didn't say they were in a relationship with each other and why they didn't seem to interact much online.

Wendy breathes out heavily through her nose as the truth hits her. She's been focussing in on the wrong man. Of course Lou's disappearance is connected to Mike's. She didn't return because she'd got a job in Malvern, she returned for him. Maybe they'd talked online and reignited a spark. They met up, experienced a resurgence of feelings and decided to go away together. It would certainly explain why Mike had disappeared without telling anyone where he was going. He'd spent nearly two decades trying to rebuild his reputation. There was no way he'd advertise the fact that he was back together with the girl who'd destroyed it.

But why did Lou ring Wendy? That's what she can't explain. Why arrange to meet her and then not show up? There was a part of her that had hoped that the girl was planning to apologise. It was certainly about time. A joke then? A twisted wind-up suggested by Mike? Payback for what she'd done to him?

Fire burns in the pit of Wendy's stomach as she gets up from her armchair, crosses the small living room and unhooks her coat from the peg in the hallway. Unhinged or not, they mocked her once but she won't let them do it again.

It's dusk and pouring with rain as Wendy pulls into the sprawling, gravelled driveway that surrounds the

271

large farmhouse. All the lights are off in the house but the Volvo and Lou's red Mini are parked outside the garage. Wendy parks her car, throws open her door, pulls her hood over her head and stomps towards the house and hammers on the door with closed fists. She doesn't wait for a response. Instead she stalks around the house, staring in at the windows and smacking on the glass with the flat of her palms as the wind whips her jacket around her. Are they upstairs – Mike and Louise, snuggled together under the duvet, laughing at her? Has he shown her the tiny wound in his thigh and told her what a psycho his ex-wife is?

Psycho. She clenches her teeth as she rounds the house. It's a ridiculous word, thrown at anyone who retaliates rather than plays the victim. How dare he throw her loyalty back in her face and ask for a divorce? How dare he strip her of everything she loved? She had every right to be angry, the way he'd treated her. The judge must have agreed too or she wouldn't have given her a non-custodial sentence. The restraining order was a joke. As if she wanted to go anywhere near Mike after what he'd done to her.

Wendy returns to the driveway, her circuit of the house complete.

'Louise!' she shouts, staring up at the master bedroom. 'I know you're in there. Open the door!'

She crosses her arms over her chest and waits, but no one appears at the window. There's no movement at all in the room.

'Lou!' She stoops down, grabs a handful of gravel and throws it at the glass. 'Open the door!'

Without waiting for a response, she stalks up to the side door and pulls the letter box open.

'I need to talk to you!'

But no one responds.

Frustrated, she returns to her car, reaches for her handbag and pulls out her phone. She jabs at the screen as she walks back to the side door and opens the letter box, then presses her left ear against the slit. Wendy holds her breath. If she hears Lou's phone ring out from inside the house she will . . . well, she's not quite sure what she'll do yet, but she won't leave until she sees Louise Wandsworth. She's not going to let her slip away again.

But nothing happens. There's no sound from the house and no dialling tone in Wendy's right ear. She moves her phone away from her ear and peers at the screen. No reception. God damn it.

She stares up at the window above the kitchen, her foot tap-tap-tapping on the gravel for one minute, two, three, then, unable to keep still a second longer, she slips between the garage and the house and walks into the garden. Her heels sink into the soggy grass as she walks backwards, keeping her gaze fixed on the house, then, as a rose bush scratches at her calves, she turns and walks up to the gate.

She shakes her head in irritation as she steps into the yard. Does all this belong to Louise too? If it was hers she wouldn't let the fields grow wild and unkempt. She'd graze sheep, grow crops, maybe buy a horse or two and she'd definitely keep ducks on the lake in the field behind the barn. Sighing with frustration, she heads for the barn with its patchy roof and broken walls. It looms over her in the half-light as she approaches. It probably housed lambs once, Wendy thinks as she pulls on the heavy metal ring on the door. She can imagine them now, bleating and crying for milk under the light of orange heat lamps and—

Scrabbling. That's the only word she can think of to describe the sound that makes her blood run cold. An animal, hurriedly getting to its feet, knocking against something metal and groaning. It sounds scared, or in pain. She backs out of the barn and slams the door shut, her heart pounding in her throat. Is it a fox? Ever since she read that story about a fox mauling a baby in its bed she's been terrified of them. If it has somehow got itself trapped in the barn, or if it's made a nest in there to have its babies, it'll feel cornered if she walks in. And it might attack.

But what if it's not a fox? What if it's a hurt sheep, lost and alone? Wendy's always had a soft spot for sheep with their stupid faces and their ridiculous running style. A sheep wouldn't hurt her. She opens the door an inch and peers inside but it's so dark she can't see a thing.

'Hello,' she whispers, braced to run. 'Hello, I just want to help.'

And there it is again, the low groan, barely feet from where she's standing.

274

'Hello?' she says again, opening the door a little more. 'I won't hurt you.'

'Help,' says a deep, rasping voice.

A scream catches in Wendy's throat as she darts back into the yard and slams the barn door shut. She leans her weight into the door to keep it closed. It was a man's voice. But why is there a man in the barn? Is he homeless? Sleeping rough for the night? An image flies into her mind, of a film she saw as a child. Some children discover a man, that they mistake for Jesus, sleeping rough in a barn. They take care of him, not knowing he's actually a criminal on the run. Wendy shivers at the thought. She could be in danger. The man in the barn could be a murderer who's already killed Lou and Wendy could be his next victim.

No, no. She forces her frantic brain to slow down. He said 'help'. And he groaned. Unless it's all part of an elaborate plan to lure unsuspecting middle-aged women into the barn, he's unlikely to be a serial killer. It's more likely that a local farmer had an accident and couldn't raise the alarm. He could be trapped under a piece of machinery, crying out for help.

Wendy glances at her phone – no signal – then pulls at the door and peers into the darkness.

'Hello? Is there someone in there?'

'Help.' A single word floats towards her, then another. 'Water.'

'You need water?'

'Yes.' The word is little more than a whisper, as though it's taking all the man's strength to say a single syllable.

'I'll be back,' Wendy barks into the gloom. 'Don't go anywhere.'

She hears the low groan of the man's despair as she turns and heads back to the gate. The sound disappears as she sprints through the garden and between the gap between the house and the garage. She pauses at the side door and hammers on it with both fists.

'Help!' she shouts. 'Someone needs our help.'

She doesn't wait for a response. Instead she darts into her car. She grabs her handbag first, then scrabbles around in the glovebox. There's no water but she does have a warm can of Diet Coke. It's better than nothing.

Panting and out of breath, Wendy yanks at her handbag strap as it slips from her shoulder. There's nothing in her bag that would come in useful if the man has impaled himself, or pinned himself beneath a piece of farming equipment, but it does contain hand sanitiser, a handful of plasters and a few other bits and bobs that might help with any minor injuries. And she could always unclip the strap to use as a tourniquet if necessary. Turning on the torch function on her phone, she pushes at the barn door.

'I'm back,' she says, sweeping the light from left to right. She sees the straw first, piled up in the back of the barn, then the bars of the cage glint back at her, then she sees what looks like a pile of clothes in the nearest cage. But it's not, it's a man, lying on his side with his back to her.

Her breath catches in her throat and panic rises in her chest. He's locked in the cage. She can see the padlock on the door. Why? She searches for a rational explanation but her mind is still fixated on the trapped farmworker theory and she can't make sense of what she's seeing. Some kind of mistake? He accidentally locked himself in? A stag do joke that went wrong? Her mind darts back to the film she saw as a child. Is the man a criminal who's been locked in by some locals? She glances behind her, fully expecting to see huge, burly farmers looming out from the fields.

'I . . .' her voice comes out as a small squeak. 'I couldn't find water but I've got a can of Diet Coke.'

The man groans and, with what seems like Herculean effort, rolls over to look at her. Wendy angles her phone so the light sweeps across his body. And then she sees his face.

'Mike?'

She takes a step forward, gripping her phone tightly. A battle is raging in her mind. One part is telling her that this wan-faced man with grey hair, stubble and dark circles under his eyes is her ex-husband Michael Hughes. The other part is telling her that's not possible.

'Mike, is that you?'

The man opens his eyes slowly. He squints, then winces as though he's in pain and slowly, slowly raises a hand to his forehead to shield his eyes from the glare of her phone.

'Dee?' he breathes.

'Mike!' She throws herself at the cage, then drops to her knees. 'Mike?' She pulls at the bars with both hands, her phone still wedged under her right thumb, but they don't so much as quiver. 'Mike, what happened?'

'Water,' he croaks. 'Water.'

'God, yes. Of course.' She takes the can from her bag, opens it, then reaches an arm through the bars.

Mike, still lying on his side, holds out a hand, but there's a good six inches between his quivering fingers and the can.

'You're going to have to sit up,' Wendy says. 'Can you do that?'

She watches, half horrified, half mesmerised, as her ex-husband tries to push himself into a sitting position. He's as weak as a kitten and he collapses back onto the cold, hard floor of his cell several times, before, finally, he's in a sitting position. He takes all his weight on one arm and reaches for the can of drink, but they're still too far apart.

Wendy presses herself so tightly up against the bars that the metal bites into her armpit but it's enough and Mike grabs at the can. His arm wavers as his fingers close around it and, for one horrible second, he seems like he's going to drop it, but he manages to regain his balance and raises the drink to his lips. He drinks without stopping, gulping and gulping and gulping, then slumps back onto the ground, the empty can in his outstretched hand.

Wendy scrabbles to her feet, rounds the cage and pulls at the padlock. It's hefty and well made, the sort her dad used on his shed, and despite its rusty appearance, it holds firm.

'Where's the key?' she says, looking desperately around the barn. 'Mike, where's the key?'

He shakes his head.

'Who did this to you?' Wendy glances back at the door of the barn. Whoever locked Mike in could return at any second and lock her in too.

She looks down at her phone, desperately hoping that at least one bar of reception has magically appeared in the top right-hand corner, but it's still showing a no entry symbol. Ringing the police will have to wait.

'Mike!' she says. 'You need to talk to me. Who did this to you and how do I get you out?'

She pulls on the cage door again. It rattles but doesn't budge.

'Mike!'

Her ex-husband is still lying on the floor with his eyes closed. His chest is rising and falling and there are no obvious signs of injury. Why isn't he answering her? If their positions were reversed she'd be screaming for help.

'Who did this?' she asks again, but she knows the answer. It has to be Lou. The barn's directly behind the house. And to think she'd suspected the two of them of having an affair.

Her ex-husband makes a strange retching sound. He clutches at his stomach, twists onto his side and retches again. The third time he retches, his lips part and he vomits violently, spraying the straw-strewn ground with a thin brown liquid, dotted with chunks of food. He vomits again and again, then finally lies still, his hands clutching at his stomach.

'Mike,' Wendy says. 'Say something. Are you okay? Mike!'

For several seconds he doesn't move, then he slowly opens his eyes and looks at her. He coughs, grimaces, runs the back of his hand over his mouth and says, 'Hello, Dee.'

Something inside her clenches. *Hello Dee?* That's it? She's his knight in shining armour. His key to freedom and all he can manage is *Hello Dee?* He doesn't even look particularly pleased to see her.

'Can you sit up?' she snaps.

Mike nods, grabs hold of one of the bars, grimaces and then slowly, painfully, pulls himself into a sitting position.

'What are you doing here?' he asks. He speaks slowly, with one hand pressed to his throat as though it hurts to speak.

Wendy ignores him, darts to the barn door and peers outside. There's no sign of Lou and no lights from the house beaming through the trees at the edge of the garden.

'Okay, Mike,' she says, looking back at her ex-husband. 'I'm going to ring the police now. I'm not sure how far I'll have to drive to get phone reception, but if I head back towards Malvern then—'

'No police.'

'What?' She stares incredulously at him.

'No police.'

280

'But you're . . . you've been . . .' She can't make sense of what she's hearing. Why on earth wouldn't he want her to go to the police?

'Dee.' He drags himself to his feet. 'You can't go to the police. Trust me on this.'

'Trust you?' She can't help but laugh.

'Please.' He shuffles across the cage, stepping around the pool of vomit. 'It's important. Listen to me.'

She stiffens at his tone. It's the same one he used on her when they were married. *Listen to me Dee, you don't need to worry about that. I've got it under control. Listen to me Dee, you're being neurotic. Listen to me Dee, the police are liars. I haven't been sleeping with anyone, never mind a fourteen-year-old girl.* She'd almost forgotten how patronising he could be. Almost, but not quite.

'No *you* listen,' she snaps. 'You're the one in the cage.'

Mike falls silent and stares at her. The muscles in his jaw pulse beneath his grey stubble and haggard skin.

'Who locked you in there?'

He sighs. 'Lou.'

She deliberately plays the fool. Mike has no idea how much she knows about Louise Wandsworth and she wants to keep her cards close to her chest for now. 'Who?'

'Lou . . . Louise . . . the . . .' He breaks eye contact with her. 'The girl . . . the girl from karate.'

'Karate? But you haven't done karate for years . . . Oh. I see. That girl. But why? I didn't even know she

281

lived round here.' Wendy is almost proud of her performance. She could definitely have been an actress in another life. Someone classy like Meryl Streep or Sigourney Weaver.

Mike raises his gaze to meet hers. 'She does now.'

'Where is she?'

'I don't know. I haven't seen her for a couple of days.'

A couple of days? She was supposed to go to Wendy's house on Friday but never showed up. Was she going to confess to her? Tell Wendy that she had her ex-husband locked in a barn at the back of her house? If so, why didn't she show up and where is she now?

Wendy runs a hand over her hair. It's started to rain and one side of her head is damp with drizzle. She steps back into the barn and pulls the door closed.

'Why did she do it?'

Mike shrugs. 'Who knows.'

Wendy stares him straight in the eye. 'You know.'

'She . . .' he sighs heavily. 'I was trying to stop her from harming someone.'

'Who?'

'A friend's daughter. She's obsessed with her. She's been to her house, followed her to school and she's been stalking her at work. I found out and tried to warn Lou off. That's when she did this.'

Wendy frowns. Quite frankly the whole thing sounds preposterous. What possible reason would a thirty-two-year-old woman have for stalking a child? 'Which friend's daughter?'

'Alan Meadows.'

'Chloe? Isn't she nine . . . ten?'

'Thirteen – I think.'

There's something about the way Mike added 'I think' to Chloe's age that chimes a warning bell in Wendy's head. Lou was only a year older when all the horribleness happened.

'How did you find out?'

'Does it matter?'

'It does if you want me to help you.'

'I was at Greensleeves, you know, the garden centre. I do deliveries for them and I sorted Chloe out with a job when Alan said she wanted to earn some money. Anyway, I was there one afternoon when Chloe came running into the yard saying some woman was freaking her out. I went to see who it was, recognised Lou and followed her home. She told me she had something belonging to Chloe in the barn that she needed to show me and, when I walked in here, she hit me over the back of the head. Next thing I knew I was in here.'

It's Mike's pseudo-earnest expression that sets Wendy off – the downturned lips, pleading eyes and cartoon sad eyebrows – and she explodes with laughter. But it's not long-lived and, within seconds, her expression is stony again.

'You're such a bloody liar.'

'What?' Mike gawps at her.

'Credit me with a little intelligence please, Michael, and tell me the truth.'

'That is the truth.'

'Okay, then. The police can find out what really happened.' She turns on her heel and pushes at the barn door.

'No! Wait!'

Wendy turns slowly, stifling a smile. Sitting in an office with Lou was nothing compared to the power trip she's enjoying now.

'She's setting me up.' Mike holds his hands up, palms pressed against the bars. 'Lou is. That's the real story. She's trying to make out I'm grooming Chloe. That's why she locked me in here, so she could convince her to go to the police or something. She's tapped, totally fucking cuckoo. Her life's screwed up and she blames me for it. But I swear to you, Wendy, I haven't done anything wrong. I haven't touched the girl. I wouldn't. You know that. You . . .' he tails off. 'I did you wrong, Dee. I'm sorry. You were there for me the whole time and I fucked you over. But I can put it right. I've got money. It's all yours. You can buy yourself a bigger house. I know how much you miss the old one. Just please . . . please . . . hear me out.'

'Okay,' Wendy says, feeling more calm and in control than she has in years. 'Okay, I'll listen.'

Chapter 36

Wendy

Forty thousand pounds. *Forty thousand pounds.* The figure whirls round Wendy's head as she drives through the dark, away from Bromyard and back towards Malvern. It's not nearly enough to buy a house as lovely as her old one, but it would be enough to move away from Clarence Road and her nightmare of a neighbour. She might even get a bigger garden, maybe a third reception room for that price if the location was right. She is *owed* that money. It is recompense for everything she's been through. And all she has to do to earn it is get a pair of bolt cutters from Mike's shed and a mobile phone that he's hidden in his house.

What if he's lying? What if he is grooming Chloe Meadows?

A loud, insistent voice shouts the question from the back of her brain. She turns on the radio and cranks the volume up. It's Queen, her favourite band, but the thought persists. Is that why Mike won't let her call the police? Only a man with something to hide wouldn't want the police to free him and arrest his kidnapper. But she so desperately wants to believe his story – that Louise Wandsworth is a mentally ill woman who has never got over her teenaged obsession with him. That she returned to Malvern because she blames him for everything that's ever gone wrong in her life and is out for revenge.

'I wish I could go back in time,' Mike had said, staring at Wendy through the bars of his cage. 'I wish I'd ignored her when she turned up to class, crying her eyes out because her dad was drunk. She said she was going to run away to France because she was scared he was going to kill her. The only thing I did wrong was to go after her to try and keep her safe. She took my kindness and used it against me. And now she's found a new weapon.'

Chloe Meadows. According to Mike, Louise had infiltrated the young girl's life and was filling her head with dark thoughts. She was the one grooming her, he'd insisted, not him. If he went to the police about the kidnapping, Lou would retaliate, dragging Chloe along with her and he'd end up in jail again. There was only one way he could prove his innocence and that was if Wendy got hold of his mobile phone before Lou did. There were incriminating text messages from Lou, he said, threatening to make Chloe press charges unless he paid her forty thousand pounds.

'It's yours,' he'd told Wendy, 'every penny of it.

Just get me that phone, get me out of here and the money's yours. You can do what you want with it. I just want this nightmare to end.'

Indecision gnaws at Wendy's guts as she turns right off New Mills Way. Logic tells her that the right thing to do is to go to the police and let them deal with the situation. But her distrust of Lou Wandsworth and the lure of the money is too great. Even if she works for another twenty years there's no way she could save up that much. But, even if she does get what Mike wants from his house, what's to stop him reneging on their deal? He can promise all he wants, but the money won't actually be hers until it's sitting in her bank account. She glances at her phone, on the passenger seat. If he gave her his details she could log onto his account and transfer the money across before she handed him the bolt cutters and his mobile. But then there's no reception out in the sticks, is there? Not unless Lou's house has Wi-Fi.

There are no spaces on Mike's road, so she parks several streets away, wriggles her fingers into her favourite leather gloves, puts on her rain mac, pulls up the hood and gets out of the car. She's only ever driven past her old house half a dozen times since the divorce, and she's never stopped. When the judge gave her a conditional discharge for assaulting Mike she was told, in no uncertain terms, that if she broke the terms of her restraining order she would go to jail. The threat of no privacy, no garden and no Monty was enough to make her keep her distance.

She stops walking when she reaches her old

three-bedroom semi. It's dark and the house next door is lit up like a Christmas tree. Before she has time to change her mind she hurries down the path with her head bent low. On the front patio, just as Mike said, are several dozen potted plants and small trees (plants and trees that didn't exist when *she* lived there). The spare key is under one of them.

Wendy works quickly, ducking down, lifting pots and feeling underneath.

'Come on,' she mutters as she moves from pot to pot. 'Come on, come on.'

She yanks at the ceramic pot holding an ornamental cherry tree but it's too heavy to lift with one hand. She bends her knees and pushes at the lid of the pot whilst simultaneously reaching down to steady the bottom with her other hand, but the weight of the tree is too great and the pot slips from her grasp. The tree bashes into the hedge, bounces off it and then crashes to the ground, taking out several pots before it lies still. Wendy clamps her hands to her ears, then ducks down low, as a shadow appears in one of the upstairs rooms in the house next door.

Her heart thunders in her chest. What should she do? Run back to the car? Hide under the hedge? She places a hand on the cold ground, preparing to run, and then she sees it – a silver Yale key lying beside one of the smashed pots. She inches forward, snatches it up, then, keeping low, heads for the hedge. She presses her back up against it, hands quivering against the smooth leaves and sharp twigs and waits. Her neighbour wouldn't blink an eyelid if a smashing

288

sound came from her front garden – he'd probably be having such loud sex he wouldn't hear it – but she has no idea who lives next door to Mike now. Hopefully not an off-duty policeman.

She starts to count, in her head. Up to sixty first. Then up to one hundred and twenty. No one comes. She inches away from the hedge and glances up at the bedroom window next door. There's no one there.

Forty thousand pounds shouts the voice at the back of her brain. *Forty thousand pounds!*

In an instant she's at Mike's front door, pushing the key into the lock.

The urge to explore the house and see how much Mike has changed it since he kicked her out is almost more than Wendy can bear. Instead she chants, 'Forty thousand pounds, forty thousand pounds,' as she heads for the kitchen, pulls open the drawer next to the oven and pulls out a steak knife. She slows her pace as she returns to the hallway and carefully counts the floorboards between the kitchen and the front door. Mike told her that the loose one was seven planks away from the kitchen. When she reaches it, she prods it with her fingers. It wobbles, ever so slightly, but doesn't flip up, so she wedges the knife between the skirting board and the wood and jiggles it backwards and forwards. She swears under her breath as the knife pings out from the gap, then grits her teeth and tries again.

What kind of man hides a mobile phone under a floorboard?

289

When Mike had asked her to grab his mobile phone, she'd imagined snatching it off the kitchen table or the arm of the sofa, not digging into the floorboards like a drug dealer trying to retrieve her stash. It didn't make sense. If someone had been blackmailing her, she would have taken the phone straight to the police to show them the messages but, according to Mike, he hadn't taken Lou's threats seriously at first. So why hide the phone under the floorboards before he went to meet her? The only possible explanation Wendy can come up with is that he didn't want to risk Lou snatching it or he didn't want his phone to give away his location. That, or the blackmail story was a steaming pile of cow shit and he was actually hiding the phone from the police.

On her second attempt the floorboard gives way and she reaches into the recess. Her fingers make contact with something smooth and solid and she snatches it up. Mike's phone. A noise beyond the front door makes her start. She holds herself very, very still, barely breathing as she listens, then she slowly rises to her feet and creeps along the hallway. She pauses when she reaches the front door and zips Mike's mobile into her right pocket. She looks at the kitchen knife, considers running back down the hallway to put it back in the drawer, then zips it into her left jacket pocket. Just in case Mike decides to try any funny business. A cool breeze drifts into the house as she turns the handle to the front door. She listens, but the only sound is the thudding of her heart in her ears. She opens the door a little wider. Outside the broken plant pots are still scattered on the patio beside the felled cherry tree but it's darker than before. Wendy chances a glimpse to her left. Several of the lights in the neighbour's windows have been turned off. She creeps forward, then runs, light-footed, down the path and onto the street. She sprints round the corner and doesn't stop until she reaches her car. She takes off her jacket, the knife still in the pocket, and shoves it under the passenger seat, then she slips into the driver seat and, with a shaking hand, shoves a key at the ignition. She pauses. She's forgotten the bloody bolt cutters.

'God damn it!' She slaps the steering wheel with the palm of her hand.

The only tools she owns are a screwdriver set, a hammer and a level. If she's to stand any chance of getting her hands on Mike's money, she needs to get him out of that barn before Lou comes back. She jumps back out the car without bothering to put her jacket back on. She's got to go back into the house.

Wendy scans the walls of the shed. She used to wind Mike up about how OCD he was about his things when they were married – his sock drawer with its neat lines of balled socks and his insistence that all the jars and cans in the kitchen faced forwards – but now she's grateful for his neatness. The bolt cutters are hanging on a nail on the far wall of the shed, next to a saw. She snatches them off the wall, re-locks the shed and runs back across the garden. With tremulous fingers she locks the back door, then hurries through the dark house towards the front door. She's barely set foot through it when she hears the wail of a police siren. She freezes. The neighbour must have rung them. Should she hide, go back into the garden or make a run for it?

She's halfway down the garden path when she realises she's still carrying the bolt cutters and Mike's front door key. She ducks down, shoves them under the bush, then speeds out of the gate. She's halfway down the street when a police officer rounds the corner and orders her not to move.

She immediately stops running, her heart pounding in her chest. As the policeman walks towards her, his eyes fixed on her face, a thousand thoughts flash through her head.

He's not after me. I'm a respectable fifty-nine-year-old woman.

I'm a fifty-nine-year-old woman with a restraining order against her.

Mike's neighbour spotted me.

I don't want to go to jail.

Mike's being kept prisoner in a cage. Say something.

Forty thousand pounds if I don't.

I can talk my way out of this.

I don't want to go to jail.

'Wendy Harrison?' the police officer says, reaching out an arm. 'Are you Wendy Harrison?'

Wendy runs a hand over her hair, pats it back into place and smiles tightly. She knows exactly what to say.

Chapter 37

Lou

I wake with a start, my brain cloudy with sleep, my eyes almost sealed shut from crying. Someone is pounding on the hotel room door. Mike jumps out of bed, hair dishevelled, boxer shorts hanging low on his hips. He doesn't make it more than halfway across the room when the door slams open and four men in navy uniforms and berets burst into the room.

'Police! Police! Police!'

Mike roars as he's wrestled to the ground. One police officer kneels on his back and another pins his legs to the ground as the third grabs his hands and slaps handcuffs against his wrists.

The fourth man speeds across the room towards me. I scream and scoot across the bed, but there's no place to hide, nowhere to run.

'Louise Wandsworth!' the man says in a thick French accent as I cower in the corner of the bedroom. 'Are you Louise Wandsworth?'

I nod mutely.

As Mike is bundled out of the room, the policeman holds out a hand. 'Come. Louise, come. You are safe now. We take you home.'

Sunday 6th May 2007

How long does it take to get discharged from a hospital? When I was woken up just after six this morning to have my vitals taken, I asked the nurse whether I could leave, seeing as everything appeared to be normal. She told me no, I needed to be officially discharged by a doctor. It's now lunchtime and there's still no sign of a doctor. When I moaned to the nice lady who brought me a tiny portion of spaghetti bolognaise with a pile of overboiled carrots and a cup of tea, she shrugged and said, 'You might be here for hours yet, darling. They're all terribly over-worked.'

I barely slept last night and not just because of the snoring ladies or the fact I had to sleep on my back because of my cast. I've got to get back to the barn. If Mike's not dead now, he will be if I stay here much longer.

No one stopped me as I slipped out of bed, shoved my feet into my shoes and stumbled across the ward. I half expected to feel a hand on my shoulder as I hurried through the never-ending white corridors and out the front door, but I didn't attract so much as a second glance. If the taxi driver I flagged down was concerned about the fact I had one arm in a sling and was dripping in sweat, he didn't let on, although he did whistle when I told him where I needed to get to.

'That's going to cost you from here.'

'I know, but it's the only way I can get home.'

A message from Ben flashed up on my phone as we left Hereford.

Just to let you know that Dad's conscious and doing okay but the doctors want to operate. He's going to need a pacemaker. How are you? Did you sleep ok? Have they let you out yet? If so are you going to the police or straight home?

Going straight home, I tap back, then pause.

Going straight home. Glad to hear that your dad is doing okay. I hope his operation goes well.

I press send, then tap out another message. In the next thirty minutes or so I'll lose reception and he'll worry if he can't get hold of me.

Don't worry if I don't reply to your texts. Normally I'd go into Bromyard or Malvern to check my phone but I can't drive because of my arm. We can stay in touch via landline though. My number is 01886 884579.

I press send, then wind down the window and sit back in my seat.

'You all right, love?' the taxi driver asks, glancing at me in his rear-view window. 'You look a bit peaky. You're not going to throw up are you? I only had a valet two days ago.'

'I'm fine,' I say, as I pop the last painkiller the nurse left me into my mouth. But I'm definitely not.

My stomach twists as the taxi pulls away and disappears down the lane, leaving me standing at the bottom of Dad's driveway. I don't want to do this. I want to rewind time and find myself back in my cosy, cramped little flat in London with a weekend of lazy lie-ins, DVD binges and drinks with friends stretching before me. But I can't. I have to open the barn door.

The smell hits me the second the door opens – piss, shit and something else, something sour and bitter. It's the scent of death. And there's Mike, lying face down on the floor of the cage with his face turned away from me. There's something dark and viscous puddled around his hair. Blood? Worse?

I thought I'd gasp, cry or shout but I don't make a sound. I feel nothing. My brain, so frantic and fearful less than half an hour ago, has gone to sleep. I don't know if it's relief or my pain meds kicking in, but all the frustration and terror I've felt over the last couple of days has gone. I don't have to count the hours since Mike last had a drink anymore. If I wake up tonight, heart racing, it won't be because I'm worrying if I can make it back on time. It's over. Mike is dead. And I'm going to prison for the rest of my life.

I close the door to the barn and wander back through the garden. I feel as though I'm in a dream as I let myself into the garage and pick my way through Dad's crap. I'm not even sure what I'm doing as I one-handedly wrestle with jam jar lids, prise open paint pots and unlatch toolboxes, but there's something soothing about the methodical way I move from one side of the garage to the other, rooting through nails, screws, washers and bolts.

When I've finished looking through all the shelves, I begin dragging the larger items out of the garage and onto the driveway – the lawnmower, leaf blower, workbench and cardboard boxes. In the gaps they leave behind I find more stuff: bin bags, plastic bags, rags, blankets and tools. I carry the bags outside, one by one, then upend them, tipping the contents onto the driveway. I almost laugh as half a dozen keys land on the gravel. But I don't. Instead I stoop to pick them up, shove them into my pocket and grab a blanket.

I don't look at Mike as I walk back into the barn, but he's still there, in my peripheral vision, prostrate on the floor of his cell. The second key I try fits the padlock and it opens with a soft click. I step into the cage, the blanket in my hands, and shake it out. I'm not sure why I'm doing this, but it feels like the right thing to do, not least so I don't have to look at him anymore. I begin at his feet, awkwardly draping the blanket over his trainers and the worn cord of Dad's trousers. As I reach his waist, a memory pops up in my brain – of finding Mike passed out on the bed in the Travelodge hotel in Birmingham. We'd been to a local supermarket and stocked up on cider, bread, ham and cheese and then returned to our room. 'A bed picnic', Mike called it. I went for a bath afterwards and when I came back he was face down on the bed, fast asleep, his right hand curled around a hunk of bread. I pulled the blanket over him, then curled up beside him and watched him sleep. As his chest rose and fell I felt happier than I'd ever been. I was going to spend the rest of my life with the man I loved and no one could keep us apart.

I pause as I pull the blanket up over Mike's shoulders. Did he just move? I focus on the soft curve of his back, holding my breath, watching for a gentle rise and fall but none comes. He's still haunting me, even though he's dead. As I move to cover his head, something glints in my peripheral vision. Something silver, red and white. I turn to look at it. It's just a Diet Coke can. Nothing to worry about—

A can of Coke?

I turn sharply. As I do, I'm grabbed round the waist and yanked off my feet.

I smash down onto the hard floor of the cage, hitting it with my elbow, hip, then head. Before I can move, Mike is on top of me. The shock of the fall and the weight of his body on top of mine knocks the air from my lungs and, for a second, I can't breathe. He shifts his weight, only a fraction of an inch to one side, but it's enough. I suck damp barn air into my lungs, press my hands to his shoulders and twist beneath him.

'Stay still,' he hisses. The skin is pulled tight over

his cheekbones, his eyes are red-rimmed and his breath is sour. He snatches at my wrists, but I twist them out of his hands and pound at his back, his shoulders and ribs. My blows bounce off him and he hooks his feet around mine, pinning my legs to the ground. For a man who's barely eaten in days he's scarily strong.

'Stay still!' He raises an arm, fist clenched. I twist my head to the side and close my eyes, anticipating the blow.

It's like no pain I've ever known – like being smacked round the head with a brick.

As Mike hits me again and again I smell the rusty scent of blood and something wet and warm trickles into my ear. I tense, eyes screwed shut, and wait for the next blow.

Nothing happens.

He's still here. I can feel the warmth and weight of him straddling my waist. I can hear his laboured rasping breath and smell the fetid stench of his breath, hair and skin. What's he waiting for? I want to open my eyes but I'm too scared of what I might see.

The pressure on my torso suddenly eases as Mike shifts his weight. I don't move an inch. Is he going? Does he think he's punished me enough? I feel the heat of his breath on my ear before I hear his voice.

'You ruined my life. Do you know that? You turned me into a man I despise.'

He pauses, waiting for a response.

'It's all your fault, Lou. All of it. You made me like this.'

Fear pulses through me and every muscle in my body tenses. He's going to kill me.

'I'm sorry.' I open my eyes and look up into his face. 'For everything. It is my fault, you're right. I'm sorry. I'm so, so sorry. Please, just let me go. Please. I'm sorry. I love you.'

His lips thin into a smile as he slips his hands around my neck. 'No you don't.'

The ground is cold and damp beneath my cheek. Something wet and rancid-smelling seeps through my T-shirt and chills my skin. I inhale sharply, desperately, but nothing happens. I try again. A loud rasping sound reverberates up from my throat, but my lungs are still empty. I can't breathe. Why can't I breathe? Panic forces me up and off the ground but my arm is too weak to take my weight and I collapse back onto my side. The fall jolts my broken arm and I cry out in pain. Grey shapes swirl around me as I open my eyes. My lungs are burning, my tongue feels too big for my mouth and my throat feels as though it's stuffed with cotton wool. What happened to me? Where am I? Why can't I—

I'm in the cage, lying on straw that smells of urine and decay. My stomach twists, my body convulses and I retch, spewing bile over my arms and hands. I vomit again and again and, just when I think it will never stop, it does. Air rattles in and out of my lungs as I struggle to breathe.

'Where is it?' The door to the barn flies open and Mike limps in, carrying a length of metal piping in his hand. 'Where's my van?'

He's going to kill me. I survived once, by some miracle, but he's not going to let that happen again. I can see it in his eyes.

'Where's my van?' he shouts again.

I try to shake my head but I can't. All I can do is pray that when he kills me he does it quickly.

Mike pulls himself up to his full height. From down here he looks huge and powerful. 'Tell me where my van is or, this time, I will snap your fucking neck.'

So he didn't mean to kill me before. He just wanted me to pass out.

'Louise!' He grabs hold of the door and yanks but the padlock is shut and it holds firm. 'Fuck.'

Still holding on to the cage, he awkwardly lowers himself into a squatting position and sweeps at the straw, muttering under his breath. He hasn't got the key. He must have dropped it after he shut me in here. He looks back at me and grits his teeth as he stands back up.

'For fuck's sake.'

CLANG! The whole cage shakes as he smashes the pipe against the padlock. It jumps.

Please, I pray. *Please don't open.*

CLANG! He smashes it again. Beads of sweat have appeared on his forehead and he's breathing heavily.

His top lip tightens over his teeth as he stares at me through the bars of the cage. 'Fuck the van.' He

301

reaches into his pocket and pulls out a set of keys. *My* car keys. He's been in Dad's house.

He smiles. 'Looks like I'll have to take Chloe on a little trip in your car instead.'

'No!' I croak as he turns to leave. 'No! No, Mike. No! No!'

I grip the bars of the cage with my good hand and, gritting my teeth against the pain, try and haul myself to my feet. I get as far as a semi-crouched position, then black spots appear in front of my eyes and a whooshing sound fills my head, making me feel as though I'm under water. Then everything goes black.

Chapter 38

Chloe

It's been twenty-four hours since Chloe Meadows last saw her mum. Her dad returned from the pub three hours after her mum left the house – stomping around and shouting Julie's name. When she didn't appear, he slammed open the door to Chloe's bedroom and barked at her to sit up. Chloe, puffy-faced and red-eyed from crying, forced herself up from her pillow and stuttered that her mum had said she was going out for a bit but didn't say why. Her dad didn't believe her. He thought she was covering. He ranted, raged and threatened then, getting nowhere, stormed across the landing and delivered the same speech to Jamie who promptly burst into tears.

After he'd torn ten strips off both his children, Alan Meadows stomped back down the stairs and rang everyone who might know where his wife had gone. Chloe stood at her bedroom door and listened as he swore at her nan, her Auntie Meg and her mum's best friend Sally. Shortly afterwards she heard the theme tune to *Match of the Day*. Then her dad swearing at the TV. It wasn't fair. Why was her mum allowed to escape and she wasn't? And why hadn't she asked her to go with her? She would have left in a heartbeat. She really wanted to text her to ask her where she was but she couldn't risk her dad discovering her rooting through his sock drawer. She couldn't text any of her friends either. Not that she'd know what to say to them. Her life was collapsing around her ears and there was no one she could talk to about it. Not her mum, dad, friends, her nan and definitely not Mike. And if she ever saw the weird skinny woman again – the woman who'd given her the diary that she'd thrown against the wardrobe and was lying splayed and curled on the carpet – she'd stab her in the heart.

It's Sunday afternoon now. Her dad hasn't said a word to her all day, not even when she went down to get breakfast and asked if her mum had come back yet. Now Chloe's back in her bedroom. Last night, before she fell asleep – broken and exhausted – she scrawled *I should have jumped* on her bedroom wall in eyeliner. She tried to scrub it off with a make-up remover wipe when she woke up but there's still a greasy stain on the wall and the word *jumped*.

'Chloe?' There's a tap at her bedroom door. 'Chloe, can I come in?'

She sighs and swings her legs off her bed. Before

304

she opens the door, she glances at the patch of carpet by the wardrobe but the diary's not there. It's under the bed, where she shoved it after her dad got back.

'Yes, Jamie.' She looks down at her little brother and his pale, pinched face.

'Where's Mum?'

'I don't know.'

'Is she coming back?'

Chloe sighs. 'Probably.'

'When?'

'I don't know.'

'Chlo?'

'Yes.'

'Can I have a hug?'

'Why?' Chloe can't remember the last time she and her brother touched, never mind hugged. When he was a baby he'd fall asleep in her arms. When he was two he followed her everywhere. She loved him back then, back before he became their dad's little mimic. She loves him now too, she's sure, she just can't feel it anymore.

Jamie tucks one leg behind the other and scratches the back of his calf with his toenail. 'Because I'm sad about Mum.'

'Okay then.' She crouches down and opens her arms. Jamie steps into the gap and wraps his arms around her neck, pressing his skinny little body against hers.

'You won't leave will you?' he says, lisping the words, something he does when he's tired. 'Promise me you won't leave too.'

Chloe doesn't say anything. She can't. But she hugs him tighter to make up for it.

Chloe is sitting on Jamie's bed, watching him play Minecraft when there's a sharp rap at the front door. She and Jamie share a look. Is it their mum? But she's got her own set of keys. Why would she knock?

'Jamie,' Chloe gestures for him to pause his game and, for once, he does what he's told.

They both listen, their eyes fixed on the gap in the bedroom door as their father's heavy footsteps carry up the stairs from the hallway. They hear the click of the front door, their dad's sharp intake of breath and then,

'Mike! Fucking hell. You look like you've been pulled through a hedge backwards. And you stink like shit. Where the hell have you been? The police have been looking for you. Chloe, Chloe! Stick the kettle on. Mike's back!'

Chloe stops dead in the doorway to the living room. Sitting directly across from her, with his elbows on his knees, is someone who looks vaguely similar to the love of her life. He's the same height with the same hands, same broad shoulders and silvery-grey hair, but his face is all wrong. There are dark circles beneath his hooded eyes. His lips are pale and chapped. His cheeks are pinched and the lower half of his face is covered in thick stubble.

'You all right, Chlo?' He smiles tightly as his gaze

sweeps the length of her body then returns to her face.

'Yeah.' She doesn't break eye contact. 'I heard you were missing.'

She can feel her dad watching her from the sofa by the window but he may as well be on the other side of the world. This is about her and Mike and no one else.

'Apparently so.' Mike raises his eyebrows. 'But I'm back now.'

'He wasn't in a ditch.' Her dad's laugh sounds too loud, as though he's dialled it too high. 'He was off with some bird. Find her on Tinder, did you?'

'Yeah.' He nods, his eyes not leaving Chloe's face. He's sending her a message. There's something unsaid behind his steady gaze, but she's not sure what it is. Another lie probably.

'You wanted me to get you some tea?' she says, looking at her dad.

'Fuck tea!' He laughs again. 'I've changed my mind. Get us some beers from the fridge. Bollocks.' He taps his pockets. 'I'm out of fags. Mike,' he points across the room as he stands up. 'Do not move a muscle. If you go missing again I'll come after you and shove you in a ditch myself! Chloe, get the man a beer.'

The second the front door slams behind Alan Meadows, Mike stands up and crosses the living room. 'Chloe, I've missed you so—'

'No.' She takes a step back into the hall, her hands raised.

'Hey,' Mike pauses, stunned by her reaction. 'I know you're angry with me but it's not true, what your dad said. I wasn't with another woman. I can't tell you where I was but—'

'I needed you.' Chloe's throat is so tight she can barely speak. 'And you didn't come. I waited for hours.'

'I would have been there . . . if I could have, I swear I would have . . .' He reaches for her, his expression pained. 'Chloe, you've got no idea what I've been through the last few days but I'm back now and—'

'Were you with her?'

'What?'

'That woman. The skinny one with the long brown hair?'

Mike's expression changes in an instant. He gawps at her, his eyes wide and uncomprehending, then he swallows and shakes his head. 'What? Who?'

But it's too late. His reaction just told Chloe everything she needed to know. He was with her – the woman who'd given her the diary– the original love of his life. It was all there in black and white – how they met, how they fell in love, how they had sex, how they planned to run away together. She didn't refer to him by name but it wasn't hard to work out that M was Mike. So many of the things he told Chloe were there, scribbled in the other woman's untidy handwriting, many of them the exact same phrases:

I've never felt this way about anyone before.

I was so unhappy until I met you.

You don't know how beautiful you are.

You understand me.

It's killing me, the way I feel about you.

I should walk away but I can't.

I love you. We're soulmates. I want to spend the rest of my life with you.

I would give up everything to be with you.

You're special in a way other girls aren't.

They all stung, but the last was the worst. She'd felt so special. Out of all the women in the world that Mike could have fallen in love with he'd fallen in love with her – a thirteen-year-old girl with a lumpy body and a ton of insecurities. There were other women at Greensleeves who fancied him, she'd heard them talking in the staffroom, but he wasn't interested in them. It was her he wanted. Her that gave him sleepless nights because of their age difference. He'd risk the ridicule of his friends and family to be with her. He'd give up everything to be with her, run away with her, start a new life with her and she . . . she'd believed him . . .

What a stupid, fat, ugly, naïve, waste of space she was.

'What is it?' Mike says now, his hands dropping to his sides. 'Why are you looking at me like that?'

'I know.'

'What do you know?'

'Everything.' She glances up the stairs as a shadow stripes across the landing. Is Jamie listening to their conversation?

'I don't understand what you mean.'

'I know about her. And you.'

'What?' He shakes his head, uncomprehending. 'What about . . . I . . . I don't know what she's told you, but I guarantee it's lies. What is it she's told you, Chloe?'

She laughs lightly. 'You'll just deny it if I tell you.'

'I'll tell you the truth.'

'No you won't. You'll tell me what you think I want to hear. Just like you told her.'

'Chloe, please! I don't know what she's told you but she's poison. And she's a liar. She's jealous of our happiness and she's trying to turn you against me.' He reaches for her hands again. This time she slaps them away.

'Don't touch me!'

'Chloe!' Mike lunges for her, reaching for her shoulders but, before he can make contact, Chloe raises her right hand and slaps him hard across the face.

He recoils, temporarily stunned, then lunges for her again, his hand reaching for her throat. As he does, the front door flies open and her dad appears, brandishing a packet of cigarettes and a blue plastic bag filled with more beers.

'Hello, hello. What have I missed?'

Chapter 39

Lou

It takes me three attempts to sit up and, when I finally manage it, I have to dip my head to stop the room from spinning. I must have passed out when I tried to stand up. I've got no idea how long I was unconscious for but my broken arm is throbbing so badly I feel sick. It's dark in the barn but I can hear the faintest birdsong from beyond the door. It's morning then. I've got to get out. If Mike managed to get to Chloe last night they could be anywhere by now.

Gritting my teeth, I twist onto my hands and knees and crawl, one-handed, across the cage to the door. Mike was in here for a long time. If he couldn't escape, what hope do I have? I turn and scan the floor, walls and ceiling for something, anything I can use to get out. That's when I see it, the Diet Coke can lying amongst the straw. It all comes rushing back in an instant – me entering the barn convinced that Mike was already dead, seeing him lying still in a pool of vomit. Was he asleep when I first saw him? I was so sure I'd find him dead I didn't think to check. At some point he must have woken up, then, when I opened the padlock, he stayed very, very still. He *was* breathing, I just chose not to believe it.

But none of that explains where the Diet Coke can came from. I crawl back across the cage and pick it up. It's empty, save a couple of tiny drops that I pour into the palm of my hand. I touch a droplet to my tongue. Where did it come from? It wasn't in the cage when I locked Mike in and he didn't have it on him. The only way it could have got in here was if someone gave it to him. But who? And why didn't they let him out? Any normal person would have rung the police and they'd have turned up by now.

I stumble back to the door and shake it. As I do, something small and silvery, nestled in the straw catches my eye. The key! Mike couldn't see it when he crouched down to search, but I can. It's too far away for me to grab, even if I press myself up against the cage. I need something to draw it closer. Bucket? Brick? Straw? I look down. My belt! The buckle is made of a cheap metal but it's solid. If I hold the other end and throw the buckle towards the key the weight might pin it to the floor. Then all I have to do is drag it towards me.

I unbuckle my belt as quickly as I can but it's tricky and painful, with one arm in plaster. When it finally comes free, I slip the leather from the loops of my jeans, then crouch down. I gather the belt in my hand with the end tucked beneath three of my fingers and the buckle between my forefinger and thumb, then I throw it.

Clunk! The buckle lands three inches short of the key. I haul it back and refold the belt. This time I don't tuck quite so much of the leather under my fingers and, when I reach my arm through the bars, I press into them with my shoulder. Three, two, one . . . throw! The second the buckle leaves my fingers I realise something is wrong but it's too late – I've let go. The belt flies from my hands and lands, curled in an S shape, on the straw outside the cage. Shit. Shit. I jam my arm through the bars but my fingers only graze the very edge of the belt. I lie on my good side and press my weight into the bars, forcing my shoulder up against the metal. My middle finger touches the belt. Nearly . . . nearly. I grit my teeth and push harder. Now I'm able to dig my fingernail into the soft leather. Come on. I hold my breath as I slowly, carefully, retract my arm. The belt shifts the tiniest bit then stops, caught on a piece of straw. I jab my fingernail back into it and try again. This time the belt slides a couple of inches towards me before it gets stuck again—

A noise in the yard outside makes me start. I don't know if it's footsteps, a bird or something else, but I don't wait to find out. I push my whole weight against the cage, grit my teeth against the burning pain in my shoulder and grab at the belt. I bend two fingers over it and yank my arm back. As I do, one wall of the barn shudders. Someone's pulling on the door handle outside. I shove the belt under my legs and pull myself up into a sitting position. A second later Mike walks in.

I scoot back on my bum as he walks up to the cage. Clang! The whole thing shakes as he slams the palms of his hands against the bars. I can smell the stench of stale booze on him from here.

'What did you tell her?'

I shake my head. 'I don't know . . . I don't know what you're talking about.'

'Chloe! What did you tell her?'

'I didn't tell her anything.'

'Look at me when I'm talking to you!'

I raise my gaze from the ground. The key's gone. It should be about half a metre from where he's standing but it's disappeared. He must have knocked it with his foot when he walked in.

'Mike I . . . I don't know what you're talking about.'

'Liar.' His top lip curls, revealing his teeth. 'She knows about us. What did you tell her?'

Fuck. The diary. Chloe's read it. She was supposed to tell someone what was happening to her, or go to the police. Not confront Mike. Stupid girl. Stupid, stupid girl.

'Let me go,' I say. 'Let me go and I'll . . . I'll talk to her . . . I'll put things right. She'll listen to me. She'll—'

He laughs, a rough grunt of a sound, and slowly

314

shakes his head. 'I think you've done quite enough already, don't you? See these?' He reaches into his pocket and pulls out two phones. One of them's mine. He must have taken it when he stole my car keys. 'You know, you really should use a passcode rather than a pattern, Louise. All I had to do was look at it under the light and I could see the greasy L shape. Ben,' he says, before I can comment, 'that's your boyfriend's name, isn't it? He's very concerned about you, Lou. He sent you a text saying he tried to call your landline last night and you didn't reply. His dad got through his operation okay though, so that's good, isn't it?'

A cold shiver runs through me. Please don't let Ben show up unannounced again. 'Mike—'

He holds up a hand. 'No need to thank me.'

'For what?'

'Putting him out of his misery.'

'What?'

He laughs at my distress. 'I didn't kill him, you stupid bitch. I sent him a text. From you. Poor Ben, I think he was quite upset to be dumped so unceremoniously. Especially with his dad being ill and everything, but he wished you a nice life.'

'No.' I shake my head. 'No you—'

'And your work were okay about you resigning. Ian, isn't it? Your boss? He left a voicemail saying he wanted a chat about your ill health and your return to work. I . . . well . . . you . . . texted him to say you wouldn't be coming back. He wasn't surprised, although you've rather landed him in the shit, Louise.'

315

'Mike—'

'What else, what else . . .' He stares up at the ceiling. 'Oh yes. Your Facebook friends are all horribly jealous that you've decided to spend the next year travelling the world.'

'No. You can't have done that. I haven't got—'

'Wi-Fi? 4G? I know. Annoying isn't it? But your phone works in Malvern, which is where I've just come from.'

'You can't do this. Someone will come looking for me. No one's going to believe that I'd just up and leave without . . .' I tail off. I upped and left London without any fanfare. Only a handful of people knew and those I didn't tell found out on Facebook. Alice might be a bit put out that I didn't ring and tell her I was going travelling but it could be ages until she starts to worry. And she might not worry at all if Mike posts regular updates from my phone. I could be dead within three days and no one would know.

Mike steps away from the door, crosses his arms over his chest and looks me up and down. 'Right, well I think that's it. Don't you worry about Chloe, I'll talk my way back into her good books and then we'll go on a lovely trip together. Now, is there anything I'm forgetting? Oh yes. Where's my fucking van?'

'If I tell you will you let me out?'

'What do you think?' He walks to the door, pauses and looks back. 'When I come back you're going to tell me where the van is. If you don't I'll get the hose out. And I'll stick it down your fucking throat.'

316

I wait for the door to close, then I scrabble to the front of the cage, praying that, somehow, he kicked the key within reaching distance. It takes me a while to spot it. It's almost completely covered in straw. And it's next to the back wall. Even if my belt was double the length I still wouldn't be able to reach it.

Chapter 40

Wendy

Wendy Harrison used to have a lot of respect for the police, back before Mike was arrested, then there was all that nonsense around her own arrest. Now she finds them to be small-minded busybodies who assume everyone they arrest are absolute thickies. Take DS Hope for instance. Before she turned on the tape recorder she was all smiles and chat and 'would you like some water?' Now she's stony-faced and reading from a long list of questions on the clipboard in her hands. What was the buttering up for? To make Wendy think she'd made a new friend? To prise a confession out of her? Wendy has nothing to confess because she wasn't doing anything wrong. Unless taking a stroll has suddenly become illegal? Something she's asked every police officer, including the custody sergeant, since she was brought in.

She was interviewed at length by DS Hope last night

(she replied 'no comment' to every question) and was then told she would be held overnight pending further questioning. And now it's begun again.

'When was the last time you saw your ex-husband Michael Hughes?'

'No comment.'

'Why were you walking down his street last night?'

'No comment.'

'It was a cold evening. Why weren't you wearing a coat?'

'No comment.'

She's aware that answering *no comment* makes her look guilty. She's seen enough episodes of *24 Hours in Police Custody* to know that it's a popular tactic with criminals and liars but, quite frankly, she hasn't got the time or the patience to answer the younger woman's ridiculous list of questions. She knows what she's trying to do – pin Mike's disappearance on her – but she's not going to find any evidence to support that and, without any evidence, she'll have to release her without charge.

There was a brief moment, yesterday evening, when she considered telling the younger woman that there was no point questioning her about the disappearance of her ex-husband because she knew exactly where he was. She swiftly dismissed the thought. If the police released Mike from his cage she would instantly lose out on her forty thousand pounds. Of course, she still had Mike's phone hidden away in her jacket pocket beneath the driver's seat of her Ford Mondeo (assuming the police had bought her story that she'd gone to his house on foot and hadn't found the car) but there was no guarantee he'd give her the money for the phone's safe return if he wasn't behind bars. In fact, she was fairly certain that he wouldn't. She'd have to blackmail him to stand any chance of getting her money and, given Mike's temper, that would be a very risky move indeed.

'Did you break into Michael Hughes's house?'

'Michael Hughes'.'

'I'm sorry?'

'Michael Hughes' house. Not Hughes's. Your grammar is incorrect.'

The police officer's lips thinned. 'Did you break into his house?'

'No comment.'

'Did you throw a pair of bolt cutters and a key under his hedge on your way out?'

'No comment.'

'If you didn't break into his house why were you running down the street?'

'No comment.'

'Do you know where Michael Hughes is?'

'No comment.'

'You don't like your ex-husband, do you?'

'No comment.'

On and on it goes. At one point Wendy sits back in her chair and sighs.

'I'm sorry,' DS Hope says. 'Am I boring you?'

Wendy glances at her solicitor, a lovely lady called Carole Dickinson, and smiles. 'No comment.'

* * *

320

Wendy glances over her shoulder, just to check that no one is following her, then hastens her pace as she hurries down the street. Ten minutes ago, the duty sergeant handed her her things, told her that she had been charged with breaking the terms of her restraining order and was being released on bail pending further investigations. He handed her a card with the date that she should return to the police station, asked her to sign something on a computer tablet and then said goodbye. Wendy thanked him, straight-faced and serious, but inside she was smirking. She hadn't expected to be charged with her ex-husband's disappearance but she had been the tiniest bit concerned that she might get attempted burglary. She'd worn gloves, there wouldn't be any prints on the bolt cutters, or the front door key, and she'd ensured she'd locked all the doors as she'd left, but she was fairly certain the next-door neighbour had seen her lurking about. Why else would the police have turned up?

Still, no time to worry about that now. There's the small matter of her ex-husband being kidnapped by Louise Wandsworth to deal with. And she's going to have to drive to B&Q to buy some bolt cutters. That's assuming she isn't followed to her car.

Nearly thirty pounds for bolt cutters! Wendy tucks the receipt back into the plastic bag, then reaches below the passenger seat for the coat. When she left the police station and returned to her car, everything was still inside, exactly where she'd left it. DS Hope had asked her why she was in the area and how she'd got to Mike's house, but she obviously hadn't sent a PC to see where Wendy's car was. She'd have found Mike's phone in her coat pocket if she had. And the knife. How very remiss of her.

Wendy takes Mike's phone out of her pocket, then presses the on button. The mobile flashes to life but the screen is locked. Wendy nibbles on her bottom lip. So tempting. So incredibly tempting. She laughs lightly. Oh who is she kidding? Of *course* she's going to have a look. She taps the screen and guesses the four-digit code.

1234.

Despite being OCD, Mike is also incredibly lazy. She can imagine him going for a number that he wouldn't have to try hard to remember. The display wavers from side to side. Incorrect.

0000.

Incorrect.

9999.

Incorrect.

4321.

Incorrect. Wendy gazes out of the window of the car and makes a soft grunting sound. What else would he use. His date of birth perhaps?

0808.

Sixteen colourful icons flash up on the screen making Wendy squeal with excitement. She's in!

Her heart flutters in her chest as she taps the messages icon and Mike's text conversations load. Strange. There's only one message thread and, instead of a name titling it, there's just a telephone number.

She taps to open it and reads the last the message sent.

I can't wait to spend the night with you either but please don't call it sex. That's intimacy without emotion. I prefer the term making love and I'll show you how much I love you with every kiss and every lingering touch. You are my life, my everything. Never forget that. X

Wendy wrinkles her nose in disgust. What is this? She'd prepared herself for a barrage of angry messages between Lou and Mike not this . . . this . . . revolting soft porn. She scrolls up and reads the previous message.

I love u Mike and can't wait to show u how much. I'm not ready to have sex yet but I do want it to be with u. xxx

Confused, Wendy reads more of the messages but they're all the same. Mike and Lou confessing their love for each other, calling each other pet names and discussing illicit rendezvous. She scrolls up and up and up the seemingly never-ending stream of messages, then gasps as a picture message appears on the screen. It's a dick. A very excited dick. And she's pretty certain it's Mike's. She almost laughs at Lou's response:

Wow. That's huge.

Huge? Mike might be a tall man, but she'd always found his penis to be disappointingly small. Not that she'd ever told him that of course. She flicks further up the messages.

Her jaw drops as she reaches a photo of a pair of naked breasts and the message attached to it.

I took this in the girls loo. Please delete it after uv seen it. I wd die of embarrassment if anyone else ever saw it.

The message above the photo is from Mike and it says: *Please send me a photo of your breasts. It would make me so happy. You'd do it if you loved me.*

With her heart in her mouth, Wendy scrolls up again. All of the messages are from Mike, cajoling and begging:

Please let me see your body.

I love your body

I want to worship you.

Don't tease me. SHOW me.

There are replies to each one:

I can't.

I'm too embarrassed.

Someone might see.

And then there it is. The photo that makes Wendy retch, yank open the driver side door and puke onto the car park. A photo of a schoolgirl, her tie pulled to one side, her white shirt unbuttoned to reveal her bra and her breasts pushed together to reveal a generous cleavage. It's been a long time since she last saw the girl but she recognises her instantly.

It's little Chloe Meadows.

Chapter 41

Wendy

After vomiting in B&Q's car park, Wendy begins to shake so violently she fears she's about to suffer a stroke. When she finally calms down she reads the entire thread of messages. They started innocuously, with a message from Mike,

Your dad gave me your number because he can't give you a lift to Greensleeves after school. What time do I need to pick you up?

And a tentative reply from Chloe,

3.30 ok? You can't park directly outside school. Most parents park a couple of streets away.

And progress to,

Are you ok? You looked a bit upset earlier.

To which Chloe replies,

Not really, but thanks for asking.

Weeks pass without another message, then there's a text from Chloe saying, *Sorry I cried on you earlier.*

After that they pick up pace. Mike takes control, reassuring Chloe that, despite being friends with her dad anything she says to him will remain confidential. It won't go any further, he promises her.

I don't like seeing you so sad. I want to help if I can. X

It's the first message to end with a kiss. Chloe doesn't immediately reciprocate. Dozens of text messages pass between the two of them before she closes her message in the same way.

Thank you for our chat today. I feel like you really understand me. x

We're a lot more similar than you think, Chloe, Mike replies. *I know I probably look like an old man to you but I don't feel one. In many ways I feel like I'm the same age as you. X*

Chloe replies immediately. *I don't think you look like an old man. X*

A middle-aged man? ;) x

Is David Beckham middle-aged? I think you look a bit like him. X

Do teenagers find David Beckham attractive? I thought they preferred his son Brooklyn? X

I don't. x

The tone changes then. Not immediately but over the next dozen or so text messages Mike drops the supportive friend act and ups the flirtation. Wendy has to stop reading several times and open the car door because she feels so sick. And that's before she gets to the picture messages again.

* * *

She can still smell vomit, clinging to her hair and skin, as she drives up the track to Louise Wandsworth's house but, for once, she doesn't care about her appearance. As she pulls into the driveway, she scans her surroundings for signs that Lou has returned but there's no little red Mini parked up outside the garage and no lights on in the house.

'Good,' she thinks as she parks up, opens the door and, clutching the phone and bolt cutters, steps onto the gravel. Dealing with Louise is a complication she doesn't need right now. She needs to talk to Mike alone.

She marches down the garden and opens the gate. Anger burns in her belly as she strides across the yard. Anger aimed at Michael but at herself too. He's a paedophile – always has been. How could she not have realised when she first met him? How could she have been so naïve and trusting that she married him? She'd always prided herself on her judgement and Mike seemed so nice, so normal. Their sex life had been normal too. She'd slept with three men before she met him, so it wasn't like she didn't have anyone to compare him to. If anything he was the most vanilla of her lovers. He wasn't into sex in public places or light bondage and he'd never asked her to shave down below or dress up in school uniform. Had he fantasised about younger women when they'd made love? Is that why he favoured doggy style, so he didn't have to look at her lightly lined face?

Wendy's stomach clenches violently and she retches, several metres away from the barn. Nothing comes up but she continues to dry heave for several seconds before she straightens up again.

He was so convincing, after his arrest, pleading with her to believe him. Swearing that he'd never laid a finger on the young woman who was accusing him of such terrible things. It wasn't a stretch of the imagination to believe that he'd gone to France to keep her safe, because everyone knew that Michael Hughes was a good man. He gave free, private karate coaching to a young lad with special needs. He mowed the lawn for old Mrs Anderson at the bottom of the road. He'd nursed his mother through the final, terrible stages of dementia and then pushed himself to the absolute limit to run an ultramarathon to raise money for an Alzheimer's charity. It wasn't that Wendy needed to believe him, she did believe him. She knew there were girls at the club who'd developed crushes on him – he'd told her all about them. She also knew how vindictive teenaged girls could be. When she was fourteen she'd plunged the sharp point of a badge into another girl's airbed at Guide camp to pay her back for a bitchy comment. At fifteen she'd started a rumour at school about another girl having a sexually transmitted disease after she slept with the boy Wendy liked.

Louise Wandsworth was an unstable, neurotic girl who'd created a fantasy world to try and escape from her unhappy home life. Her father was an alcoholic, her mother was a stuck-up city girl and neither gave her enough attention. She'd latched onto Mike because he was the only adult to show her any kindness. She tricked Mike into travelling to France with her, then threw herself at him. When he'd refused to sleep with her, insisting they should return to the UK, she'd cried rape.

Only she hadn't, had she? That was all a lie, invented by Mike to keep Wendy by his side while he went to court, to ensure he received his commissary every month, and he had a home to return to at the end of his jail sentence. How many more young women had there been since their divorce? He was a monster, a vile, perverted predatory monster luring young women into his arms and his bed. She shouldn't have stabbed him in the leg with the knife. She should have aimed straight for his heart.

She yanks open the door to the barn and storms in, a barrage of accusations and insults primed in her brain, ready for launch.

She stops dead after a single step.

Her brain scrambles to make sense of what she's seeing. The cage still holds a prisoner but, where she expected to see the large, broad-shoulder shape of her ex-husband, there's a decidedly thinner figure with long, slender limbs and mousey brown hair. In the split second it takes her brain to name her, Lou, lying on her stomach with one arm reaching through the gap in the bars, turns to look at her.

'Wendy?'

Lou darts away from the bars, scoots into the centre of the cage on her bottom and gathers her long limbs together, making herself as small and compact as possible. She reminds Wendy of a monkey, with her big fearful eyes and her tightly wrapped arms. She knows who she is. It's written all over her face. If she still believed that Wendy was a potential client who just happened to have driven to her house and stumbled into her barn she'd have reacted with shock, then relief.

'Wendy?' Lou says again.

Wendy stares at her and says nothing, then, as sudden and unexpected as a hiccup, she laughs. She'd braced herself for several different scenarios before stepping through the barn door. Mike morphing into a woman was not one of them.

'Where is he?'

'I don't know.' Lou scrabbles to her feet and points through the door of the cage. 'But the key's over there, by the wall. Please. Quickly. Before he comes back.'

Wendy follows the angle of Lou's outstretched index finger, crosses the barn, dips down and brushes the straw away from the wall. It doesn't take her long to discover the key.

'Quickly!' Lou opens her hand, reaching for it, then glances towards the barn door. Her eyes are wide and fearful. 'Quickly!'

Wendy takes a step towards the cage, then pauses. She opens her hand and looks at the key. She should open the door and let Lou out. That's what any normal person would do in this situation, so why is she feeling so conflicted? She looks from the key to Lou with her desperate, pleading face. Louise Wandsworth is as much Mike's victim as Chloe

Meadows, so why does she still feel a stab of anger when she looks at her?

'I'm not a robot,' Wendy says, more to herself than Lou. 'I can't just turn off my feelings.'

Nor should she ignore them. She's made a lot of rash, snap decisions recently and there's something inside her, niggling away in her gut, telling her not to let Lou out of the cage unless she's absolutely sure it's the right decision.

'Please.' Lou presses herself up against the bars of the cage and extends her fingers. 'Wendy, you need to let me out.'

'No,' she pulls back her shoulders and straightens her spine, pulling herself up to her full five foot six. 'I don't. I don't have to do anything.'

'Wendy, please. Mike's dangerous. He tried to strangle me.'

'Did he lock himself in the cage?'

'What?'

'I'm just trying to work out which of you is the most dangerous. He was in that cage before,' Wendy nods at it, 'and I'm pretty certain he didn't lock himself in.'

'I . . . I did. I locked him in. I didn't mean to, it was an accident. He tried to attack me and I defended myself. Please . . . Wendy . . . we haven't got much time. You need to let me out.'

'Again with the orders.'

'I'm not ordering you, Wendy. I'm begging you. Please.'

Wendy presses her fists against her face – one

331

hand still clutching the bolt cutters and the mobile phone, the other holding the key – and closes her eyes. She needs to blot out Lou's pleading face and think clearly but it's all so overwhelming. There's a part of her – a big part – that still blames this woman for ruining her life. If Mike had never met Louise Wandsworth, Wendy could be a mother now. He would have turned up at the clinic and given his sample and Wendy would have started her IVF. If it had worked – and she knows it would – her eldest would be doing his or her A-levels now. There might even be a second child, a year younger, desperately trying not to be eclipsed by their elder sibling's shadow. But there aren't any children. They're a figment of Wendy's imagination and they always will be. Meanwhile Louise Wandsworth has a loving boyfriend, enough time left to have children and a huge house to bring them up in. Less than an hour ago the imbalance in their lives was going to be corrected. Wendy was going to hand over the bolt cutters and phone to Mike and, in return, she would receive forty thousand pounds and Louise Wandsworth would be arrested for false imprisonment and blackmail. Their lives would be reversed – Wendy would have the nice house and Lou would have nothing. And Mike . . .

Wendy screws up her face as an image of Chloe Meadows with her big, worried eyes, her awkwardly unbuttoned shirt and the deep line of her cleavage flashes up in her mind.

Mike is the bad person here, says a little voice in

her head. *Lou hasn't done anything wrong. You have to let her go.*

'Wendy,' Lou's soft voice cuts through the noise in her head. 'Wendy, please listen to me. I know . . . at least I think I know how you feel about me. I ran off with your husband. I ruined your marriage. I sent him to jail. I'll be honest, when it was all happening I didn't give you a second thought . . .'

Wendy flinches. She wants Lou to stop. She wants to scream at her to STOP TALKING but she can't. Her throat is so tight, she can't speak.

'You were never a real person to me,' Lou continues. 'You were the bad guy, the annoying obstacle preventing me and Mike from being together. I thought he was my soulmate and I was his. I thought it was true love and that we were meant to be. I didn't give you a second thought when Mike said he wanted to take me to France for the weekend. I was so excited, I thought we were going on a romantic getaway. But that wasn't what he had planned, Wendy. He tried to abduct me. He told me we were never going back to England and we were going to live the rest of our lives in France, then when I tried to escape, he tied me to the bed and gagged me. He nearly killed the man that tried to help me.'

Wendy shakes her head. 'No, no it's not true.'

'It's true. It's all true. I've never told anyone any of this before because I was too scared. That's why I didn't testify against him. Not because I loved him but because I was afraid of him. I've spent the last eighteen years terrified that he'd come after me after he got out of jail. I didn't go to university for *months* after he was released because I was so scared I'd turn round on the tube and see him standing behind me, or come out of a lecture to find him waiting by the door. I missed so many lectures I failed my exams and had to retake my second year. He never loved me, Wendy. He groomed me so he could control and dominate me. He strangled me during sex because he got a kick out of seeing me pass out.'

'No, no.'

'He's doing it again, Wendy. He's been grooming a little girl called Chloe. I tried to warn her. I gave her my diary so she could see for herself what a dangerous man he is but she's too deeply under his spell to believe me. He's going to abduct her and do to her what he did to me, or worse. We can't let that happen. Please, Wendy. I know how hurt and angry you are. I can see it in your face. And I'm sorry, I'm so, so sorry that Mike fucked up your life as much as he fucked up mine but it's not my fault. I was fourteen years old. I was as much of a victim as you. If you're looking for someone to hate, hate Mike. He's a paedophile. He abuses young children and he's doing it again. Please, I know you hate me but you have to open this door and let me go to the police.'

Lou stops speaking and the barn falls silent. Beyond its walls a wood pigeon softly coos and thunder rumbles in the distance. Wendy doesn't move. She can't. The slightest motion and her legs will collapse from under her and she'll fall to the floor. She feels like a statue, shattered by Lou's words, and the only thing stopping her from falling apart is the glue of snot and tears that fills her clenched hands. The last couple of minutes were the most painful of her life but she has her answers now. It's over, eighteen years of waiting, wondering and torturing herself. She never has to do that again.

She raises her eyes to meet Lou's. Forty thousand pounds is a lot to say goodbye to, but some things are more important than money. A *lot* more important.

'Okay,' she says. 'Okay.'

Chapter 42

Chloe

Chloe touches the scalpel to the paper. She cuts through the top edge then, slowly and carefully, drags the blade down its length. There's something so satisfying about the ccccch sound the scalpel makes as it slices through the A4 sheet. It helps her blot out the sound of Mike's voice, and the look on his face when she slapped him. Surprise. Disappointment. And then anger. He'd scared her when he'd lunged for her. She didn't recognise him. When her dad burst into the small hallway with his fags and beer in a plastic bag, she almost cried with relief. She didn't. She ran straight up the stairs and didn't look back. Her dad's laughter followed all the way to her room. She could hear Mike and her dad talking and laughing until about three o'clock in the morning. When she crept downstairs after they finally went quiet they were both passed out on the sofas. Her dad was still asleep but Mike was gone when she and Jamie slipped out of the door in the morning, dressed and ready for school.

Cccccch. Cccccch.Cccccch. She runs the scalpel over the page again and again.

'Chlo,' Kirsteen nudges her elbow. 'What are you doing? You're supposed to cut out your design, not slice through it.'

Chloe ignores her best friend and carves out another long strip. It's Design and Technology, her favourite class, but she didn't feel a rush of pleasure as she walked into the classroom ten minutes earlier. She didn't feel anything at all.

'Have I done something wrong?' Kirsteen asks.

Chloe shakes her head.

'Then why have you stopped talking to me?'

'Because my dad took my phone.'

'I'm not talking about Snapchat. I mean now. You've been really quiet today. Are you sure I haven't done something wrong?'

Chloe shakes her head again. Normally she'd be quick to reassure her friend that of course she hadn't done anything wrong and she'd apologise for acting weirdly. Normally. Normal. What even is that?

'Chloe?'

She jumps at the weight of a hand on her shoulder and spins round, scalpel raised.

'Woah!' Mr Harris, her Design and Technology teacher, jumps back, both hands raised. 'Careful!'

'Sorry, Sir.' Chloe puts the blade on the desk and forces a smile.

'So you should be. You could have had my eye out.

337

Or worse. I just wanted to see how you were getting on.' He steps forward and peers over her shoulder. 'Bad day?' he asks, nodding at the pile of thin strips of paper in front of her.

'I made a mistake.'

He smiles kindly. 'Bit of a drastic solution isn't it, destroying the whole thing instead of trying to fix it?'

'No.' She looks him in the eye. 'No, I don't think it is.'

Mr Harris presses his lips into a thin line and raises his eyebrows. 'It's your work,' he says as he moves away and peers at Kirsteen's neatly cut out prototype.

'Yeah,' Chloe says under her breath as she reaches for her scalpel and slides it off the desk and into her school bag. 'And it's my life too.'

When the bell rings Chloe is the only student to turn right rather than left as they file out of the D&T studio.

'Chlo?' Kirsteen tugs on her arm and gestures in the other direction. 'We've got biology now.'

'So?'

'Aren't you coming?'

'No.'

'Where are you going then?'

'I don't know.'

'Why are you being so weird? You're really starting to piss me off.'

'You and the rest of the world.' She yanks her arm free and starts to run towards the emergency fire exit.

Kirsteen doesn't run after her. No surprise there.

* * *

338

Chloe takes off her blazer and lays it down on the ground. It's cold, tucked away in the bushes, away from the warmth of the May sun, and she pulls the sleeves of her jumper down over her hands as she lies down.

For several minutes she does nothing apart from stare up into the leaves. There's nothing much to look at apart from an abandoned spider's web and a greeny-black beetle that marches along a branch like it's on a mission. When it disappears from view, Chloe sits up. She opens her school bag and takes out the scalpel and her mobile phone, stolen from her dad's sock drawer while he slept.

It's nearly time.

Chapter 43

Lou

I take a step away from the door, keeping a wary eye on the heavy bolt cutters in Wendy's right hand as she approaches the cage. Her face is pale and puffy, her nose red and swollen and her eye make-up is a black stain around her bloodshot eyes. She's a mess now but she came back to the barn to let Mike out. That's why she brought the bolt cutters. But how did she know he was here in the first place? Did she come to the farm looking for him, or for me? I don't know if Mike was lying when he said Wendy stabbed him in the leg but I need to be careful.

Wendy unhooks the padlock, lifts it from the door and takes a step backwards. I can't read her eyes. I've got no idea if she's angry, fearful or upset. But she doesn't look away when I meet her gaze. She looks at me steadily, watching, waiting for me to do something, and she's still gripping the bolt cutters. If she attacks me when I walk out of the cage, I don't know if I'll be able to fight her off. I might be twenty odd years younger than she is and I'm a lot lighter, but I haven't got a weapon. And one of my arms is broken.

'I'm going to come out now, Wendy.' I raise my good arm as though in surrender and wait for her to respond. When she doesn't, I take a step forward.

Wendy tightens her grip on the bolt cutters.

'We're on the same side.' I push at the door and step out of the cage. Now there's nothing but two or three metres of air separating us. 'I need to go to the police. I should have gone a long time ago.'

Wendy doesn't reply. She's still staring at me with that same strange, intense expression on her face. She reminds me of the fox I found in the porch – backed into a corner, unsure whether to attack or run.

'I'm going to leave the barn now, Wendy.'

I breathe shallowly as I walk towards the barn door, my shoulders tense, my good hand twitching at my side. My body feels like it's on red alert, waiting for the sound of Wendy's shoes skirting over the straw, the touch of her hand on my shoulder and a blow on the back of the head. I can already feel the weight of the bolt cutters smashing into my skull, my knees giving way beneath me and the rough sensation of the barn floor under my palms and it's all I can do not to duck and run with my fingers cradling the back of my head.

I keep walking. No sudden movements. No loud

sounds. As soon I'm out in the yard, I'll run for my car.

I touch a hand to the barn door and pause. What if Mike's waiting for me outside? What if he sent Wendy in to set me free so he could—

'Louise?'

I freeze at the sound of Wendy's voice.

'Before you go to the police there's something you need to see.'

I scroll quickly through the texts, skimming rather than reading. Wendy watches my face, waiting for a reaction. She doesn't get one until I reach the photos.

'Where did you get this?' I click out of the messages and hand the phone back to her.

'Mike's house. Under a floorboard.'

That's why the police couldn't find any evidence of grooming when I reported him for kissing Chloe – as I thought, he keeps it hidden when he's not at home – and they must have missed it when they searched his house. It makes me feel sick, the idea of him poring over a young girl's messages with the curtains closed, hidden away from the world.

'He told me to get it,' Wendy says, misreading my shock. There's a defensive note to her voice that suggests it wouldn't be entirely out of character for her to creep around Mike's house uninvited. 'He said you'd been blackmailing him and there were texts on there that he needed to take to the police.'

'Weren't you suspicious? Who hides their phone under a floorboard?'

'Of course I was. Why do you think I checked it? I'm not stupid.'

I raise an eyebrow. Wendy's moods are so mercurial it's hard to predict how she'll react from one moment to the next. 'I know you're not stupid, Wendy.'

'So what happens now?'

'I take the phone to the police and tell them everything.' I correct myself as she raises her eyebrows, 'Almost everything. I'll say he had the phone in his jacket or something. He needs to spend the rest of his life in jail, Wendy. I won't let him do this to another girl. I can't.'

'Fuck.' I pause as I reach the barn door. 'Mike's taken my car.'

'So we go in mine.' She smiles tightly. 'Don't worry. I'm not going to kidnap you, Louise. I think you've got that particular life skill covered, don't you?'

Neither of us says very much as we drive from my house to Malvern. Wendy seems lost in thought but there are a hundred questions I'd like to ask her.

'Wendy—'

I'm interrupted by the sound of a mobile phone bleeping.

'Sorry.' She slips her hand into the plastic pocket in the driver side door and pulls out her phone. She frowns as she glances at the screen. 'That wasn't mine.'

We share a look.

'It was Mike's,' she says. 'It's in the glove compartment. The code's 0808.'

343

I unclip the glove compartment, take out the phone and key in the code. The messages icon is showing one new message.

'Wendy,' I say. 'You need to pull over. Now.'

The photo is of Chloe Meadows. She's in her school uniform with the sleeves of her white shirt rolled up to the elbow. She's sitting cross-legged on the ground, surrounded by leafy green undergrowth. The photograph has been taken from above and she's angling her chin to one side, staring sulkily into the lens. It could totally be a normal selfie except for two things – the word 'Goodbye' overlaid on the image and the scalpel she's holding in her left hand with the blade pressing into her wrist.

'Oh my god.' Wendy covers her mouth and nose with her steepled hands and stares at me over the tips of her fingers. 'What do we do?'

'Ring the police. Give me your phone.'

She reaches into the door, then shakes her head. 'No, we need to text her. Tell her not to do anything. Use Mike's phone. She'll listen to us if she thinks we're him.'

'This is my fault.' I look in desperation at Wendy. 'When Mike came back to the barn, he said I'd turned Chloe against him. They must have had an argument about what I wrote in my diary, that's why she's threatening to kill herself. Or maybe it's something she read.'

'You don't know that. Just text her,' Wendy prods the phone in my hands. 'Send her a message. Tell her

344

not to do anything stupid because you're on your way.'

'I can't.'

'I'll do it then.' She reaches for the phone.

'No, you don't understand. Mike's got two phones. Chloe texts them both. If we reply *and* Mike replies, she'll know something's up. She'll ask him why he's texting from both phones and he'll realise we've got the other one. He might run.'

'So we go with your plan and tell the police.'

'But if Chloe has texted Mike's other phone he might already be on his way to meet her. By the time we get to the police station he could already have . . .' My neck spasms as I turn my head to look out of the window.

'What?' Wendy says as I press a hand to my throat. There are four tender spots on the left of my neck and one on the right, bruises left by Mike's fingers. 'He could what?'

I love you, Lou. You know I'd never hurt you, don't you? Promise me you'll never leave me, no matter what.

'Louise.'

Your love keeps me sane, Lou. It makes me feel human. I don't know what I'd do without you.

'Louise?'

If you ever left me I wouldn't be responsible for my actions.

'LOUISE!' Wendy taps me on the shoulder, making me jump. She waves the phone at me. I didn't even notice her take it.

'What is it?'

'We don't have to go to the police. I know where she is.' She drops the phone in my lap. 'See that bush, behind Chloe in the photo? It's a *Viburnum arboricola*. It's not native to the UK. It's from Taiwan. The head gardener goes abroad each summer to gather unusual plants. He tells me about them whenever I run into him. Chloe's in Priory Park.'

Chapter 44

Lou

'This way, quickly!' Wendy leads the way, running past the bandstand, over the bridge and along the pathway that loops around the pond. We sprint over a wide patch of grass, past a huge oak tree and through a gap between the hedges. Each step makes my broken arm bounce in its sling and I have to hold it against my body with my other arm to dull the pain.

'Chloe!' I shout, as we run over another patch of grass. I'm scanning the bushes for the one in the photo but they all look the same. She could be anywhere.

'Chloe!' Another shout carries across the park. It's faint but I recognise the voice instantly.

'Shit.' I look at Wendy. 'It's Mike. Chloe texted his other phone and he's looking for her too.'

We speed up, weaving between willow trees and zig-zagging around dozens of small paths. I follow Wendy through a gap between two hedges, then almost plough into her as she stops abruptly. We're standing on the edge of a small square of grass, surrounded on all sides by trees and bushes and hidden from the rest of the park.

Standing in the middle of the clearing with his hands cupped around his mouth is Mike. The shocked expression on his face when Wendy and I burst out of the bushes gives way to a slow smile.

Wendy, standing beside me, makes a sound that's half scream, half sob.

'You bastard. You contemptible, lying, dirty bastard.' She lunges at him.

'Don't.' I grab her by the wrist and yank her back. 'Don't rise to it. It's what he wants.' I lower my voice. 'We can deal with him later. We need to find Chloe first.'

'That's right,' Mike says, nodding at me and raising a hand as though in thanks. 'You hold that psycho back. Where's your knife, Dee? Come to stab me in the other leg have you?'

'I hate you!' Wendy tries to pull away from me, but I've got hold of the back of her coat, as well as her wrist. 'I hate you. I fucking hate you.'

'Oooh, would you listen to the mouth on that. Vile language. Filthy. You see that, Lou? You see what I had to put up with for all those years?'

I scan the clearing for any sign of Chloe. The bushes are so thick she could be anywhere. But if she can't see us she can definitely hear us.

'Is it any wonder,' Mike says, 'that I ran off to France rather than live here with *that*?'

'You're the worst kind of monster,' Wendy screams.

She snatches at my fingers with her free hand, yanks her arm free and slips out of her coat. 'You abuse children. How could you—'

She flies at Mike, arms whirling, landing punches on his face, his neck and his chest.

'Wendy, no!' I start towards them but, before I'm close enough to pull her away, Mike grabs her by the throat and pulls back his right arm. There's a terrible crunching sound as his fist smashes against her jaw, and Wendy's head snaps backwards. The second Mike lets go of her she drops like a stone, her limp body crumpling onto the grass.

'Wendy!' I drop to my knees beside her and touch the side of her neck. Her lips are parted and she's breathing but her closed eyelids don't so much as flicker. I crawl away, reaching for her dropped jacket. She put both phones in the right pocket before we got out of the car.

'Oh no you don't.' Mike weaves his fingers into my hair and yanks me upwards. I howl with pain and grab at his hand, but he's too quick and strong and he twists my good arm behind my back.

'Is my phone in there?'

'No.'

'Liar!' He yanks on my broken arm, making me groan with pain. 'I know she's got it. Now, nice and carefully, get the phone and give it to me.' He lets go of my wrist and dips me back down towards the coat, still holding me by the hair.

I reach out a hand and pluck at the zip on one of Wendy's pockets.

'Just the phone.' He tugs on my hair, jerking my head back sharply. 'Don't even think about calling the police.'

'Got it?' he says as I slide two phones out of Wendy's pocket and grasp the one that's not in a butterfly blue case.

'Yes.'

'Okay, now up we come.' He pulls me back onto my feet. 'The passcode is 0808. Unlock it but *don't* do anything after that.' He gives a warning tug on my hair. 'Now,' he says after I enter the code, 'go to the messages, hold your thumb down on the thread and select delete all.'

I hesitate. If I do that all the evidence that he's been grooming Chloe will disappear. She could be lying in the bushes right now, bleeding to death. If Mike finds her and takes her phone no one will ever know that he was responsible, but if I threw the phone into the bushes he'd—

'Hello Mike.'

Chloe steps out of the bushes. As she moves towards us, Mike lets go of my hair and grips the bicep of my broken arm. At the same time he grabs my right wrist. The phone slips from my fingers as he twists my arm behind my back. There's a faint *thunck* as it drops onto the grass.

'What's she doing here?' Chloe stops about three metres away from us. Her face is pale, there are dark circles under her eyes and her hair is wild and unkempt as though she just got out of bed. But it's not her face I stare at. It's the silver scalpel blade pressed into the thin skin of her left wrist. 'Who's that?' She looks dispassionately at Wendy, still unconscious on the ground.

'My ex-wife,' Mike says. 'She's not very well.'

Chloe swivels her strange, glassy eyes in my direction. 'Why are you doing this?'

'I'm not doing—' I gasp as Mike digs his fingers into my damaged arm.

'If you say another word,' he hisses in my ear, 'I'll whip the scalpel out of Chloe's hand and slit her throat with it. Do we understand each other?'

I nod.

'What was that?' Mike asks, his stubbly cheek pressed against mine, his warm breath in my ear.

'I understand.'

'Good girl. No one needs to make this any more complicated than it already is. All I want to do is take Chloe home to her dad, safe and sound, and then we can all forget this ever happened. You want that don't you, Lou? To forget all this ever happened.'

'Yes,' I breathe.

'What are you whispering to her?' Chloe takes a step closer, tears shining in her eyes. 'Are you telling her that you love her?'

I shake my head but she's not looking at me anymore, she's completely fixated on Mike.

'No, sweetheart,' he softens his voice. 'God, no. Chlo, how can you even ask that?'

'You loved her. You loved her more than anyone in the world. I read it, in her diary.' Her hand twitches and a tiny pool of blood appears on her wrist.

My chest tightens and my breath catches in my throat.

'You were lying, weren't you, Lou?' Mike presses on my bicep. 'You had a crush on me, didn't you? Made up stories in your diary? Fantasies.'

'Yes.' I glance round the clearing. I could risk it. I could scream for help. Mike would be startled enough to loosen his grip on me. I can probably still outrun him. But . . . I look back at Wendy, still unconscious on the grass and Chloe with her big, desperate eyes and the blood snaking around her wrist.

'You're the one who's lying,' she says and, for a second, I think she's talking to me. 'I googled you. You ran away to France with her. The article said you had sex.'

'Lies,' Mike says. 'She set me up because I wasn't interested in her. I went to prison because of what she did. I don't love her, Chloe. I hate her.'

She smiles, ever so slightly. 'Say that again.'

'I hate her.'

She looks at him for the longest time, her big, green eyes still and impassive, the blade still pressed to her wrist.

Mike shifts from one foot to the other.

'Let me take care of you,' he says softly. 'I know you're unhappy and I'm sorry I haven't been there for you like I promised, but it was Lou's fault, Chloe. I didn't want to tell you this last night in front of your dad, but the reason I went missing was because Lou locked me in a dog cage. She's a psychopath.

She's jealous of what we've got, me and you. She's obsessed. Always has been.'

Chloe doesn't so much as glance at me. Her attention is so focussed on Mike it's as though she's forgotten I'm even here.

'I love you, Chloe Meadows. You're my world, my special girl. I'd do anything for you.'

A smile flickers at the edge of her lips. 'Let go of her then.'

'What?'

'Let go of her. I can't stand the way you're snuggled up to her. You should be SNUGGLED UP TO ME!' Rage, or pain, shines in her eyes.

'Okay, okay.' Mike shoots me a warning look, then lets go of me. 'There you go, Chlo.' He pushes me roughly away and reaches an arm out to her. 'She means nothing to me. Come here, sweetheart. Come here, my love.'

'No.' Chloe swerves out of his reach. 'Not until you say it.'

'Say what?'

'Say you never loved her. Say you never fancied her. Say you never touched her. Say she's not special. Say that you hate her.'

'All those things.' Mike holds up his hands palms out. 'I never loved her, never fancied her, never touched her and she's not special.'

'You didn't say you hated her.'

'I hate her. I already told you that, Chloe.'

'I know. I just wanted to hear it again.' She walks up to me and stops less than a foot away. The scalpel isn't pressed up against her wrist anymore. She's holding it in her hand, pointed towards me and she's less than a foot away.

'Do you know what I hate?' she asks. 'That you got him first. That you kissed him first. And I really, really hate that he loved you first.'

'Chloe!' Mike darts towards her and gathers her into his arms. 'Stop!'

'I love you,' she says, pulling away so she can look up into his face.

'I love you too.'

She smiles and stands up on tiptoes, craning her neck for a kiss. All the tension in Mike's face seems to melt away. She's back under his control again – calm, subservient and willing. He smooths the hair away from her face, cradles the back of her head with his hand, then leans in and lowers his lips to hers. As their mouths meet, Chloe slides her left hand over his chest and onto his shoulder. She pulls him closer, so he's bent over, leaning his weight into her, then she whips up her right hand and plunges the scalpel in his neck. She stares up into his anguished face as he roars in pain, then she pulls out the blade and stabs him again.

'Liar,' she says as the blood spurts from his neck and coats her hand. 'You're a fucking liar.'

'Chloe, stop!' I scream. 'Stop! Stop!'

It's like a scene from a horror film playing on a loop. There's blood everywhere, on Chloe's hand, on Mike's hands, on his shirt, his jacket, his throat and his face. There's blood on his trousers, the grass and on me. He's gone quiet. The only sound is the wet squelch of the scalpel going in and out of his neck.

'Stop!' I kick out at Chloe's legs, smashing the heel of my foot against her left knee. Her leg crumples and she tips to the side, arms outstretched. As she falls, the scalpel flies from her hand and lands in the bushes.

There's a soft groan from behind me. Mike has dropped to his knees. He's clutching his neck and blood is pouring over his hands and dripping off his fingers. His face is ashen.

'Mike?' Chloe crawls towards him. 'Mike, I'm sorry. I'm so sorry.'

'No.' I try to pull her away from him but Wendy is calling my name. Her voice is weak but her eyes are open. She's trying to get up.

'Wendy?' I crouch beside her. 'Are you okay?'

'I can't see properly.' She touches a hand to her face. Her right eye and cheekbone are so swollen I can't see more than a tiny slit of eyeball and there are violent red scratches on her skin.

'We need to call an ambulance, and the police. Chloe just stabbed Mike.'

'I know. I saw.' Wendy winces as she props herself up on an elbow. As she cranes her head to look around me, her lips part in shock.

'What is it?' I twist round.

Six or seven feet away Chloe is sobbing and rocking back and forth, cradling Mike's head in her lap. His

355

eyes are open but he's not looking into her face, he's gazing, unseeing at the sky.

He's dead.

I thought I'd feel relieved, vindicated, free. Instead I feel nothing.

'Lou.' Wendy tugs at my sleeve. 'Louise!' She tugs harder. 'We need to get out of here, before the police turn up and arrest Chloe. Her life will be over. We can't let that happen.'

'I'll say it was me.'

'What?'

'I'll say I stabbed him. The police don't need to know that Chloe had anything to do with it, not if we get rid of both Mike's phones.'

'But she's covered in blood.'

'So we'll wrap your coat around her and smuggle her out of the park.'

'Her DNA will be all over him. Look at her. Her hair's all over his face.'

'So we try and get him out of here too. We drive him somewhere in your car and we burn his body or we . . .'

I tail off. It's a ridiculous idea. There's no way we can get a man of his size, covered in blood, out of here unnoticed, but there has to be an alternative to Chloe spending the rest of her life in jail. If that happens he'll have destroyed her life twice.

'The scalpel's in the bushes,' I say, getting to my feet. 'The police might not be able to pin this on Chloe if they can't find a murder weapon. I need to find it so we can—'

356

'Wait!' Wendy pulls on my sleeve. 'I've got a better idea.' She reaches for her jacket then looks up at me. 'Get me a leaf from that bush over there. The one with big leaves. But don't touch it with your fingers, pull your jumper over your hand.'

'What?'

'Just do it.'

I run to the bush, pluck off a leaf, making sure I don't touch it, then run back to her. Chloe has stopped crying and rocking. Mike is still slumped across her lap but she's not staring down into his lifeless face anymore. She's watching me.

'Right,' Wendy says, angling her body towards me. 'I want you to reach into my left coat pocket and pull out what's inside. Do it *carefully*, with the leaf. Do not touch it.'

I peer into the pocket, then look at Wendy. 'It's a knife.'

'Correct. It belongs to Michael.'

'Why's it in your pocket?'

'I took it when I went to his house. Anyway, what's important is that the only fingerprints on it are his.'

'C'mon, c'mon, c'mon,' she says as I slowly withdraw the sharp kitchen knife from the pocket, handle first.

A police siren sounds in the distance. Whatever Wendy's got planned, we need to be quick.

'Now what?'

'Give the knife to me, carefully. We don't want any fingerprints on it. Chloe!' She raises a hand and beckons the girl over. 'Come over here now.'

I expect Chloe to ignore Wendy, to refuse or to shout something abusive but she doesn't. Instead she pushes Mike off her lap and stands up, her shoulders slumped and her eyes on the ground. As she drifts towards us, Wendy looks back at me.

'Okay, you need to leave now.'

'What?'

'Go.'

I stare at her, aghast. There's no way I'm leaving. Chloe needs my help. They both do.

'Lou,' Wendy says. 'You need to get out of here. When the police turn up they'll arrest us all and seize our clothes, phones and cars. Then they'll search our houses. Your car has Mike's DNA all over it, your barn's covered in his piss and shit and god knows what, and you're covered in his blood. If this plan's going to stand a chance of working you can't be here.'

'Tell me the plan and let me decide.'

She talks rapidly – machine gun fast – leaving no gaps for me to interject then, as suddenly as she started, she stops. There's a second of silence as she takes a breath then she says, 'I know I've given you no reason to trust me, Louise. And I've got no reason to trust you, but if we don't do this right, Chloe is going to go to prison for a *very* long time.'

I stare at her in shock as I process everything she's just told me. 'Saskia Kennedy? The woman who told Ben I was dying. That was you?'

She shrugs awkwardly. 'Yes.'

I step backwards, hands raised. I don't know what's

going on. I don't know who she is anymore. 'But why would you—'

'Please.' Wendy steps towards me, hands outstretched. 'I know it sounds strange and it . . . well, it probably was . . . but I was never going to hurt you, I just wanted to—'

'You left the flowers too, didn't you? And the deepest sympathy note.'

'I thought it was funny.' She grimaces, apologetically. 'I've got a . . . slightly unusual sense of humour.'

I don't want to hear anymore. I want to get the hell away from her, and this park.

'No!' someone shouts as I turn to leave. Chloe walks towards me, blood-stained and shivering, her arms wrapped around her body.

'Please,' she begs. 'Please go through with her plan. I don't want to go to prison.'

I shake my head. 'I can't. I can't trust a thing Wendy says.'

'So we all go to prison?' Chloe says. 'None of us deserve that. Not me, not Wendy and definitely not you. I know what Mike did to you. I read your diary, remember?'

'You hate me.'

'No I don't.'

'But you said—'

'Lou,' Wendy touches my arm as a police siren rings through the park. It's getting closer. 'I know I've given you every reason not to trust me but this really is the only way we can get through this. If we don't, Mike wins, again.'

I glance at his lifeless body. I couldn't escape even if I wanted to. He's got my keys and mobile in his pocket.

'So take them back,' Wendy says as I point this out. She crosses the clearing, plucks Mike's phone from the grass and rubs it on her skirt. 'Fingerprints. We need to switch this with your stuff. Make sure you pull your jumper over your fingers before you make the swap.' She pauses. 'It's your decision, Lou. Are you going to do this or are you going to run?'

I'm nearly at the exit to the park when a blood-curdling scream makes all the hairs on my body stand up. Chloe's just been stabbed.

Chapter 45

DS Anna Hope

DS Hope sits back in her chair and crosses her arms over her chest. She looks from the girl, pale-faced and tear-stained – her shoulder heavily strapped – sitting across the desk from her, to her mother, tight-lipped and wringing her hands in her lap. It's not ideal, having the mother present. From the way the child keeps glancing at her, she can tell that she's anxious. Another appropriate adult would be better in order to get full disclosure, one the child isn't so closely connected to. Still, better the mother than the obnoxious arsehole of a father who turned up at the desk and screamed abuse at the duty sergeant.

'Okay.' She nods at DC Wilson, sitting beside her, then shoots what she hopes is a friendly, reassuring smile at Chloe Meadows. 'Why don't you tell me what happened, starting with your relationship with Michael Hughes.'

'Chloe,' says Simon Arnold, the solicitor sitting on

the other side of the girl, 'you don't have to answer that, or any other questions that DS Hope asks you. Remember the chat we had before.'

The girl looks from him to her mother.

DS Hope says a silent prayer. *Please be a talker.*

'It's okay,' Julie Meadows touches her daughter on the shoulder. 'Just tell the truth.'

'You'll hate me.'

'There's nothing you could say that could make me hate you. I love you. You're my little girl.'

'Dad'll kill me.'

'He won't do anything of the sort. I promise you. When this is all over, we're going to go and live with your Auntie Meg. Me, you and Jamie. If you want to.'

'Of course I want to. I didn't know where you'd gone, Mum. I didn't think I'd ever see you again.'

'Oh, Chloe. I was always going to come back to get you and Jamie. I just needed to get away for a bit, sweetheart. Your dad . . . he . . . I . . . I couldn't take it anymore. I'm so sorry I left you behind, Chloe. I'm so, so sorry.'

As Chloe bursts into tears, Julie shuffles her chair closer to her daughter's, then pulls her into her chest.

'Sorry,' she says to DS Hope as she strokes the girl's hair. 'Things at home have um . . . they've been difficult. Me and her dad are splitting up. I haven't been living with them for the last couple of days. It all got a bit much, so I went to stay with my sister.'

'Right. I see.' DS Hope pushes a box of tissues and a glass of water towards the girl, waits for her to calm down then says, 'Are we okay to continue, Chloe?'

The girl looks at her mother who smiles reassuringly.

'Yeah,' she says. 'I am.'

Simon Arnold sighs audibly but Anna ignores him.

'Okay then. So, talk me through your relationship with Michael Hughes. How you met him and how your relationship progressed.'

Anna Hope listens intently as Chloe explains how her relationship with Mike Hughes morphed from apathy ('He was a friend of my dad's. He seemed nice enough but he was . . . you know . . . *old*') to confidante ('He let me talk without judging me or calling me names') to 'boyfriend and girlfriend'. The girl's expression changes when she talks about her feelings for him. Her eyes swim with emotion and she looks impossibly young.

'It sounds like he meant a lot to you,' she says.

Chloe nods. 'He was my world. I loved him.'

'But something changed?'

Chloe runs a bitten fingernail back and forth along the desk.

'It's okay, love,' her mum says. 'You can tell her.'

Chloe's gaze remains fixed on the white Formica table that separates them. 'I thought he'd gone off me. He stopped replying to my texts. I thought it was because I'd got sacked from work and he was annoyed that he wouldn't be able to see me every day or because . . .' she presses her lips together and frowns, ' . . . because I wouldn't sleep with him.

When we went on holiday, me and my family, I . . . um . . . I was . . .' She brushes her hair forward with her hand, a flimsy barrier so her mother can't see her face. 'I was going to throw myself off the balcony. I just wanted to die.'

Julie Meadows presses a hand over her mouth and stares at Anna with startled, uncomprehending eyes, but she doesn't say a word.

'That must have been very hard,' Anna says softly, looking up at Chloe, 'feeling like that.'

Her heart goes out to the girl. How broken and lost must Chloe have felt to have considered suicide? When she was thirteen the worst thing to happen to her was her best friend dumping her to be friends with Jayne Ashton. She was miserable for weeks, but killing herself never even entered her mind.

'Yeah,' Chloe says. 'The only reason I didn't go through with it was because I fell off the table. Then I heard Dad on the phone saying Mike had gone missing.'

'Did you see Mike again? Before the incident in the park?'

'Yeah.' She nods. 'He came round the house. Mum wasn't there. She'd left the day before and Jamie was in his room. Dad said Mike had been on a "dirty weekend",' Chloe makes quotation marks with her fingers, 'with some woman, then he told me to make tea for them. Before I could make it Dad changed his mind and said he wanted beers instead. When he went out to get some fags I tried to go up to my room. Mike followed me into the hallway and he attacked me when I told him I didn't want to see him again.'

DS Hope's eyebrows flicker upwards. DC Wilson sits further forward in his seat.

'What exactly did he do? Where were you?'

'We were in the hallway. I was trying to go up to my room and he came after me. I told him that he was a liar, that I'd read Lou's diary. That's when he tried to grab me round the throat and Dad came back in.'

Anna glances down at her notes. Louise Wandsworth, the girl Michael Hughes groomed eighteen years earlier. She was the one who came in a couple of weeks earlier with an allegation that Michael Hughes was grooming Chloe. She'd given a different name, called herself Louise Smith. Anna puts a star by Louise's name. One of the team needs to make sure she comes in for a chat. The DCI's already got half a dozen of them trying to track down any other kids Mike might have come into contact with over the last eighteen years. Anna's not a betting woman, but she'd put money on the fact that there are more victims out there, too afraid to speak up. Sounds like the bastard had violent tendencies too. More reason for the kids to keep quiet.

'How did you get hold of Lou's diary?' she asks Chloe.

'She gave it to me. I was waiting for Dad to pick me up from school and she showed up.'

'Why did she give it you?'

'I don't know.' Chloe shrugs. 'She said she wanted me to realise the kind of man that Mike was. I thought she was a weirdo and I didn't want to read it. Not at first.'

'But you changed your mind?' DC Wilson asks.

'Yeah. I thought it might help me find him.'

'She gave you the diary when he was still missing.'

'Yeah.'

'When was that?' Anna asks. 'Can you remember?'

She notes down everything Chloe says. She didn't work on the Mike Hughes missing person case but she's spoken to PC Bray about it. His house-to-house enquiries didn't lead anywhere and, when Mike Hughes eventually did reappear, he didn't report to the station. He went straight to Alan Meadows' house by all accounts. Alan's version of events seems to match his daughter's. He said Mike had given him the impression that he'd gone off with some woman for a bit of fun. He did that a lot he said, disappeared off for the weekend without telling anyone where he was going, although he did say that when he turned up he smelt like shit – literally, like shit. They've tracked Mike's last movements – several delivery jobs in the Malvern and Worcestershire area that were confirmed by his receptionist Joy, his customers and his mobile phone records. Data from the phone company showed he received a phone call from a public phone box just outside Bromyard, then several text messages and a phone call from Chloe Meadows in the Acton Green/Acton Beauchamp area on Monday 30 April. Sightings of his van in the area confirm he was there. There was no further activity on his phone until he made a call to Chloe's house from Worcester city centre on Wednesday 2 May. After that, he completely disappeared off the grid. Wherever he was, he wasn't with Chloe Meadows, that's for sure. But his disappearance ties in with his murder, she'd put money on it.

'So you think that if your dad hadn't walked in when he did, Mike would have hurt you?'

Chloe nods. 'He went for me, after I slapped him. I thought he was going to strangle me.'

'Right. And you didn't think to tell anyone—'

'Tell who?' Chloe jolts forward, reaching across the table as she stares Anna in the eye. 'My seven-year-old brother? My psycho dad?'

Anna registers the way Julie seems to fold into herself as her daughter speaks. She feels guilty for abandoning her daughter when she needed her most.

'A friend maybe? A teacher? The police?'

'Yeah right.' Chloe slumps back in her chair. 'Like anyone would have believed me.'

'I would,' Anna says.

'No you wouldn't. I'd already told you that I wasn't seeing Mike and you believed me. Remember?' She gives her a defiant glare.

Something inside DS Hope twitches. Chloe's right. She should have pressed her more.

'I can only go on what you tell me, Chloe. I'm not a mind reader.' She softens her tone as she hears how brittle and defensive she sounds. 'Anyway, let's get back to that night and how you were feeling.'

'Destroyed.' Chloe brushes a tear from a cheek. 'My mum had walked out, my dad was . . . my dad

'. . . and the only person who said they could rescue me from all that shit hated me.'

'You think Mike hated you?'

'He tried to strangle me, didn't he?'

'Is that what made you decide to try and kill yourself again? Mike attacking you?'

Chloe sighs heavily. 'Yeah. I thought if I killed myself everyone would be sorry for the way they'd treated me. Mike especially. I wanted him to know how much he had hurt me. That's why I sent him the photo.'

'It wasn't a cry for help?'

'Fuck off. Sorry,' she glances at her solicitor then back at Anna. 'Seriously, though, that's really patronising.'

Anna raises her palms. 'I'm sorry, Chloe. I didn't mean to patronise you. I'm just trying to understand what happened.'

'Well I didn't want him to come after me and I didn't want him to stop me. If I had I'd have told him where I was.'

'But he did find you.'

'Yeah. I heard him shouting my name and I came out of the bushes.'

'What happened then?'

'We had an argument.' For the first time in the interview Chloe glances away, up into the corner of the room. 'I told Mike that he was a paedophile. That he'd groomed me the same way that he'd groomed Lou and that, if he didn't leave me alone, I'd go to the police.'

'And what did Mike do?'

'He called me a bitch and he stabbed me in the shoulder with a knife he was holding behind his back.' She touches the top of her left arm and winces. 'I thought he was going to kill me so I stabbed him in the neck.'

'With the scalpel?'

'No, with a carrot.'

'Chloe,' Simon Arnold says. He leans across and whispers something in her ear that makes her sigh.

'Yes,' she looks at Anna. 'I stabbed him with the scalpel.'

'Multiple times.'

'It was self-defence.'

DS Hope waits for Chloe to continue her story. When she doesn't she says,

'What happened then? After you stabbed Mike?'

'He . . . he fell. He dropped down to the grass and I freaked out. I knew he was hurt but I didn't think he . . . he . . .' Fresh tears roll down her cheeks. She reaches for the tissue box, pulls out two tissues and presses them to her face.

Anna Hope waits for her to compose herself again.

'Can we talk a bit about Wendy Harrison?'

Chloe shrugs. 'If you want.'

'She was in the park and saw what happened . . .'

'Yeah. She came over when I was down on the ground with Mike. She tried to calm me down and then rang the police.'

'How did she react when she saw you?'

'She was really shocked. She screamed a bit when she saw Mike's face.'

'Did you know he was her ex-husband?'

'Not until she said, no. I'd never seen her before.'

There is so much about the Mike Hughes case that doesn't quite add up, not least the fact that Wendy Harrison just happened to be in Priory Park at the same time as him when she'd been arrested for breaching her restraining order just days earlier. According to Wendy, she'd been walking her dog when he suddenly ran off. She'd stumbled upon Mike and Chloe when she was looking for him. It all sounded a bit bloody coincidental but Hills & Coleman vets in Malvern had confirmed that Wendy's dog Monty was handed in to them by a member of the public after it was found wandering the streets. Unfortunately, the Good Samaritan didn't leave their name.

If Chloe Meadows is sarcastic and fearful, then Wendy Harrison was the complete opposite. She was cold and reserved, answering no comment to any probing questions about her relationship with Mike and her feelings about what had happened, but she had given her a full account of what she'd witnessed in the park. She was more reticent when Anna asked her about her black eye – 'I walked into an open cupboard door' and who the passenger was in her car – 'a Polish farm worker hitching a lift', but they had no way of disproving her 'cupboard door' injury (even if it did look like a punch) and the CCTV they'd got from a shop near the park was so blurry they couldn't even make out the gender of the person sitting beside Wendy in her car. Anna's instincts told her that Wendy was involved in the murder, but Mike's DNA and blood hadn't been found on her clothes or her skin and there was no evidence she knew Chloe Meadows. They'd been through Wendy's phone records and the girl's number wasn't listed. Interestingly Louise Wandsworth's number *was*. Anna's interested to hear what she has to say when she interviews her next.

When pushed, Wendy had admitted going to Louise's work under the pretence that she was a new client. 'There's no law against that, is there?' she snapped.

'There is,' Anna retorted. 'It's called stalking.' There was so much about the case that didn't add up, but when it came down to it, there was no evidence to suggest that Wendy Harrison or Louise Wandsworth played any part in Michael Hughes' murder. Chloe Meadows, on the other hand, openly admitted to stabbing him and the evidence backed up her claim.

'That girl can't be more than five foot four,' Wendy had said when Anna asked her whether she believed Chloe's life had been in danger. 'Mike was well over six foot. He could have killed her. I don't blame her for defending herself. And I doubt any jury would.'

Anna Hope agreed. If she had a daughter Chloe's age she'd want her to retaliate too. Not least because paedophiles were the scum of the earth. But as DS Hope she had to put aside her personal feelings and investigate the incident. A man had been killed and Chloe Meadows had openly admitted to stabbing him. It wasn't her job to decide if there were mitigating circumstances. She had to find enough evidence to send it to court and let a jury decide.

'Okay, Chloe,' she says now, laying down her pen. 'We're going to take a quick break, then we'll carry on. There's just a few more things I need to ask you.' She presses a button on the tape recorder, then glances at her watch. 'Interview terminated at 16.07. Okay?' she says as she looks at the girl.

Chloe doesn't reply. Instead she slumps onto the desk, rests her head on her hands and sighs with relief.

Chapter 46

Wendy

Two weeks later

Wendy Harrison bends over her newspaper. There's a hideous photo of her on page five, leaving the courtroom yesterday after she gave evidence as a witness for the defence. She responded 'no comment' to the journalists who crowded around her, desperate for a soundbite, but they've written about her anyway, as she knew they would. It's largely speculation – about her so-called 'fragile state of mind' having seen her convicted paedophile ex-husband bleed to death – and a few quotes from 'friends and neighbours'. The reporter doesn't mention any names, but she's pretty sure the comment about her being 'a loner who only socialises with her dog' came from the idiot next door.

Wendy looks up, sensing someone watching her, and smiles tightly as a tall thin woman walks down the steps towards her. Wendy gives the smallest of nods, then lifts her handbag from the space beside her on the bench. The viewing gallery at Worcester Crown Court is packed and she's had to defend the small space from irate journalists and members of the public ever since she sat down. The thin woman says thank you, then sits down. Neither Wendy, nor the woman say a word. Instead they stare at the small, round-shouldered figure in the dock.

It's day five of the trial and, in a couple of minutes' time, the jury will retake their seats and give their verdict. Hundreds of pairs of eyes will be fixed on the young girl's face, watching for her reaction, then they'll swivel towards Wendy, the ex-wife of the murdered man. Wendy shudders. Going to court once was bad enough, it brought back all kinds of horrible memories and she really doesn't want to run the gamut of journalists and photographers again as she leaves. But she couldn't not come. Not after everything that's happened.

She glances, warily, around the court. Have any of the journalists noticed that she's sitting next to Louise Wandsworth? No doubt they'll be frantically scribbling in their notebooks if they have. Screw them and their speculation. She has nothing to be ashamed of. Neither has Lou.

Wendy cups a hand to her mouth, as though preparing to cough, and leans slightly to her left. 'How did it go yesterday?'

Lou, also a witness for the defence, angles her head towards her. 'It was horrible. I had to relive everything

374

that happened in France. But I let them know what a monster he was.'

'Good. Well done. And this morning?'

'Okay, I think,' she says, keeping her voice low.

'Did the prosecution barrister give Chloe the third degree?'

'Hmm, yeah. He really pushed her.' Lou raises a hand to her mouth. 'He tried to get her to admit that she was angry rather than scared. He said she wouldn't have stabbed him so many times if she wasn't. The defence barrister kept standing up to object.'

'But he didn't break her? She didn't change her story?'

'No. She was amazing.'

Wendy allows herself a small, self-satisfied smile. She'd had to think quickly, that afternoon in Priory Park with Chloe a quivering mess, Lou trying to play the selfless hero card and Mike bleeding out on the grass. All the evidence pointed to Chloe being the one who'd driven the knife into Mike's neck. Wendy had watched enough episodes of *Dexter* to know that blood splatter analysis would reveal that she was standing directly in front of Mike when he was stabbed. There was blood on Louise too that proved she was nearby. Wendy was the only one who hadn't been contaminated with the stuff as she'd been flat out on the grass several metres away when the stabbing took place. She had to act quickly. The longer she took to ring the police, the more suspicious it would look. No one else had appeared on the scene, but that didn't rule out witnesses who had heard something unusual. The police would try to pinpoint what time the attack had taken place.

She knew that it would look suspicious, her magically appearing on the murder scene. That's why she'd come up with the idea of pretending that she'd been walking Monty when she heard a commotion. Obviously there would be no dog when the police turned up. That's why she'd told Lou to collect Monty from her house and take him to the vet, saying she'd found him wandering the street.

If getting rid of Lou had been tricky, the most difficult part of her plan was convincing Chloe to let her stab her in the shoulder. It didn't matter how many times she explained that it would only be a flesh wound; the girl remained unconvinced. It was only when she pointed out that, if Chloe was sent to prison for Mike's murder, she'd be over forty when she got out that the girl's glazed expression faded and fear filled her eyes.

'That's old,' she whispered. 'That's really old.'

It was all Wendy could do not to roll her eyes.

'Mike attacked you with the kitchen knife first,' she told the girl. 'And you acted in self-defence, stabbing him in the neck. You threw the scalpel into the bushes, then realised what you'd done and tried to save his life. I heard the commotion and ran over to see what was going on and rang the police. Have you got that? Can you repeat it back to me?' She stared into the girl's pale, terrified eyes wondering whether any of it had gone in but, after a couple of seconds' pause, Chloe robotically repeated the words back to her.

'Good. You have to stick to that story, Chloe. Do you understand? The police will put a lot of pressure on you. They'll suggest that something else happened. They might even suggest that Lou and I were involved. You need to tell them that you were feeling suicidal and you sent a text to say goodbye to Mike but you didn't expect him to turn up. When he did, you got into an argument. You told him it was over between you but he wouldn't accept it. He stabbed you when you said you'd tell someone if he didn't leave you alone.'

Chloe nodded mutely. Her gaze kept flicking back to Mike's lifeless body.

'Chloe!' Wendy took her by the shoulders and shook her. 'You have to get your story straight. If you don't, you'll spend the next twenty-five years in prison.'

She stared into the girl's glassy eyes. She was in shock. When it wore off she'd get emotional, crumple under police questioning and tell them the truth. If that happened, Chloe wouldn't be the only one who ended up in prison. Wendy and Lou could be arrested as accomplices to murder. It was already a risk, her claiming to be a witness and breaking the terms of her restraining order again.

'Forget it.' She released Chloe's shoulders. 'Forget everything I just told you. Just tell the police the truth. A good barrister might be able to get you a reduced sentence because of the abuse you've suffered.'

'No.' Chloe grabbed her arm as she turned to walk away. There was a defiance in her eyes, a steadiness that hadn't been there before. 'I can do this. I can. I know what to say to the police.'

Wendy nodded, impressed, as the girl repeated her story back to her, almost word for word.

'Do it,' Chloe said, gesturing at the knife. 'Do it now. Quickly.'

'If you're sure—'

'Do it now!'

Wendy braced herself, then drove the blade into the young girl's shoulder before she could change her mind. It was a thoroughly unpleasant experience and she'd derived no pleasure from inflicting pain (unlike when she'd stabbed Mike in the leg).

All that was left to do then was transplant the knife into Mike's hand, throw the leaf into the bushes, wrap her jacket around Chloe's lightly bleeding shoulder and call the police.

Less than five minutes later they arrived.

Now Wendy jolts in her seat as Lou gently nudges her.

'The jury are coming back in.'

Seven women and five men walk slowly through a door in the side of the court and take their seats on the benches. Wendy tries to read their expressions but they all look terribly sombre. Is it bad news? She presses her fingers into her mouth and bites down on her nails. She feels sick with fear, as though she were the one on the stand, not Chloe. Lou, beside her, is deathly pale but she seems to be holding it together. There was a part of Wendy that worried Lou might crack under the strain of everything that had happened but she's stronger than she looks. There was one awful moment, when Wendy was being interviewed by DS Hope, when she wondered whether she could really trust Lou Wandsworth. For all she knew she could be in another interview suite claiming that Wendy was an accessory to Mike's murder, or even that she was solely responsible. But no, Lou did everything Wendy told her to do. Not that Wendy found any of this out for several days. She couldn't ring Lou because there was a possibility the police might monitor her calls, despite releasing her without charge. But she suspected everything had gone according to plan when she received a phone call from the vet telling her that her dog had been handed in by a member of the public. On the fourth day after her release she drove to a public library on the outskirts of Birmingham and sent Lou a Facebook message from Saskia Kennedy:

Message me if all is okay.

A couple of hours later her phone pinged with a reply from Lou. *I'm okay. How are you?*

They couldn't risk saying more than that to each other, but it was enough to reassure Wendy. She just had to pray that Chloe Meadows was as strong as she claimed to be. Everything rested on what she said to the police.

'Ladies and gentlemen in the gallery,' a loud voice says from below, making Wendy jump again. 'Could we please have silence? Court is now in session.'

There are coughs, creaks and whispers but, very quickly, the huge room falls silent and the court clerk stands up. Wendy reaches for Lou's hand and squeezes it tightly. Her heart's beating so quickly she's sure she's about to have a heart attack.

'Ladies and gentlemen of the jury,' the court clerk says. 'Could the foreperson please stand up?'

A middle-aged woman in a blue jumper stands up and smooths down her skirt.

'Has the jury reached a verdict on which you are all agreed?'

'Yes,' she says. 'We have.'

'On the count of manslaughter, do you find the defendant Chloe Meadows guilty or not guilty?'

Wendy stares at the back of the girl's stooped head and holds her breath. *Please*, she prays. *Please*.

The foreperson clears her throat.

'Not guilty.'

Chapter 47

Lou

Three months later

'Was that Wendy again?' Ben calls from the kitchen as I put the phone down. 'I'll have to have a word if she's stalking you again.'

'Nope.' I laugh. 'Not Wendy. Estate agent.'

'Good news?' My boyfriend pops his head round the door, a pair of tongs in his hand. The pan on the hob behind him spits and sizzles. The whole flat smells of cooked bacon. Not difficult when you could fit all four rooms of Ben's flat into Dad's living room.

'I've finally got a buyer!'

'Yessss!' Ben bounds towards me, crossing the tiny living room with two steps and whips me up and into his arms. 'That's brilliant news,' he says as he sets me back down on my feet.

'I'm so relieved. Obviously there are a lot of stages to go yet. Their mortgage application needs to be approved, then there's exchange and completion, but then I'll finally be rid of it.'

Mike's dead, Chloe's free and the house is my final link to the past. Once it's sold I won't ever have to go back to Malvern again.

It all happened so quickly after Wendy set her plan in motion. She'd told me she'd been a nurse in her youth and that she'd only scratch Chloe. 'It won't be more than a flesh wound,' she said. Still, I nearly turned back when Chloe screamed – she sounded as though she'd had part of her body gouged out. Logically I knew that Wendy's plan made sense, but I still panicked as I searched the streets for my car. What if Wendy was secretly arranging with Chloe to set me up for Mike's murder? Or worse, what if she'd killed Chloe rather than wounding her and I was next? It was a distinct possibility given the fact she'd just admitted to being Saskia Kennedy and leaving creepy flowers at my door.

I tried to push my doubts to the back of my mind as I finally located my car. Wendy had no reason to kill Chloe and if she was setting me up for Mike's murder she would have let me leave my fingerprints on his knife and phone and my DNA on his body. The one thing that convinced me to trust her was the first thing she'd asked me to do – drive to her house and collect her piebald springer spaniel, Monty. Even if Wendy was a psychopath, there's no way she would have let me take her dog. I'd seen the way her face lit up when she said his name. And besides, Monty was her alibi.

'I'll tell the police that I was driving through town with Monty in the back and he started whining for a wee,' she said. 'I detoured to the park and let him out. With no lead with me I had no choice but to let him run free. And that's when he ran off. You need to go to my house, get the spare key from under the bin and let yourself in. Get Monty, then take him to the vet's, any vet's, and say you found him wandering the streets. Don't tell them your name. When you've done that, go back to your house, wash down the barn with bleach and burn anything Mike wore or touched, including that stinking bucket. And make sure you wipe anything he may have touched in your house, particularly door handles. When that's done, go and get your car valeted – thoroughly – inside and out. Then wait, do nothing until you hear from me.'

It was astonishing – and slightly terrifying – the speed with which she came up with the plan.

I didn't hear anything from her for three long, torturous days. My guts turned liquid when I turned on the news and saw that two women had been arrested for the murder of a forty-nine-year-old man. Wendy's plan had failed. She and Chloe were going to spend the next twenty-five years of their lives in prison and it was only a matter of time until the police came for me too. The fear and guilt I felt was incapacitating. I could barely move from the sofa and I spent all of the first day cycling between the different news channels on Dad's TV. By the second day I felt as though I was going insane from inaction so I tackled the garage. I sorted everything into piles – save, charity shop, burn. My landline rang at lunchtime. The police wanted to talk to me. Could I please visit the station that afternoon, sooner rather than later? I felt sick with fear as I arrived. The only thing that stopped me from puking all over the floor was the knowledge that, if I was a suspect, I'd have been arrested not invited to help with enquiries. Somehow I held it together through my interview and answered every question they threw at me. What was my relationship with Mike Hughes? When had I last seen him? Why had I visited Chloe Meadows at home? Why had I given her my diary? Had I encouraged her to kill Mike? Did I know that Mike had gone missing for several days before his death? Did I have any idea where he might have gone? Why had I given DS Hope a fake name when I'd reported the kiss between Mike and Chloe? What had Wendy Harrison and I discussed on the phone? Why did I think she'd turned up at my work pretending to be a client? Why didn't I want to press stalking or harassment charges? Was Wendy Harrison planning Mike's death? Was I? Each time the officer paused between questions I felt as though my heart was going to beat straight through my chest. When the interview finally ended I was utterly convinced that I was going to be arrested and charged with conspiracy to commit murder. Instead the officer nodded curtly and said, 'Thank you for your help, Miss Wandsworth. We'll be in touch.' They didn't ring me again. But Chloe's defence barrister did.

The day after my police interview I drove into Worcester to check my Facebook messages in a café. Saskia Kennedy had left me a message saying she was okay. If Wendy was able to go on the internet she obviously hadn't been charged. The plan was working. I just had to pray that Chloe's plea of self-defence would be accepted and she wouldn't be found guilty of manslaughter or murder.

Before I drove back to the farmhouse I called Ben. It went straight to voicemail, as I suspected it might. The last time he'd heard from me – or thought he had – it was a text saying that we were over. I left a garbled message saying that Mike had sent that message, not me and that he was dead. Less than thirty seconds later Ben rang me back. He'd seen the news reports about Mike and Chloe and wanted to check that I was okay. I was fine, I said, but there was a lot I needed to tell him and I couldn't do it over the phone. He went quiet then and I braced myself. This was the moment where he told me that he'd had enough. He couldn't deal with any more drama. He'd felt something for me once but things had changed. He didn't. Instead he said he'd drive down that evening. His dad was out of intensive care, and recovering well on the ward. He was only really staying up there to keep his mum company.

'It sounds like you need me more,' he said. 'I'm coming down whether you like it or not.'

For once I didn't put up a fight.

I told him everything that evening – including what

385

had happened with Mike in the barn and how he had died. It was the first time I'd completely opened up to anyone and the words poured out of me. I wasn't afraid of him sharing my darkest secrets. I wasn't afraid of being judged. I wasn't afraid at all.

I didn't look at him as I spoke. Instead I stared out of the living room window as the sun dipped down and the sky darkened and all I could see was my own reflection, silently spilling my secrets. When I finally finished speaking I was surprised to see Ben sitting across the room from me. I'd forgotten he was there.

'Jesus,' he breathed. 'Jesus Christ, Lou.'

His eyes were so full of love and concern that I started to cry.

The next day he helped me ferry all the charity stuff to Bromyard and Malvern, then we visited an estate agent and I put Dad's house on the market. We were both knackered by the end of the day but neither of us wanted to spend another night at the farmhouse so I packed up all my possessions and we loaded them into both our cars. We were halfway down the M40, me trailing Ben's car, when I suddenly remembered the van. Every other trace of Mike had been eviscerated but the van was still in the lake. I'd need a crane to get it out of there and some kind of truck to tow it away. It wasn't something I could do in secret. I'd have to pay people to help. Alternatively I could just leave it. I'd had to swim several feet under the water to try and get in. The chance of anyone accidentally discovering it was tiny but I wasn't sure it was a chance I wanted to take. I rang Ben, to ask what he thought.

'Leave it,' he said. 'Mike's dead and Chloe's free. Even if the next owner did discover it it's not like they'd run a check on the licence plate.'

'They might report it to the police though.'

'Would you? If you bought a new place and found a rusty old car? You'd be pissed off with the previous owners but you'd get it towed away or sell it for scrap or something.'

'I guess.'

'Lou, it's just a van. Forget it. This is a new start. Remember? Clean slate and all that.'

'If you're sure.'

'I am. Now get off the phone or we'll both be arrested.'

I've been in London ever since. I was only supposed to stay at Ben's for a few days until I'd found a place to rent but days became weeks and then, one night, when we were lying in bed he asked if I wanted a hand packing. I was so shocked I pulled away and tried to get out of bed.

'Wait!' He grabbed my wrist. 'You didn't let me finish my sentence. I was going to ask you if you wanted a hand packing or if you'd officially like to live here full-time. As my girlfriend?'

I punched him lightly on the arm. Then I wrapped myself around him.

Ben was only joking when he asked whether Wendy's started stalking me again, but we have been in touch a lot. She's moved too, from Worcestershire to Herefordshire. She received a phone call, a couple of weeks after Chloe's trial, from one of Mike's friends – a guy called Brian Davies. He was the executor of Mike's will, he said, and he wanted to meet at the solicitor's for a chat. Wendy being Wendy demanded he tell her there and then so he did – Mike had written a will several years earlier but he hadn't passed it to a solicitor. That meant his first will, the one he wrote when they were still married, was the only one that was legal. She'd inherited everything. The house she'd loved so much and over sixty thousand pounds in savings. The will wasn't contested. Mike was an only child and his nearest living relative, a second cousin, couldn't be traced. Wendy put both houses on the market – hers and Mike's – and they sold quickly. Last time I spoke to her she was following a removal van towards Ledbury.

'It's huge,' she said of her new place. 'Five bedrooms, *enormous* garden. Monty's going to think he's died and gone to doggy heaven. And it's the sweetest little village. I'll be sorry to leave my neighbours on Clarence Road, but I left them a little gift.'

'What did you do?'

'Left my stereo plugged in in the bedroom. I put a Queen CD on, pressed it right up against the bedroom wall, turned it up to full volume and programmed it to play "We Are the Champions" on a loop. The new owners don't move in for two weeks.'

I had to laugh.

I haven't spoken to Chloe since what happened in Priory Park. I got hold of her number from Wendy but, when I rang, she wouldn't talk to me. Her mum wouldn't talk to me either but, when I explained who I was and that I'd been through the same thing as Chloe, she slowly opened up.

'It's all been a bit much,' she told me. 'The trial and me and Alan splitting up. Chloe's refusing to go back to school and I can't say I blame her. I thought I might take her away for a little holiday, just me and her. I feel so guilty about what happened. I was so miserable with Alan I had no idea what she was going through and I need to make it up to her. She says she understands why I ran off to my sister's and left her behind with her dad, but I think she's still angry with me.'

I told her not to be too hard on herself, that Mike was clever and shrewd and there was no way she could have known. I suggested she take Chloe to a psychologist who specialised in post-traumatic shock syndrome and that she should be there for her when she wanted to talk, and to give her space and time when she didn't. And I asked her to give her daughter my number, saying she could call me any time of the day or night.

Three nights ago Chloe finally rang. It was just after two in the morning and, for several seconds I couldn't work out who was sobbing down the phone to me. And then it clicked. I slipped out of bed and curled up on the sofa with a blanket over my shoulders and the phone pressed to my ear. We talked until the sun came up.

'So you hated him too?' she asked.

'Yes,' I said. 'Even though, in a weird way I still loved him.'

'Even after everything he did to you?'

'Even after that. I know it doesn't make sense.'

'Actually it does. Do you still love him now?'

I glanced towards the closed bedroom door and pictured Ben curled up in bed, one lazy arm slung over the duvet, the other folded under his head.

'No, not anymore.'

'That gives me hope,' she said softly. 'I still think about him and how things were before . . .'

'You will. But those feelings will fade and you'll move on. Are you seeing anyone, a psychologist?'

'Yeah. I saw her today. I think that's why I couldn't sleep. Too many thoughts going round in my head.'

'How are you feeling now?'

'Better.' I could almost hear the smile in her voice. 'Lou, do you mind if I ring you again sometime?'

'Whenever you want. Honestly. I'll always be here for you, Chloe.'

'Thank you. That means a lot. One more thing, Lou, before I go.'

'What's that?'

'I don't hate you. I want you to know that. I couldn't see it before but we're the same, you and me.'

'We are,' I said, 'but you're definitely braver.'

Chapter 48

Mavis

One year later

Mavis Horne shuffles down the aisles of her local Co-op, her handbag and basket hooked over her right arm. She's not moving slowly because she's got arthritis and can't move any quicker, she's killing time, hoping Elaine Fairchild will show up. They often have a little chat when they run into each other and Mavis looks forward to it. It's not that she's a gossip per se but she does enjoy sharing the little snippets she hears on the radio and sometimes a conversation or two that she happened to overhear. It makes her happy, keeping other people entertained and informed. She's pretty sure that, if she could rewind her long life, she'd make a pretty damned good disc jockey herself. Maybe even a news reporter. That Angela Rippon did it for years and she's still on the telly even though she's in her seventies.

Mavis completes her slow circuit of the shop and sighs. No sign of Elaine and she really can't justify dawdling much longer. Her granddaughter's bringing her new great-grandson over later and she has sandwiches to prepare and a Victoria sponge to bake. She ignores the shorter queue for Brenda's till and joins the line to be served by Edward instead. Mavis likes Edward. He must be late twenties or early thirties but he's got a lovely twinkle in his eye and an amusing turn of phrase that reminds her of a young Terry Wogan. God rest his soul.

'How are you today, Mavis?' he asks as she loads the conveyor belt with the contents of her basket. 'Hot, isn't it?'

'Hottest summer since 1976,' she says. 'According to the weatherman.'

'Feels like it.' He wipes the back of his hand across his sweaty brow, then scans her flour, packs it in a plastic bag for her (he never charges her the 5p) and then reaches for the strawberry jam.

'Cold drinks. And putting a fan in front of the window. Only way to survive it.' She pauses. 'I don't suppose you heard the news this morning did you? On Three Counties radio?'

Edward shakes his head. 'I listen to CDs in the car.'

'Music? Oh, well you won't have heard then. Do you remember the murder case last year? The one where young Chloe Meadows stabbed a man in the park. Mike Hughes he was called.'

'Yeah, I do.' He passes a box of eggs in front of

the scanner. 'Deserved what he got by all accounts.'

'Quite.' Mavis feels a fizz of excitement building. She's approaching the climax of her story. She mustn't mess it up or get her words in the wrong order and spoil the impact. 'Well they found his van. In a lake not far from here. The family who own the lake went for a swim and one of the children discovered it.'

'What's a dead man going to want with a van—'

'Anyway,' Mavis says, not appreciating the interruption. 'They got the van taken out of the lake and transported to a scrapyard, but when the proprietor looked it over he discovered . . .' she pauses for effect ' . . . a secret panel in the back. Between the . . . the . . . what's it called . . . the floor of the van and the underneath. You'll never guess what was in there.'

Edward shakes his head, one hand holding the plastic bag open, the other poised in the air with the box of eggs.

'The body of a young girl,' Mavis says with a flourish. 'Fourteen they think she was. Horribly decomposed apparently, but they could tell she'd been strangled. Do you know what the police think?'

Edward shakes his head again. He looks enrapt. So does the woman standing behind Mavis in the queue. And annoying Brenda on the next till. They're all staring at her, waiting for her to finish her story. Mavis feels amazing, like she's on stage.

'That she's not the only girl he's killed,' Mavis says. 'They're looking into the cases of half a dozen teenagers who've gone missing in Gloucester, Birmingham and Somerset over the last eighteen years or so. They think he travelled round the country in his van when he was supposed to be off doing deliveries.'

Edward's jaw drops and a woman at the back of the queue gasps.

'Do you know what's really strange?' Mavis breathes.

'What's that?'

'The dead girl had a dark bob with a heavy fringe, a round face and hazel eyes.'

Edward frowns. 'So?'

'She looked just like that one that stabbed him, Chloe Meadows. The psychologist on the radio was saying that he thought it was all sparked off by the one Mike ran off to France with back in the eighties. What was it the psychologist called her? The one that got away.'

ACKNOWLEDGEMENTS

Huge thanks to my amazing editor Helen Huthwaite for being such a support during the writing of this book, for her insightful and spot-on (as always) editorial comments and for her enthusiasm and encouragement. Thank you Phoebe Morgan for the seamless takeover when Helen went on maternity leave. I couldn't have asked for a safer pair of editorial hands and I really appreciate all the time and energy you put into getting *The Fear* ready for publication. Thanks also to Jade Craddock for doing such a great job with the copyedit, Henry Steadman for the amazing cover, Hannah Welsh for being a sales goddess, Sabah Khan and Deborah Elliot for being PR mavens, Elke Desanghere for digital marketing magic, and Kate Elton and Oli Malcolm for steering the good ship Avon. Thanks to Simon Cowell, I mean, Charlie Redmayne for his support and bonhomie.

Thanks, as always, to my amazing agent Madeleine

Milburn who didn't run shrieking when I told her I wanted to write about the power play between a female captor and a male prisoner, but instead asked questions that helped the idea take shape. Also for taking all of my moans, tears, frustration and jubilation in her stride and supporting me every step of the way. Thanks to the rest of Team Milburn – Hayley Steed, Alice Sutherland-Hawes and Giles Milburn for all their hard work and general loveliness.

Huge thanks to ex-detective Stuart Gibbon for his police procedural expertise (he has a book out on the subject, all crime writers should buy it) and to Rebecca Bradley and Neil White for patiently answering my questions about sex offender legislation and what happens after they get out of prison.

A big high five and 'oh my god I can't believe you did it' to my friend Scott James. For years Scott's asked when I was going to dedicate a book to him. I told him I'd only do it if he got a tattoo of one of my books (thinking that would never happen). He got the tattoo – the cover of *The Accident* on his calf – and, as promised this book is dedicated to him. Scott, you're a loon but we wouldn't have you any other way.

All the love in the world to my amazing family – Reg and Jenny Taylor, David Taylor, Sophie Taylor, Rose Taylor, Rebecca Taylor, Lou(bag) Foley, Sami Eaton, Fraser, Oli, Great Nan, Steve and Guin Hall, Ana James, James Loach and Angela and Nick Aspell. You keep me sane, you make me laugh and you share my books all over social media. Thank you! Sadly we lost two members of our family this year. Derek (Sam) Griffiths and Margaret Harris you are hugely missed.

Big love to my second family – the huge army of authors that make me laugh on a daily basis and constantly wow me with their generosity, kindness and ability to drink until the sun comes up. The loss of Helen Cadbury, one of our own, is still so keenly felt. Massive hugs in particular to Julie Cohen, Rowan Coleman, Miranda Dickinson, Kate Harrison and Tamsyn Murray for being the best friends I could ever ask for.

Then there's my own little family – Chris and Seth. I love you both ridiculous amounts. Thank you, for everything.

Finally, a HUGE thank you to the tireless bloggers who promote my books, turn up to my events and cheerlead every step of the way (and without being paid). You guys are AMAZING. You're like book fairies – spreading the reading magic all over the web (was that cheesy? Sorry, it was a bit). And you my readers. You're the reason I do what I do. Your emails, letters and social media comments mean the absolute world to me. Knowing that I entertained you, scared you, moved you or kept you gripped is such a huge compliment and when you tell me you can't wait for another C.L. Taylor book it spurs me on to write more. Thank you for reading this book. I hope you enjoyed it.

To keep in touch with me on social media follow me on:

Facebook: http://www.facebook.com/CallyTaylor Author

Twitter: http://www.twitter.com/CallyTaylor

Instagram: http://www.instagram.com/CLTaylor Author

And if you'd like to receive quarterly updates with all my book news then do join the free C.L. Taylor Book Club. You'll receive THE LODGER for free, just for signing up.

http://www.callytaylor.co.uk/CLTaylorBookClub. html

READING GROUP QUESTIONS

1. How culpable were Lou and Chloe's parents in what happened to their daughters?

2. Lou admits that she actively pursued Mike, even when he refused to kiss her and that she didn't give his wife a second thought. She was fourteen years old. Sixteen is the age of consent. Would you have judged her actions differently if she were fifteen and a half?

3. How do Lou, Wendy and Chloe change over the course of the book?

4. Why do you think Lou pushes Ben away from her even though she knows he's a good person?

5. Do you think Lou does the right thing when she re-opens her past by trapping Mike? What would you have done in this situation?

6. How important is the fact that Mike was Lou's teacher?

7. How do you think Wendy feels about Lou by the end of the book?

8. Who do you think is the real victim of this story?

9. Do you think the authorities dealt with the issues in this book appropriately? Could they have done anything more to help the girls?

10. Why do you think people like Mike behave in the way that they do?

Keeping this secret was killing her . . .

She trusted her friends with her life . . .

Get the *Sunday Times* and number one eBook bestseller, now in a brand new look for 2018.

You love your family. They make
you feel safe. You trust them.

Or do you . . .?

Get the *Sunday Times* and number one
eBook bestseller now.

What do you do when no one believes you . . .?

Get the *Sunday Times* and number one
eBook bestseller now.